SOPHIA
and
CASSIUS

Anna Canić

SOPHIA *and* CASSIUS

Addison & Highsmith

Addison & Highsmith Publishers

Las Vegas ◊ Chicago ◊ Palm Beach

Published in the United States of America by
Histria Books
7181 N. Hualapai Way, Ste. 130-86
Las Vegas, NV 89166 USA
HistriaBooks.com

Addison & Highsmith is an imprint of Histria Books. Titles published under the imprints of Histria Books are distributed worldwide.

All rights reserved. No part of this book may be reprinted or reproduced or utilized in any form or by any electronic, mechanical or other means, now known or hereafter invented, including photocopying and recording, or in any information storage or retrieval system, without the permission in writing from the Publisher.

Library of Congress Control Number: 2023948270

ISBN 978-1-59211-378-1 (hardcover)
ISBN 978-1-59211-399-6 (eBook)

Copyright © 2024 by Anna Canić

To the one who remembers…

You who deny me, confess me,
and you who confess me, deny me.
You who tell the truth about me, lie about me,
and you who have lied about me, tell the truth about me.
You who know me, be ignorant of me,
and those who have not known me, let them know me.
(Thunder: Perfect Mind)

The queen of the south shall rise up in the judgment with this generation and shall condemn it.
(Matthew 12:42, KJV)

PROLOGUE

I am Sophia, the first woman on Earth. Created by God together with the first man, as one being. Separated from him to meet him again. Born to be my husband's companion, not a maid. A lady – neither a wo-man, nor a fe-male. Made to love, and to be loved.

I was the first and only, then only the first, eventually deleted, but forever perfect. She, whose faithfulness resisted the devil's temptation. Hated by the other one who did not resist it. Rejected and demonized by her descendants. Later, glorified under false names. I've always been the biggest challenge and mystery to people, but now it's time to finally tell you the truth.

In the beginning, it was Love. On the sixth day, our Father Adonai made the first man out of four elements – earth, water, air, and fire. A human being, dressed in light – male and female in one. As one, we felt infinite gratitude for the Father, and as two halves we loved Him from the moment He breathed the immortal soul into us. As we were so sincere and blessed, God gave us gifts unknown even by the angels – the free will and earthly love.

We lived in the Garden of Eden – a beautiful oasis in the heart of our flat Earth. We have given names to all the lower beings – beasts, birds, fish and plants... We ate the sweetest fruits and drank water from the purest sources. We didn't know about the pain or sadness.

One day we noticed that each creature has a different, separate being – to live with, and to be attracted to.

"Why does everyone around me have its mate, but I'm alone?" one of us asked.

"You're not alone, we're two, locked in the same body... I just don't understand why. Why can't we look at each other, touch each other – just like every being around us?"

"Surely the Father had a reason for this."

"Remember, He gave us the free will."

One of us, who could talk, wondered aloud, "What should I do?"

"Just ask Him nicely."

"Will you help me?"

"It is weird – Father gave you the opportunity to talk, and you can't even speak to Him without me."

"Then, you must be my better half."

"And you're my other self."

Suddenly an indescribable, blinding light scattered all around us. We felt a sudden, pleasant warmth that penetrated our very depths. We could not see or understand anything anymore, but flew towards the light, dissolving in its embrace.

"You are ready now."

When I came to myself, I saw my husband, Adam, and three angels, messengers of God – Senoy, Sansenoy and Semangelof, beside him. It was a strange feeling – being alone in one's own body. It was easier and harder at the same time – for me, and, hopefully, for the man next to me.

I thought, how beautiful he is, and how I probably look like him. With the smile on Adam's face, I realized that the same thing went through his head.

"Our Creator always knows our wishes – even before we ask of them. By the will of God the Father, whose name is ineffable, you are no longer one but two," Senoy started, and Sansenoy continued:

"The name of the husband," He said, "shall be Adam – for he is the strength to his wife. And the wife shall be Sophia – to be her husband's wisdom. Love each other, multiply and inhabit the Earth."

"For the God has loved you much, He gave you freedom to do by your will. The only thing you may not do is to commit adultery. If you deceive each other – you deceive God. That is a sin, and it brings a curse," finished Semangelof, before all three have disappeared in heaven.

First, we just looked at one another in the eye. Slowly, we started to look around as I noticed delight in my husband's gaze. We exchanged smiles, and then Adam grabbed me by the arm and pulled me toward him – a little rougher than I expected.

"What are you doing?" I asked him in confusion.

"You are my wife," he answered, squeezing my arm even harder. "I want to have children with you, like all other beings."

"Do you love me, Adam?" I snapped, a little disappointed.

"Of course, I do," replied my husband. "Father commanded us to love each other."

"You want me – just because you're ordered to?" I tried to catch his glance. "Or you just want me at your will?"

Adam took time to think.

"My will, my wish, depends on Him," he replied. "I want to be as perfect, as He is."

"A creature will never be like the Creator," I riposted, "and you and I, we are the same, equal."

"You make a lot of noise," he said. "Like any other female."

I felt offended and moved away from my twin husband. "If you just want to own me," I said firmly, "it's not love, and I'm not going to be a part of it."

Bewildered, Adam tried to get closer to me, but I turned my back. "Sophia, where are you going?" he exclaimed indignantly, watching me leave. "I love you, Sophia!"

I turned around. "And I don't know yet if I love *you*," I replied. "I need some time and space to think."

"Stay!" Adam screamed. "I promise, I won't touch you until you feel love for me."

So, I agreed. Together, we built a hut, met water and fire, started picking and storing. The sun was always mild, the rain cool, the flowers fragrant, and the fruits sweet and delicious. Hand in hand, we enjoyed the endless meadows and starry heavens, but I still felt no love for my husband. Days, months and years passed, but the union of Adam and Sophia had not yet been consummated.

"How much longer do I have to wait?" my husband asked, lighting the fire. "I want our happiness to be complete."

I didn't feel ready. Beside Adam, I felt warmth and comfort, but my body did not crave for him. "Love is like fire." I looked sadly at the flames. "It will not last unless it's hot."

"Fire is burning too fast," he sighed, and threw two branches into blaze. "A big one can ruin."

I disagreed, but I kept silent and simply dropped my head on his shoulder.

And then came the day when Senoy, Sansenoy, and Semangelof warned us about a renegade, a fallen angel who imagined himself godlike and persuaded a third part of the heavenly beings to rebel against the Almighty.

"Once, Mithras was an Archangel, closest to God," Senoy began, "until his pride made him want to overthrow the Creator."

"But there was Michael, faithful Commander of the Celestial Army," Sansenoy continued. "With a fiery sword, he overthrew the enemy and his followers, and drove them into darkest depths of Earth."

"From then on, they are doomed to tortures in inferno – a burning lake created by their pride," finished Semangelof.

For the first time in our carefree life, we heard bad news. They told us not to trust anyone but the three of them, because that cursed one, who was jealous of people, sought to destroy us from the very start.

"Mithras hates you," the angel explained. "God loves you more than angels because you are perfect in your duality… And your ability to love is most disturbing for the enemy. Beware of him, for he is cunning, and he knows your weaknesses."

When we were alone, Adam wondered. "Why, if Mithras was punished, would the Father allow him to roam the Earth, to attack us?"

"Nothing in the world happens without God's permission," I concluded. "The renegade must not hurt us, but he will do his best to deceive us – to do something forbidden… Adultery."

"And become like him? No, never!" Adam shouted. "I'm just wondering, why God does not protect us if he knows we won't forsake Him?"

"We need to prove it," I replied. "Remember, God has given us free choice? Now is the time to choose."

My husband shrugged. "Still, I don't understand, how should we choose eternal torments over bliss? Why should we betray God?"

Feeling his fear, I reached out to hug him. "I would never cheat on you."

He laughed. "Sophia, what comes to your mind? With whom can we deceive each other? We're the only people in the world! Of course, there will be our children, and they will love one another…"

I sighed. My husband did not understand me again. "I know, but if there was another woman who is all I'm not –" I wanted to ask him, but I was interrupted.

"I won't think about that which is impossible. My wife is you."

Suddenly I remembered something I saw in the woods the other day.

"Come here," I said. "I want to show you something."

Adam agreed but asked that we not stay in there long, as he was hungry.

It was the last time we walked hand in hand by the lake. What I wanted to see was our reflection in clear water. Two beautiful humans in light gowns, more similar than twins, red-haired and azure-eyed, were watching us from the lake's glistening surface.

"Amazing!" Adam exclaimed in admiration.

"So perfect in their duality, aren't they?" I asked, recalling the angels' words, but, again, my husband did not listen.

"From the first day, I have been exploring nature," he said thoughtfully. "I went around every corner of Eden, but I somehow missed this treasure... It's a game of light!"

I stiffened in place, feeling a change in my husband's behavior. I did not hear him as he marveled at the creation of God around us. I no longer cared that the sun came up in the morning, that a cricket started its song at dusk, that an owl flew at midnight and a nightingale at dawn... My very first tears were dripping down my face.

"Sophia?" I heard a gentle note in Adam's voice. "What is it, my dear?" Softly, he caressed my cheek and asked me, "Are you crying?"

"I'm scared, Adam." My voice suddenly quivered.

He got earnest. "Tears in a place where no one cries... Not a good sign." He hugged me tightly and whispered in my ear, "My dear, you have no reason to worry. With me, you are safe."

Nevertheless, I didn't feel safe... or loved.

"It's time to go back."

That night, we slept facing opposite sides of our bed.

At early dawn, while my husband was still sleeping, I got up carefully and tiptoed from the hut. I picked up a clay tray and a jug from the table and walked down the familiar path to the lake.

I picked large violet figs – my husband's favorite fruits. I went by myself, as I did not heed the angelic warning.

What can he do to me, I thought, *that Mithras?*

After I filled my jar with juicy fruits, I knelt by the lake to catch some more water. Suddenly, steps from behind me made me feel anxious.

This was not Adam.

In the mirror of the lake, I saw a stranger. He was tall, dark-skinned, and black-eyed. I dropped the jug with a splash of water.

"Hail, Sophia," he said, sounding refined. "I'm bringing some good news for you."

An angel stood in front of me – with wings as bright as the sun, clothed in a gleaming dress.

Trust only in us three. I recollected the words of our guardians and looked into the stranger's eyes. His gaze was arrogant, and his presence, instead of trust, brought me fear and disgust.

"Don't be afraid of me." He reached out to me. "I'm your friend. I know your pain, and I want to help you."

I took a fast step back.

"I know who you are," I said roughly. "From you, I don't need help or anything at all!"

His laughter sounded horrible. "You are so defiant for a female," he said. Then, suddenly, his pensive face softened into a gentle and spiritual expression. "I know you don't love Adam. Leave him, and follow me –"

"I do not love you either," I interrupted him. "You are disgusting."

"You have no clue, you stupid thing," said Mithras, clenching his fists. "You don't know who I am, nor what my powers are. If I wish, I can crush you. But if you bow down to me…" his voice grew crafty, "I will raise you to the ninth heaven, as a goddess, equal to myself."

I looked at him with contempt and turned around to find the jug. "Don't lie, Mithras, and don't tempt me with what you don't have. I only worship God, for he's the only ruler of the Universe."

The foreigner shook with fury.

"You female ape!" he roared, raising ahead a cloud of dust. "You will pay dearly for your insolence!"

He can't do anything against the will of God, I thought, embracing my jug, and turned around to leave.

"You will regret it," Mithras laughed in a thousand voices. "You'll remember me!"

I closed my ears not to hear that demonic echo.

I made my way to the hut unbelievably fast. Adam stood on the threshold, turning me away with a sole gesture.

"Go back where you came from."

I did not take it seriously.

"Here you are," I said, handing him the jar of figs. "I picked them to surprise you."

He pushed my hand away, spilling the fruit out.

"You've been picking figs all day? Why are you lying to me, woman?"

He had never addressed me like that before.

"What do you mean?" I looked up at the sky, astonished. It was sunset, dying the blue horizon purple. *So, he can move the time.*

"Sophia, you betrayed me," Adam said disgustedly. "Rejected me for Mithras!"

I realized the power of demonic threats.

"An angel visited me," he continued angrily. "He told me you are evil, and I have to banish you!"

Through tears and pain, I tried to tell the truth, but he did not believe me.

"God, I don't need a woman who is not obedient!" Adam exclaimed, raising his hands to the sky. "What is the use of a woman who does not give birth? All you can do is to demand some – love?"

I leaned against the date palm tree. I was speechless, but the worst was yet to come. I noticed *her*, stepping out of our house. Another woman – someone to replace me. Adam's unconstrained choice.

Tall, blond, and slim, she had snake-like green eyes. God named her Eve, meaning – life. My husband had got a new life, where there was no space for Sophia.

I turned my eyes upon him.

"*You* betrayed me. Devil seduced you, not me."

"Shut up, woman!" Adam growled. "I'm not your *stronger half*, I am her *man*!"

Humble Eve had hidden behind Adam's back, watching us closely.

"So be it!" I smiled bitterly. "Farewell."

My husband didn't answer me. Pushing Eve out of his way, he turned back to the hut that once was mine.

I went away. For days, I wandered through strange roads without rest or purpose.

"Why was I created?" I asked, sobbing. "Why can't I love and be loved back?"

Semangelof, my guardian angel, gave me the answer.

"We have no right to question God's decisions. Father gives us happiness, and we make sorrows ourselves. Your human love is great, but it is infinitely smaller than our heavenly love."

The angel took me in his arms, as a caring mother rocks her ailing child.

"In heaven, there is no love other than holy, divine. Us angels are always happy."

"I didn't love him," I confided to my guard. "But I did not betray him. Every day I prayed to God that I could feel some love and to be loved by Adam."

"I'm sorry, Sophia." Semangelof sighed and spread his huge wings so we could leave the ground. In a moment, I was just flying among the clouds. My body became light, like a feather, and that freedom of the blue, cloudless sky awakened joy in me. Joy, but not happiness.

"Your home is now land between two seas," my angel said. "Here, on the highest rock, shall be your habitation. Your land will be forever yielding, and your stream will not dry up. For you have never violated God's commandment, you will never die. Your home is now surrounded by the impassable forest and deep sea – as to protect you from the world you left."

"What else can Mithras do to me?" I shrugged.

Semangelof lowered me to the ground.

"For now, he is no longer interested in you, Sophia. The damage has been done, so the outlaw is quite sure of his victory. You need protection from the human race. Eve hates you; so will her descendants."

I saw a magnificent house, carved in stone, in the shade of tall trees, and a waterfall emerging from the rock, and various flowers… I saw the deep forest that surrounded my new home, and the dark blue sea… This was where I had to live forever – all alone. This didn't seem like a reward for faithfulness, it was a punishment.

The angel read my mind.

"Don't be ungrateful," he said roughly. "Your afflictions are yet nothing to the punishment of infidelity."

I felt like unatonable things had been happening during my wanderings.

"How is Adam now?" I asked worriedly. "Is he happy with another woman?"

Semangelof fell silent, looked up to heaven and whispered, "Adam and Eve have been exiled. The Garden of Eden is submerged, and the human race is cursed."

The pain, almost physical, bent me in half. "Is Eve… as well? What do you mean – cursed?"

The angel took my hand and led me into a new house. "Adam's fall has led to Eve's adultery," he said. "A woman, created from his rib, has been seduced by Mithras."

I remembered her serpent-like gaze.

Perhaps it's my fault, I thought with sadness. *I did not give Adam children; I did not support his desire to discover new lands and crafts… I was only guided by love.*

"You are not to blame," the messenger of God replied. "You're sinless."

The punishment for Adam and Eve was to live a kind of life they choose themselves. Existence outside of Eden was hard and dangerous – rains and droughts hindered the man's work; the woman was doomed to give birth in anguish. Everything in their life was transient; even life itself had its end. And after that were mist and darkness…

Eve had been carrying twins, but Adam was not their father.

The angel left in silence, leaving me to spread out on my new soft bed – asleep at last.

I was awakened by gentle rays of morning sun. I was hardly an early riser, but I was pleased with what I saw. The sun appeared to be born from the calm sea, spilling bright colors across the sky one by one – red, orange, pink and yellow. A couple of white clouds floated, uniting in the air like lovers.

It won't be me, I thought. *I'll never know what love is.*

Suddenly, I heard a shudder behind my back. I turned to see a big owl sitting on the table and looking at me sleepily. It had large orange eyes and small black ears.

"Lilith[1]," I patted her, "we're much alike – both prefer night to day, and neither of us knows how to make a nest. Come on, I'll find you something eatable."

That bird was a very smart creature. She had bonded with me and loved sitting on my shoulder. I was telling her about Adam, and the owl nodded as if she understood each word. She often flew away at midnight, but when the bird was back – and wasn't sleeping – she always kept an eye on me.

One day, I found her feather on the floor, dipped it in juice of a pomegranate, and guided by heavenly power, wrote the first verse on the bark of a tree.

> *You wonder who I am,*
> *Coming to you as your shadow,*
> *Like an owl in the middle of dark night?*[2]

I looked at the letters, read them, and my heart filled with gladness. I found it strange what I'd been doing. I didn't know why or to whom I was writing, and I didn't even understand the meaning of my words, but I went on.

> *I sleep on the ground and play in the trees,*
> *Lie on the sand and fly with the breeze,*
> *I step to heaven and drink with the bees,*
> *I sing… and do whatever I wish!*

I loved my new skill and felt thankful to God for the talent He bestowed me with. My days went on by writing, but I was still lonely.

---

[1] (hebr.) Owl.
[2] From the Apocryphas of Solomon.

"Why do you need other people, Sophia?" the angels asked me. "Here at his place, you are safe and comfortable. You know neither hatred, nor disease."

"I only want to love and be loved," I responded. "With the earthly, human love."

"Adam has chosen Eve," Senoy expounded. "He forgave his wife for infidelity and gave her more children."

"Eve is jealous," Sansenoy continued. "She is envious of your immortality and faithfulness. She convinced Adam and her children that you followed Mithras and became a demon that kills newborn babies and seduces men."

"Take a look around you, Sophia, and tell me," questioned Semangelof, "do you really love human pain and sorrow more than godly happiness?"

I did not give in. "Without love," I answered, "there is no difference between heaven and hell."

> *Only a Hero can tame me,*
> *The one who loved me yet before my birth…*

I found solace in writing.

> *He is my offspring in due time,*
> *And my power is from him.*
> *I am the staff of his power in his youth,*
> *He is the rod of my old age.*
> *And whatever he wills happens to me.*

My pursuit of love and searching for someone who did not exist led me straight to the edge of reason.

"Adonai!" I called the ineffable name of the God, "I beseech you – end my suffering!"

I broke the vow. Guardian angels never visited me again. In an instant, everything I had – the house, the wellspring, and the rock – were gone… I was standing on the shore of the rough sea with a wild steppe behind my back. With the first trespass, my light gown disappeared. Bare and alone in the wasteland, with neither single drop of drinking water, nor a saving shade, I slowly faded…

I am strength in trembling;
I am she who is weak,
And I am well in a pleasant place,
I am senseless and wise,
I am unlearned,
And they learn from me...

With my last ounce of strength, I wrote on moist sand – between hot stones and chilly water. I thought death was coming, the death my guards told me about.

Straight away, the ray of vivid light ran through my fingers, blinding me for a while. When I received my sight, in front of me I saw Michael – an archangel with six blazing wings.

He helped me get back on my feet, and I felt relief.

"Sophia," Michael said mildly, "the one who preserved in faithfulness to a man, proved her fidelity to God as well. From now on, you are a mortal, but for your love, you will return to live again – to love and to be loved."

I noticed a fiery sword of gemstone in his hand. I was amazed at the perfection of this strange tool's shape.

"Archangels are the warriors of Heavenly Kingdom," he said, revealing a secret, "and your mate will be a soldier of an earthly kingdom."

I wanted to fall at his feet, but the angel stopped me.

"Kneel only before God; give thanks to Him, for this is His will."

As I calmed my crazed heart, I asked the archangel about the future of Adam, Eve, and their descendants.

"For those who deny love, the punishment is a loveless life. A man who does not love his mate cannot love God either. Those who will repent and turn to the Almighty, they will find the way to their salvation. Everyone will have to fight for love in order to perceive the greatest gift of God to people."

I was glad there was hope for humanity.

"However, Sophia," he continued in a thunderous voice, "Eve's deceit will follow you for generations. Through your name, Mithras will try to lead people astray. They will regard you as a demon and a goddess, a myth and a nebula. But earthly glory is all void and vain, as well as the outlaw's rule. Your love will live for the duration of the world, and by the end of time your story will be told."

"So be it," I said. Then, I asked the archangel if I could see Adam one more time.

"Not now," he said, and disappeared into the pillar of heavenly flames.

For nine hundred years, I lived on hope alone, on my very own in the wild. I made shelters, gathered food and prepared it with the help of water and fire. I was neither afraid of the cold, nor the heat, nor predators. I never felt tired. I took care of the beasts and the birds, with love and without fear, and they responded to me with fidelity. Owls and feral cats constantly accompanied me – free, smart, and skillful creatures. I shared my food with them, nursed them, and mourned my friends when they died.

The places where I lived were magnificent. High hills, clear rivers, green woods… I did not stay in the same place for too long; I was looking for a path that would lead me to my loved one. The angels were silent. I had to talk to myself not to forget our language. And I was writing, thinking to my destined one.

I'm the barren one
And many are her sons.
I am peace,
And war has come because of me.
My husband is the one to give me life,
And to take it away…

One night, in my dream, a strange voice spoke to me one word: "Calvary." I realized immediately – there I had to go. It hurt my heart, but still, I could not believe this presentiment.

I left at dawn, when my animals were still asleep, passing all my food supply on to them.

The first seven days were the hardest, as I ate and rested poorly. My feet were bleeding, and Sansenoy's words about higher love were spinning in my head, but I did not give up, even with the fever stirring up my nightmares with my verity.

I am the one whom they call Wisdom,
and you have called me Death…

Every time I lost and regained consciousness, I thought it was the end. When I finally came to myself, I felt a soft bed and a warm blanket. The room I found myself in seemed better than my angelic home on the rock. Next to me sat a woman, holding my hand.

"Thank God you woke up. How are you?" Her voice was gentle and full of care, but she was not an angel, but a human being – Eve's daughter.

I had no strength to talk until the stranger fed me some soup.

"You saved my life," I whispered, looking at her face. She resembled neither Adam nor Eve. Her hair was dark as night, and her eyes were a deep dark blue like the sea.

"When we found you, you were lying motionless. My husband believed you were dead, but I knew you were alive," the stranger smiled. "I'm Sharon."

I responded with a smile. I realized I didn't know any of their female names. There certainly was not another Sophia on earth.

Sharon took my hand and whispered intimately. "You are free to tell me who you are. If you are hiding from someone, don't be afraid – I will never betray you. Neither will my husband, nor my son."

I was fascinated by her kindness. For the first time in my life, I had a friend, and I didn't want to lose that feeling. I didn't want to lie to Sharon either, for she was my source of confidence.

"Sophia."

"What a lovely name!" she admired. "I have never met a woman named like that."

She appeared to have completely no idea.

"Where are you from, Sophia?" Sharon stared at me. "Loose hair, short dress – you don't look like a woman from our Calvary."

The last word got me back me to feet.

"Easy, my dear," the woman stopped me. "You are not yet strong enough to walk."

"Do you know where this place is?" I asked.

Eve's daughter looked surprised, and then she laughed out loud. "You're joking, aren't you? Who of us doesn't know where the Calvary's hill is?"

This darkened my eyes, so I had to go back to bed.

"You'll be fine." She covered me with a blanket. "Have a rest. I'll bring you some water."

"I have to go there – now."

She saw I was serious, so she began to doubt. "You're not of Seth's lineage, are you?" Sharon's expression quickly changed. "You are… of Cain?"

"I am neither."

"How is that possible?" wondered my rescuer. "Abel had no offspring, and you are too young to be a child of Adam."

Despite my mortality, I still remained young-looking.

"I am as old as Adam. We were born together."

The woman opened her graceful eyes wide. "God!… You are Lilith!"

I nodded. She promised I'd be safe, whoever I might be.

Thank you for the nickname, Eve. I thought. *You could've come up with something worse.*

However, Sharon seemed so… happy.

"Har'El! Har'El!" she called her husband's name. "Come here!"

"What happened?" I heard a male voice from the other room.

"You'll never guess who our guest is!"

A tall red-haired young man stood at the doorway, quite resembling Adam. He was holding a little boy in his arms.

I got out of bed, no longer needing rest. The man was staring, and the woman and the child were smiling.

"As far as I can see, you're not from Calvary," he said, embarrassed by my look.

I laughed. By God, these people had succeeded in something even the angels had not – to cheer me up, at least for a moment.

"She doesn't know where it is," Sharon hinted. "She's Adam's coeval."

Har'El shrugged, unaware.

"I'm Sophia, called Lilith," I said at last. "But I am not a demon who kills children and seduces sleeping men. I've never met a single child or man except Adam."

Red-haired man accepted me with verve as well. "We have never believed those stories. The late great-grandmother plotted them as to convince everyone there had been someone worse than her and Cain."

"Eve? Has she died already?" I asked with mixed feelings.

"Long ago," Sharon replied. "Adam did not grieve at all, though. Azura, one of Seth's wives, told us Eve had cried a lot before she died. I guess she felt remorse for you."

"Women live shorter than men," Har'El added. "Men don't give birth to one child after another and, honestly, we never have that many obligations... As for me," he went on, embracing his wife, "I do cherish and protect my loved one, but unfortunately, the rest of them are not like us."

I felt pitiful. Angels had described death as darkness, loneliness and murk. I didn't want this, not even for foolish Eve.

"You two were equal – you and Adam," Sharon whispered excitedly, as if she was afraid of someone listening. "Where we came from, a wife is a man's servant. Women have no rights for... pleasure," she blushed. "But we do understand, and we stand by you."

Finally, someone was on my side.

"Who is that Cain?" I asked. "Why doesn't he live at Calvary?"

Har'El was the first to answer.

"Cain was the eldest son of Adam. He killed his younger brother, Abel, out of envy. He was then banished to the end of the world, together with his wife."

So, Mithras' heir had raised his hand to other human being, his own brother. This was probably the price for Adam and Eve's infidelity.

"Abel was a shepherd and Cain a farmer," Har'El continued the story. "They both seemed to be pious and devoted to the Almighty. Cain laid wheat flour as a sacrifice, and Abel gave his lambs. Each time they did, the smoke from the Abel's altar turned white, and was rising straight to the sky, unlike the smoke of Cain's harvest, black and stuffy. So, the Lord himself had indicated which of the brothers pleased Him more. But Cain was evil."

This was the right moment to tell them the truth.

"Mithras was the one to blame. He seduced Eve, and she gave birth to a murderer."

"What do you mean?" the young couple wondered. "Did not the devil, in the form of a serpent, deceive Eve into biting a fruit of the forbidden tree and giving it to Adam?"

"An apple fairy tale," I guessed, "was probably made up so descendants would not hate the ancestors." I told them about my adventures from the very start.

A hearty Sharon wept, and their son approached me, handing me a big pear. "My name is Daniel," he smiled. "Be my friend."

I gently hugged him. Never, ever would I hurt a single child!

Come forward to childhood,
and do not despise it because it is small and it is little.
And do not turn away greatnesses in some parts from the smallnesses,
for the smallnesses are known from the greatnesses.

Har'El suggested I stayed with them. "They'll hurt you there. Adam is old and probably doesn't remember you. The patriarch of our family is Seth – his youngest son, our grandfather. Seth and his children are more dangerous for you than Eve was."

"Because of them, we ran away from home," Sharon went on. "Since our childhood, we have been in love, but Seth betrothed me to another man, and found another bride for Har'El. We did not let them break our hearts, so we came here to be together."

"God knows how hard it was in the beginning." Har'el hugged his wife. "We went through quarrels, illnesses, and fears. But love overcomes everything. Indeed, of all the earthly and heavenly loves, the greatest is the one between the spouses."

They knew I couldn't stay. For seven days, I shared with them a roof, a table, and a prayer. I was picking flowers with Daniel, knitting wreaths and making toys for him. Sharon sewed me a white dress like those worn by her chaste cousins. She did not try persuading me to tie and cover my hair, because she knew I would never do it, regardless of 'almighty' Seth's opinion.

"I am so happy there's a place on earth where you can be yourselves, and love, and be loved," I told them, when it was my time to leave. "Where true friends live."

Sharon gave me a hug, and Har'El handed me a small sack with bread and fruit. I gave him a scroll of bark with my poem. *The Thunder: Perfect Mind*, so said the title.

I kissed all three goodbye, forever leaving the place that one day would bear my name.

Calvary was a hilly grove where Adam and Eve had settled down after their exile from Eden. Wandering in the desert had made them see this place, with a small river and somewhat fertile land, as their salvation.

Cain was their first-born son, followed by his twin sister Naomi – bitter fruits of mother's sin. Within a year, Eve had another son named Abel, and another daughter Na'El. The older children grew selfish and vicious, while the younger were kind-hearted and good-tempered.

When the time of first sympathies came, Abel and Na'El decided to get married. However, Eve did not let a family be founded out of love. Although Adam had rejected me and chose her, she was always aware that she wasn't loved. Therefore, she hated love itself, repeating the same lie – as if this feeling distracts man from God. Adam respected the mother of his children and supported her, but their relationship went cold and tight. His pride did not allow him to acknowledge his injustice.

So, Cain had to marry Na'El, and his younger brother reluctantly took Naomi for his wife. Na'El was broken, but she couldn't oppose her parents' will, which was god-like to her. Abel grieved as well, but soon forgot his sweetheart once he experienced Naomi's charms. Naomi had inherited all the worst traits from their mother. She became Cain's lover, inflating his hatred of innocent Abel. Together, the wicked couple wanted to get rid of their parents and take everything Adam and Eve had gained through hard work, making a slave of poor Na'El – but God did not allow this to happen. When Cain killed Abel, Adam saw Senoy, who told him to beware. At the angel's behest, he banished the murderer and his wife, leaving treacherous Naomi at his house as a maid.

For 130 years, Adam mourned his beloved son. He did not touch his wife and slept alone in his tent. From then on, the place of Abel's death was called Calvary – a skull. There, by the place of his boy's burial, the hopeless father decided to live and to die.

Graceless Naomi, worrying lest Eve vent all the anger on her, made up a story of Lilith, whom she allegedly saw overnight by her father's tent. As the suffering Eve was afraid to question her husband, Naomi kept lying to her mother. Thus, guilty without guilt, I became a witch who slept with Adam to give birth to giants.

When the mourning time was over, Adam and Eve had a son named Seth. His father blessed him to be a leader to all tribes because he no longer considered himself worthy. Seth grew up in austerity and became sanctimonious. Adam and Eve had seventeen more daughters, and Seth married each of them, even including Naomi. He demanded obedience from his wives and endeavored to have as many children as possible. This way, he thought to obtain God's blessings, and thought the sins of the father would be atoned, and his sons followed him.

Many women were dying at childbirth, and their mothers blamed Lilith. Men used to curse me when they had dreams of defilement, and to beat their wives and children for the slightest disobedience. Oppressed wives hated their spouses, so, in many houses, adultery and infanticide occurred. Most of them regarded love as weakness, valuing their possessions higher than their families. Soon, people's hearts were filled with avarice and envy.

One day, Seth son, Enos, had learned that his children Har'El and Sharon were very attached to each other, and he immediately summoned all the elders, with Seth at the helm, to thwart this young love. Seth chose the right young man – in his view – for Sharon, and a humble and meek girl for Har'El. The siblings had to be separated as soon as possible. They could no longer see each other without a witness, so the lovers rebelled and escaped from Calvary. My friends found their new home far north – beneath a magnificent mountain and beside a wide river, with no one to find them.

I thought of that story when my feet refused to go, swollen and heavy as two stones. I went where my heart led me, ignoring my hurt body and clouded mind.

I knew Adam was dying… and that I was going to die with him.

I came to the settlement at dawn. I didn't need a bunch of bearded men around the big tent to sense Adam's presence. His sons, grandsons and great-grandsons had been discussing some irrelevant things, waving their hands and trying to outdo one another in vanity. Women were staying in the tents, and, judging by the scents, cooking a meal. I heard children's cries from several huts.

A tall and thin old man noticed me first. He wore a long robe and held a stick in his hand. His oblong face and icy gaze gave him away. Seth was Eve's image and likeness.

"Who are you, woman? What are you doing here alone?" he asked me harshly. "Where's your husband?"

The others looked at me with curiosity.

"I am Sophia," I said loudly. "I came to see Adam."

Seth goggled at me. Men began to rustle.

Seth went on, "How dare you call our father by the name and harass him on his deathbed?"

"Chase her away, Father," Enos said. He raised his voice before continuing, "Nobody knows her; she must be from Cain's lineage."

"How insolent she is!" Kenan, his son, shook his head. "She looks you in the eye!"

I approached the crowd fearlessly. "Adam was my husband," I said, turning towards Seth, "before you, and your brothers, and even your mother were born."

The bewildered old man mouthed, "Lilith…"

"I am compassionate and cruel," I said, smiling. "I never attack first, but I know how to defend myself."

The crowd protested scarily. Through their noise, I heard the words "bitch," "demon," and "infant killer."

"You'll enter the tent over my dead body," Seth hissed. "Go back to where you came from, or I swear by my wives, I will send you to hell with my own hands!"

The others lined up like a wall not to let me in.

"Don't swear by others, Seth," I answered firmly, "for you will not stop me."

I pushed away the tough old man and headed for Adam. Seth did not expect an insult and, instead of opposing me, froze in place and stared. Firm Enos and fiery Kenan were stomping in place and grumbling something about "a harlot who wanted to ride a man."

"Don't let her in! She is Death!" Seth screamed in vain.

The wall of his descendants did not move. It was obvious – I frightened them.

Suddenly a hoarse voice called from the tent.

"What is it, Seth? Who is it you offend this time?"

I recognized my husband and hurried to get in.

Adam looked decrepit. His hair and beard were white. I found him lying on a wide bed, wrapped in several sheets. With trembling hands, I lifted a thin curtain.

"Sophia…" he said, barely holding back tears. Deep wrinkles changed his face, but his gaze remained warm and lucid. "Forgive me."

I could not help crying. "At the very moment I left home," I gently stroked his hand, "I did forgive you."

Adam kissed my hand. I closed my eyes for a moment. Paradise lost was coming back to me again.

"I'm old." He rose with effort. I helped him sit and took my place right next to him.

"I've met your children, Adam."

"Snooty roosters," the old man whispered in my ear. "They claim to be better than women, wearing colorful gowns and losing their hair!"

We laughed like we used to.

"I admit my guilt," Adam continued seriously. "Devil had persuaded me to substitute my love with a silly, greedy creature. Abel was killed because of me – my pride and foolishness… And then… I handed everything to Seth, who has grown up under the influence of his mother. There you go." He coughed. "I haven't died yet, but I hear them arguing about my funeral."

"I'm mortal, too." I looked into his eyes, and told him everything that happened to me while we were apart.

"I knew," he groaned. "You have always been faithful to me!"

"I've been faithful to myself, Adam."

His breath went heavy. He rejected to drink water, nor to lie down to have some rest.

"Eve was jealous…" He spoke persistently, realizing that his time was running out. "I chose her, despite loving you. I would not have been able to bear it if you had left me, so I chose an easy way – without love. But without love, one does not live, he just exists."

My heart was ready to stop beating, but this wasn't the end yet.

"Har'El and Sharon... I remember well those children. We could have been like them." He leaned his head on my shoulder.

"It's nobody's fault, Adam," I whispered to him, hugging him like a child. "Everything is as it should be."

He gave me one more vivid glance and said, "I got what I was asking for, but you, Sophia... You deserve your happiness."

I suddenly felt indescribable lightness in my body and grace in my soul. I wanted to hold that moment, to live it forever... Until I remembered the archangel's words.

"I will be happy," I said, barely audibly, "In another body."

Then, there fell darkness.

PART I
IBIS REDIBIS...

I

I am Julia Drusilla, a sister and a former favorite of the emperor Caligula. I was born on April 13, AD 13, in the Abitarvium military garrison, during the war with the Germans. My ancestors by matriline were Caesar and Augustus, and Mark Antony from the spear side. I went down in history as an impersonal victim of the mad emperor, and this was very far from truth.

The Caligula I knew was a visionary and benefactor, a great fighter against injustice. And I, Drusilla, was the first woman in the Empire, raised to the first counselor and co-ruler.

No, my story will not be like scandalous lies you have been used to. Do not look for the descriptions of wild orgies and atrocious tortures that my brother allegedly enjoyed, nor any evidence of his madness, for you will certainly not find them here. The official history is *not* written by the winners. Victory is like a racehorse – it is never tamed by a tyrant, but the noble knight. The annals are written according to the needs of losers, who exult in dancing on the corpses of the victors.

I was four when I watched my father's triumph in Rome. My people were celebrating Pyrrhic victory, because the battles with Arminius[3] had cost us thousands of lives. Although Romans did not actually conquer even a third of the Germanic lands, some huge victories brought enough glory to the governor Nero, called Germanicus, to exceed the fame of Caesar.

---

[3] Arminius – a chieftain of the Germanic Cherusci tribe.

On that day, the triumphant was riding a large quadriga,[4] pulled by four white horses. A tall slave held the laurel wreath above my father's head and whispered in his ear *memento mori*, in accordance with tradition.

Gaius Caesar, a five-year-old boy, was sitting next to a Germanicus, wearing an alba,[5] a red sagum,[6] and a pair of small wedge sandals.[7]

He looked at me with his big blue eyes, full of childish verve and pride. Our people were dancing and singing around, praising the winner and his 'lionet.' Nero and Drusus, our older brothers, enthusiastically followed the parade route from the Campus Martius to the Capitolium. Our sisters Agrippina and Livilla were already bored, and our mother looked depressed. She understood what it meant to receive triumph from the ruler.

"One day you will ride a gilded chariot alone," I told Gaius when the parade was over.

"As a winner?" my brother asked me with a moving smile.

"As the emperor of Rome."

The boy opened his eyes wide. "How come, Drusilla? Tiberius is the emperor!"

"Tiberius is old," I answered. "And he needs an heir. Our father is his stepson, and you are an heir of Germanicus."

"I know our father doesn't want to rule. He quelled the legion uprising to stay loyal to our Caesar,"[8] he said earnestly. "Still, I'm the youngest."

I laughed. I couldn't quite imagine any of our brothers on the throne. Nero was ill-mannered, interested mainly in wrestling and gambling with legionnaires. Drusus had studied works of famous philosophers for days and nights, cherishing his ambitions to become another Cicero.

"Believe me; you will wear the crown one day."

---

[4] A chariot drawn by four horses abreast.

[5] A plain white toga, worn on formal occasions.

[6] A short soldier's cloak.

[7] Gaius was given his nickname Caligula, meaning "little (soldier's) boot" in Latin, after the small boots (caligae) he wore.

[8] The rulers of the Julian-Claudius dynasty used the name of their ancestor – Julius Caesar – as an imperial title.

Gaius giggled cheerfully and hugged me gently. "If you are right, you will become Augusta."

I was right.

But until that… a lot of things had happened.

II

The emperor appointed our father to a position of proconsul[9] of all the eastern provinces, sending him on the way with no return. Germanicus fulfilled the task fairly. After he incorporated the provinces of Cappadocia and Commagene, and appeased Armenians, he had been preparing to go to Cyprus, where he could rest with his family. All of us could hardly wait to enjoy the turquoise sea and walk around the ancient buildings our teacher Zaleukos told us about.

Calpurnius Piso was aware of it. The governor of Syria, whom we were visiting, was known as a descendant of an influential Roman family, and the emperor's former favorite. Cunning and unscrupulous by nature, Piso was the kind of person Tiberius needed to eliminate his younger rival stepson.

I remember when Piso, playing a good host, asked our father to delay the voyage because of the incoming storm, reportedly predicted by his astrologer.

"Roman ships are made to withstand a thousand storms," my father answered. "I don't trust these hierophants[10] as much. From my experience, here where we are, in summer, storms are quite rare."

"If my astrologer is lying to me, I'll have him whipped. I must admit, the rogue has never failed me, though," Piso went on, and then beckoned his cellarius[11] for more wine. "After all, Nero, if you planned a fun trip for your kids, why not bring them to Egypt?"

Germanicus laughed.

"Quod dicis?[12] Without Tiberius's permission?"

Piso toasted. Thirty years spent at the Senate were enough to teach this scoundrel how to deceive people well.

---

[9] An ancient official with notable delegated authority.
[10] (Anc. Gr.) A person who brings religious congregants into the presence of that which is deemed holy. Here: in a mocking manner.
[11] (Lat.) A cupbearer.
[12] (Lat.) Excuse me?

"Do not worry about Caesar," he winked at his guest. "I won't give you away; even lend my entourage to you."

Father straightened and got serious.

"You're asking me to deceive the emperor, aren't you?"

Calpurnius didn't even wince.

"I just want you to have a good time. For all your deeds to Rome, you surely deserve an adventure." Piso blinked again, and patted Germanicus on the shoulder. "Believe me, the old fool won't even notice."

"He's not stupid." Germanicus rose from his klinē – upholstered sofa. "I have no intention to violate the law for the sake of a province where they practice incest and worship cats!"

To avoid an altercation, Piso had to fall back. As soon as he left the exedra, he ordered his servants to find the best Egyptian books, and he secretly sent them as gifts to the important guests' children. Nero received a manuscript about the great warriors; Drusus got the very rare Book of Wisdom scribed by Ptah-Hotep. Agrippina and Livilla found under their pillows Cleopatra's written secrets of eternal youth and beauty. Both Gaius and I discovered an uncommon legend of Isis and Osiris. A desire awakened in each of us to explore the mysterious and forbidden land of Egypt, like all children. Yet we didn't understand why our father seemed so abstinent, our mother so disturbed, and the host so generous.

"I'm not afraid of Caesar," Germanicus said, trying to comfort his wife. "If not me – who would stay loyal to the emperor? The Senate looks like bestiarium[13]... Praetorians are getting more arrogant... Without my support, he is in danger of collapse."

Finally, to Piso's delight, Germanicus fulfilled our wishes. We spent five days in Alexandria, disguised as a family of traveling Greeks. The acting was necessary because of the ingrained hatred between the Egyptians and the Romans. Octavian, our great-grandfather, took from this ancient and wise nation their land, their independence, most of their beautiful women – and he destroyed the queen.

---

[13] (Lat.) A room in the amphitheater where wild animals were kept for the games.

Antonia Minor, our paternal grandmother, used to tell us, "The Greeks are best in warcraft, the Egyptians in arts, the Jews in trade and the Romans in intrigues and conspiracies."

The daughter of governor Mark Antony hated Rome to such an extent that she welcomed to her house Princess Selena, her half-sister – despite Octavian's wish to throw a girl to the arena. Later, taking advantage of the uncle's love for her, Antonia assured Selena further security by marriage with the King of Mauritania.

I remember the ruins of Cleopatra's palace and the once magnificent Temple of Isis. Gaius and I had been there, accompanied by Zaleukos. That night we crossed the threshold of the destroyed sanctuary, our teacher tried to tell us the whole truth about the fall of Egypt.

"Augustus stabbed them in the back. He conquered Khem[14] for deceit. Rome was disturbed by their freedom… and love." He continued in Greek, as if he was afraid of someone overhearing, "Namely, Mithras can't stand either… And what bothers him the most are smart women."

"Who is that Mithras?" Gaius wondered. "And why does he hate women?"

Zaleukos raised a wooden torch, which lit a large sun disk painted on the wall.

"He is the Sun God. Alexander had conquered the Orient, but still couldn't overcome Mithras."

I was astonished. I had read every possible scripture about the great king, but none of the authors has really mentioned a god with such name. "Father says – gods don't exist," I said. Then I recalled the words of Germanicus: "If they existed, they would certainly not have allowed Tiberius to become emperor!"

Zaleukos suddenly grew silent, and then, thoughtfully, said something the two children were not prepared for.

"Germanicus worships this god, and so does the Army, the Senate, and the emperor himself."

My brother cried, "You're lying! Our father would never worship such a hideous deity."

---

[14] Ancient original name for Egypt.

"Hush!" The Greek squeezed his hand, looking around fearfully. "We have to leave as soon as possible. You are not ready for those stories."

Gaius did not protest, but told him to release his hand. I thought about my father. Zaleukos would never lie to us. Our whole family considered him an honest, wise and loyal man.

Leaving the dark hall, I swiftly stopped and gazed at the fresco, which depicted two main deities – Osiris and Isis.

"Here in Egypt, a brother can marry his sister," Gaius whispered to me cautiously.

"Your father is right, though," Zaleukos went on anyway, "Gods are created by men – to deceive other people. They cook up pretty legends to destroy love and rule the world. Conspiracies are born of hatred, and hatred is born of fear."

He had never spoken to us so earnestly before. Amazed, we didn't dare to ask him anything. On the way back we just kept quiet, holding hands. The night was slowly fading, kissing the golden yellow coast of the Nile, taking away our childhood by the first breath of Egyptian dawn.

III

AD 19

After we returned to Antioch, Piso had made a feast. His generosity became increasingly suspicious, but Germanicus stayed calm and witty.

"Our miser-Caesar wouldn't spend a wealth on all those dishes, balladines, and gladiators," he referred to Zaleukos, while the vestiplici[15] dressed them. "If he wanted to get rid of me, he would have found a cheaper way."

The teacher answered with Menander's words, "Whom the gods love dies young."

Father laughed bitterly. "Ananke[16] has already shot her poison arrow."

That night, I couldn't fall asleep. Since I was born, I had been plagued with unbearable spinal pain unknown to physicians. My mother was ashamed of me; my sisters mocked me. Only Gaius always had some sympathy for me. As the night fell, he stealthily entered the cubiculum[17] to console me.

"Your heart is beating hard." He gave me a strong childish hug. "When I grow up, I'll find the cure for you, even in Caledonia!"[18]

"Thank you, Caligula," I muttered, shaking inside. "Armida makes a decoction of boiled mint, but it doesn't seem to work."

"I hate my agnomen," Gaius frowned. "And that Germanic whore. How do you understand each other? She doesn't even speak Sermo Vulgatis."[19]

I smiled and inhaled deeply. It was growing faint. Fortunately, those night attacks didn't last, unlike my morning headaches. "Get accustomed to it," I whispered. "Under this agnomen, you will make history."

The boy looked at me dreamily and somewhat shyly.

---

[15] (Lat.) Valets, skilled in the art of draping a toga.

[16] Ancient Greek goddess of necessity and inevitability.

[17] (Lat.) Small bedroom.

[18] Modern-day Scotland.

[19] (Lat.) Vulgar, "common" version of Latin.

"It's not Armida's fault that she's the daughter to Arminius," I went on, nodding towards my nursemaids' room. "She's silly, but that makes her a good nanny."

My brother caressed my cheek. "I know you love foreigners… Zaleukos, Armida, and that Jewess, given to our father by Antipas[20] – Susannah?"

"Whatever they are," I answered, "they are certainly better than Romans."

"That's right," Caligula agreed, then turned aside and instantly fell asleep. He had an annoying habit of falling asleep while we were having a serious talk.

Before the dawn broke, my brother quietly scrambled out of my room, merely passing Cassius Chaerea. The centurion walked with wide steps to cubiculum, frightening my sleepy nursemaids.

"Cassius?" I asked, astonished.

Chaerea was the only soldier in the army who had gained my father's endless trust and friendship. Since he was a sixteen-year-old legionnaire, Cassius had always accompanied Germanicus in war and peace. During the Battle of the Weser River, the young man saved my father's life but suffered a bad wound. Rumor had it, the injury was serious enough to make him infertile, and so he couldn't stand children – with the exception of me.

From my birth, when Cassius was guarding the woman in labor like a Vigile,[21] until my death in his arms, that man strove to protect the only being who had managed to soften the heart of a warrior.

"Your Highness, I was commanded to take you away." He stood quietly near my bed, dressed and armored. "Forgive me if I woke you up, but you're no longer safe in here."

I was frightened, but not of him. Two visions lingered in my head – my father's conversation first with Piso, then with Zaleukos.

"Susannah!" I got up. "Take off my coa vestis,[22] and dress me in my tunica and peplum."[23]

---

[20] A son of the Judean client king Herod the Great, and ruler of Galilee and Perea, who bore the title of tetrarch ("ruler of a quarter").

[21] (here) A night watchman.

[22] (Lat.) A nightgown.

[23] (Lat.) A woman's loose outer shawl.

Nursemaids, Susannah and Armida, were in a panic.

"Why the hell are you staring at me?" Cassius shouted at young women. "Help the princess!"

"What is going on?" I asked quietly when the slaves were done with my clothes.

Chaerea crouched in front of me, and gently put his big male hand on my shoulder. "Drusilla," he said, "our world is cruel, and things you've seen north are nothing to that which is yet to come."

I timidly touched his arm, silently asking him to take me in his arms.

"Do not worry," he continued, shifting me over his shoulder. "You are as strong as your name is."[24]

I nodded and hugged him. Cassius rushed across the corridor with Armida and Susannah following us. It seemed like there was no one in the whole of Piso's villa, not even a servant.

"Gaius!" I cried out suddenly. "Where is my brother?"

"Easy, infantula," the soldier replied. "We. re taking your brother and sisters with us."

"If we get out of this house alive," Armida grunted.

"Look who's talking!" Susannah giggled, trying to cheer me up.

In the meantime, I felt like I was going to faint. "Susannah," I moaned helplessly.

"What's wrong?" the Jewess asked, taking me by the hand. That was the last thing I heard before I lost consciousness.

---

[24] DRVSILLA – (Lat.) a strong one.

IV

"My dear Agrippina," Piso addressed to my mother, when the ministrants[25] brought a big tray with roast venison into triclinium.[26] "I've always wanted to ask you something, but my innate shyness did prevent me."

"If the question is decent," my mother replied with a discreet smile, "be my guest."

Piso grinned, then turned to my father, handing him a golden goblet filled with scarlet wine. "Laodicean wine – best in all of Syria."

Germanicus raised a goblet, followed by the host's sly smile, and drank to the bottom. "It's gorgeous."

"So, I've been curious," Piso continued, looking at my mother. "Have you, Julii, really borrowed that Antonian custom of taking peregrines[27] and freedmen to the feast?"

Visitants, mostly patricians, found this jest extremely funny. Cassius and Zaleukos, umbrae[28] of Germanicus, realized they were not wanted. For my father, this had been an unprecedented insolence.

"What do you think you're doing, man?" he roared, and banged his fist on the table, bringing the rich treat down.

The teacher reddened, while disciplined Chaerea seemed forbearing.

Piso rose lazily. "What is the matter, Nero? Shall we fight for a joke like savages?"

"Savages?!" Germanicus exclaimed. "Many of the barbarians I've met had more consideration than yourself!"

"Please, darling," Agrippina tried to intervene, but father stopped her with one gesture. Piso's friends were watching the argument like an attraction from a circus.

---

[25] (lat.) Servants helping at the feast.

[26] (lat.) Dining room.

[27] (Lat.) Freeborn foreigners, living in Rome.

[28] (Lat.) "shadows" – uninvited guests, who sat behind the important invited guest on the bed.

"Whom are you calling a peregrine, Piso?" Germanicus inhaled heavily. "Indeed, a war hero who became a centurion in his twentieth?"[29]

The host gave Cassius Chaerea a disdainful glance. "A son of Hispana," he continued to provoke. "An offspring of a bastard daughter…"

"That's enough!" my father shouted. "For this insult, Calpurnius Piso, I immediately strip you of your positions!"

Piso stared at him, upset, letting his relative Coccaeus Nerva, known as the imperial jurist, speak. "Do not exaggerate, Germanicus. The punishment for injuria verbalis[30] in this case is merely conditional."

The others began to nod.

"Nero, please, withdraw your words," Plancina, Piso's wife, said humbly. "What will become of us? We have a son… We will pay damages to both Chaerea and… Callinicus."

My father laughed bitterly, and then referred to Piso, mimicking his voice and gestures. "In *this* case, right? Do you optimates[31] really think you can buy forgiveness for your vice?"

Piso cowardly looked down, seeking Nerva's support.

"I know you are righteous, Nero," the jurist went on steadily, "as well as you're stubborn. I do not impugn, because these qualities have made you who you are. Our people have spent centuries bringing the law and obeying it implicitly, to make Rome what it is. If you populares[32] had an opportunity to change it, there would be chaos. So, for a public insult of a distinguished soldier, my relative will stand before the Senate… and so will you – for entering Egypt illegally."

Musicians stopped their cheerful playing. Guests fell silent. Agrippina turned pale, and, following Germanicus' volant advice, left the feast escorted by Zaleukos. Piso, with a single nod, sent his piteous wife away as if she was a maid.

---

[29] Generally, a legionnaire had a right to advance to centurion rank from the age of 29.
[30] (Lat.) Verbal abuse in public.
[31] A conservative political faction during late Roman Republic and early Empire.
[32] A progressive political faction during late Roman Republic and early Empire who favored the cause of the plebeians.

"So be it," Father broke the silence. "Let the Senate and the emperor himself judge me. But don't you think, o Janus,[33] that you've taken me aback. I was aware of your depravity, and it was me to let you show the limits of your vice." His look struck Piso down and made the others cower. "I am not afraid of any punishment, nor do I regret fulfilling wishes of my children. All I rue about is wasting my time in your company." Then he returned to Nerva. "You, o Lady Justice,[34] do not care about the law, but wealth and fame. I must admit the right to one young Gallic druid, who foresaw Rome's fall for vanity."

Followed by evil and envy looks from their enemies, Germanicus and Chaerea left the coenaculum.[35]

"I know who is behind all that!" Cassius cried with fury when they stepped out into spacious peristyle,[36] decorated with caryatids and mosaic flooring. "The old pederast."

"Silentium!"[37] my father cut in like a severe commander pacifying a rapturous soldier. "He is not worth your career, or life. As for me, it is unfortunately far too late."

"Commander," the centurion continued boldly, "in the name of our oaths, and all that we have gone through, I will stay loyal – whatever it takes."

Germanicus gave him a listen, and then put his hand on a young man's shoulder, and whispered, trying not to get noticed by the janitor behind the colonnade, "Then you do what I will tell you. Equip yourself, find my three daughters and Caligula, and take first ship to Antium. Tiberius and *those above him* will not spare my family."

Cassius, horrified by his assumption, nodded.

"Take my children to the Empress Mother, Livia," the governor continued. "I don't like her, but she is the only person to have influence on Caesar. Try to act naturally in the harbor – as long as I am the proconsul, your way is still clear."

"At first, I thought I had a nightmare," Chaerea told me, when I asked him what had happened then.

---

[33] The two-faced Roman deity of transitions and duality; a figurative synonym to a hypocrite.

[34] An allegorical Roman personification of the moral force in judicial systems.

[35] (lat.) Another name for an eating-room.

[36] A continuous porch formed by a row of columns surrounding the perimeter of Roman house.

[37] (Lat; mil. comm. ord.) Silence!

There were a million questions in his mind, but he was running out of time. Suddenly, recollecting Piso's golden goblet, he suggested the commander to vomit or to find a port physician.

"When my children are safe, give report to the praetor," Germanicus said, then turned his back, ignoring the warning. "I believe in you. Now – vale."[38]

Chaerea did as he was commanded.

---

[38] (Lat.) Farewell.

V

Sailing the sea had worsened my condition – I got a fever. From time to time, my nursemaids woke me up from a deep and heavy dream to nourish my half-conscious body. I remember chilly wads on my forehead and bitter tinctures given rather off-handedly by a naval surgeon. I remember Gaius arguing with Cassius about which of them was going to watch over me at night. I also remember my sisters grudging for the lack of attention.

"What am I supposed to eat?" my older sister Agrippina asked Chaerea in her regular, annoying manner. "Musty bread, warm cheese – and drink some vinegar?"

The centurion had been patient for quite a long time – until he heard Livilla snuffing.

"You're on a warship, Princesses," Cassius warned the girls. "Your father is now out of grace." Then, he nodded towards wicked-looking sailors. "You better be quiet, otherwise neither my reputation, nor your kinship with Tiberius will save you."

"You silly geese," Caligula joined in. "Instead of mourning for our father, you are crying for your gingerbreads and toys!"

"You only care about Drusilla!" Agrippina replied tauntingly, as timid Livilla hid behind her back. "This unhandy being!"

"Hold your tongue!" Gaius snapped at her, but she fell back behind the younger sister to avoid a slap. "She is more beautiful and clever than you both!"

"I doubt it," Livilla spoke nervously. "Mother says –"

"You two, shut up!" Cassius stopped the children's quarrel. "Get out of my sight before I go a verbis ad verbera!"[39]

The girls ran to a tiny room under the deck.

"And you, Caligula," he went on warmly. "Don't lose your temper because of the fools. Go get some sleep before we step into the city of insomnia and insecurity."

---

[39] (Lat. prov.) From words to blow.

Gaius replied with an intransigent look. Pallor and eye bags slowly swallowed all his cuteness.

"Have some rest, my Prince," Licinius, the captain of the ship, said as he came over. "It's October, the sky is clear, the sea is calm. Any day now we get ashore. My oarsmen are like gladiators." The boy grinned, and Licinius gave him a small lagena[40] of wine. "Here you go... A sleeping cure."

Unwillingly, my brother took a couple of small sips and returned a vessel to the owner. "I don't like it," he said honestly.

"Well, there are many things *I* do not like; the same for Cassius and all the fellows on this quadrireme,"[41] the captain sighed, "but that's the way life is. Better get used to it – the sooner the better."

Fatigue and wine made Gaius feel vertigo. "My life will never be like yours," he replied earnestly, slowly bringing himself down to the bench.

Licinius giggled and sat next to him. "You're full of spirit, boy." He gently elbowed Gaius like an old friend. "Make sure you don't lose it."

Gaius nodded and leaned his head on the captain's shoulder. Sleep had overcome him.

"I'm sorry for this child," the sailor whispered to his companions. "Gods keep him!"

"If there are any." Cassius took my sleeping brother in his arms to place him somewhere better. In the lower room, he found an empty bed. "Just dream," he said. He covered Gaius with a lacerna[42] as a thick blanket. "She'll be fine, believe me."

---

[40] (Anc.Gr.) A narrow-necked, two-handled vessel of bellying-out shape.
[41] Ancient Roman warship with four rows of oars.
[42] (Lat.) Soldier's cloak.

VI

"There it is, our Italy." Licinius showed me a barely visible green coast. That morning, when the galley arrived in Antium, I was standing in the stern with my head clear and a smile on my face. I was happy to live.

Gaius held my hand with a firm grip. "I cured you," he said. He was pleased he did.

"Omnes ad arma!"[43] Licinius summoned the sailors.

"Get ready to disembark," Cassius told us. "We have to get to the Palatine before salutatio[44] is over. Augusta receives no one after noon. When it comes to me, if I don't show up to the praetor today, at best, I'll be discharged."

"What do you mean?" Agrippina was confused. "Will our great-grandmother receive us as clients?"

"Has anyone notified her at all about our arrival?" Livilla asked nervously. "Will she send a carriage for us?"

Chaerea looked up at the sky, counted to ten, and turned his back – to step aside. My sisters, messy-haired and ruffle-dressed, began to weep.

"How can you be so dumb?" Caligula exhaled.

"Cassius, wait!" I cried at the top of my lungs.

The centurion stopped.

"The little thing has temper," Licinius laughed. "She reminds me of someone."

"Tell me everything ab ovo,"[45] I demanded, stepping towards Cassius. "Why did we have to escape?"

"Tiberius," he replied violently. "It's all because of him."

"Damn him!" Gaius stamped his feet. "Gods damn Tiberius and nasty old man Piso!"

---

[43] (Lat.) Everybody get to work!
[44] (Lat.) The formal morning greeting of the Roman patron by his clients.
[45] (Lat.) From the very start.

"By all the gods, be quiet!" the captain whispered, heavily gesticulating. "You have no idea whom you're dealing with."

"What is about our mother?" I went on with questions. "Brothers? Zaleukos? What about them?"

The tone of Cassius' voice suddenly changed.

"I understand you, totally. You all are hungry, tired and scared. I also lost my father as a child, soon after that my mother died of grieving. You must not surrender. Your only hope is Empress Livia. Be polite and even humble, and, if needed pretend to be silly."

We listened to him carefully, forgetting our reprimands and quarrels. Agrippina wiped her tears off and embraced me. Livilla followed her, as usual.

"We are family," our brother said excitedly.

"Together, we are stronger." Agrippina nodded.

"We will survive," I whispered, hugging my sisters. "We will make it."

"Well done, friends!" Chaerea praised us. "Concord is important in both – war and in peace."

"Armida! Susannah!" I called my maids. "Dress my sisters up and do their hair!"

Young women ran to me and let delighted Agrippina and Livilla drag them to the utility room. Caligula asked the captain to show him the oarsmen and other naval things before the sailing was over.

"An emperor can't kill so many people, the Augustans, without trial and error." Then I heard him talking to Licinius. "Romans will tear him apart. I believe our mother and brothers are safe."

And I hope you are right, I thought, looking to the distant harbor.

VII

Livia the Exalted was a very old but lively small-boned woman with lucid almond-shaped eyes. For her age, she had a surprisingly clear mind and perfect posture. Since she had become a widow, she has replaced colorful silk and rich jewelry with long pallae[46] over neat stolae,[47] using neither cosmetics nor even perfumes. She led an ascetic life, also requiring high discipline from all the slaves. Rumor had it, she was a Domina who skimped on everything but whipping for her servants. In public, the dowager empress was regarded as a prominent and independent woman, who had elevated both her sons to higher titles, and advised Octavian himself.

Barely seventeen and eager for power, Livia left her first husband for Augustus, completely separating children from their father. Fearing that this misdeed might cast a shadow over the emperor's reputation, she accused her abandoned spouse of violence, although this was the last thing unfortunate Claudian would have done. To gain more influence, the empress sent away her son's beloved wife and forced him to get married to the daughter of Augustus. Livia didn't like her other daughter-in-law either, but Antonia was too persistent and loved by her uncle to fall.

"Will this Clytemnestra[48] give us shelter?" I whispered to Cassius as we were waiting in the atrium.

"She'll do it rather out of spite," he answered. "Caesar and his mother hate each other like cat and dog."

A husky-voiced nomenclator announces our arrival, and two other servants opened the door of the tablinum.[49]

"Gaius Caesar, son of your grandson Germanicus," he said. "And his sisters, accompanied by…"

---

[46] Palla – a rectangular-shaped shawl usually made of wool or cotton.
[47] Stola – a long dress-like garment, usually with short sleeves, held together with clasps a flounce on its bottom; fastened by the girdle high above the waist.
[48] In Greek mythology – the evil and greedy queen of Mycenae, metaphorically a bad wife and a possessive mother.
[49] In Roman houses – a study and a reception room of the head of the family.

"Cassius Chaerea." Livia finished impatiently, looking at our companion curiously. "The knight who saved my grandson's life."

"Salve,[50] Noblissima."[51] Cassius took a step forward. "It's my honor to serve the emperor Tiberius and Rome."

The old matron smiled slyly.

"I'm here because of my governor's will," the soldier continued as he was reporting. "I ask for protection for the prince and princesses… "

"I understand." Livia rose from her wide seat, interrupting him with a gentle gesture. "Nero must have done some stupid thing, so now he is afraid of my son's anger." She sounded irritatingly calm and somewhat flippant. "Fiery personalities should only fear their own unrestraint."

Cassius looked through her with no emotions on his face.

"Tiberius is a hard man," Matron continued, studying us. "Still, he is no villain, who spills kinly blood. If Nero broke the law, he would receive no greater punishment than ademptio civitatis[52] while his children remain innocent."

"The Governor would never betray his Emperor," Chaerea tried to explain. "He fell a victim to someone else's betrayal."

"What do you mean – fell?" Livia's expression became serious. "Is he dead?"

Cassius nodded.

"Requiescat in pace,"[53] the old woman whispered steadily, not to say indolently. "What a fool!"

"Noblissima," Centurion protested. "The late Governor has always been our noble role model."

"That's why he died as an innocent man," Livia said ironically. "And irresponsibly sent his children through Mare Nostrum[54] – for me to babysit them?"

---

[50] (lat.) Be greeted.
[51] (lat.) The Noblest One (imperial title).
[52] (lat.) Depriving someone of his citizenship.
[53] (lat.) May he rest in peace.
[54] (lat.) The Mediterranean Sea.

That instant, when my sister started trembling with fear and fatigue and Gaius clenched his fists distressed, I remembered my father's conversation with Piso that I had accidentally heard, passing by the triclinium. Since my early childhood, I had been shortsighted, but my sense of hearing was owlishly sharp. Piso's guards could not imagine that the child, so carelessly hopping around the atrium, could hear through the closed doors. Suddenly, everything became terribly clear to me.

"Augusta, please listen!" I exclaimed desperately. "Senator Piso has betrayed my father! He convinced him to go to Egypt – without the imperial permission!"

Stunned by my audacity, dowager empress fell silent for a while, and then ordered all the servants to leave tablinum. Caligula squeezed my hand, and Cassius' gaze told me not to be afraid.

"Princess is right," he told the royal lady, surprised by my boldness. "At the feast, where I was present, Nerva mentioned self-willed visit to the province, and then Piso…"

"I don't care about any Piso!" Livia yelled. "Germanicus received the highest honors from Augustus and Tiberius, and how did he reciprocate? O, my first grandson!" the empress moaned pathetically. "It's Antonia's fault! Instead of raising her children properly, she spent her time on reading and planting flowers!" Then, with a theatrical sigh, she sat down and looked at us. "What should I do with those four brats?"

I wished I could interrupt her again, mentioning the damn books Piso lured us to Egypt with. I wanted to address Augusta as to my great-grandmother, just to seek a crumb of understanding and assistance. In the end, as I looked at this fragile woman, possibly too aged to bear that awful news, I even wanted to console her… until our eyes met.

Bitterness – that's what I saw in her gaze, a feeling overflowing her whole being, hidden under the veil of love and concern for children. I mean, her own children. She divided people into "worthy" and "unworthy." She followed those 'worthy,' stronger ones with hidden hatred, and destroyed the weaker ones with ease. And now, having gained all the power and glory, Livia felt indignant about those who would never go her way.

I looked away disgustedly.

"I have made a decision," she said formally, reaching out to Gaius, commanding him to help her rise from her seat. "You, fellow, stay with me."

Gaius looked at me, realizing the threatening separation.

"What about the girls?" Cassius asked.

The dowager empress looked at him with disdain.

"Who are you – a soldier or a nursemaid?" Her anger turned to sarcasm. "You are disrespectful, like this little one…" She pierced me with her hazel eyes. "What is your name?"

"Julia Drusilla," I replied indifferently. Actually, I hated my name. Greek names were the ones I admired, for being more sweet-sounding and imaginative. Zaleukos called me Glaucula,[55] and this nickname was dearer to me than all the diminutives.

"This name should be borne by the lady – do not stain it with your insolence." She walked on, with her skinny hands crossed, to the column decorated with Tiberius' bust. "Do you know how to spin and weave?"

"No, I don't," I answered.

"Of course, your parents didn't teach you to be a lady." She sounded saturnine.

I shrugged my shoulders.

"Drusilla is too young and sickly," Agrippina suddenly elucidated. "But Livilla and I know everything about household –"

Livia tiredly raised her hand to stop her. "Oh, if I paid attention to my illnesses, I never would become what I am now – a mother, an empress, and an independent woman," she continued superciliously. "In my life, I only count on myself, and I am fine with it. Parents die, husbands leave, siblings can kill you for legacy… even your children always want some gain."

These cruel words and squeaky voice became unbearable.

"I don't know anything about household," I spoke. "But I am fluent in Greek, and I love history. Zaleukos, my brothers' tutor, also teaches me."

Livia waved aside. "You three," said to my sisters and me, "Go to Antonia. You will get lectica[56] and escort. Tribune?"[57] The old matron looked away. "There is no

---

[55] (anc.gr.) Little owl.

[56] (Lat.) A kind of litter or portable couch.

[57] An officer of the Roman army who ranked below the legate and above the centurion.

reason to be worried about *my* great-grandchildren, as long as I live. As for Nero," she finished nefariously, "I feel no pity for a man who disappointed me the most."

Cassius nodded and took my hand.

"No!" I screamed. "I am not going anywhere without Caligula!"

Livia's face flushed with rage; her eyes turned coal black. She resembled Medusa, a mythical creature whose gaze turned its subject to stone.

"Who are you, little bitch, to set your face against *me*?" Even her whisper sounded like a roar from hell. "You are suggesting *me* in my own house what I am to do?"

"We're leaving." Chaerea slung me over his shoulder and headed to the entrance hall. My sisters followed him scared, and Caligula, aware of our separation, cried my name out.

"Drusilla!"

I tried to break away, but Cassius was holding me tight.

"Don't make a scene, infantula," he whispered in my ear. "Everything will be in order."

"You don't understand," I burst into tears. "I cannot live without him!"

Soldier sped up his pace.

"Of course, I do. You think I'm dumb?"

"No," I rested my head on his shoulder. "Help me, Cassius… Please."

I didn't even notice when he placed me into the basterna.

"Better be careful with her," he said to the four carrier slaves. "Otherwise, you'll have to deal with me."

Armida and Susannah, who were waiting in the vestibule, rushed to help me.

"Get off!" Agrippina pushed the Jewess, taking a sit next to me. The harmony between us three never lasted long enough to call it real.

"I'll ride ahead." Cassius put his head under the colorful velarium.[58] "Don't be afraid, Caligula will be back soon. Old witch won't bother him for long."

I'd always trusted him.

---

[58] (lat.) A canopy/curtain over/in the lectica.

"If only Caesar had a little bit of your courage." He gave me a smile. "There still would be a hope for him." Then, he deftly bestrode his horse, and exclaimed.

"Villa Claudiana!"

My father's mother, so unlike her mother-in-law, did not ask any questions. She always *knew* and *understood*. When Chaerea leaded us into her atrium, Antonia, despite her age and status, hurried to give me a hug.

"O grandma's flower! Welcome home."

VIII

AD 22

Three years without Gaius had been very hard to me.

I remember when my mother, Nero and Drusus arrived at the Palatine, carrying the urn with my father's ashes. People at the Forum mourned the famous governor, demanding punishment for the culprit. Conspirators, in fear with possible rebellion, decided to sacrifice Piso. The poisoner was initially banished to Rhodes, where he was forced to commit suicide.

In order to remove all doubts and suspicions, Emperor Tiberius forgave his stepson for 'the Egyptian affair,' and organized a majestic funeral. This double-minded man also gave honor to Chaerea – 'soldier who has saved his grand-nephews' and promoted him to the rank of tribunus angusticlavius.[59] He also ordered Cassius under four eyes to do his duties far enough from the Romulus hill.[60]

Poor teacher Zaleukos had disappeared the day after my father died, leaving me eager to study his words…

My sisters kept on mocking me, always supported by our mother. Only my grandmother, grieving the loss of her son, found some relief in my company. We often had breakfast together in her chamber, joking about Agrippina the Elder and Livia.

"They say you look like me," Antonia once told me. "Same blue eyes, big and mournful, and shiny dark hair… You have not inherited anything of the Julii – you are as bright, fiery and persistent as your great-grandfather – Mark Antony. That is the way we all are – me, Germanicus and you. We do not care of what the others think; we go through life as warriors…"

---

[59] (Lat.) Literally – "a narrow-striped tribune; a senior officer of the Roman army who ranked below the legate and above the centurion, usually of Equestrian (knightly) rank.
[60] The Palatine Hill.

I listened to the matron carefully, staring at her smooth, round face with no wrinkles. This plump woman had never been considered a beauty, but she was strong and wise enough to gain respect of the Augustants.[61]

"Did you love your husband, granny?" I asked her, while Antonia was silent, recollecting something dear.

"Unless I loved your grandfather, I'd have never stepped into that serpent lair – Livia's house."

I started laughing, but my suppressed pain had reached me soon. When I was a child, I thought I would always love no one but Gaius. It was insane to hope that anyone in Rome could understand that feeling. Since the time of Numa Pompilius,[62] marriages between closest relatives were strictly forbidden. Augustus banished his daughter Julia to the semi-wild Pandataria Island mostly because of the rumors of their alleged incest.

"I will never get married," I said earnestly, moving my dinner plate aside. The very thought of marrying someone else caused me nausea.

"What?" Antonia wondered. "Am I raising a Vestal Virgin?"[63] Then, with a giggle, she added: "Today, even whores are more white-handed than these arrogant tribas."[64]

"I don't want to be a Vestal Virgin." I felt a little bit offended. "But I want no husband either."

Antonia looked me straight in the eye, and her voice suddenly lost its softness.

"What is it, Drusilla? You are a princess; it's your obligation to get married and give birth to the new royals. Usually, it's up to Caesar who will marry whom, but if I kindly ask him, there would be a chance for you to choose a husband by yourself."

Like all the forlorn children, I had a habit of interrupting my interlocutors, especially when I was feeling bad.

"Tiberius would never let me…" I cut myself off, realizing that I had said too much.

---

[61] Members of the Familia Julii, relatives of Emperor Augustus.

[62] The second Roman ruler from the Age of Kings.

[63] (in ancient Rome) a virgin consecrated to Vesta and vowed to chastity, sharing the charge of maintaining the sacred fire burning on the goddess's altar.

[64] (lat.) Lesbians.

Matron sighed, moved toward me and hugged me.

"I understand. You love someone who is forbidden to you, don't you?"

I fell silent. My truth could have been unbearable even for my liberated grandmother.

"You won't even tell me, right?" Antonia became concerned.

I thought about what would happen if someone found this out. Terrifying visions started hovering in my small head, so I broke into tears. "Granny, I can't!" I murmured, crying.

"Alright, you don't have to." Antonia kissed me on the forehead, then took her silk neck scarf off and dried my tears. "O, poor child! Forgive your foolish grandmother if I made you sad."

It had been a long time since we talked about my marriage again. Grandmother was very attentive, and she always did her best to comfort me after the things we had both survived.

"You are the only hope of mine, Drusilla," Matron used to say. "Nero is gone. My younger son Claudius is a complete idiot, that's why both his marriages have failed… My daughter Livilla would sell me for power and wealth if she could. I'm afraid, your sisters are becoming much like her, as they already asked me to arrange their marriages. You are the only one to understand me, girl."

Antonia was probably the only Roman lady who valued other women's charisma and intelligence much more than their zeal for housekeeping. She had a large library of very rare books in Latin and Greek, presented to her by Augustus. Grandmother held this room as a sacred treasure, keeping everybody out of it but Uncle Claudius and me. My father's brother was the only male descendant of Mark Antony who did not aspire to military service. Born with physical disabilities, Claudius spent his days among the books, studying the history of the Etruscans – the first inhabitants of Italia. Living in his older brother's shadow turned this merely intelligent man to a constantly envious, infantile, mean and self-absorbed bookworm.

"What are you doing here?" he shouted like Cerberus[65] every time he saw me entering the library.

---

[65] In Greek mythology the three-headed dog, Cerberus, stands guard at the entrance to the underworld.

"Antonia allowed me," I replied with pride, so my uncle reluctantly left me alone.

This room, with its vivid frescos, neat shelves, and hundreds of scrolls, was my place of worship and escape. Virgil, Varro, Cicero… I missed no one of these mighty literates who built the memory of Rome. I read everything – historical writings, Greek mythology, foreign legends, dramas. I dreamed that one day my own creative works would be scribed in the Argiletum, and performed on stage.

My biggest role model was Ovid – creator of divine stories and poems. At the time of Augustus, his books were banned and destroyed, because the writer openly extolled love and criticized haughty patricians. Tiberius did not have mercy on Ovid himself, forcing the poet to the inhospitable coast of Pont-Euxin.[66] Nevertheless, Antonia was brave and mad enough to keep a copy of his *Amores*, for she also found salvation in the world of manuscripts and fantasy.

---

[66] (Anc.Gr.) The Black Sea.

IX

On the eve of the spring holiday Parilia,[67] we received news that Livia had fallen ill. Namely, only her physician, jurist and balneator[68] knew about the nature of those health issues, but it was rumored that the dowager empress could barely get out of bed, constantly groaning. To my pleasure, the suspicious old lady had shortly sent Caligula 'where he belongs' – to Villa Claudiana.

On that day, Roman women, in accordance with tradition, decorated their houses and gardens. Antonia and Agrippina the Elder were knitting floral wreaths for doors and hearths, and I was busy decorating the atrium fountain with ribbons. My sisters went to Carinae[69] to help our aunt with holiday preparations. Once a famed beauty, Livilla the Elder had managed to win the favor of Tiberius' the only son, Castor, and strengthened her position in the court with the birth of a baby boy, Gemellus.

At noon, the courtly herald Fabius greeted my grandmother, and conveyed sad news. A young man couldn't help his gaze of curiosity.

"If you expect me to rejoice, I'll disappoint you," Antonia said. "I am the wife of her late son. Augusta can always count on me."

"We wish the Mother Empress to get well as soon as possible!" Agrippina excitedly added.

"I'm sorry, my ladies." Fabio carelessly tossed a paenula[70] over his shoulder. "Noblissima strictly forbade you to visit her. Lady Antonia is the least welcome."

"Then, let Libitina[71] take her!" Triumvir's daughter exclaimed, then grabbed a rare vase of Sidon glass from the table and threw it against the thick column. "Convey to your Domina my words. Heard me?"

---

[67] Roman religious festival related to the foundation of Rome (celebrated on April 21st).
[68] Keeper of the baths.
[69] A Roman area of the most exclusive neighborhoods, where many of the senatorial class lived.
[70] A thick hooded-knee length cloak.
[71] An ancient Roman goddess of funerals and burial.

The young man lost his courage, nodding like a boy, and grandmother raised her hand as if she was threatening him again.

"Get lost, before I throw it at your head!"

The guest hurried to leave. My mother, timidly watching her mother-in-law, began pedantically picking up the pieces of colored glass from the floor. This scene was so comical that I burst out laughing.

"She didn't mourn my son like the damn vase!" Antonia smiled back to me. "And now she is doing my slaves' work!"

"That is not funny." Agrippina frowned, confused. "I'd rather not teach my children to rely on slaves – too much."

"You read about Spartacus[72] too much." The old woman's expression turned sincere. "Only the damn gods know how my heart bleeds... My grief will last until my last breath, but I have no intention to spent time hanging around the house and playing damn Hecuba.[73] My family needs me."

My mother bit her thin lip and looked away, ill-humored.

"Tiberius didn't allow me to attend my son's funeral," Grandmother went on thoughtfully. "The old witch has been keeping my grandson on house arrest for four years. If you think they're done with us, you're wrong. It's the beginning of our nightmares."

"I was warning him, mother," Agrippina tried to explain herself, making sad grimaces. "I begged him, I beseeched him not to go to Egypt, but my husband has always been stubborn... "

"I know better than you, what Nero was," Antonia stopped her. "Not everyone is born to crawl before the rulers, and especially – the worst ones. When a bold eagle has to share the sky with vultures, his devastating fate is obvious."

"My husband neither cared for me... nor for our sons," my mother whispered.

Antonia did not reply to her.

"Let's go back to knitting wreaths," she said severely to the maids instead.

---

[72] The Thracian gladiator, who was the leader in the Third Servile War.
[73] The mythical queen of Troy and mother of 19 children all killed during the Trojan war.

That moment we heard the door of our oecus[74] opening.

"Domina!" Actaeon, grandmother's secretary, appeared at the entrance. "Prince Gaius is here!"

"Caligula, my little grandson!" Antonia exclaimed happily. Mother loudly praised Juno, and I threw my wreath into water and hurried to meet my brother.

He had changed. Now he was taller than me, more slender, and… hesitating to hug me. Nevertheless, I didn't wait a second.

"How I missed you!"

I felt how my hug and kiss brought him back from his nightmare. Finally, he looked at me with tenderness, reciprocating my love.

"I had to be strong, Drusilla," my brother whispered in my ear. "You gave me strength."

---

[74] (lat.) Hall or the large room in a Roman house.

X

Tiberius was not interested in women. The biggest bit for that did his ambitious mother Livia, as well as Julia, his second wife. Augustus' daughter had a troubled childhood. When her mother Scribonia was pregnant, all the Roman augurs and auspexes[75] claimed that Octavian would have a son. However, to his disappointment, a princess was born. The vain ruler was enraged. Unfortunate Scribonia was immediate divorced and had to leave the palace all alone soon after giving birth. It was rumored that Livia, his then lover, played a major role in that infamous event. Moreover, from the very day she was proclaimed an empress consort, Livia had been trying her hardest to make her stepdaughter fall from grace. Alas, she succeeded.

Trice married of convenience; Julia was trying to find relief in casual relationships. Tiberius could hardly tolerate his wife's deception, mostly because it made him a fool of in the eyes of all the Romans. When he became an emperor, unfaithful Julia was sent into exile. Thus, my great-uncle Tiberius spent the rest of his turbulent life spouseless. Imperial loneliness and disappointment were then treated with perverse amusement. Disapproval of the crowd was half-muted with high taxes and some other forms of punishment.

"Stay away from women, Caesar," the court astrologer Thrasyllus foretold him the day my father died. "Pandora's[76] daughter will bring you demise."

Nevertheless, there was a lady who enjoyed Tiberius' respect. Antonia Minor, whose son and husband fell victims to the games of power, had the rare right for personal correspondence with Caesar, and even for visiting him without invitation.

"If you want to survive in the male world, my dear," Grandmother taught me, "you need to have an attitude and to express it without mentioning the others' mistakes. And, if you're exposing someone anyway, just have no fear and be sure of yourself."

---

[75] Roman fortune-tellers or interpreters of omens.
[76] In Greek mythology, Pandora was the first human woman created.

When Nemesis[77] took from Caesar his mother and son, one after another, Antonia was the first to express sincere condolences. The loss of closest relatives and the fear of assassination forced the tyrant to move to the island of Capri, leaving the Imperial administration to the praefectus urbi[78] Aelius Sejanus.

"I'm not going back to the capital, sister," the emperor wrote to my grandma. *"I'm leaving this cloaca to my deputy, whom I don't trust at all. But you, Antonia, have never disappointed me. Thus, I appoint you my secret adviser. I want to know everything they talk about at the Forum and discuss in Curia Hostilia.[79] You will have access to aerarium, and fiscus,[80] to keep me informed on a regular basis. Keep your eye on Sejanus – ambitions can spoil him. In order to reward your loyalty, I will fulfill your every plea."*

"Salve, Divus![81] All of us, nobles to slaves, are born to serve you," Antonia responded wisely. *"It is an honor for a woman to fulfill this duty. As long as I'm alive, I will not let you down. I have the only plea for you, Caesar. Protect my grandchildren."*

---

[77] The Greek Goddess of retribution.

[78] The high-ranking official of the early Roman Empire who was responsible for police and criminal prosecution in the City of Rome.

[79] The meeting place of the Roman senate.

[80] The public treasury and the Roman Emperor's treasury.

[81] (lat.) The divine one – Roman Emperor's epithet and title.

XI

"In fact, I haven't seen Livia since we parted," Gaius said when we were sitting alone in grandma's garden. "I was a hostage, not allowed to leave the room, except for using bathroom. Food was brought to me by slaves as unpleasant as our great-grandmother. I had a dozen books around, no less disgusting. To keep my head clear, I started scribbling poems and changing my small cell arrangement."

"Oh, my dear." I hugged my brother, stroking his dark hair. "It should be me to suffer."

"You don't say," he stopped me. "You wouldn't hold on."

"If I lived through grandma's talk about my marriage, I could make it through at Domus Livia."

Caligula looked up and stared at me with sky blue eyes.

"I said I wouldn't –" I explained myself.

"That is not possible!" he interrupted me. "You are just nine!"

"I have nothing to do with it."

It seemed like I was trying to justify myself, so my brother got angry.

"What did you tell her – when she asked you why you don't want to get married?"

"I didn't say anything about us," I burbled fearfully. "But she found out I am in love."

"By Mars[82] and Rhea Silvia,[83] Drusilla!" Gaius exclaimed. "Do you want us to be separated again?"

"It's not my fault!" I tried not to cry, but I couldn't help weeping. "She doesn't know it's you…"

"Don't whine, little sister," Caligula rolled his eyes. "I can't stand women's tears."

---

[82] The Roman god of war.

[83] The wife of Mars, and mythical mother of the twins Romulus and Remus, who founded the city of Rome.

I rose from a large alpinum,[84] where I loved to sit and headed for a small waterfall on the opposite side of the garden.

"Where are you going?" He grabbed my arm. "You think you can get rid of me?"

I tried to free myself, but his gaze, strangely wild, made me motionless. I felt his kiss – hot and humid.

"What are you doing?" I barely managed to jerk. "I am your sister!"

Gaius laughed.

"So what should I do when I share parents with my loved one?"

I looked at him a little shyly and smiled.

"Will we love each other – till the end?" I asked excitedly, trying to meet his gaze.

"Until the end, forevermore – these words are used by losers," he said knowingly. "Love only acknowledges – here and now." I disagreed but passed that over. Suddenly, Gaius fell thoughtful, and then whispered in my ear, "I have no choice. I must become an heir."

I recollected my childish prophecy on the day of my father's triumph and embraced him.

"That's the only way to save my family," Gaius went on, leading me into the shade of a large oak. "And for us to be together."

I felt admiration and fear. "What are you up to?"

"Don't worry, I've planned everything." He sounded earnest. "First, I will get closer to Tiberius."

"Our father was an heir," I reminded him.

"Germanicus was just a fool," Caligula concluded. "That's why he ended up so miserably. As for me, I am no threat to our great-uncle. I made Livia think I was a weak and silly child, and she undoubtedly conveyed that to Tiberius. Therefore, I'm going to seek the emperor's invitation and play his fool until I please him."

This sounded a bit naive, but somewhere deep inside my heart, I had a feeling he would accomplish the feat. A kind of strange thought then occurred in my head.

Caligula would need my help.

---

[84] An artificial hill planted with alpine plants.

"Do you want to be my mainstay, Drusilla?" my brother asked half-loudly.

"If you take me with you," I smiled.

Gaius knit his brow.

"Is it blackmail? Do you think I would put you in danger?"

"The ruler is not on his own," I tried to make it clear. "He is supported by the Senate and the army. Don't you forget, you're just a little boy?"

He giggled at my words. "How can you, little girl, help me?"

The answer to that question had been wondering around my head. Conspiracy... Mithras... Women... I recollected the last words Zaleukos told us.

"Hate is actually born out of... fear."

"Still, Tiberius is just a human being," I went on more confidently. "He has his fears... of women, for example."

Caligula looked up, amazed. "Do you know something I don't know?"

"For now, it's just my guessing." I shrugged. "What I know for sure is that you shouldn't rush to Capri until we finish our investigation."

"Is it because of the prophecy?" Again, in Gaius' voice I heard some disbelief.

"Like, the emperor is going to be killed by some – Pandora? That's ridiculous! Great-Uncle doesn't keep a single fresco of a female in his palace, but he is surrounded by the dozens of praetorians[85] that can't be fought by Bellona[86] herself!"

I spoke the first thing that came to my mind, and this was the last thing my brother expected to hear. "Why have women always been forced into submission by men?"

"Women are tender creatures, and they need protection and care," Caligula replied uncertainly.

"Indeed?" I squinted, feeling the urge of rebel rising inside me. "What kind of protection is it, when they choose you a husband, who would decide how many children will you have? Do you, men, care why women live significantly shorter than you do? We have no rights – why?"

---

[85] The Praetorian guard was an elite unit of the Imperial Roman army whose members served as personal bodyguards and were often used as an army reserve at the battlefield, aiding their emperor defend the empire.

[86] Ancient Roman goddess or war.

Caligula was blinking in astonishment, wondering what had happened to his sweet Drusilla, so she talked this way.

"That is, probably, the role of all the women – to be wives and mothers," he responded doubtfully.

"Oh, sorry, we can choose – among a stranger's house, a lupanar,[87] and the Temple of Vesta." I sighed at my bitter joke. "You don't know what's worse."

"I've never thought about it." He shook his head.

"Only Grandmother had the audacity to tell Augustus to his face she would be happier if Cleopatra ruled the Romans." I remembered Antonia's words.

Caligula began to laugh.

"She was as young as you then. Do you think Augustus could be angry at a child?"

"That's not the point." I turned away. "He felt her courage and respected it."

"Octavian is not my idol." My brother got nervous again. "But how can you compare a hero to a whore?"

I was aware that our discussion could easily turn to a quarrel, but I couldn't give it up.

"You mean – a weakling and a plotter to the real heroine? Remember, what we learned from our teacher there in Egypt! Rome is in the hands of a new religion! They choose our rulers and suggest how we should live."

At once, I noticed a spark of curiosity in his eyes.

"What should *I* do?"

"Just wait." I gently touched his arm. "We'll search for the answers in Grandmother's library. Tiberius will not escape, but if you go there unprepared, you'll ruin us all."

He nodded.

"It sounds interesting. Maybe, you are right."

I felt gladness – not only for my brother finally agreed with me. Undoubtedly, this mystery was going to play a great part in my life.

"O Prince! O Princess! Where are you?"

---

[87] (lat.) A brothel.

We heard the voice of Antiochus, our friend. Born as the lawful heir of Commagene, he was brought to Rome as our father's hostage and protégé.

"It's dusk, they're serving cena!"[88]

"Why are you yelling? We are here!" Caligula stood up and headed towards the young man.

I looked at the sky. Evening was slowly falling upon the Campus Martius.[89] The scarlet sun had hidden behind the gable of the Great Mother Temple.

"Domina!" I saw Armida gasping on the run. She was treading on Grandmother's flowers like a true barbarian. "Familia is... has... eating! Your mother... to scold you!"

"Calm down, I'm coming!" I replied and gave my German nursemaid a small bunch of violets.

"For you have ruined my grandmother's flower bed, you will be carrying this bouquet all the way back home."

Fair-haired Armida looked at me in confusion, and in a moment burst into laughter.

"You're learning quickly," I praised her. "Like me... From now on, no one will be scolding me. Guess why?"

She spread her arms like she had no idea.

"I will not allow it."

---

[88] (lat.) The main meal of the day, held in evenings.
[89] (lat.) The Field of Mars – in Ancient Rome, a floodplain of the Tiber River, about 2 square kilometers in extent.

XII

AD 24

Agrippina the Younger was fifteen and Livilla two years less when Tiberius announced their engagement to the two consuls. After reading the emperor's letter, Antonia has brought the family together for a dinner. Despite the rules and customs, in her triclinium women did not sit on chairs, but shared soft benches with the men.

"Your wish is coming true," Grandmother said to my sisters. "You couldn't wait to settle down by some senator's side… So your great-uncle chose for you the worst of all the candidates."

"Mother, please!" Agrippina the Elder timidly interrupted her speech. "Don't ruin their moment!"

My sisters, who looked bright a cheerful just a moment ago, now were staring at Antonia fearfully. My brothers, Nero and Drusus, who often played jokes at vinculum matrimonii,[90] were barely refraining from laughing. Uncle Claudius was gazing at his plate, waiting for the sign to start a meal. Aunt Livilla, the fresh widow, didn't look interested either.

"Ahenobarbus is a gambler and a lecher," the matriarch went on, ignoring her daughter-in-law. "He'll never miss a comissatio.[91] No need to be a sorcerer to tell the future of my Agrippina. If she lets this boar on a binge, he'll dress her with gold and silver, and when she finally gets sick and tired, he will cover her with bruises."

"Why are you doing this?" my mother asked in an unpleasant whisper.

"Because I love my grandchildren," Antonia said calmly and continued. "Vinicius is an orator-to-be. He doesn't need a wife, but someone to enjoy his unborn speeches. My Livilla won't be cursed and beaten, but one day she'll die of boredom – that's for sure."

My aunt spoke next. So unexpectedly, she seemed to agree with my mother.

---

[90] (lat.) Bond of marriage.
[91] (lat.) An orgy.

"Marriage is not fun," Livilla said. "They are no longer children."

"Who of us was free to choose her destiny?" My mother plucked up courage. "Which woman got married by love? Love and happiness come later, after a child is born…"

"O shut up, both of you!" Grandmother raised her voice. "And don't compare me to yourself. I married the one I loved, gave birth to as many children as I wanted to have, and no one even tried to suppress me."

"Mother dear, don't you forget, you were Augustus' little niece?" Aunt Livilla reminded her, but Antonia Minor was not in the mood for a dispute.

"Augustus did appreciate me mainly for my character. A woman, who knows what she wants, but doesn't tread on corpses, is respected and untouchable," she said, "However, our conversation is becoming meaningless, so let's begin with hare stew. Between the courses we'll discuss the dowry for the girls."

As Antonia mentioned the dowry, my sisters became high-spirited. My uncle and brothers were eagerly awaiting meat. Agrippina the Elder pretended she was not hungry and took Livilla's son Gemellus at her knee.

"I'm sorry for our sisters," I whispered to Gaius. "If Grandma is right…"

"They wanted it – they got it," he returned phlegmatically, digging in the stew.

What if… tomorrow is my turn? I thought, and cowered. *No! I will not let it happen.*

I looked at my grandmother, who had already been chatting with her eldest grandchild, Claudius' daughter Antonilla.

Maybe I can't avoid the marriage, but if Grandma helps me, I'll be free to choose, I went on thinking. *It's impossible… Would anyone agree to be my spouse on paper only? Would anyone like to play family in the daytime, sleeping alone by night? Who can I trust?*

There was only one name in my head. *Gaius will kill me.* I stood up abruptly, squinting.

"What is it, Drusilla?" my brother asked me, scared.

"I wish all the best to Agrippina and Livilla," I began uncertainly, nodding at my sisters. "I admire their courage, but I couldn't marry a complete stranger."

"Who asked you?" Mother blushed with discontent.

"I am asking her." Antonia stood up as well. "At last, I see another clever head around."

"So…" I said, almost breathless. "With your help, Grandmother, I will ask the emperor's permission to marry by love."

"Well done!" Antonia exclaimed with joy. "That is my girl!"

The others were too astonished to speak.

"What is his name?"

I didn't have the strength to look at Gaius, but it was too late to turn back.

"Cassius," I replied. "The military tribune Cassius Chaerea."

XIII

"No, that's impossible," Agrippina the Elder protested. "My child, a great-granddaughter of Augustus, and a knight of dubious descent! Is Drusilla smart enough to choose? She has been tagging along with that centurion since she started walking, but Chaerea... I don't know whether he's mad or greedy."

Grandmother was just laughing. "I would be really surprised if you told me something else. Fortunately, you are not the one to make decisions. Caesar is."

"A childless marriage is a shame! This man does not deserve my daughter."

"And who does?"

"Some young patrician, one of the Augustans. What about Asinius?"

"The youngest son of senator Salonin?"

"What is wrong with him? He's healthy, tall, and handsome, like Phoebus[92] himself, and extremely ambitious."

"That's perfect! I will send him to the emperor." Antonia ended the argument. "Old wolf is waiting for young meat."

What happened then? My sisters, occupied with their wedding preparations, finally left me alone, but Caligula... had been avoiding me for mere three days.

"I cannot find a name for you." It was the first thing I heard when he finally opened the door. "You're worse than Livia." His words hit harder than a slap.

I hugged my brother. He was mad, but he did not reject me.

"Cassius is a eunuch," Gaius grumbled, recollecting the foul rumor.

"You're an idiot," I laughed through tears. "Even a fool would understand."

Gaius returned my hug. He smiled.

"So, you pretended all the way, didn't you?"

"I did, and I will," I replied, somewhat angry with him.

---

[92] Another name for Apollo – Greek and Roman god of sun, medicine, music, poetry, and sciences.

"Are you sure that Chaerea will consent to a sham marriage?" Gaius looked at me suspiciously. "You would break the law."

"Cassius is a good man," I explained. "And he saved us."

"Whatever, I just don't trust soldiers," Gaius went on, frowning. "They kill people."

"Vivere est militare,"[93] I said earnestly. "He is born a knight. What else could he become? He lost his parents very young…"

"Oh, I don't care." My brother sneered. "I'm more concerned with you, Drusilla. You have changed. I knew a fragile and a gentle girl who turned into a trouble. It is so Antonia!"

I found myself speaking my mind… and surprising myself.

"I'm afraid, I'm finally figuring out who I am."

"Oh, little sister…" Gaius sighed, and pecked me on my forehead. "Only I can love you. No one else can understand and tolerate you."

"I'm aware." I shrugged my shoulders. "I got used to it."

---

[93] (Lat.) Life is a struggle (Seneca).

XIV

In the lower area of the Campus Martius was once Goat Lake – a deep, dark swamp, which had been considered as haunted since the time of our ancestors – the Latins.

They said our first king, Romulus, had disappeared without a trace along with his entourage, passing through the stormy wood by Goat Lake. There, Numa Pompilius allegedly encountered the wellspring nymph Aegeria, who advised him to raise the Pantheon[94] near the swamp. The temple was built, but the dark magic of the place had been scaring people for many more years. In my time, there were no hunters to meet, although the wood was full of hares and chamois.

That was the perfect place for my secret appointment. With the help of Actaeon and his wife Photice, I learned that Cassius was staying at the Esquiline military camp, where he was training recruits. Without prejudice, I wrote him a short letter, asking him for a meeting and some help.

"This girl is crazy like a fox," Actaeon whispered to his wife, when we were quietly preparing to sneak out. "Even Medea[95] herself wouldn't go to this wasteland."

Photice nodded. She could barely manage to dress me up in the light of a small oil lamp. No one, including my nursemaids, was aware where I was going and for what.

"I'm not fond of the Argonauts[96]," I smiled. "Because of the sad ending. Every time I read a tragedy, I'm crying."

"Me too," Actaeon said. "When I was young, I loved "Perseus,"[97] he continued sleepily. "He kills the monster, saves the daughter of the king, marries her and they live happy ever after… But, alas, life is not myth, especially when you and your Andromeda were born as slaves."

---

[94] (Anc.Gr.) A temple dedicated to all the gods of pagan Rome.

[95] In Greek mythology – the Princess of Colchis and a powerful sorceress, who helped the legendary hero Jason obtain the Golden Fleece.

[96] A band of heroes in Greek mythology, who accompanied Jason to Colchis in his quest for the Golden Fleece.

[97] A famous Greek hero, best known for beheading the Gorgon Medusa and founding Mycenae.

"Will you stop talking?" Photice sighed, obviously annoyed. "Luckily, we serve Lady Antonia – the only mistress who keeps the ergastulum[98] closed."

"Ah, *Photiki*," Actaeon replied. "You've always kept your feet on the ground, while I've been a hopeless daydreamer…"

"You are a scribe, and I'm a cook." The Greek woman chuckled and put a hood over my head. "I've finished, Princess. We can go now."

"The shortest way to get there is to go down the Cacus staircase all the way to the Temple of Pales, and then to take the old path to the wood," Actaeon turned to me and said in muted tones. "When we reach the old grotto, we'll have done it."

I hugged them both.

"When I succeed," I said excitedly, "When Gaius becomes Emperor… You have my word – you'll get your freedom."

Actaeon kissed my hand.

"Ah, prikipessa,"[99] Photice went on chuckling, "you're a greater dreamer than my husband. Please Gods, let her dream come true!"

As we walk through the vestibule, I looked up to the compluvium.[100] The dawn was breaking. The big moon was fading, letting rose-fingered Aurora pull away the curtain of a morning mist.

"Dreamers never count on the gods, but on themselves," I muttered earnestly.

"And on true friends." Actaeon winked and opened the front door.

Cassius was waiting for me near the grotto overgrown with ivy, lost in his thoughts. He wasn't dressed in military uniform but wore an equestrian cloak over a long tunic with a narrow crimson stripe. He looked very handsome. Corax, a crow horse, was lazily grazing grass beneath a strange evergreen shrub.

"Cassi Chaerea!" I greeted him, imitating old Livia's voice.

"O salve!" He jumped to his feet and headed towards me. "Is that you, infantula?"

The tribune seemed confused, but happy.

"You've grown up… How old are you?"

---

[98] A Roman private prison, where slaves were punished.
[99] (Anc.Gr.) Princess.
[100] A rectangular open space in the middle of a Roman house, which collected rainwater.

"Eleven."

"You don't say!" He smiled. "I wish I could take you in my arms and play with you like we did in the East... But now I can't – you're almost a girl for marriage."

I felt shiver down my spine. I took Cassius by the hand, squeezing his big palm.

"That is the reason... I am here."

"What do you mean?" He became worried. "Why are you scared?"

Sleepless nights and walking made my thoughts a little blurred and scattered. The tribune spread his cloak onto a wide piece of rock so I could take a sit, and he sat there beside me.

"Caesar..." I said, gasping, "gave my sister Agrippina to that ape – Ahenobarbus... Livilla's wedding is one month from now."

"I know it," Cassius replied. "Antonia sent me an invitation."

"I did not see you at the ceremony..."

"I do not like weddings," he explained with a grin. "And I like your sisters even less."

I smiled back as I remembered their quarrel on the ship.

"Neither do I," I sighed, "but I suppose I will be next."

"Oh, take my condolences." Cassius tried to stay witty, but he couldn't hide his disappointment. "Marriage is a voluntary bondage."

I understood him better than anyone else. My wider family was mostly known by scandalous divorces and intrigues. Those idyllic love stories from the books unfortunately couldn't happen anywhere in Rome.

"Still, Antonia said I might choose my husband... like she did."

Cassius still didn't understand... or at least it seemed. "She got married during the reign of Augustus, not Tiberius."

"Man, does it matter at all?" I started to get nervous. "She promised me, and I believe her. Actually, the point is... would *you*, Cassi Chaerea, marry me?"

Women did not propose men even in pre-Hellenistic Egypt, where equality prevailed. I held my breath, with my eyes on my chosen one.

Cassius was too manly to murmur a cowardly 'I don't know what to say.' He cared for me too much to stand and watch me without saying a word either.

"I know they're talking about me a lot – a lot of lies." He smiled. "But I'm not wounded in my head to reject you."

I felt ashamed. "Don't flatter me, tribune, or I may think you're doing it by interest."

"I'm not a senator," he said sincerely. He finally noticed Photice and Actaeon, who were waiting by the other side of the grotto. "Who are these two, after all?"

"Servants of my grandma."

"Look like Greeks."

"They *are* Greeks."

Cassius waved to the slaves, and they replied with a slight bow of their heads.

"Greeks are good people," he went on half-loudly. "I remember, in the cohort, we had a Cretan soldier named Alcaeus… When I was wounded hard, none of those Roman dogs were there to help me. I would have bled to death, had Alcaeus not saved me."

"But where was my father then?" I asked him carefully.

"Probably chasing Arminius."

I could feel my heart pounding somewhere in my stomach.

Why am I doing this? I thought. *This man had gone through deepest hells… I cannot break his heart.*

However, Cassius knew more than I could guess. "I, too, am wondering what I am doing…" The tribune pressed me to his chest. "But have no fear, for I won't leave you even if it would cost me my head."

"I guess, it should cost *me* my *heart* first," I spoke softly, led by mixed feelings, timidly returning a hug. As Chaerea felt my doubt, he instantly loosened his hold.

"I know you don't love me, infantula. I know what you really want to avoid by this marriage."

Shame started choking me. I wanted to explain myself, tell him everything about me and Caligula, but tears overflowed me.

"You have a poetic soul, and you believe in love," he continued. "You live in a world of your own, far away from intrigues, childish cry and dull weaving. I won't let some bastard strangle you."

"My father... loved you," I said in a weeping voice.

"If Marcus and Helvilla were alive, they would adore you," Cassius replied, thinking of his deceased parents.

"It sounds like a joke." I sighed, trying to imagine myself as a daughter-in-law.

"It does not." He wiped away my tears. "You helped me understand what they were telling me..."

I wasn't able to listen to him attentively.

"There's something else," I said, breathing heavily. "There is a conspiracy... always has been. Zaleukos, the teacher, told me... We are all in danger. We need you, Cassius – me and Caligula. And you need us too."

He took my hand and pulled it to his heart.

"I give you the word of a soldier. I will stand by you – until my last breath."

This was what I wanted to hear.

At that moment, Actaeon reminded me of the time. "Your Highness, we must turn back by negotium.[101] If I'm not there before the first client arrives, Domina will be upset."

"I have to oversee the younger cooks," Photice added worriedly. "Those Egyptians girls always mix up the ingredients when it comes to the refined Greek dishes."

Cassius helped me get up and placed his cloak over my shoulders.

"Let me give you a ride home, Drusilla."

"We will ride Corax together?" I asked, looking curiously at his dark horse.

"Undoubtedly," he winked. "How can I leave my promised one to go afoot?"

I noticed tiny wrinkles under his Iberian[102] gray eyes.

He must be less than thirty-five, I thought. *He is more handsome than Asinius or any other Augustan... Even more handsome than Caligula.*

He carefully helped me sit upon a horse, and then joined me in the saddle.

"Hold on tight and don't look down. If you feel sick, say it."

---

[101] (Lat.) Business time; time of the day meant for public activity.

[102] The Iberian Peninsula, peninsula in southwestern Europe, occupied by Spain and Portugal. Its name derives from its ancient inhabitants – Celtic migrants.

"I will try." I hugged him from behind and closed my eyes.

"I'm glad they made it." I heard Actaeon's voice behind me. "I'm so happy prikipessa will be riding. The road uphill is awful."

"I wish I had another horse, so I could lend it to you, friends. You are nice people," the tribune said to the Greeks.

"Don't worry, noble knight," Photice replied, surprised by his kindness. "We are accustomed to long walking."

Then, she whispered to her husband in their language, *"He is worth proposing."*

"She is worth marrying," Actaeon replied, and wished us an easy ride.

XV

"I guess Praetorians are not a good sign."

I opened my eyes. In front of the gates of Villa Claudiana stood ten guardsmen, dressed in red and black and formidably armed.

"It should have taken you to the Esquiline," Cassius said, as he dismounted the horse. "Stay here until I find out what has happened."

The sight had me out of breath, muttering something inaudible.

Cassius approached a grey-haired officer called Quadrigarius and saluted him.

"We're here at the behest of Tiberius," the guardsman responded. "Lady Julia Agrippina is accused of murdering the Imperial Prince – along with her sons."

Everything darkened. I often heard Mother blaming Caesar for my father's death, imprecating godly curses on the murderer, but Agrippina seemed incapable of that vile vengeance. Late Prince Castor, so unlike his father, did not seem arrogant. I remembered him doing his best to reconcile our family.

Through my torn thoughts, I heard Chaerea mentioning Sejanus.

"Our prefect only fulfills the will of Caesar," another guardsman spoke lazily.

"Who was in charge of the investigation? Was there any evidence?"

The Praetorians remained silent, and Quadrigarius pointed his crooked finger at the scorpion emblem – the symbol of a reckless murder.

"What about the little one?" Cassius asked. "Was he also arrested?"

"No." the guardsman replied, "just two elder brothers."

So Gaius was safe. I slowly regained breath. Cassius turned around to see me.

"Princess!" he exclaimed. "You are as white as parchment!"

"Take me home," I whispered, almost senseless. "Please."

The tribune took me in his arms and signaled to the guardsmen to let us pass.

"Open the gate!" Quadrigarius ordered the janitor. "Princess Drusilla is coming."

In the atrium, I saw my frightened nursemaids running towards me.

"Oh thank the gods!" I heard Armida. "Domina alive and well!"

"Tell Grandma I'm... We're..." I grabbed Susannah's hand.

"Lady Antonia is bad," the Jewess said. "When they arrested Lady Agrippina and our Princes, she sent little Lady Livilla to her husband-to-be, and locked herself in her chambers."

"Where is Gaius?" I muttered.

"He's gone, Domina," the young woman replied. "We couldn't follow him in this crowd. I'm afraid he's gone looking for you."

I looked up at Armida, but she was just shrugging.

I touched my aching forehead. Nursemaids were tubling nervously all around me, and Cassius headed to the peristyle,[103] carrying me in his arms.

"Where is the princess' chamber?" he asked the women, and then spoke quietly to me. "Who knows where your brother is now, and what kind of stupid mistake he is making!"

"Gaius is not my father," I replied. "He doesn't do anything stupid – even for my sake."

In the hall, we met panic-stricken Claudius.

"Drusilla, w-w-what is g-g-going on?" When nervous, my uncle often stuttered. "First they t-t-took your mother, then you s-s-suddenly appear with H-h-h –"

"Good morning to you, Claudius," Chaerea interrupted, kicking the door open. "I guess Sejanus wants the throne, so he is stirring up bad feelings in Tiberius – against us."

"Have you just told 'us,' or have I misheard you?" Claudius hesitantly followed him into my chamber.

"Today I have proposed to your niece at Goat Lake," the tribune responded honestly, "but do not worry, I'm not here to visit you. As soon as I make sure Princess is fine, I'll leave. Those geese will do the rest."

Susannah was silently making my bed, while Armida was making reluctant grimaces.

"What you mean, p-p-p-proposed?" My uncle opened his eyes wide.

---

[103] (here) An intimate part of the Roman house.

"Have a rest, my dear," Cassius told me, ignoring the rhetorical question. "I will find your brother."

I felt like I had been run over by a chariot.

"Did C-C-C-Caligula, too, d-d-disappear?" My father's brother looked completely wretched. "Oh, mother! We are done!"

"Don't lament like an old woman, Claudius! Come on out!" Cassius pulled him by his toga.

"Antonia, she locked herself in her ch-ch-chamber, letting no one in, not even me!" I heard my uncle moaning from the hallway.

"She is bored by you."

"By my father's shadow, I am serious! If my m-m-mother doesn't know what to do, we are done!"

I turned my face to the wall and threw a quilt over my head. My fatigue was stronger than my fear.

Cassius will find Gaius... I thought, falling asleep. *Grandma will persuade Tiberius... We've suffered enough... This Wheel of Ixion[104] must stop...*

---

[104] In Greek mythology – a winged fiery wheel that was always spinning; probably most terrible punishment of the underworld.

XVI

None of the household servants knew where had my brother gone. Actaeon had questioned all the slaves in vain. Not even the wide-awake janitor had seen him going out that morning. I remember Cassius telling me what happened afterwards... or maybe I just saw it in my nightdream.

"Now that the culprits are pulled in, why don't you go back to duties?" he asked Quadrigarius.

"Not yet," the centurion replied. "The rest of the family is placed under house arrest till the end of the trial."

"Caesar believes the widow had some accomplices," the other guardsman spoke.

"Who do you mean?" Chaerea couldn't hide his anger. "Could it be Antonia – a spotless, virtuous lady? Maybe, Claudius, that clumsy fool? Or probably Caligula, a boy of twelve?"

"Go your own way, tribune," the third guardsman said arrogantly. "Unless our prefect treated you with some respect..."

"What would you do?" Cassius laughed. "Would you attack me like a herd of dogs a lone wolf? Fight the unarmed one – just because he tells the truth? Tell your Sejanus, that I spit on his respect!"

"I see you're eager to end up like your commander," Quadrigarius replied, watching him saddling the horse. "Go ahead, but don't get us involved! We don't kill madmen!"

"Nor do I kill cowards!" Cassius shot back before he rode away.

How did he manage to sneak out unnoticed? He asked himself, passing through Porta Esquilina half an hour later. In this part of Rome, known as a military district, also lived Sutorius Macro – prefect of the Vigiles.[105]

---

[105] The commander of watchmen and firemen.

Macro had a talent for sensing fire where there was no smoke before one took an oil lamp to light it. People said he could predict the wind direction and the streamflow of the Tiber River, unpredictable even for his father-in-law Thrasyllus. With the help of his wife – a famous courtesan and gossipmonger of the house Ennii – Macro was able to orientate in high society, balancing between optimates and populares. It was rumored that even Sejanus was a little bit afraid of Macro, for there was no spy in the Empire to reveal his darkest secrets.

I don't trust Macro as far as I can throw him, Chaerea thought, greeting the janitor. *But, unless he helps me, no one can.*

Ennia welcomed him in the atrium, yawning and stretching like a cat.

"I'm looking for your husband," the tribune said earnestly. "The case is urgent."

"Sutorius is resting in a steam bath," the hostess replied. "You can wait for him in the oecus, if you wish. Slave girls will bring us breakfast."

Cassius refused politely and sat down on the client's bench. Ennia gazed at him with curiosity.

"I hope you are in order, tribune. You look like you have met Trivia."[106]

"A certain family, extremely dear to me, got into trouble," he returned unwillingly.

"Oh, Agrippina the Doe and her kits…" she said sloppily, playing with the skirt of her expensive dress as if she was counting its wrinkles. "Macro can't do anything about it. Tiberius has evidence."

I know that story, Cassius said to himself. *Caesar is too busy having fun on the Capri to see Sejanus playing dirty.*

His thoughts were interrupted by the low and deep voice of the host. "I see we have a guest, don't we?"

The prefect of Vigiles, dressed in a thin robe, entered the atrium, escorted by four dark-skinned slaves.

"I'm sorry to have kept you waiting, tribune." Macro welcomed the guest and gave his wife an irate look. "Why don't you offer the knight a bath in our new tepidarium?"

"No need to go mad, Sutorius." The tribune stood up. "Ennia has kindly offered me to share breakfast, but I wasn't hungry."

---

[106] Roman goddess of sorcery and witchcraft, who haunted crossroads and graveyards.

"Good." Macro's lips formed a cunning grin. "Who cares about the Forum gossip?"

"After all, I would decline a bath as well," Cassius added. "I'm an early riser, and I have my bath and meal at dawn."

"I understand," the host nodded. "I think I know the reason of your visit. Let's continue to tablinum. We can have a glass or two, and no one would disturb us."

The hostess quickly disappeared as if she got the message. Chaerea followed Macro to the study, arranged too lushly for a working room of a watchman.

"I need help," the tribune began, as a slave man closed the door. "They say, even a rat from the basement of the Imperial palace can't hide from your eyes."

"Come on, I'm just vigilant." Macro half lay on a wide, soft bench. "Everything else is just a matter of experience. If you ask for my opinion about your proposal to Drusilla…"

Cassius was thunderbolted.

"You wonder how I know, don't you?" His interlocutor smiled again.

"Antonia has been lauding you for about a month. Alas, I would not hurry with congratulations, for I am absolutely sure that Caesar…"

"Tell me, what will become of her mother?" the tribune interrupted him.

Commander of the Vigiles gestured her decapitation and continued quietly.

"Sejanus proposed to Livilla – the imperial daughter-in-law. It is strange, isn't it?"

"Castor's widow," Cassius recollected. "She poisoned her husband to help her lover take the throne… Then, she calumniated Agrippina in the eyes of Tiberius!"

Macro asked a slave man for more wine. Cassius was upset.

"So, you will sit and watch injustice to be done, won't you?"

"What can I do, Chaerea?" Macro shrugged. "In Rome – you either kill, or die. I hate Sejanus much more than you do, but he's the *Hand of fucking Emperor*!"

Cassius took a breath and sipped some wine. It tasted sweet, just like the drink he'd had in Syria. Unwillingly, he recollected the last words he exchanged with Germanicus.

"My late commander knew they wouldn't let his widow live," he thought aloud.

Sutorius turned away thoughtfully and said, "You know, Chaerea, I admire you. Your deep devotion to that madman and his family is worth a Vigile's poem."

The tribune said nothing to restrain a quarrel. His plan to get a useful companion was already to ripen in his head.

"Don't get me wrong," Macro sighed, "I've known you both since my late childhood. You are a dreamer like Germanicus, but he is also unresponsible. His rebellious ideas put his family at risk…"

"Sutorius, are you an optimate? I thought a peregrine couldn't be an optimate…"

The only way to provoke cold-blooded Macro and disconcert him was to mention his father Nevius' Gallic descent. All the peregrines, even those free and wealthy, have always been considered second-class citizens in Rome. A man of foreign roots could neither enter the Senate, nor get promoted to a higher military rank. The only one exception was Chaerea, for his father had become a member of equestrian order by the grace of Augustus.

"So what?" Macro stood up, nervous. "Should I start rebellion like Germanicus? No, thank you. I have no desire to be cut."

Cassius smiled. The ice was broken.

"Wouldn't you like to be praefectus urbi – instead of Sejanus?"

"Watch your mouth," the host warned him with a raised finger. "It's already a conspiracy."

"Isn't cutting down the innocent a damn conspiracy?"

The watchman thought a little, sent his cupbearer away, and lent Chaerea an ear.

"Tell me where could Caligula go after they took his mother and two brothers to praetorium?" Cassius asked.

"At the port, I suppose," the host replied. "Waiting for a ship to the Capri. My fellows have seen him this afternoon riding to Ostia."

"By all the Lares and Penates!"[107] the tribune exclaimed. "Why didn't your Vigiles stop him?"

---

[107] Groups of ancestor-deities, or gods, who protected the family and the Roman state.

Sutorius gave him a look full of irony. "Who in the world can stop a prince without the order of Tiberius himself?"

"If he leaves for the Capri without the order of Tiberius, he won't survive," the guest retorted.

Macro tried to prove him that the destiny of Germanicus' son was already determined, but he did not give up.

"Come with me to Ostia, please. I have to stop him. I have to protect –"

"And what do I get for it?" the Vigile interrupted him. "Why would I risk my life and my prosperity for a damn brat?"

"I know Gaius well," the tribune responded. "He's a fighter. He would grow into a good emperor, and promote you to Praefectus praetorio… Unless you want to stay a watchmen and firefighter all your life."

Macro burst into laughter. "Who, Caligula?! He is as silly as a log! If he was not, he would be dead. Thrasyllus told Tiberius that this boy's chances to become an emperor were poorer than to build a bridge across Mare Tyrrhenum."

"Your father-in-law also told him a tale of a weaponless girl who would kill him," Cassius reminded him. "Do you believe in that, too?"

Sutorius shook his head. The idea of new Caesar and promotion tickled his imagination. The emperor's stinginess led Rome to the economic crisis and caused numerous uprisings in the provinces. The people hated their ruler and were longing for the change.

"To fight Sejanus or Tiberius," Macro finally said with excitement, "we will need a serious ally."

"What do you think of Antonia?" the tribune propounded. "She is very influential and yearns revenge on both Sejanus and the emperor for everything they took from her."

"Antonia won't turn against Livilla – no matter how evil she is, it's her daughter."

"You are wrong, Sutorius. She's never stood by criminals, and she would love to see her grandson on the throne."

"This I believe," Macro sighed agreeably. "And I can't wait to get away from this graveyard[108] and Ennia."

"So, are you with me?" Cassius smiled triumphantly.

"Aut Caesar, aut nihil,"[109] the host raised his goblet. "Now let's go and save that Caesar."

---

[108] The Esquiline Hill was mostly known for its Necropolis.
[109] (Lat.) [To be] either Emperor or nothing: all or nothing.

XVII

In my half-sleep, I felt a gentle touch of a warm hand, stroking my hair. It was Antonia, who woke me up. Her loose nightgown of rich silk looked even funnier in the light of her small oil lamp.

"Drusilla!" Grandmother called out. "You scared me half to death, sleeping all day and almost all night long."

A thorny question started swirling in my head. "Where is Caligula?" I rose up with impetus.

"I should have beaten the hell out of your brother," the matron replied angrily. "He fled to Ostia, sneaked up to a grocery ship, and almost ended up in Tiberius' paws!"

I lost my breath and put my head on a pillow as I felt familiar nausea.

"Don't worry, he's already home," she calmed me down. "We should thank your betrothed, Cassius Chaerea, for finding that driveller and bringing him home."

So, he tried to do what he once planned, I thought. *He tried to save our mother, Nero and Drusus. He probably thought they found me first. Why didn't I tell him I was safe with Cassius?*

"Are you alright, my flower?" the matron asked quietly. "I have to feed you."

Through nausea, I felt thirst and hunger.

"Anat!"

I saw an Egyptian slave girl, nimble as a viper, shaping out of the dark.

"Go and wake Fotis! Haven't seen that lazy Greek since yesterevening! She would better start with making breakfast!" Domina exclaimed.

Anat nodded obediently and fell back.

"Fotaki is not guilty," I said regretfully. "She and Actaeon followed me to the Goat Lake… I ordered them."

Antonia burst out laughing nervously.

"Did Chaerea propose to you… in the backwoods?"

I shrugged my shoulders.

"I just didn't want us to be seen."

"Not worth it," Grandma shook her head. "The emperor's spies will follow us even to Hades."

My stomach ached in a terrible hunger. I imagined a crunchy, oily pie with fresh cheese and olives; I could almost smell it… Fotis was the perfect cookmaid.

"Still, my flower," the matron went on earnestly, "I think a girl who hasn't bled yet is too young for dates. Besides, engagement doesn't work until the emperor approves it."

"Will you write to him, Grandmother?" I asked humbly.

Antonia stood up abruptly and looked at me somewhat… differently.

"We will speak of that later. First you have to eat and rest a little more, for this will be a long talk."

Even her voice sounded sharp to me. I remembered stone-cold faces of the uninvited guests and shivered.

"Caesar will not spare them, will he?" I looked at Antonia. "My father knew it wouldn't be that long."

I stopped as I noticed Grandma's tears – quiet and sublime. She was dignified, even in grief – her face did not turn red, nor mouth distorted.

"Listen to me, girl. We are strong women," she had always told me. "Strong women may cry, but never gripe, they don't play martyrs, nor use tears as weapons."

Slowly, I got up to hug her. She kissed me in my forehead.

"Drusilla, I will talk to you like to an adult," she continued hoarsely.

"We live in the empire of injustice, surrounded by challengers, but we must not let evil change us. Our life is not worth living if our conscience is not clear. If you fight the truth, you have lost in advance, even with an army by your side. My father and my son had given life for truth, while other people prefer lie – for money, fame, or pleasure. Now, it is my turn – to prove that I am worthy of my name."

"You… want to sacrifice yourself?" I asked her, startled. "Do you want to leave me?"

Antonia shook her head.

"Maybe I'll have to, but it won't be fast. Unless I had you, I would say – unfortunately. Gods do not demand of me my soul, but my heart… Another child of mine."

"My aunt Livilla?"

"Damn Sejanus made her go completely out of her mind and turned against her family. She killed her husband and slandered your mother to Caesar."

Brutus stabbed Julius in the back, Augustus betrayed Anthony, Piso turned traitor to Germanicus… Treason in Rome was not considered a crime, but a life mode.

"Why – our family?" I asked, too weary to be frightened.

Antonia didn't say anything, but took me by the hand, and led me back to bed.

"What will become of us?" I was persistent.

"Nothing, if Tiberius finds out the truth in time."

Grandmother had to choose – she either could protect her daughter, or the children of her dead son. How hard it must have been – to make the righteous choice! How pure must be a heart to save the innocent for the price of your own flesh and bone!

"I admire you, Grandmother," I whispered, and reached out to kiss her hand, swelling up from the summer heat.

"Don't play your mother. I'm not Livia." She frowned. "You better save your kisses for the future husband."

I thought of Cassius Chaerea. I admired this man even more, but, still, I couldn't imagine us kissing… I was not yet ready.

It didn't take the cookmaid long to bring me my breakfast on a big copper tray.

"Don't call her nursemaids," Domina told Photice. "This time you will serve her breakfast. When you're done, bring me your husband. I want to write a letter to the emperor."

"Yes, Domina."

With the first bite, I felt better. Unlike lowbrow Armida, Photice had been patient with my childish voraciousness and daydreaming while eating.

"This is so… delicious." I looked up to her, as I took another piece of honey cake.

"If we survive," Antonia smiled bitterly to Photice, "you will follow my granddaughter to the Esquiline. She needs a good maid."

"It will be an honor, Domina."

"Actaeon stays with me," the matron continued, "but he will have days-off on nefasti and festi."[110]

"Gods may bless you, Lady."

"Go and get your husband." Grandma waved aside. "Anat will clean this up."

When Photice left the room, old woman turned to me again.

"Those two are very dear to me. It has been two decades since Selena, my sister, sent them to me, and they never disappointed me. The Greeks are believed to be lazy, but, unlike the Romans, they are loyal and sincere."

I nodded, but my thoughts have already been gone to Gaius. I could bet he was angry at me, but I wasn't sorry. I wanted to support him and to comfort, but not to explain myself. Suddenly, I wished I was alone again – as soon as possible.

"Do not tell anyone, not even Gaius – about my intention," Matron warned me as if she could have read my thoughts. "He's young, and he can hardly see the difference between the heroism and madness. When the time comes – I'll tell him myself."

"May I see him?" I asked quietly.

"No, you can't." She shook her head. "It's night out there, and everyone is sleeping. I'll tell the secretary to find you some book. Anat will light some more lamps here."

"Can I get a forbidden book?" I smiled. "Banned writings are the true ones, and the best."

"Your great-grandfather would be proud of you." The old woman sighed. "There is a book I keep in my old chest. It's a collection of some legends… It's in Hebrew, but, as far as I'm concerned, you have a Jewish nursemaid…"

"Yes, Susannah," I replied excitedly. "She is literate, and she will translate it to me. Sometimes, she is annoying, but I'll bear it."

"Fine." Antonia stood up and walked toward the door. "I'm going to the tablinum. Get well."

I sat up comfortably on the bed and thought about what would happen if I snuck into my brother's room.

---

[110] (Lat.) Days of religious and state holidays.

"I'd better not tempt fate, he must be angry as a hundred Furies," I said to a large mirror. "I'll stay here and read until he calms down. The legends of the East are very interesting."

I had no idea that the book Actaeon brought me in a hurry might have changed my life forever.

XVIII

"Where did you get these writings, Domina?" Susannah asked, staring at the old roll of parchment.

"Most likely, from the Library of Alexandria," I answered half-jokingly. "Fortunately, Augustus didn't understand your language; otherwise, he would have burned them."

The Jewess looked at me fearfully.

"This should have ended up in fire, Domina."

"Love story, right?" I assumed. "Your people hate them."

"Domina!" she exclaimed, wide-eyed. "The book is cursed. In Galilee, such books are believed to be deadly for their owners."

"Come on, Susannah, who can punish us?" I laughed.

My nursemaid started whispering some kind of spell in Hebrew. That annoyed me very much.

"Translate this to me now, or you'll be whipped like a bitch dog!"

Susannah looked confused. I've never threatened her before, even then on a ship, when she and Armida were feeding me with tasteless soup.

"Our holy Torah[111] says, the first man, Adam, had the only wife, named Eve. Nonetheless, legend has it, God created Lilith first. She was extremely beautiful, but yet too proud to obey a man…"

I smiled. "Why would she? Are men any better than us women?"

Nursemaid looked at me sternly without saying a word.

"What?" I frowned at her.

"You're acting strange, Domina," she said suspiciously, reminding me my brother's startled gaze.

---

[111] First section or first five sacred books of the Jewish Bible (Books of Moses).

"You're not the only one. Caligula complains about how I've changed. Don't worry, I will never hurt you."

The Jewess became more cheerful and continued, "A woman was created to support and comfort her husband, to give birth to their children... and to satisfy her husband's needs... Lilith refused to be obedient, and she wanted to be equal to her man."

"What's wrong with that?" I wondered.

"She broke the divine order."

"Your God is a misogynist like Caesar!"

Susana placed her pointer-finger to her lips. "Please, Domina, do not blaspheme. Our God is an avenger. He sends punishment on both the Jews and pagans."

"And especially on women," I sighed. "So, what happened to Lilith?"

"God condemned her to exile. They say, in revenge, she turned into a demon who kills newborns and seduces married men in their sleep."

This part sounded especially bizarre. "So, Adam took another wife, compliant as a puppy bitch."

Susannah couldn't help laughing, as she nodded to me, but for me this was no longer funny.

"I don't believe Lilith was evil," I suddenly claimed, surprised by my own certainty.

"The rabbis[112] say she was a myth. Perhaps, she didn't exist at all."

"Why is this book damned then?"

Nursemaid carefully unwound the yellow scroll.

"May God forgive us both, Domina... You are stubborn, but you have a good heart."

"Thank you," I replied ironically. "Now that I've heard your mind, I want to know what the book says."

"It's a testimony of a man named *Har'El* who lived before the Great Deluge. He claimed that our Book of Genesis had been rewritten, with many facts banned and

---

[112] Jewish scholars or teachers, especially ones who studies or teaches Jewish law.

distorted. Then, he mentioned the conspiracy, which put our teachings under doubt..."

The C-word made me shudder... again. What if this plot, regardless of the time and space, was related to the cabal Zaleukos told me about? As much as I believed my nursemaid, at that moment, I wish I knew Hebrew.

"First, there goes a poem," Jewess said, slightly relaxed. "Allegedly conceived by Lilith, where she claimed that she was wrongfully accused."

"I want to hear it. Take your time – translate it to me literally. If you do it right, I'll free you straight after my wedding. You will be able to return to Galilee and have the real home and family."

Dark-haired Susannah laughed bitterly.

"I had a family once, Domina, – a husband and two sons," she opened her heart unexpectedly. "I led the life of an ordinary housewife, which I was raised to be, until the day Antipas noticed me at the agora. He was young and fiery, so sure of himself. I saw him riding a splendid chariot – a handsome prince... All the girls were simply fascinated by his person, and the fellows wanted to be like him... Antipas didn't yet resemble that monster – his father... or so it seemed to me then. When he took me away, I couldn't even look at him, but I was begging him to let me go... I wept, refused to eat... But he was patient, silver-tongued, and finally I fell in love with him as his main favorite."

I knew the end of that story. Susannah's happiness had been short-lived. Antipas soon inherited a third of Herod's kingdom and married a noblewoman. A favorite was given to my father as a gift to please a Caesar's heir. Germanicus thought that a literate mother of two would have been a great nursemaid, and here she was.

"Would not your family welcome you back?" I asked. "You didn't leave them willingly, you were abducted."

"To them, I'm an adulteress." She sighed. "According to our law, such women must be stoned to death."

This startled me. "What about men?"

Susannah raised her shoulders.

"When the time comes, I will make Antipas pay for what he's done to you," I promised her. "And you will get your freedom."

Susannah, still astonished by my strange behavior, finally began to read the wicked poem, skillfully translating it to Latin.

> *I was sent forth from the power,*
> *and I have come to those who reflect upon me,*
> *and I have been found among those who seek after me.*
> *Look upon me, you who reflect upon me,*
> *and you hearers, hear me.*
> *You who are waiting for me, take me to yourselves.*
> *And do not banish me from your sight.*
> *And do not make your voice hate me, nor your hearing.*
> *Do not be ignorant of me anywhere or any time. Be on your guard!*
> *Do not be ignorant of me.*

While I was listening with my eyes closed, I imagined a beautiful woman in a dark dress, whose long hair fluttered in the wind like a cloud of red butterflies. I recognized the sadness, reflected in her clear blue eyes. There was no attributed vice, only the endless longing for love. This woman saw love as freedom, pleasure, faithfulness and devotion. In my time, such things were mentioned only in the Hellenic songs about gods and heroes. The Lilith I saw was neither bloodthirsty nor lustful, but unhappy and misunderstood – like me.

"She threatens us, Domina," Susannah broke my vision. "We should be aware…"

"Don't be a fool," I whispered absently. "She's warning us."

The Jewess continued reading.

> *For I am the first and the last.*
> *I am the honored one and the scorned one,*
> *the sister of my husband,*
> *and the utterance of my name.*
> *Don't laugh at me!*
> *Do not separate me from the first ones whom you have known!*
> *For I am the one before whom you have been ashamed…*

These verses seemed absurd to me, but at the same time there was something so familiar to me about what I'd heard.

"What is the meaning of her name?" I asked.

"An owl." Susannah frowned. "An ominous nocturnal bird."

My teacher Zaleukos called me that.

"In Greece, it is a symbol of pure wisdom," I recalled, a little bit offended. "Doesn't matter now. Why does she say that people are ashamed before her?"

For a certain while my maid was silent, meditating.

"Did Adam's second wife turn out even worse than Lilith?" I assumed wittily.

"Well, in a certain way she was. Eve tasted the forbidden fruit and gave it to her husband. For breaking the God's law, they both were banished from the Garden of Eden."

That was worth a laugh.

"Oh, was this really about a stupid fruit?"

Susannah looked away and exhaled heavily.

"One legend, which I shouldn't mention either, says her sin was far heavier. Eve got allegedly seduced by an evil spirit. Even so, I never understood why God abandoned Adam if the woman alone was to blame."

The ancient poem unexpectedly gave us an answer.

"I am the one who is disgraced and despised scornfully," one of the verses said.

I had no doubt it was Adam, who left Lilith – his first spouse, and asked the Lord to give him someone better.

"He deceived…" I thought out loud.

"Who, Domina?" Susannah asked, rubbing her tired eyes.

All of a sudden, I heard violent sounds in the hall. It was my brother, giving names to Ioh, Grandma's guardsman, and to Anat. They were seemingly unmoved to curse words, so he couldn't enter.

"Tell them I'm not sleeping." I looked up at the Jewess. "Have some rest, we will continue later."

My nursemaid fell back, leaving me to prepare for an unpleasant conversation.

XIX

Gaius climbed onto my bed and said straightway, "I was vexed at you and Chaerea. You disappeared without a trace, and he returned me here as if I was a child!"

"You *are* a child," I answered earnestly. "O, did you think Caesar would welcome you with open arms?"

He gave me his famous grin, followed by a hug and a kiss – even more daring than the one in Antonia's garden the other day.

That time I returned it.

"Cassius will help me overthrow the emperor," my brother said, confusing me with an intent gaze. "Macro is on my side as well."

I didn't know the Prefect of the Vigiles personally, but I heard various stories, which had always ended with the words 'a spiv' and 'another Pompilius.' Namely, Macro was crafty and resourceful like a king, who had succeeded in tricking Jove[113] himself.

"Be careful," I said thoughtfully. "This man is working for his own benefit."

"I've noticed." Gaius winked at me. "Therefore, as soon as I get the throne, I'll think about what to do with him… And with Chaerea."

"Don't you even think about Cassius that way," I frowned. "He is my friend."

I felt his arm about my shoulders drawing me closer.

"I hope you are right… sister dear."

I leaned my head against his shoulder, calm and ready to slumber away.

"I have to go," my brother whispered. "It's dawn. Grandmother asked to join her at ientaculum,[114] and after that, I will be visited by my new teacher."

"Is he Greek?" I opened one eye curiously.

---

[113] According to the ancient legend, the Roman supreme deity ordered Numa Pompilius to sacrifice a head. The king offered him a head of garlic, but Jove told him that he wanted something human and living. When clever Numa put a tuft of hair and a small fish to the altar, the god burst into laughter and received the gift.

[114] (Lat.) Breakfast.

"He's Egyptian," Caligula replied. "Antonia is mad about the Land of Khem."

"A pity." I turned to the other side of the bed, and then recalled. "How did you get out of the house with all those guardsmen at the gates?"

"Ask Arminius' daughter. She lent me her dress and cosmetics."

"You are joking me!" I jumped out of the bed, but Gaius was already out. Anger made me scream so loud that my ears hurt. "Armida!"

Anat came in.

"Where is my nursemaid?" I attacked the woman as if she was guilty of my Germanic slave's behavior.

"Princess," she began, self-collected as usual. "Lady Antonia said…"

Some nasty feeling mastered me, and almost made me faint. The Egyptian, frightened by my yell, fell silent and ran out of the chamber.

Armida didn't make me wait too long.

"Help me change my clothes, and dress my hair," I told her, barely calm.

She nodded.

"Bring me the dress my brother wore yesterday," I ordered with irony. "I'd like to have it."

Armida dropped an ivory comb to the floor. Her icy-green eyes flashed.

"You went behind my back… didn't you?" I continued in the same tone.

"Prince Caligula asked me for help," she replied. "He was desperate… "

"So you took care of him." My pretended calmness went sarcastic. "You helped him put himself in danger, and then lied to me."

"I did what I thought was right." The German sounded arrogant.

"Do you know what the punishment is for that?" I exclaimed, as I lost my patience.

The nursemaid insolently mentioned Gaius, pretty sure he would protect her.

"Do you really think my brother cares about a slave?" I giggled brashly.

"Well, I am the firstborn daughter of a prince," Armida raised her voice. "So I could be alumna, like Antioch and Agrippa,[115] but your father put me in chains – to please his little daughter."

"Whatever my brother has told you, you'll be whipped – for lie and insolent behavior," I stopped her even louder. "If you fail again, I'll kill you. Don't compare yourself to the true princes. Their fathers bent the knee before Tiberius, unlike your father, who rebelled against us. It's Arminius you are to blame, not me, nor my late father."

"Caligula can hardly share your opinion," the blond girl sighed. "And, honestly, I'm not afraid of death."

"You're not a warrior, Armida," I reminded her. "You won't get to Valhalla."[116]

"Sorry?" She became a bit confused.

"I read about your customs in a book." I used the moment to cut the German down to size. "I'm literate."

She joined me in my laughter, making our quarrel comical.

"Dress me the hell up," I waved aside. "You are forgiven. It is not your fault, that my big brother is an idiot."

"I hope, you understand me, Domina." Armida looked at me like nothing that serious happened. "I cannot be tamed like Susannah. The Germans never lose their pride, and that is what Caligula probably likes about me."

She said my brother's name too many times. An awful feeling suddenly came back to me. "What do you mean?"

Armida's oblong face changed its expression into merely confused but satisfied. I realized what it was all about, but instead of anger, I felt pure disdain.

"Pride means nothing if you have no honor," I said flatly. "I no longer want you in my service, German. Pack your things and go away."

"Would you like the last advice from someone who is twice as old as you?" she asked.

---

[115] A hostage and protégé of Germanicus, later – the last client king of Judea.
[116] In Germanic and Norse mythology – a majestic hall in heaven, into which the souls of heroes slain in battle and others who have died bravely are received.

I turned my back but let her talk.

"Don't get attached to anyone, my Domina. They all will make you cry. Men's love is so deceptive. When they're young, they need a whore. Mature ones need a fool to bring them dowry and as many sons as possible. The old ones hardly care for us at all."

I barely could remember what she told me next. I didn't notice when she left. Slowly, I lifted my comb from the carpet, and began to do my hair in front of the mirror.

"I should change the color of my hair," I said to my pale-skinned reflection, framed with dirty-brown curls. "And, damn, I need cosmetics."

At noon, well-dressed and unusually cheerful, I joined my grandma, uncle and Caligula for prandium.

XX

Macro delivered Grandma's letter personally to the emperor, and the very same day became Praefectus urbi. Notorious Sejanus ended up in a dungeon of the praetorian camp, soon beheaded by a deaf-mute lictor.[117] Aunt Livilla, as Tiberius' niece and daughter-by-law, was allowed to take poison.

My mother, Drusus, and Nero lost their lives as well. Imperial accusations were considered godly and could never be withdrawn. They were expelled to Pandataria, an island where my mother's mother, Julia the Elder, had been imprisoned and starved to death.

AD 30

"I did a vile thing, sister dear," Tiberius wrote to Antonia six years later. *"I killed the innocent. Since I sent my kin away, I've lost small traces of my peace which still remained in me until I sentenced Agrippina. When I closed my eyes, I got attacked by Furies,[118] devastating maidens lurking in the darkness. I feel their icy breath behind my back right now, writing this letter. There is no escape from my misdeeds, so I decided to redeem myself by making my great-nephew Gaius my lawful heir. By this letter, I invite him to Villa Jovis as soon as possible to grant him necessary education and protection. Besides, I've finally made a decision regarding my great-niece's engagement. Therefore, I demand Drusilla's presence on Capri as well, alongside Tribune Chaerea."*

"Is it a trap? What do you think?" Grandmother asked Actaeon, when the three of us were having supper in triclinium.

"It doesn't seem so to me, Domina." The Greek sighed. "In any case, we do not have much of a choice. It would be even worse to disobey the emperor."

"Let him kill me!" Antonia exclaimed. "I'm not sending my grandchildren to Charybdis![119] I'm not mad to trust that bastard!"

---

[117] (Lat.) An executioner.

[118] In Greco-Roman mythology, the chthonic goddesses of vengeance.

[119] A mythical sea monster (living whirlpool), which dwelt in the Strait of Messina.

As for me, I didn't see a catch in Caesar's words. Regardless of the number of his victims, Tiberius was incurably ill, and his reputation was beneath redemption. I believed he wished to ease his conscience before death.

"I'm not afraid of Caesar," I spoke decisively. "I know he's not lying this time. I also know Tiberius is not our only enemy. Caligula must get the throne and save our family. We must go to Capri and play loving fools until we take what is lawfully ours."

The matron listened to me intently, with her expression slowly changing from sad and angry to hopeful and moved.

"That is the great-granddaughter of Mark Antony, the daughter of Germanicus! How could you be different?" her whisper cried.

"I knew from the beginning, that our prikipessa is a fighter," Actaeon admitted. "She will save us all."

"Caligula will save us," I corrected him. "I have a plan, but everything depends on him."

"Your brother couldn't wait for Caesar's invitation. I remember how this silly thing snuck out to the harbor dressed in women's gown." Grandmother sighed.

I remembered that day like the worst in my childhood. Gaius had begun avoiding me for an unknown reason.

Secretary chuckled, probably imagining his Prince dressed in a servant's paenula over a motley tunic. Domina looked at him severely, and the Greek fell silent.

"You," Antonia referred to me. "Remind your brother that his games with fire are not going well on Capri. Every guest who looks suspicious to Tiberius, is fated to be thrown off a cliff into the sea. Unless the victim breaks himself to death, he is still doomed by hungry sharks or slaves, waiting down there to finish him with sticks."

Once, in the East, there was a little girl who was afraid of her own shadow. If she heard those stories, she would tearfully beg Granny to stop telling them... I wasn't *that* Drusilla. I could neither feel uncertainty, nor fear.

"Please, don't worry," I responded. "I had a good mentor."

XXI

Licinius was glad to see us all again.

"I hope this sailing won't be difficult for you, my Princess." He addressed me, watching proud young sailors, busy raising white sails on a large galleon.

"I can survive that," I smiled. "I've grown up, got stronger, and, my sisters say, I even gained weight."

"Cybele", quinquereme[120] of Augustus." Licinius put his big hand on a rudder. "There is no better ship in the Empire."

"You've prospered, Captain." Cassius patted him on the back.

"Tiberius was generous the other year." The seaman said.

"Extremely," Gaius muttered through his teeth. From the very morning he was out of his mood.

Licinius looked down at him, recalling our first meeting.

"One decade ago, my Prince, you said you wouldn't be like us. And here you are – the heir, the future Emperor… "

"First leap, and then say – hop." My brother replied absently. "They say it's easier to come back home from Hades than from Villa Jovis."

"Don't be downhearted," I said softly, reaching out to stroke his hand.

"Don't be naive." He looked at me worriedly, and moved a little further.

I had always understood him… He could hardly even try to get me.

"I need some rest." I turned to Susannah, already waiting for me with a peacock feather fan.

Licinius took us to a comfortable room, which did not resemble a tight space on our Syrian ship. There were silk curtains, a long mirror in the silver frame, and cashmere blankets on a big soft bed gave away the name of the woman who once owned

---

[120] The largest Roman ship, with three banks of rowers, two each for the upper two oars and one rower on the lower oar.

this chamber. Atia, Augustus' mother, took this ship to bring her faithless son-in-law, Mark Antony, back home.

"Atia returned to Rome pale, weak and miserable," Grandma told me once. "She crossed the whole Mediterranean in vain. Queen Cleo didn't want to open the front doors for her, and, if you ask me, she was absolutely right."

"But Anthony was married to Octavia!" I rebelled first, too much accustomed to the bookish happy endings. "And they had you!"

"My father didn't want that marriage," she explained. "He was forced to it by the Old Caesar and Octavian. The alliance with the ruler and his heir was too important to the proud and ambitious consul, so he couldn't scorn it. My poor mother was known neither by her looks, nor mind. A quite widow, a mother of three, who worshiped her brother, was the exact opposite of her spirited and captivating rival Cleopatra."

"You took your stepmother's side, don't you?" I wondered.

"I always take the side of love and truth," Antonia replied. "When you grow up, I bet you'll do the same."

Grandma was never wrong. I've always done the same.

"Domina," Nursemaid brought me back from daydreaming. "Just before we left, I've bought an interesting thing for you."

I reached out and felt a papyrus scroll beneath my fingers, wrapped in her linen shawl.

"The Book of Wisdom,"[121] she whispered excitedly. "Unchanged."

My headache, born of weariness, had left me in an instance.

"Unbelievable," the Jewess smiled. "It seems that you were right, my Princess."

I had the scroll unwrapped and handed it to Susannah.

"Do you remember the story of Solomon?" she asked.

"The king with seven hundred wives, who thought he was wise?" I said jokingly.

"The whole nine hundred," the nursemaid waved aside. "But he loved only one of them."

---

[121] One of the books of the Apocrypha – a Jewish text, composed in Greek, created in Alexandria (Egypt), traditionally attributed to King Solomon.

"Maqueda, Queen of Sheba," I remembered our bedtime stories.

"The king marveled at her wisdom and compared her to Lilith," Susannah went on quietly.

I shook my head and rubbed my eyes.

"Oh, he was really a clever man!"

It had been six years since I started searching for the answers to my questions in Grandmother's library. My eyesight worsened from that frantic reading, but there was no word about the first woman and the plot of Mithras. I had almost learned by heart the only evidence of Lilith's innocence, believing there would be a trace of what Zaleukos warned us about.

"Tell me, nanny." I took Susannah by the hand, and offered her a seat right next to me. "What else did Solomon think about Lilith?"

The nursemaid spoke half-loudly: "Once two women came to the King and stood before him, both claiming to be the mother of the child they brought to court. Wise Solomon suggested cutting the baby in two, so each woman could receive a half of it. One of the women agreed imperturbably, but her rival went to tears, begging the judge to have mercy on an infant, even by giving way to her companion. Solomon understood who of them was the true mother, and returned the baby to the gracious woman. All the Jews know that story, but only in this book King Solomon revealed the names of the two rivals – Naomi and Lilith."

"Lilith was the good one, right?" I asked, horrified with the false mother's behavior.

She nodded, and went on.

"As far as I'm concerned, Naomi was the older daughter of Adam and Eve, the twin sister of Cain. She was believed to be vile-natured like her brother, as if her true father was the Devil himself."

Therefore, true Lilith was wise, like Maqueda of Sheba, compassionate like that merciful mother, and more fair-minded than the better part of Eve's descendants. Still, even Solomon could hardly dare to justify her, but in riddles.

"There is another poem, where the King admired an enigmatic woman named Sophia. Our priests interpret it as the praise to God's wisdom, but I don't think so. The author calls Sophia the interlocutor of the Lord, which means she was a human being. Also, Solomon's veneration for that woman is kind of…"

"Sensual?" I guessed as if I knew the book's content.

"Yes," Susannah replied, slightly surprised. "Sensual and lyrical, but also sublime."

"Sophia means wisdom," I said thoughtfully. "What is the symbol of wisdom?"

"An owl," the Jewess smiled. "A sinister nocturnal bird."

"You say this book had been transcribed?"

"Some parts of it were removed, replaced by lies, or added to another books."

"That sounds familiar." I sighed. "Augustus had burned down a third of the Alexandria Library. He destroyed the scrolls that could endanger him and his allies…"

"*…to rule the world,*" the words of Zaleukos flashed in my mind like lightning. "*They hate love and women…*"

"Damn Susannah, where did you get this?" I asked, startled.

"You won't believe me, Domina," she said excitedly.

"That day, when you sent me to the market, I met my fellow countrywoman Rachel. Her father was a wealthy merchant, and he had no other children beside her, or living brothers. When he died, Rachel succeeded him, and continued the trading tradition so she could gain her independence, which is barely impossible for any Jewish woman."

"So she's spreading the forbidden scripts now, right?" I wittily concluded.

"In her store, she has a lot of things," the nursemaid whispered. "From rare spices to expensive silks – all the goods Augustus banned for selling."

"She's like Macro!" I exclaimed. "I want to meet her when we're back to Rome."

Susannah nodded, and began to make my bed.

"You really need some rest, my Princess. Capri is not Syria, but you are not accustomed to sea voyages."

"That's true, and you may sleep as well. If I get hungry, I'll call Photice. Fortunately, Grandma let her go with us, so I won't eat pig's wash made by a ship cook."

"Domina, I think you're wrong." The Jewess shook her head. "Boiled food is healthy. Pies and roasted meat can make you ill."

"Oh, don't be boring, Susannah!" I turned my back on her. "Leave me alone. When I wake up, we will continue our secret studies."

When the nursemaid left, I slowly came up to the window and moved the thin curtain aside. The ship was on its way, sliding slowly on the calm waters of the Tyrrhenian Sea. The eager captain was giving orders to the sailors, constantly gesticulating in a funny way. On the bow I saw Cassius, thoughtfully looking into the distance. To the right of the mast there was Photice, arguing aloud with the ship cook about boiled buckwheat with bacon and onion. I strained my eyes to see my brother, but I couldn't see him.

He must be sleeping in the other room, I thought, as I darkened the chamber, and lay down on the bed.

Oh, please, Caligula, be smart... I told him in my spirit. *Everything depends on you.*

XXII

Tiberius' mansion was perched on a rock, at the very top of a massive mountain, surrounded by deep caves and lush vegetation. One look at the steep cliff made my head whirl.

Macro met us at the shore. His colors now were red and blue instead of black.

"The view from above is even worse." He smiled wryly. "Welcome to Tartarus, sirs."

"It's pretty high." Cassius raised his head. "And precipitous, too."

"I am afraid, we cannot ride the ascent." Macro jerked his chin upward. "Our road is rocky."

"Do not worry." Chaerea turned around and winked at me. "I'll carry you."

"Are you sure, tribune?" Gaius muttered. "She is heavy."

Cassius looked at him with a certain disdain, and easily lifted me up.

"He said, we shouldn't hurry," I heard Macro say. "But I don't advise you to get late, either. We will have a brief rest by the Black Cave. There are horses, and some drinking water waiting for us there."

"I need a horse for my freedwomen, too," I told him earnestly.

The prefect couldn't hide astonishment, but quickly nodded.

"Can you ride a horse, Susannah?" I turned to the stunned Jewess.

"I know," Photice replied instead. "In Mauretania, they teach us, girls, to ride like boys."

When we got to the first flat meadow, Gaius asked the tribune to let him speak with his sister alone.

"Tell me, Drusilla," he began tensely, with arms crossed over his chest. "That slave of yours, Armida – where is she?"

I looked at him - a little careless, and turned aside to wash my face with icy spring water.

"What a refreshment in that heat!" I smiled, and took a sip, pretending I ignored his question.

"Hope she's alive…" He looked at me worriedly.

"Who knows…" I shrugged. "But she is free."

"Drusilla!" My brother touched his head as if he was in pain. "Why have you driven her away? Where could she go in that big Rome? She's stubborn, and she hardly knows our customs! She must have ended up in a brothel!"

"Good," I answered calmly. "She belongs there."

"Is it you, Drusilla?" Gaius cried with disappointment. "Do you know how much the maiden suffered?"

"Maiden?!" I repeated mockingly, alluding to their love affair.

Caligula fell silent for a moment, and continued quietly, but angrily.

"If it was all about her love for me, you are no better than the one up there." He pointed a finger at the gates of Villa Jovis.

"You said – l-love?!" I asked in disbelief.

"Now you remind me of Claudius." Gaius rolled his eyes and whispered, "What did you expect of me, sister? Did you think I'd sit and watch you and your Cassius behaving like two lovers?"

"I do not love Cassius," I answered out of habit. "You are the one for me."

"Drusilla, it's just words!" his whisper screamed. "When I was in despair, Armida gave me comfort and support. And where you were that day, when they took our mother to Praetorium?"

"The truth is that we – Cassius and me," I somehow managed to respond in the same tone, "we saved you from sharing our mother's fate!"

"Let it be so," Caligula turned back on me. "At least I tried to save our mother, while my sister was daydreaming in the library, with her ears full of Antonia's rubbish!"

Tears welled up in my eyes. I heard Armida's outrageous laughter echoing in my head.

"Don't speak, Gaius. Please…" I came up to him. "Don't forget where we are now."

"I don't give a damn. I'm already in Hades." My brother pushed my hand away.

I felt vertigo and fever attacking my body, ready to start their torturous, demented dance. I reached out for Susannah. Both of my maids took me by the hands and led to the grotto, where Macro and Cassius were resting.

"I am sick." I looked at Gaius.

"It's no wonder." He stepped up to me. "What about Armida? First, *her* father left her mother for the sake of a trollop Thusnelda,[122] and then *our* heroic father captured her."

"She betrayed me!" I moaned.

"Don't be stupid," the prince went on. "She has taken care of you for eight years, and never heard a single 'thank you.' Was she worse than these two cows, you treat like friends?" He nodded towards Susannah and Photice.

"What took you so long to ask for her?" I asked with my eyes squinted.

Brother took his grey horse by the reins and saddled it without a word.

"Easy, my Prince!" Macro stood up. "We go together, don't we?"

Chaerea, realizing I was losing consciousness, ran to me and took me in his arms.

"What's going on?" she shouted at Photice.

"Looks like sunstroke, tribune." The Greek touched my forehead, frowning at Gaius.

"Fetch her some water!" he ordered and carried me into the shade of tall cypress trees. Susannah carefully moistened my mouth, and my face with water.

"She needs something harder," Macro spoke, and handed a small lagena to Cassius. His drink had pungent smell and bitter taste.

I have to come to my senses, I thought. *No time for self-pity, Drusilla.*

Finally, Caligula's concern for me overcame his anger. He dismounted his horse, and came over, but I pushed his touch away.

"It's better now," I turned to Cassius. "It's time to ride."

"What?" Gaius opened his eyes wide. "You can hardly drag your feet!"

"It's not my first time," I replied. "Let's go. Caesar is waiting."

---

[122] A Germanic noblewoman, who was a wife of the Cheruscan chieftain Arminius.

XXIII

"Quis venit?"[123] We heard the large janitor standing by the huge stone gate.

"Efutue!"[124] Macro called out, as he got off his horse.

The wakeful giant saluted us, letting the prefect introduce him.

"This is Anicetus. His looks may be frightening, but he is reliable. "

"My Prince," the janitor bowed to us. "My Princess."

I looked up at him. His face was sharp to ugly, but his eyes were full of almost childly kindness.

"Podapos ei?"[125] I asked him curiously.

Anicetus smiled, as he recognized his mother tongue.

"From Cyprus, Your Highness, the village of Akaki."

"Look, they've already made friends!" Macro addressed to my brother. "It's for the first time I see that bear smiling."

The prefect's arrogance became disgusting. I knew well what it was like when someone mocked you.

"And you, Sutorius? Which animal are you?" I cried out furiously. "You remind me of a skunk."

The prefect fell silent, took my brother by the hand, and leaded him to the vestibulum.[126]

"May all the Gods guard you in this awful place, Your Highness," Anicetus whispered to me as I followed my brother.

"Don't worry, Argus.[127] She's no coward." Photice whispered back to him, nodding at me proudly.

---

[123] (Lat.) Who goes there?

[124] (Lat.) Fuck off!

[125] (Anc.Gr.) Where are you from?

[126] (Lat.) A corridor between the gate of Roman house and the atrium.

[127] The many-eyed mythological guardsman.

"Meanwhile, I've made a lot of useful acquaintance." The prefect winked at Gaius, trying to turn the attention away from his effrontery. "We'll talk about that later, for, I think, Nerva is watching us."

In the atrium, I saw a familiar figure of an elderly man, wearing a toga with a broad purple stripe. He was observing my brother with a curiously derisive smile.

"He was there, too," I recalled. "One of those who killed my father."

Cassius, as if he sensed the flow of my thoughts, grabbed me by the wrist.

"I know what's on your mind," he warned me sharply. "Nerva is an imperial jurist. A single word of his would be enough…"

"Let go of my hand," I whispered angrily. "He won't do any harm to me, but to himself."

The tribune looked to me in astonishment. Scared by my own words, I grabbed my head.

"I don't know what I'm saying, so forget it."

"Please, Drusilla," Chaerea went on earnestly. "We must not make mistakes."

I reluctantly nodded, and we passed through the atrium. The entrance hall was large, surrounded by the oak-like pillars. Mosaics on its walls reflected some well-known Greek motifs. There were Achilles and Patroclus, Orestes and Pylades, and of course, immortal Phoebus cuddling his lover Hyacithus.[128]

"Nice to see you, Prince," Coccaeus Nerva spoke restrainedly, stepping forward. "You certainly do not remember me… When we last met, you were a child."

Caligula, bewildered, hardly mumbled words of salutation.

"Do you recognize *me*, Consul?" I stepped forward, ignoring Chaerea's warning. "I'm a daughter of Germanicus."

Nerva's narrow, wrinkled face suddenly put on a perfidious smile.

"Princess… I did not expect you were invited… Usually, women stay away from here."

"Caesar is a god," I answered coldly. "There's no 'usually' for the gods."

Nerva coughed anxiously, and then turned towards Gaius.

---

[128] Mythical heroes, known, among other things, for their homosexual love.

"Caesar is waiting for you in the ceremonial hall, my Prince."

Caligula was lost and still upset with me – I saw it in his eyes.

"Noli sollicitus esse,"[129] I replied to him in my mind. "Te amo."[130]

"This way, Your Highness." Macro gestured toward the dimly lit hallway between the atrium and the peristyle. Gaius followed precariously, and three of them quickly disappeared in the spacious porch.

My heart started beating like a hammer again and my breath became shallow.

"What about us?" I spoke. "What are *we* going to do now?"

"For now," the tribune sighed, "all we can do is to wait and to stay quiet."

"I don't see a soul in here…" I looked around. "Weird, isn't it? Like on the night we escaped from Syria."

"Far be it, Domina." Susannah shook her head and looked at Cassius with hope.

"Your Domina is out of control," he smiled. "Caesar himself will be afraid of her."

"The big, bad wolf? I chuckled, as I noticed a particularly dirty fresco on the wall. "If he ever touches my brother, I will…"

"Caesar won't touch him," I was interrupted by an unfamiliar male voice at the dark corner of the hall. "He is aware of his illness, and will never risk his only heir."

Cassius took a defensive position in front of me, ordering the maids to watch my back.

"Don't be afraid." The stranger said half-loudly. "I'm your like-minded friend."

In the light of the wall torch, there emerged a young man, dressed in a short tunica, which gave away his slave status.

"I am Callistus." The dark-haired man gave me a nonchalant bow. "I will take care of Your Highness during your stay at Villa Jovis."

"Look, he's Greek!" Photice chortled. "Well, these Trojans[131] are obsessed with us."

"Easy, compatriot!" Callistus frowned. "You're referring to the Imperial Secretary."

---

[129] (Lat.) Have no fear.

[130] (Lat.) I love you.

[131] The Trojan hero Aeneas was considered the ancestor of the ancient Romans.

"I'm married to a secretary." Photice replied proudly. "And, first of all, I'm a freed-woman."

"Enough, both of you!" I yelled in Greek. "If we are really like-minded friends, let's see what we can do."

The woman fell silent immediately, and the secretary burst out laughing.

"Macro warned me, that you are a bit of shrew, Your Highness," he said sincerely, without a trace of slavish humility. "I like it, but for now, I'd rather recommend you and the tribune to have some rest. I'll show you your rooms."

"A good idea," Cassius agreed. "I'm afraid we've already drawn too much attention to ourselves."

"No, you haven't... yet," the Greek replied, lighting a lamp. "Tiberius does not take our Princess seriously, and old Thrasyllus doesn't even know she's here."

"Do you know what is he planning – for Caligula?" I asked him worriedly.

"Well, today he will adopt him, and declare him his successor."

Suddenly I recollected our cousin Gemellus, another grandson of Tiberius.

"It's strange that Caesar doesn't mention little Gemellus... He is indeed blood of his blood."

The Greek covered his mouth slightly with his hand.

"The emperor thinks that Gemellus was born of Livilla's adultery, but he can't kill the boy, because he can never be sure."

His voice gave me composure. I realized I was tired. Callistus escorted us to a neatly furnished room, adorned with a large bookshelf.

"This time, dominus spared no expense." The secretary winked at me, pointing toward the shelf. "The most exquisite Greek works on the best parchment."

"Very considerate of him," I said enthusiastically. "I've always told my teacher, Zaleukos, how I wished I was born Greek."

"One doesn't become Hellen by birth, but by his education," Callistus said proudly. "They told me you've been speaking Greek since early childhood."

"Since age four." I smiled. " Mia glotta oudepopote ikani."[132]

Callistus agreed, and returned to the practical matters.

---

[132] (Anc.Gr.) One language is never enough.

"For your maids or whatever they are, I prepared rooms in the west wing – with windows and without floor heating."[133]

"No way!" I shook my head. "Photice and Susannah will stay with me."

"As you wish." The secretary nodded. "But I'm afraid, Tiberius would not allow the tribune Chaerea… "

"I would've never thought of that!" Cassius spoke out angrily. "I know I haven't been promoted to that rank for my success in war, but I still have my honor!"

"Sorry, I am too excited," Callistus replied, a little bit ashamed. "You will be staying in a separate room in the guards' house. It's not cozy, but I guess it sounds much better than the chamber for the favorites."

I was the first to burst into laughter. Cassius, almost ready to get angry at the secretary for another inappropriate joke, suddenly changed his mind, and joined me. So did Photice, Susannah and Callistus himself.

"Laugh, Drusilla!" I recalled Grandmother's words again. "In hardest times – do not give up, but raise your head, straighten your back and – smile! Believe me, child, you'll hit *them* hard like that."

"Callistus," I asked the Greek, as he and Cassius were leaving. "Why is Nerva here?"

"Well, he's the suffect consul, and his presence at the ceremony of proclaiming the Crown Prince is obligatory." The secretary turned around. "By the way, I've heard he was complaining of his poor health condition, so there is a chance he'll be replaced by a younger jurist."

This news should have cheered me up, but a question, born in my head all of a sudden, filled me with insecurity.

"Like whom?"

"Lucius Longinus," he replied. "Caesar's former… very close friend."

I didn't know that man, but I felt really unpleasant about him.

Better the devil you know than the devil you don't, I thought.

My intuition did not fool me.

---

[133] The Roman traditional patrician house was separated from the world outside by thick walls with no windows. Small windows for ventilation were only placed in servants' rooms, or in the insulas – many-floor houses for the poor.

XXIV

The next day, Cassius and I were honored with a reception at Caesar's.

Tiberius, dressed in a gorgeous purple toga, sat on his ivory throne, watching us intently. The laurel wreath of pure gold gleamed on his grey and balding head, but no jewel or attire could cover the signs of the hideous disease on his face and neck.

"Ave, Caesar!" We greeted him almost in one voice.

Tiberius greeted us back, gesturing to come closer. I stepped forward.

"So, Drusilla," he spoke huskily. "I heard, you hadn't made a good impression on my late mother."

"Neither had she on me," I replied in the same humorous manner.

Tiberius' fell silent, his ironic smile suddenly faded. Cassius looked at me with an emotion, probably unknown to him before – a kind of fear… for me. And I… I didn't even blink.

Finally, the emperor's loud laughter filled the room.

"I really love honesty!" He clapped his hands, and sighed. "That virtue runs away from all the rulers…"

"Always out of fear," I explained. "Fear breeds lies… and hatred."

"You're right." His curiosity turned to astonishment. "And you, Drusilla, do *you* fear the ruler?"

"No, I don't." I shook my head. "I have no reason for it, Caesar."

"You're the same as your grandmother!" A sardonic smile was on his face again. "Speaking of Livia, I'm not angry at you. I hated her as well."

"I hated Agrippina," I confessed him unexpectedly, feeling no shame.

"We understand each other," Caesar sighed. "That's a nice start."

I noticed a trace of compassion in the old man's eyes, and I believed it.

I should not.

"Tribune," Caesar said abruptly to Chaerea. "Do you really wish to take my grand-niece as a wife?"

"Aye, Caesar," Cassius replied immediately.

"You are not a patrician, but the son of a knight and a peregrine," Tiberius went on sharply. "Julia Drusilla is a princess. I can understand your reasons, but, as far as I'm concerned, the wound you sustained on the Rhine left you sterile. For my Augustan grand-niece, a childless marriage wouldn't be a decent choice."

Right then I had no other choice than interrupting him.

"Exalted Caesar," I spoke calmly. "The issue matter doesn't mean that much to me. I love that man, and he loves me."

"You don't say so!" the old man sneered. "I wouldn't recommend it. Love destroys more people than all wars, intrigues and plagues together."

"Love does not," I objected. "Her absence does."

His piercing gaze ordered me to fall silent. If I had to play his game, he wanted me to do it by his rules.

"You're not as stupid as the rest of womanhood." Tiberius said through his teeth. "With you, I can converse."

Then he looked up and went on dolefully. "I wish, my dearly beloved Vipsania could be that brave..."

"And you, my Caesar?" I asked fearlessly. "Were you as brave as that?"

I saw wildfire in his sight. I barely calmed my heart, showing him neither fear, nor tears. My great-uncle sensed it, and stopped himself as well, and... smiled to me.

"Young lady, you deserve your Cassius."

Chaerea took my hand, believing that we made it. As I felt the joy in his big heart, I squeezed his palm, and looked up to thank Caesar.

But, the emperor stopped me with his right hand raised. Then, he exclaimed "Come in!", referring to someone outside the throne room.

The guardsmen opened the doors, and I saw two men entering. An old one and a younger one, they stood before Tiberius.

"Lucius Cassius Longinus." My great-uncle introduced to us his younger guest. "A friend of mine, new consul-suffect of the Empire, and a future life companion for you, Drusilla."

I could not believe my eyes and ears. Middle-aged Longinus resembled a bat – he was my height, but slender like a boy. He tried to hide his thinness behind overly wide toga, but that made him look bizarre and clumsy. Consul-suffect's gaze was dreamy, giving away his short sightedness. His leisurely posture made him look like someone suffering from frequent fevers.

"Aren't they look-alikes?" Tiberius asked Chaerea, even more struck dumb by his decision than myself. "Just like two siblings!"

You natty freak! I thought, looking at Caesar, who just started dancing merrily in place. *All the goodness you might have, was ruined by your odious mother.*

"Bring the musicians!" Tiberius yelled rapturously, waving his wiry hands. "I want to celebrate my great-niece's engagement!"

Longinus also seemed to share my frustration, but his timid nature never let him oppose anyone, especially the emperor.

"I'm not euphoric, lady," he whispered to me as Tiberius reached for another glass of wine. "I've always been attracted to… another kind of women."

"I see," I whispered back with some relief. "I'm not offended."

"Cui bono?"[134] Longinus smiled disappointedly, yet unaware that this very phrase, spoken in some other place and other time, would make him famous.

"Stop bitching and accept your destiny," Cassius said in his ear. "You don't have a choice."

Tiberius heard our conversation very well.

"You're a good man, tribune," he said refinedly. "You serve your emperor and you would give your life for his familia. And now that I have broken your heart without scruple, you are acting more than dignified. For that, I'm letting you accompany Drusilla to Antium, where she will get married next month."

Next month, I thought desperately, *I'm marrying a dwarf, who, thankfully, already hates me. And what am I supposed to do? I sacrifice my life for Gaius, who now hates me even more…*

With a heavy heart, I went out into the porch, where Callistus and Susannah were waiting for me. I felt too broken to answer their questions. I didn't even turn around

---

[134] (Lat.) To whom is it a benefit?

when Cassius called my name. I was painfully absent, as my mind was carrying me far away – into the world of myths and dreams… And, in an instant, I occasionally overheard the conversation between Caesar and his older guest.

"O Divus." The stranger sounded bitter. "Why did you invite her here?"

"I knew you were going to wail, Thrasyllus," My great-uncle hadn't lost his humor. "That is why I didn't tell you about her arrival. Do you really think that my grand-niece is the Pandora, who will cut me down one day?"

"My Lord." The astrologer's voice was trembling. "She is not Pandora… She is *Libitina*."

XXV

"*I loved Sophia and sought her out from my youth; I desired to make her my spouse...*" Susannah read forbidden verses of King Solomon to me. "*I preferred her before Scepters and Thrones, and esteemed riches nothing in comparison to her... Yea, the Lord of all things Himself loves her.*"

"Your god is not as bad... as people – men... represent him," I spoke, fighting tears. "He must be better than Jove... or Mithras."

"All the pagan deities are evil," the Jewess sighed, "but that Parthian bloodsucker is the worst."

"What do you know about him?" I got out of bed. "I've turned the library upside down, but I haven't found a word about him."

"I don't know too much either, Domina," she answered. "They call him 'Unconquered Sun' and claim he is a god of virtues who promises his followers eternal bliss in the afterlife... and secretly requires human sacrifices."

I had heard the same from my Greek teacher.

"That makes him a hypocrite," I thought out loud. "The worst of his kind."

"Us Jews call all the heathen gods – daemons." She wrapped the scroll tightly, as we finished reading. "However, Mithras is believed to be the darkest and meanest fiend."

"So it was he – the one who seduced Eve?" I suddenly recalled.

"Damned be his name!" Susannah frowned and hugged me to take me back to bed as if I was a child. "Come on, let's wipe those tears away."

"Don't call me a Domina." I leaned my head against her chest. "I freed you."

"What do you want me to call you then?" She smiled. "By name, by title or... just – Little Owl?"

Why did I find her boring? I thought, looking at my caring nanny. *She was always there to comfort me.*

"Little Owl, definitely," I replied.

"Then, Little Owl, you better wash your hands for dinner." She began to set a small, skillfully carved wooden table.

"It's a good idea," I sighed, slowly coming back to my reality. "Where is the Greekess?"

"She is coming. First she had to wait for other cookmen to prepare some meal for Caesar."

I washed my face and combed my hair in front of the mirror. *I am stout*, I thought, looking at my curvy body. *That's why my brother chose that bony German over me.*

Susannah read my mind by the expression of my face and began to palaver.

"Could you imagine what that Greek, Callistus, told me yesterday?"

I looked at her with curiosity.

"He is a bigger gossip than a Jewish woman," she continued. "He claims that Caesar welcomed a new favorite the other day – some young patrician named Asinius."

"I know this softie." I recalled the man. "My mother wished I married him. Longinus may be ugly, but Asinius is a disaster."

Susannah insensibly covered my back with a blanket of thin wool. "The Consul-suffect is a good man, Little Owl. I think, he's honest, and, perhaps his heart is broken too."

"I do not care about his heart." I whispered tiredly. "Nobody cares for mine."

I got more and more hungry. Photice wasn't showing up. I looked at the clepsydra[135] – she was getting pretty late. A shiver attacked me.

"I'm going for the Greekess." I stood up, wrapping myself in a blanket. "In this goddamn palace, anything can happen."

"I will follow you." The nursemaid lit two lamps. "I know where the kitchen is."

We stepped out to the empty hallway, holding hands. The doorless relief walls, lit by four torches, looked like the entrance to Hades. We couldn't hear a sound, but the water dripping into the impluvium,[136] and our own steps.

---

[135] An ancient time-measuring device worked by a flow of water.

[136] The sunken part of the atrium in a Greek or Roman house – a shallow pool that caught rainwater which filtered through the porous stone and into a cistern below.

The imperial aedicule, I thought, facing the marble altar under the bright fresco, representing a handsome deity. It was a young man, eyes coal-black, with a sun-shaped crown on his head.

The Jewess turned aside with abhorrence. I raised my lamp and read under the fresco – 'SOL INVICTVS.' Sudden fear made my hands tremble. The sun-god's face seemed spiritual and good-looking, but there was a kind of greed and shamelessness in his dark beauty.

"Let's get out of here," Susannah pulled me by the sleeve. "Demons are dangerous."

"I know." My fear gave way to earnestness. "His worshipers have killed my family."

Then, I swiftly took the other lamp, brought it to Mithras' face, and... spat between his eyes. The nursemaid grabbed her head.

"Drusilla!" she called out. "What if there's someone here?"

"There is." We heard a familiar voice in the dark. "I knew you were looking for trouble."

I turned around and lit up Callistus' slender figure.

"We're looking for my cookmaid. Where is she?" I asked him worriedly.

The secretary nodded toward the atrium.

"Come with me – now."

I squeezed Susannah's hand in panic, and we followed the Greek slave without a word.

"Fortunately, all the company is down there in mithraeum." The man spoke, as we were leaving the palace. "Celebrating the death day of the first woman – Layla."

"Where are you taking us?" The Jewess asked him anxiously.

Callistus said nothing, and accelerated steps.

By the annex house for the slaves, we met Anicetus.

"I'm sorry, Princess," he said sadly.

A weak moan came from the sleeping room. I pushed the janitor away and rushed inside. Photice lay on the bed under a thin blanket, trembling in fever. The imperial physician, also Greek, stood motionless over her body, murmuring something about Charon's obol.[137]

"Photice!" I exclaimed, running to her tiny bed. "What is it, Photice? What have they done to you?"

"I found her on the floor in a triclinium." The medic said with sorrow. "She was lying in a pool of blood with her dress torn… I have tried my hardest, Princess… but she can't be saved."

I knelt in front of her, and I took her palm in my hand. The hand that fed me was now cold and sickly wet.

"It hurts, Actaeon … Hurts…" Photice groaned like a child, looking somewhere up.

"It will pass, soon," I replied in Greek. "Actaeon is on his way… I hear him coming."

She turned her head and looked at me lucidly.

"Sorry, prikipessa… Photice left you hungry."

I put my head on the edge of her bed and wept. Tears were choking me, as I felt Photice' hand, caressing my hair with her last ounce of strength.

"Take Her Highness away, Callistus." I heard the old physician's voice. "One shouldn't embrace with the dying. Thanatos[138] is lurking…"

"O, fuck Thanatos!" I screamed, jumping to my feet, and pushed the medic away. "There are no gods! I will avenge you, Photice, I swear!"

Callistus and Susannah took me by both hands and pulled me carefully toward the corridor.

"Do not look. She's already in agony," the nursemaid said, covering my eyes with the other hand. I let them take me to the antechamber, where Anicetus was guarding. Susannah helped me take a seat and covered my back with the blanket again.

---

[137] The coin placed in or on the mouth of a dead person before burial. Greek and Latin literary sources specify the coin as an obol, and explain it as a payment or bribe for Charon, the ferryman who conveyed souls across the river that divided the world of the living from the world of the dead.

[138] In ancient Greek mythology, the personification of death.

"Tell me the truth." I turned to Callistus. "Who dared to raise his hand on my familia?"[139]

"Marcus Asinius." The secretary sighed. "While Caesar and his company were in Mithraeum."

Gritting my teeth and clenching fists in pain, I spoke.

"Asinius will pay for what he's done."

"Why – she?" Susannah joined me in crying.

"Well… perhaps, the bastard thought he's brought to Caesar at Antonia's recommendation," Callistus explained, as he himself went pale.

"You," I referred to the Jewess quite sharply. "From now on, you will stay by me! I do not want to lose you, too."

Susannah nodded and sat down next to me. The rain outside brought the cold to the house.

"And you," I continued, pointing at the secretary. "If you consider yourself Hellen, help Anicetus and me bring justice to your decent fellow countrywoman!"

Anicetus, slightly surprised, gave me a nod. Callistus goggled at me.

"Do you want me to kill a patrician because of a servant?" He spoke out in disbelief. "A woman?"

"Photice is a human being, you moron!" I yelled at him. "Man, woman, nobleman or slave – we're all the same! We're all descended of Adam and Eve!"

Caesar's secretary, stunned, got down to the chair, and Susannah glanced at me with an approving smile.

"You're right, Your Highness," the tall guardsman spoke. "Who are these Latins to oppress us? Our Hellenic art and science are centuries old, and what about them? They only conquer, steal and murder…!"

"Take it easy, colossus!" Callistus frowned. "Don't forget that Her Highness is Roman."

"Let him be," I waved aside. "I wish I could choose my origin."

---

[139] Unlike the modern conception of the family, the Roman familia referred to the entire household, including the slaves and servants.

The secretary sighed, turned aside toward the door, rubbed his temples, and said.

"We only have tomorrow. The day after the feast Tiberius usually fasts and does not leave his chambers. When everything gets done, I'll tell him that his favorite, persuaded by his too conservative and pious parents, jumped off a cliff to kill himself."

I approved the plan. Photice wasn't just a servant in my eyes – she was my honest and devoted friend. Her murderer had to be punished, and so had it happened.

We buried her in the old Greek cemetery in the southern part of the island. Then, struggling with tears, I wrote to Actaeon, and Callistus made sure the letter went to Rome unnoticed with the morning ship.

The morning before my departure for Antium, I found Gaius in the garden. He sat on a bench by the statue of an athlete, watching the amber sunrise above the sea.

"You're not having breakfast with Caesar?" I asked, trying to smile.

Caligula turned his head.

"He hasn't invited me. Maybe, he's not in the mood. And you," he looked at me, trying to seem indifferent. "You have an early start today, why?"

"After that, what's happening to me, I cannot sleep," I told the truth.

My brother moved aside, making some place for me to sit.

"I heard about your cookmaid… I am sorry. I know you are very attached to your servants."

The mere thought that she was gone stroke me right to the heart.

"She was more than a maid to me. She treated me better than our mother did."

As he recalled Agrippina the Elder, Caligula frowned and turned his back on me.

"Are you avoiding me?" I brought myself closer to him. "Don't you understand how miserable I am now – without you?"

Gaius looked at me – slowly, patiently, as if he was studying me. His blue eyes, as before, radiated with love, while his words and posture told me something different.

"I know you cannot stand on Longinus." He went on, as if he hadn't heard my questions. "But us, people, grow used to everything. You'll move to Carinae, start a family… I bet a jurist's wife enjoys more comfort than the soldier's…"

"O, are you still my brother, my Caligula?" I interrupted him with disappointment.

"I am the heir to the emperor." He became earnest. "I will have to marry a suitable lady, who would give me sons as soon as possible."

My maid and friend was dead... My love was ready to abandon me. Was this another test of my endurance?

"Do you remember what you said to me in Grandma's garden?" I asked him.

"Little sister," Gaius smiled and looked away, "I was ten years old."

Suddenly I saw Lilith or Sophia with my minds' eyes again. She was the first to cry a sea of tears, longing for love and happiness, but didn't find them.

"*I am disgraced... and exalted one.*" As though she was talking about me... But why?

The sound of footsteps drove away my vision.

"I hear Macro and Callistus coming. Don't embarrass us," my brother whispered, reaching out to grab me by the hand.

"Don't worry." I stood up, and I stepped to the colonnade – towards the secretary and the prefect.

"Princess!" Callistus was gasping. "Caesar calls you to say goodbye."

Macro greeted me with his well-known crafty smile. Looking at him contemptuously, I turned to the secretary and spoke softly but audibly.

"Take care of my brother, filo mu.[140] Don't let him fall under the faulty influence."

"At the cost of my life, Princess," he replied in Greek, touched with the way I called him.

I sealed our friendship with a hug. I believed, Callistus would never let me down...

"Do you want to say goodbye to me, Drusilla?" Gaius called, watching me leave.

"Vale," I said calmly, as I didn't even turn around. "Propediem te videbo."[141]

---

[140](Anc.Gr.) My friend.
[141](Lat.) See you soon.

XXVI

My wedding day was hot and muggy. The invitees, the members of my husband's family and their friends and optimates thronged the Temple of Liber and Libera.[142] The monotonous ceremony and long standing made me feel like I was going to vomit.

"Ubi tu Gaius, ego Gaia,"[143] I finally said, followed by the curious looks and rehearsed smiles of the bridegroom's relatives.

Lucius Longinus was getting married for the third time. His first wife left him for a younger and more handsome lover, and the second one – for someone older but wealthier. As his caring mother Lucia Verginia, Longinus loved them both, and greatly suffered his divorces. My mother-in-law didn't hide another bitter fact of his biography – the Consul-suffect used to live in Villa Jovis, where he was entertaining Caesar by playing harp and doing all the things favorites do… So, his soft heart was broken more than once.

"My son may not be marrying out of love," Verginia said, when I was made matrona Longini, "but he respects you, and won't have another woman beside you."

"I'm sorry, lady," I spoke honestly. "As for myself, I do believe in love, so I can't promise him the same."

Verginia, shocked by this statement, would surely give me names or even slap me in the face… unless I was Tiberius grand-niece. She left the temple heavily upset.

"Why are you doing this?" Longinus whispered bitterly. "I do not understand you, Julia Drusilla."

I just shrugged, exhausted by nausea and vertigo.

"Worst of all, I'm getting married on dog's days[144] like a barbarian!" He was complaining. "Caesar must be really angry at you."

---

[142] In Roman religion, a pair of fertility and cultivation deities.

[143] (lat.) Where thou art Gaius, I shall be Gaia – the vow recited by brides.

[144] The hot, sultry days of summer, which were historically the period following the heliacal rising of the star system Sirius, which Greek and Roman astrology connected with heat, drought, sudden thunderstorms, lethargy, fever, mad dogs, and bad luck.

"Send some slaves to bring me lectica," I moaned. "Unless I have a seat, I'll faint."

Longinus holds me by the elbow, and his look got warmer.

"Do not worry; you will have some rest now. I will cancel the feast if you like. You and I, we suffer the same anguish… by the game of fate."

I took him by the hand. The Consul half-smiled sympathetically, and helped me out of the temple.

"O, Drusilla!" I heard a deep female voice in the crowd, which looked smaller now.

I turned around and saw Domitia Lepida – my grandmother's niece, the elder sister Ahenobarbus.

"I congratulate you, dear," she said to me with a half-hug and a restrained smile. "Seventeen is the high time to start a family."

I nodded slightly and replied "Benigne."[145]

"I wish my daughter Messalina found her place by some respectable man." The aunt sighed. "She is thirteen, but she can't stand on talking of the wedding."

I remembered Messalina as a red-haired little thing with bright green eyes and waggish nature. We didn't play together much when we were kids, for Mother didn't like haughty Domitia, but I had always wanted to be friends with this my second cousin. I believed, I was the one to understand her resistance to marriage that day.

"Excuse me, kinswoman, but my bride is not feeling well," Longinus uttered to Domitia. "There won't be any feast. We're going home."

"O, dear child…" Aunt sighed in disappointment. "To a woman, being sickly is a curse. Our kind must be healthy and strong – to give birth and to raise many children."

Her speech was unbearable for Longinus, too.

"Kinswoman, please!" He spoke out, losing his natural equanimity.

Domitia stepped back, with her eyes wide and dubious.

"I would be glad if Messalina visits us one day," I said before she left, and she replied with a reluctant nod.

"Are all of the Antonii so discourteous?" My groom smiled, taking me to the terrace. That question, even more discourteous than its cause, sounded bitterly familiar.

---

[145] (Lat., inf.) Thank you.

"She got it from Octavia," I muttered, unable to walk on my own.

"Oy, Domina!" I saw Susannah running upstairs, willing to help me get to lectica.

"Call me 'Domina' again, and I will slap you in your muzzle!" I said panting, leaning on a pillow. "Climb in, damn you!"

The nursemaid hesitantly glanced at her new "dominus."

"Do what your Lady says!" Ordered Longinus. "She needs to wash her face and drink some water."

Susannah did as he said, and called out to the four muscular carriers to lift up the litter.

"The Consul-Suffect should be sitting next to you, Drusilla." He told me discreetly as we were being carried through the bridge. "He's of poor health, and customs say…"

"Flocci non faccio!"[146] I waved aside. "Longinus is a man, a senator… He will survive."

A sip of icy water and a fan were slowly bringing me to life. My tireless nursemaid cooled me with one hand and massaged my swollen feet with the other.

"Why the hell did the old wolf send us to Antium?" I sighed, wiping the sweat off my forehead. "He knew returning home at noon could kill that bat and me…"

As Susannah nodded, I noticed her lovely heart-shaped face becoming nervous and gloomy.

"Little Owl, they have brought you a letter this morning… from Rome."

"Actaeon?" I got scared, imagining the worst. I knew what a sensitive person could do if he lost his loved one.

"No, no!" The Jewess calmed me down. "He's mourning, but he's not that bad. Lady Antonia is ill."

So, Grandma sent Domitia… She thought her presence could bring me some comfort that day.

Why didn't she tell me? I thought of my aunt. *She just annoyed me with her talk.*

"What is it?" I asked, hoping it was a cold or some other two-day weakness.

---

[146] (lat.) I don't give a damn!

"No one knows," Susannah said sympathetically. "She's losing weight and complaining of abdominal pain. The medication lessens pain, but it returns…"

"Please, gods, let that be anything but poison." I shook my head as if I tried to drive terrifying thoughts away.

"Don't worry." The nursemaid stroked my hand. "Actaeon mentioned that physicians didn't even suspect poisoning."

I sighed with relief. After all, no situation was really hopeless for fearless Antonia.

"There's something else, Little Owl." My freedwoman went on, taking a piece of parchment out of the hem of her dress. "Before we left Capri, Callistus asked me to give you this letter, but not until you return."

I grabbed the tiny scroll impatiently.

"Princess dear," Callistus' handwriting was nearly calligraphic, *"Please don't get angry at that poor thing Susannah for hiding this letter for more than one moon. It's for your safety, I demanded she wait until your wedding day."*

I smiled at my nursemaid, and then glanced at the bulky marriage token on my ring finger.

"For the twenty years I spent with the Romans, I've experienced a nightmare. I would rather not speak of the punishments, tortures and deaths that I witnessed, as well as all the ways I was humiliated to survive. I had no hope in any better change, so I lived from day to day, and prayed I wouldn't join hose miserable things in ergastulum. Fear made me flatter, lie, bewray… I lost my dignity and honor. Even now, I conspired against Caesar for personal gain, as Macro promised that Prince Gaius would free me. I was a bad man, Highness – until you came to remind me I was Hellen. When I faced your courage, justice and compassion, I desired to help others, and to fight the evil like you do. I'm even ready to die for my men, who were chained and weakened by the enemy. I have faith in you, Drusilla, and I believe that your brother will make Rome a better place for all the people, regardless of their status and origin.

Take care, Your Highness.

Your friend and servant,

Callistus.

Post scriptum. It's obvious that your role model is Alexander the Great, and I admire that, but, as for me, a princess shouldn't curse like a centurion, or give the gods names like a drunk popular."

Deeply moved by his words, I read the last sentence aloud.

"He is right." Susannah nodded. "Your idea of equality is good, but, no, vulgarity does not adorn a lady."

"Yeah," I whispered, as I tore the parchment to small pieces, and strewed outside. Then, I moved the motley curtain, and called out to the carriers, already tired of the long walk and the heat.

"Villa Claudiana!"

XXVII

"Thanks be to gods, prikipessa!" Actaeon ran to meet me as I crossed the threshold of my maiden house.

"Thanks be to Longinus for the litter," I answered with irony, as I greeted him with a warm hug. "Now I hate weddings more than Chaerea does."

Actaeon gave me a slight smile. His good-natured face wore traces of the deepest pain, and his face got deadly pale.

"Actaeon," I whispered in astonishment, stroking his bearded cheeks. "Pariemai, filo mu... Metamelei moi."[147]

"Don't blame yourself, Your Highness," he said impassionedly, leading me through the atrium. "Fate is inexorable, and you were so kind and fair to Photice. You freed her, avenged her death, and buried her according to our customs, even risking your own life, like Antigone!"[148]

"Leave the 'Theban Cycle'[149] alone." I waved aside. "Where is my grandma?"

"She is resting now," he said, already in a better mood. "Seems, that Asclepius has brought her back some sleep and appetite. I cook for Domina myself, Your Highness!"

"You know how to cook?" I marveled, imagining him with a kitchen spoon in his hand instead of a stylus.

"My father was a rich man, but a drunkard and a gambler," Actaeon began. "He even got into debt to King Juba, and when it was the time to pay him back, my parent sold me as a boy for everything. Fortunately, Queen Selene, who was Greek herself, had mercy on a poor boy, and sent me to her sister – your grandmother."

"And Photice?" I asked, sorrowed by the story.

---

[147] (Anc.Gr.) Forgive me, my friend. I am sorry.

[148] (myth.) The daughter of the Theban king Oedipus, who buried her brother, in violation of the king's order.

[149] Four lost ancient Greek epic poems that chanted the mythical history of the Beotian city of Thebes.

"She was the cookman's daughter," he explained. "Her father taught me everything, and when she saw me beaten by the other slaves, she wiped my tears and healed my wounds. When I was finally to leave for Rome, Photaki knelt before Selene, begging her to let us go together. Well, the queen agreed…"

"And you got married – out of love," I sighed, looking at the well-known fresco representing Paris and Helena.

"I used to be handsome… twenty years ago," Actaeon recollected, a bit rapturously. "All the chambermaids were mad about me, but I had chosen Photice… Let her rest in Elysium!"

I smiled. The image of an estranged widower failed to suppress the good old Actaeon.

"Well done!" I pushed him gently with my elbow. "If you boast, it's not that bad with you."

Greek smiled like a child caught stealing figs.

"As life goes on, everything changes." Susannah spoke sophisticatedly. "Nothing is really eternal…"

"It depends," I interrupted her when we got to the hostess' chambers. "Go to my maiden room and have some rest."

The nursemaid fell back, and Actaeon knocked on the door.

"Veni!"[150]

Antonia half-lay in her wide bed of wood and ebony, surrounded with soft silk pillows. Her loyal servant Anat stood by the matron, cooling her with a big fan. By the other side of the Egyptian-fashioned bed, there sat the keeper of the chambers Ioh, reading aloud *The Orations of Cato the Elder*.[151] The slave was nervous, as he made mistakes in almost every sentence.

"What a fool!" Grandmother grabbed her forehead.

Ioh, pretty sure the Domina referred to him, began to murmur some excuses about his poor knowledge of Latin.

---

[150] (Lat.) Come in!
[151] The famous Roman senator and writer from the period of the late Republic.

"Not you, fool, but the ugly bumpkin Cato!" she explained ill-temperedly. "He was talking about women like we're beasts who need a chain! It's been two hundred years since he passed on, and those male trollops of the Senate keep on quoting him!"

"I see you're feeling better, Grandma." I smiled. Antonia looked neither pale, nor bony.

"I will outlive Tiberius – that's for sure," she answered, reaching out to me. "Come closer, little flower. I worried to death about you and Caligula."

Anat and Ioh fell back to the servant room, and I took a seat on the edge of the bed.

"When I found out you were to marry that Longinus, I was lost." The Matron spoke with slight head tremor. "One of his ancestors, named Longinus, murdered Old Caesar, and another Longinus was there to justify my father's death. They hate us, and I know you hate your husband, too!"

"Well, Lucius is not that bad," I said, a little bit confused. "He canceled the celebration when he learned I wasn't feeling well."

"The groom went home alone, didn't he?" Actaeon asked curiously.

"Yes, he did, leading the wedding convoy."

"Ha! He had it coming!" Grandma clapped her hands. "I hope you'll spend your prima nocta[152] here as well."

"Or even on the Esquiline." The secretary chuckled, alluding to Chaerea, who lived there.

"Watch your mouth, you Greek," Antonia threatened him with a finger, holding back a laugh. "Looks, like Drusilla cheered you up." She turned to me again. "I don't know what was worse to me the other day – my illness or his sour face!"

"I'm sorry, Domina." The Greek looked down bewildered, and then, glancing at the blue clepsydra, changed the topic. "Otium is here, my Ladies. Would you like to have some dinner?"

"Good idea." Grandma smiled and winked at him. "You better bring us something big, delicious and unhealthy."

---

[152] (Lat.) The wedding night.

"What do you think of a shellfish appetizer, followed by the steak in almond sauce, and some pastries with pepper and honey?" The servant asked without thinking.

"To some good wine." Antonia approved his choice, and slowly gotten out of bed. "I've had enough of witchy soups and stews!"

This tempting offer made my mouth water. Since Photice left us, I could hardly eat. To my surprise, Actaeon turned out to be a better cook than his late wife.

Uncle Claudius joined us for dinner in triclinium.

"Why are you not resting, M-m-mother?" he asked, looking at his merry mother, dressed in a new blue gown.

"I'll rest in Hades." The old woman waved aside. "If there is one."

"When are you going to remarry, uncle?" I jokingly sent him the question he hated the most.

"I hope, n-n-never," he said, frowning. "It's hard to please me."

"I doubt your opinion matters." I sighed. "I didn't choose to marry that old tortoise – Cassius Longinus!"

Claudius replied with an apathetic look, and plunged into his plate.

"Don't worry, little flower." Grandma patted me on my shoulder. "You will get divorced as soon as the Old Wolf goes west. And even now, you are a princess. Who can stop you from going wherever you want, even to the Esquiline?"

Actaeon and Susannah, who, much to my uncle's displeasure, shared table with us, burst into an unlabored laugh, infecting me as well.

"Oh, mother dear!" Claudius grabbed his head as if embarrassed.

"Did I say something wrong?" Grandmother wondered. "We Antonii do not believe in loveless marriages."

"That's right! Opa!" Actaeon exclaimed, smashing his glass on the floor. His Domina and I enjoyed this custom, which spiced up all the Greek feasts.

"You need a barber, Actaeon," Grandmother said mirthfully. "You cannot join a respectable familia looking like a homeless man!"

The Greek goggled at her, trying to guess what she meant.

"I give you to Drusilla," Matrona explained. "I don't need a secretary anymore."

"And your d-d-duty to Caesar?" Uncle got worried. "Doesn't he need an a-a-a-advisor?"

"The emperor has already a new advisor, fili mi."[153] He smiles mysteriously. "A younger, smarter and more beautiful one."

As I got lost among my thoughts, the Jewess, sensing who the girl was, gave me a stunned look.

"Long live Julia Drusilla – the second woman in history, named an imperial advisor!" Grandma got up and toasted. "I don't know, Drusilla, what you did on Capri, but Tiberius is satisfied."

"I certainly did not bring shame on you, or the Antonii," I said in wonder of the breaking news. "I thought he hated me, and the old astrologer incited him against me –"

"Thrasyllus has committed suicide," Actaeon interrupted me. "And Nerva, too – on the same day. Something is going on there, Domina."

I bottomed up my glass. To me, that all sounded unbelievable and doubtful. I suddenly thought of Caligula and wondered how he was and what was he doing.

"What about Gaius?" I looked at Antonia. "Did Caesar mention him in a letter?"

"He found him a betrothed," she replied. "Senator Silan's daughter, Junia Claudilla. They two will wed in three years – when she is mature enough for marriage."

I was ready to hear it, but the news hurt anyway. The thought of my loved brother and some sniveler together, in a *real*, consumed marriage – made me sick.

It doesn't matter, I said to myself, trying to find some solace in this lie. *Caligula loves nobody but me.*

Memories took me back to the magical moment of our first kiss. I could almost feel my brother's gentle gaze, the touch of his warm lips, and the rapid pounding of his heart... even the sunset of the scarlet sun above the Palatine.

"Don't forget, it is a huge responsibility." Actaeon woke me up from the daydreaming. "You will be dealing with both – the Senate and the Army, which are Roman Scylla and Charybdis."

---

[153] (Lat.) My son.

"Tomorrow is the Sitting of the Senate," Grandmother recalled. "Claudius will take you there."

My uncle looked at her, a bit confused, and turned to me.

"If you need my a-a-advice, I'll help you, niece. After all, I'm an aedilis c-c-curulis."[154]

"Now, it's time to sleep," Matrona said, and left her sofa. "We've had a busy day today."

I thanked Claudius for his goodwill, kissed Antonia goodnight, and headed to my cubicle. Finally, after those terrible nights on the island, I was longing for some sleep. Susannah took me by the hand, and Actaeon followed us there.

"Go, get some rest." I stopped him. "The adventures that are waiting for us now are much more dangerous than in your legends."

"You mean, in *our* legends, Domina?" My secretary lit a lamp of painted terracotta. "Aren't you, too, a Greek now?"

"First, I am not your *Domina*," I answered, patting him on the broad back. "From this day on, you are a free man."

---

[154] The magistrates (high civil-servants), responsible for maintenance of public buildings and regulation of public festivals. They also had powers to enforce public order.

XXVIII

"Hu-hurry up, or I'll be late for s-s-sitting!" Claudius got nervous, waiting for me in the vestibule. Narcissus, his constant companion, stood by my uncle, adjusting his praetexta[155].

"It couldn't be faster," I responded wittily, as I entered the atrium. "I am a woman, after all."

"He's coming, too?" The aedilis curulis nodded towards Actaeon, neatly shaved and barbered, carrying my codex.[156]

"Of course," I answered sharply. I trust him more than I trust you."

Claudius sighed desperately, and limped outside, where eight slaves and two litters were waiting for us.

"Do not forget, no one should see you, Princess," dark-skinned Narcissus reminded me. "No woman should exceed the threshold of Curia Hostilia."[157]

"I know." I smiled. "I'll try my hardest not to swear."

The Parthian man laughed in a high voice and opened the door for me.

The famous building, erected many centuries ago by King Tullus Hostilius, looked small and untidy in comparison to the tall and quaint Temple of Vesta, rising high by the gates of the Forum.

"There's a back entrance on the other side," Claudius whispered anxiously, when we stepped down from the litters – in the middle of the square, beneath the statue of Augustus.

"You will c-c-come in, when Narcissus gives you a sign," my uncle continued. "I will do my best to t-t-turn their attention at c-c-comitium."[158]

---

[155] A toga with a broad purple border worn by certain magistrates.
[156] Essentially an ancient notebook, consisting of one or more quires of sheets of papyrus or parchment folded together to form a group of leaves, or pages.
[157] A building that served as the meeting-house of the senate of Rome
[158] A space for political decision-making and a speaker's platform.

"Don't worry, uncle, I'm not as clumsy as my sisters think," I whispered back staidly.

The senators were gathering near the rostrum.[159]

"These – are mostly Optimates," Actaeon informed me. "Unlike the Populares, they just talk, and never act."

"Unfortunately, they are all the same," Narcissus interjected. "The end of the sitting is the same for every one of them."

These words made me feel chill in my body.

"What do you mean?" I asked worriedly. "My father was a Popularis, and…"

"O Narcissus!" Claudius called his slave, pointing towards the city hall.

The Parthian nodded, and followed his master.

"Too arrogant for his status," the Greek murmured as he covered me with my peplum, carefully adjusting the hood. "Let's go down through the basilica as if we went to the market."

I took his hand, and headed down the Via Sacra,[160] watching the senators climbing up the stairway of Curia Hostilia. In the first place, I recognized my husband, Cassius Longinus, who was explaining something to Vitellius, the legate of Syria.

Fortunately, he's nearsighted, so I won't be recognized, I thought, accelerating my steps.

"See that guttler over there?" The secretary showed me the stout senator, yawning by the entrance of the hall. "This is Silanus – Junia Claudilla's father. He prattles around about how he wants to feed all the poor of the city, but in fact, he only thinks about his stomach…"

"And Claudilla?" I asked, trying to hide my jealousy. "Is she a daddy's girl?"

"No way," Actaeon chuckled. "She's scrawny and freckled like a hyena. And, despite her tender age, she's known for doing all the household chores herself – to please her future husband."

"I'm already sick." I looked away toward the Arch of Augustus. "You'd better follow what is going on at the back door."

---

[159] (Lat.) A raised platform on which a person stands to make a public speech.

[160] The Main street of ancient Rome.

"Excuse me, Princess," he said openheartedly. "I never meant to upset you… I thought you wanted to know, but if you ask me…" He held his breath and went on in a whisper. "You are the most beautiful noblewoman in this city."

"You, Greeks, know how to flatter." I sighed, realizing that my secret was revealed.

"We, Greeks, know what true beauty is," Actaeon said earnestly. "And what true love is."

"Now that you know it all, please keep it," I said gently, in a friendly way. "I am afraid to lose him, or to disappoint him even more."

The Greek fell silent, and then looked at me with his dark, piercingly lucid eyed.

"We have a saying – to love is nothing, to be loved is something, and to love and to be loved in return is everything." He spoke.

"What do you mean?" I was confused, but didn't get the answer.

"Here comes the Parthian," Actaeon nodded toward the back entrance of the building.

Narcissus stood by the small door, which was extremely low, and looked sealed or even walled. He was gesturing us to come in, and make no sound.

"It's quiet now." He whispered, as he took a look around. "The sitting has begun."

What I saw inside looked like a blind corridor, half-littered with sand and rubble.

"It's a little narrow and dirty, but safe enough," the Greek assured me, lighting the lamp. "Lady Antonia was always joking that Tiberius wanted to save money, even while making that passage."

I smiled to myself, imagining my chubby grandmother making her way through that mouse hole, cursing all the known gods.

"Watch the stairs." Narcissus took me by the hand, and led into a strange semicircular chamber, similar to the enclosed apse of the temple, with a small opening in the wall.

"Can you hear anything, Your Highness?" The secretary asked me hardly audible.

Shaking the dust off the peplum, I came on my toes up to a semicircular wall and pressed my ear against the opening in the stone slab.

"Rebellion broke out in the eastern provinces… The Dacians refuse to surrender … In the north, the Germans crossed the Rhine again." The harsh voices were heard from the other side. "Financial crisis in the city… Money disappears."

"Now, look through the opening," Narcissus said.

A small void of the size of the human eye opened the scene for me. I watched from above hundreds of men in white togas with purple borders, listening diligently to the speech of the presiding magistrate. The magistrate, a balding middle-aged man with short neck and legs, was sitting on the podium, flanked on both sides by a row of marble benches for the other members of the Senate.

"Who is this?" I asked Actaeon, referring to the speaker in the center of the hall. "He is disgusting."

The Greek peered through the opening, first with one eye, then with the other, and looked at the Parthian bewildered.

"Tribune Vespasian of the Flavii." Narcissus sighed, as if he heard the speech below.

"How is it possible, for a tribunus militum to sermon about the state of the treasury or foreign policy?" I asked him, startled. "Aren't the Quaestor and the Praetor really responsible for that?"

"They basically are." The secretary nodded, obviously muddled like me. "But it seems like something's changed."

"And Flavii, aren't they really Plebeians and descendants of the eastern newcomers?" I suddenly remembered the notes of my grandma's archive.

"Don't forget why you are here, my Princess." Narcissus nodded towards the wall. "You will find out more if you look and listen by yourself."

Tiberius… I thought with irony, putting my cheek against the cold slab. *At first, he underestimated me, and now he overestimates me.*

Vespasian was talking about commonalties like they were the livestock, and he had the rights to control their living conditions and issue. He was supported by a tall and lanky man with an aquiline nose, who added that the populace of Rome needs soldiers and manpower.

The other senators stayed mostly silent, occasionally speaking when asked by Vespasian or the other arrogant man.

"Titus Sabinus, his brother and, too, Tribune," Actaeon said, still in a state of shock. "They both once served in Syria at the Parthian border."

Among the others, I noticed Claudius's friends – Valerius Asiaticus and Publius Regulus, who often came to the Palatine hoping that friendship with the Caesar's nephew would help them advance their political careers.

"Tiberius has chosen a successor." Asiaticus spoke disappointedly. "The son of Germanicus."

"Since this familia gained little power, they've always done everything wrong," Vespasian replied irritably. "They swear to serve our brotherhood until they die, enjoy the goods that only our chosen order can provide, but, suddenly, they fall in love, get struck by conscience, or just overcome by senile cowardice, and then betray us overnight."

"I heard Prince Gaius is naive and immature," Regulus said intently, leafing through some scripture. "We can influence him."

"If our Pater Artabanus[161] wanted a fool on the Roman throne, I would rather recommend him Claudius!" Vespasian roared, tossing the end of his pallium over his shoulder. "Shall we let a fucking sniveler ruin the empire, built for centuries?"

The semi-amphitheater was vibrating with the noise the statesmen raised. The magniloquent Optimates were talking about the necessity of the experience of war and politics, while enthusiastic Populares were sure that the son of Germanicus would help them gain the favor of the populace.

"With the help of little Gaius, we will easily control the commonalty as well as the whole Army." I could hear the younger senator, Aemilius Lepidus, speaking.

Vespasian gave him a skeptical look, but suddenly his brother Sabin raised his hand to silence other legislators.

"I agree!"

Junius Silanus plucked up courage to remind everyone in attendance that his daughter was engaged to Gaius. One by one, Vitellius, Regulus, even Asiaticus supported him. After thinking for a while, the self-proclaimed high magistrate stood up and turned to Claudius, as always frightened in advance.

---

[161] Artabanus II incorrectly known in older scholarship as Artabanus III, was the King of Kings of the Arsacid Empire.

"Get up, Aedile and listen to me carefully. Your task is difficult, responsible and, if the Lord wills so, ungrateful, too. Tiberius has made a big mistake, and you are chosen to amend it – even if it takes your poor life."

My terrified uncle stood up and, with his knees trembling, bowed to Vespasian and whispered something indistinct. I heard a muffled laugh in the hall, which was immediately silenced as the magistrate raised his right hand.

"When your brother's son becomes the ruler of the empire, you must be close to him, follow him, and gain his trust – at all costs."

Claudius nodded, muttering something that resembled some ancient pathetic oath, and the magistrate replied with a satisfied grin.

"If you succeed, you'll become one of us," Tribune Sabin added mysteriously, followed by the mockery from the first rows.

"There are four years for you, Aedile. Four years will have your nephew – to grow up into a man of Lord or to get dead. If you dare to disappoint me, you will share his fate."

At that moment, I felt Narcissus pulling me by the arm. "It's getting dangerous here, Princess, we should go back now," he whispered anxiously.

"Wait!" I rubbed my eyes, tearful from squinting. "They are talking of my brother!"

"I know," the Parthian shook his head, "that's why we have to leave."

I looked bewildered – first at my Greek secretary, then at Narcissus. Actaeon nodded and reached out to hold my hand. The room was getting cramped and fuggy, so I hurried to get out.

"Don't worry; I'll explain it to you later on," the young man said, as he closed the door with some deft movements, so it looked like barred over again.

I lifted up my hood. After the dark, barely visible room, the rays of midday sun stung my wet eyes. Without a word, we quickly went out onto the always crowded Via Nova walkway.

"Good." My uncle's slave smiled with relief. "No one is chasing us. Now you can ask me anything, Your Highness, but do not forget that dominus will need me soon."

I looked around. None of the passersby, dressed in colorful robes, really paid attention to the girl in a closed dress alongside two foreigners, who led her by the hands.

"First, *you* tell me," I said, frowning at Actaeon, "how come you knew nothing about this vulgarian?"

"Vespasian came out of the shadows after Lady Julia Antonia has fallen ill," Narcissus spoke, as the Greek shrugged his shoulders sadly. "After they have returned from the East, Vespasian and his brother became very influential in the Senate, letting no one get in their way."

"What secret society was this man talking about?" I asked him in the ear, tapping myself nervously above the chest. "Why does he call our enemy – the King of Parthia – the father? Is it all about Mithraism?"

Narcissus suddenly turns pale and looked at me scared.

"You better tell her." Actaeon pushed him slightly with his elbow. "She knows much more than her grandmother."

"I… I have to go," the Parthian muttered. "I guess the sitting is now over. Dominus is waiting for me, Princess."

Therefore, he knew, and he could tell us … But he was afraid.

"You promised me." I tried to keep calm, not to discourage him. "I ask you not because Tiberius ordered me to; I'm worrying about my brother!"

"Forgive me, Princess – I cannot." He shook his head. "And you yourself should stay away from the abyss, Your Highness."

"I'll do what *I* want to do," I answered earnestly. "For now, I can persuade my uncle to free you… if you help me in return."

"Quicquid erit fuerit."[162] Narcissus sighed deeply. "If you so desire, you'll find out by yourself."

Before I argued, Narcissus had disappeared into the multicolored crowd. I closed my eyes and pressed the palms of my hands to the eyelids, as I felt fever closing around me.

"Take me home, filo mu." I leaned against Actaeon's shoulder. "It's even worse than I thought. I don't know whether I must talk to Grandma first or… write to Caesar."

---

[162] (Lat.) What will be, will be.

The secretary, holding me the way an adult helps his baby walk, turned towards the big altana, where the carriers were resting.

"Gods forbid you tell the emperor!" he whispered worriedly. "He is not a friend. There may be greater enemies than he, but he will never be your friend."

Struggling with vertigo, I barely made my way to the altana, and took my sit on a litter. The Greek wetted his hand with fountain water and put it on my forehead.

"You will be fine, Your Highness. You've already made it through 'the Iliad.'"

"I have." I smiled bitterly, slowly coming to myself. "Now it's time to face 'the Odyssey.' When I get home, I swear, I'll make that Claudius puppy speak."

The problem was that 'home' for me no longer meant my maiden house, but the Bat's cave.

"To the Carinae!" I exclaimed, and then, as I looked once again at the Curia, I added ironically. "To my dearly beloved husband."

XXIX

My new house greeted me with surprises. Lucius Longinus was already at home, and looking moody.

"Quid agis, Helen?"[163] He asked with an indolent grin, and handed a scroll with his sitting notes to a slave.

"Valeo,"[164] I replied, taking off the peplum. "I was at my grandma's."

"I know." He nodded. "I heard Antonia is already recovering."

"I'm sorry, Lucius. It's turned out that way," I told him almost honestly. "I learned she was ill by the moment we left Antium."

"Don't worry, Drusilla," he went on more earnestly. "I've just returned from Curia Hostilia, and I'm going to take a bath. It would be proper if you welcome our guest – he's waiting in your chambers."

"In my chambers?" I repeated in astonishment.

"Your brother is here," Longinus explained, heading for the tepidarium.

I looked at Actaeon, as if he had the answers to all the questions in this world. The Greek smiled discreetly, and offhandedly adjusted my hairdo.

"Susannah!" I called out of habit, before I recalled I had left her in Villa Claudiana.

"I don't think your funny Jewish maid has arrived yet," Longinus responded from the corridor. "Orla will show you your chambers."

A slim and petite Gaul emerged from the portico and greeted me with a kindly smile and a slight bow.

Another barbarian, I thought, remembering Armida.

The slave girl looked fragile and sweet. She looked nervous, but her Latin was clear and rich and her dexterity could surpass even Anat's.

---

[163] (Lat.) "How are you, Helen?" Here, Longinus jokingly compares Drusilla to Helen of Troy, who, according to the Greek myth, escaped from her husband, King Menelaus, shortly after their wedding.

[164] (Lat.) I'm fine.

"Would you like to change your clothes first, Domina?" The Gaul asked me in a ringing voice, leading me to the peristyle. "The other day, pronuba[165] brought your dresses."

Although after a hard morning I rather needed a clean and fresh tunica, I replied "not now", and hurried to see my brother.

"Where is *my* chamber, Orla?" Actaeon asked with a seductive smile, which confused the young Gaul even more than getting a new Domina.

"At the end of the corridor…" She replied, looking down shyly. "Next to the guest room."

"What do you think you're doing?" I wondered, watching this fresh widower trying to attract a beauty, much younger than him.

Actaeon looked at me with a bewildered, muffled laugh.

"Men, you are all the same." I sighed, exasperated.

"You are mostly right." The secretary nodded. "But every rule has an exception."

Suddenly, in my mind, occurred a picture of an April-sky-grey eyes, reflecting understanding and devotion.

"This is your room, Your Highness." Orla's childish voice made my pure vision fade. "I'll be there when you call me."

Affected by my 'thank you,' the Gaul left with a joyful smile. Actaeon followed her, and I, still in a blissful disbelief, entered the chamber on my toes.

Gaius was there. He was lying on my bed, lit by the afternoon sun, having a nap.

He changed… I thought, watching him breathlessly. He was still sleeping like a baby – on the side with his legs curled, but his body looked well-built, and his face had become manly. His tender black curls, which I loved to stroke, were cut to make a formal short hairdo, as the violet boyish robe was now replaced by a lavish attire with a wide golden hem. *The future Emperor…* I said to myself. *Most handsome the world has ever seen.*

At that moment, Caligula opened his eyes.

---

[165] (Lat.) A bride's matron of honor.

"You're here, little sister," he murmured, waking up and stretching. "I felt like someone was watching me."

Out of happiness, I forgot where I had been and what I'd heard in the Senate, even our bitter farewell on the Capri. Hardly controlling my emotions and raw senses, I embraced my sleepy brother, and began to kiss him – on the face, neck and shoulders.

Gaius rubbed his eyes in wonder and smiled contentedly.

"What did you do with my sister?"

I didn't even know what had been happening to me. I felt an unfamiliar fire, wild and strong, created to crush everything in its way. It was not a young girl's longing for the offspring, nor the recklessness the mature women used for their vain and dirty goals. All I wanted now was Gaius – and the fire, which was burning in his eyes as well. Fire with fire – that is how Ovid described true love in his forbidden works.

"Is it possible that you read my mind?" he asked, taking me into his arms.

"For us… everything is possible," I whispered, giving in to his gentle touches, freer and freer. There was no fear, no pain. This wonderful burning slowly gave way to the feeling of lightness and verve, finally drowning in a sweet fatigue. "I love you." I leaned my head against his chest. Squinting with pleasure, I heard my lover telling me the same.

"It was so magical," he said, caressing my neck. "You surprised me."

"How?" I sat down in the bed, wrapping myself in a blanket.

"I can't explain it," Gaius replied thoughtfully. "They say, in the cubiculum a woman should be Terra, goddess of the Earth, while a man is Caelus, father of the Sky. A man is born to be like heaven – strong and agile, and a woman is created to be grateful and submissive. But you are… completely different, as if you don't belong to our world."

"So, I am different from Armida?" I chuckled. "As far as I'm concerned, there are no women in the Villa Jovis."

"Actually, there is one," Gaius smiled in an embarrassed manner. "Caesar allowed Macro to bring Ennia."

This news was like a jug of icy water spilled right on my head. I knew enough about Macro's wife to hate her even more than the arrogant German. "That woman laughed at our mother when guardsmen took her to jail," I exclaimed in disgust as I got out of bed. "She made jokes about our family!"

"How do you know?" My brother frowned. "You've never met her."

"Luckily to Ennia." I turned towards the mirror. "But I heard this from the man I absolutely trust."

"Cassius Chaerea?" He squinted with one eye – just like Tiberius.

"Yes."

Gaius burst out laughing. He was always ready to make jokes about Cassius, but suddenly he changed his mind, as he remembered that our friend would never lie to me.

"That Greek, he warned me too," Caligula said thoughtfully, putting his wrinkled dress on. "He thinks I should beware of them both – Macro and Ennia."

"But she seduced you anyway," I sighed.

"Oh sister, if you went through all these things I had lived through – for just a month, you wouldn't fault me," he said bitterly.

In fact, Gaius was right. Since his first day on the island, Tiberius had tried his hardest to pervert his young great-nephew and to drive him mad, in order to raise 'a serpent for Rome, and a Phaethon[166] to burn the rest of the world.'

By day, Caesar took my brother to the ergastulum, where his slaves were mercilessly tortured and killed. By night, Caligula was forced to watch his ruler's orgies with the boys in the baths. When the young prince was sick with anguish, Tiberius treated him to more wine, and ordered to dance before him and his favorites, dressed as a harlot.

"When a delirious feast was over, I couldn't wait to get myself into cubiculum to fall into a salvage dream," Caligula went on with a sad smile. "Fortunately, there were days when the Old Wolf just wanted to rest, so he let me read or take a ride. He even gave me a horse – a white mount with wild, but handsome eyes. I named it Incitatus."

No heart could blame him even for the number of Ennias and Armidas, especially a loving heart.

"How did he let you come to Rome?" I asked, hugging him from the back.

---

[166] A son of the Greek Sun-god Helios who borrowed the chariot of the sun and drove it so close to earth that Zeus struck him down to save the world.

"I convinced him that he had achieved his goal," he answered, as his timid smile changed to a well-rehearsed grin of an artist. "Well, he didn't send me to see you, but to have fun."

"And did you follow his advice?" I asked ironically, resting my head on his shoulder.

"You must obey the emperor," he whispered, as he turned to kiss me. I felt the fire between us ready to consume our bodies once again, but the picture of the Roman Senate in my head let it die down.

"Wait, no!" I moved aside. "I can't."

Caligula looked at the water clock.

"Looks like we've lost ourselves... Don't worry; the Bat is harmless to you."

"Of course, he is," I replied confidently. "I'm a princess and the only woman in our family, married sine manu."[167]

"Not because of that." His smile turned sly. "A crown prince actually whispered something in his ear."

I held my breath, a little shocked. "What did you tell him?"

"Keep your hands off my woman. That's what I told him." There was a sound of satisfaction in his voice.

"Are you insane?" I exclaimed. "Longinus is an Imperial jurist!"

"I know who the Bat is," the prince waved aside. "He knows who I am... and, as far as I'm concerned, he won't be grieving, so don't worry."

"Factum est quod factum est."[168] I shrugged my shoulders. "I guess it's time to have some dinner."

"It's a good idea." Gaius smiled, putting his sandals on. "Call that new maid of yours."

"Don't even think of that!" I threatened him with my index finger. "Orla is a child."

---

[167] In a *cum manu* Roman marriage, the wife was placed under the legal control of the husband. In a *sine manu* marriage, the wife remained under the legal control of her father.
[168] (Lat.) What's done is done.

Caligula giggled merrily. I quickly put my hair in a ponytail and opened the door to call Actaeon.

"By the way, where were the two of you this morning?" Gaius winked, as he saw my freedman coming.

"In Curia Hostilia," I answered honestly.

"Where?!" He was stunned. "Longinus told me you were at our grandma's."

"I was there yesterday – right after confarreation."[169]

Actaeon looked with curiosity at our rumpled clothes and bed, and silently began with preparations. While he was busy with the plates and cutlery, I recollected everything that had been lately happening to me – the wedding planning at the old Imperial summer mansion, that awful wedding itself, the news of Grandma's illness, the incomprehensible Tiberius' decision, and, of course, my first task at the Hostilia. Caligula was listening attentively, stunned by my story even more that with his own experience on the Capri.

"So, all we were taught was a lie?" he whispered dejectedly. "Roman Empire is ruled by Parthia, with a little help of a couple of plebeians?"

"Exactly." I sighed and put my hands under my chin.

"Drusilla." Gaius hugged me tight. "How could Tiberius get you involved in all that?"

"He took me aback too," I replied. "Still, isn't it better to *know*? Imagine, what it would be like if we stayed blind?"

Caligula shrugged thoughtfully. "However, this duty is not for a girl. How can I go back to the island, knowing you are constantly in danger?"

"Excuse me, Prince, for interfering," Actaeon spoke, serving the table. "Her Highness is right. No matter how mad it may sound, you are going to be safer with Tiberius than here in Rome."

"So, that dog Claudius is one of them now, isn't he?" Caligula became furious, ignoring the Greek's words.

---

[169] A traditional patrician marriage ceremony.

"Fortunately, he is still more afraid of his mother than of Vespasian." Actaeon smiled. "Lady Antonia is the real Amazon! Let the gods grant her hundred years of living!"

"Nobody lives that long," my brother muttered, and continued earnestly, "We need to gain stronger allies. There on the island we have Macro, Callistus and guardsmen."

"Don't forget about Ennia," my jealousy joked through me.

"This couple is not quite... reliable," the freedman said. "Rumor has it, Macro is prostituting his wife to the men of power in order to keep his influence."

"Shut up." The prince frowned. "You better pour us wine if you are playing a cook now."

"Here you are, Your Highness." The Greek moved a small prandium table toward us. "Will you be so kind as to wash your hands?"

"You are annoying." Gaius rolled his eyes. "Hand me a bowl."

The hot pie and juicy chicken with black plums and pomegranate arils were enough to cheer us up for quite a while. Caligula enjoyed drinking Falerno wine, so he had two full glasses.

"Now it's time to have some fun." He winked at Actaeon. "Tell me, Ganymede,[170] where is the nearest brothel?"

The freedman looked at me, confused.

"You're right, my sister wouldn't let me." Gaius waved aside.

"Don't worry; soon you'll turn to Ennia," I said ironically.

"Without her, I could go twisted like Tiberius," he answered in the same tone.

In the midst of our merry conversation, Orla slightly knocked. "Domina," she said shyly, "Dominus Lucius invites you and the prince to join him at the dinner."

"We are honored." Gaius gave the young Gaul an assessing glance. "But Actaeon has already fed me to death."

The secretary giggled, with his eyes, too, wandering around my bashful maid.

---

[170] A divine cup-bearer in Olympus.

"I'll join the Ba… I mean, beloved husband," I said quietly, bored with their silly mating games.

"Yes, it would be appropriate." My brother nodded.

"Please, comb my hair and bring me a fresh dress," I asked the girl, then referred to Actaeon.

"I want you to accompany Prince Gaius to Antonia's."

Actaeon nodded readily, and hurried to clean the room after the dinner.

"Why?" Caligula protested. "Grandma is already well…"

"It's for your safety, Prince," I said with a sardonic grin.

"So, I'll be spending time with an old woman, Claudius the Idiot, and a bunch of Egyptian slaves – for ten more days?" he exclaimed disappointedly. "Deodamnatus!"[171]

I shrugged and turned my head to the toilet table, already sunk in thought. There were some words I had heard lately repeating in my mind, over and over. I knew I had to act, to find an answer, a solution, but the danger was too big to deal with it alone. I needed help…

There's only one thing stronger than the evil, and the power – wisdom, I spoke in my mind, and grabbed a sheet of parchment, quill and ink from the bookshelf. Then, I quietly leaned my elbows on the desk, and wrote: *Find Rachel, and bring her to me.*

"Actaeon," I called the secretary and handed him the rolled-up letter. "Give it to Susannah. I need her here tomorrow morning."

"Will you visit me at Grandma's?" Gaius asked, leaving the room.

"Well, it depends on your behavior, Prince," I smiled.

"And, little sister…" He turned for a moment. "Sorry about the things I told you on the Capri. I didn't mean it."

"Doesn't matter," I said, lying to us both. "Take care!"

The Greek, a little clumsy with wine, followed Gaius, and Orla approached me with a comb and a golden hairnet.

"You don't have to make me a goddess," I told her as I sat in front of the mirror. "It will be enough not to scare Longinus off."

---

[171] (Lat.) Damn it!

"Domina, you are beautiful," the Gaul replied softly but earnestly. "You are kind and wise as well, but not self-confident."

"You are right, girl." I sighed deeply and straightened my back. "And where do I find a cure for self-confidence?"

"There's only one," she smiled. "One day, he'll find you."

XXX

The mysterious Jewess was an early bird. I'd barely managed to put my house dress on after a bath when Orla told me I had a visitor.

"Pax tecum,[172] Princess." A plump, black-eyed woman in a motley dress saluted me. "I'm Rachel bat Benjamin."[173]

"Suave te cognoscere est,"[174] I replied kindly. "Susannah told me about you, and I'm impressed with what I've heard."

"O please, Your Highness, I am an ordinary shopkeeper." Rachel smiled. "I had a little luck in my life, and I used it well. It's you who can make an impression, *infantula*."

She called me the way only Cassius did.

"Let's all go to the tablinum." I took both – the guest and Susannah – by the hand. "Longinus allows me to read there when he's out."

"Do you want me to serve breakfast now?" asked tiny Orla, opening the door to the jurist's office.

"That would be great," I said. "Bring something light, with no meat. First, tell Actaeon to join us, and then make sure that no one can bother us."

"Do you want *me* to keep a watch?" the Gaul wondered with her eyes plate-wide. "Dominus Lucius always called Falcon or someone stronger…"

"I don't trust that Falcon, nor do I have time to meet," I interrupted her. "When you see someone wandering around, just come in and let me know."

"Yes, Domina." She fell back.

The Bat's tablinum was larger and brighter than my grandma's. I took a seat at the wide, pedantically set desk, and offered my interlocutors the guest chairs.

---

[172] (Lat.) Peace be with you!
[173] (Hebr.) Benjamin's daughter (patronymic for women).
[174] (Lat.) Nice to meet you.

"Rachel," I began calmly, "I am aware that what I ask of you is risky and almost impossible. I keep in mind that maybe you will decline my plea, for I'm a heathen, and you have that right. And yet, by the irony fate, you are the only person who can help me."

"Vey, Princess, why so gloomy?" the woman asked me with a knowing smile and went on whispering. "Aunt Rachel has something to tell you – the whole legion wouldn't have brought me here unless I wanted to help."

I sighed with relief and leaned against the back of the chair.

"I told her everything, Little Owl, about the books we read, about your courage on the Capri, and that duty that the emperor has assigned you," Susannah explained.

"Not all the women are made to be mothers, whores or maids." Rachel spoke enthusiastically, pointing her painted fingernail at me. "You, Highness, you can help all those who were born different, break those male rules and be free."

"That's my goal too," I replied. "But our enemy is strong and numerous. The priority is saving the lives of the innocent – women, men, children… With your knowledge and my influence, we can do something for those people, chased by the same enemy – Mithras."

The shopkeeper nodded and took a thin scroll out of soft leather bag.

"That's all I could find, Princess. Please, make sure no one finds it, or we're done," she said earnestly, handing me a roll of parchment.

"Her former neighbor, David, is a merchant from Judea," Susannah added cautiously. "For this thing, he gave a lot of money and risked his life to take it to Italy."

"Unfortunately, he's too young and decent." My guest sighed. "David is the only man I call – worthwhile."

"I'll give you two pouches of gold," I said thankfully. "One for yourself and the other – for David."

Rachel burst out laughing, and said softly, "Not all the Jews are greedy, birdie. I have enough resources to become a Roman citizen, and David owns four houses and a hundred heads of cattle. I am not here for your money. I believe in you."

Her words got me moved almost to tears.

"Do you really believe I can… change anything?" I asked.

"You even made that hoyden think like us." The merchant nodded towards Susannah. "So you're omnipotent."

Callistus wrote me he believed in me as well… so told me my grandmother. But, before that all, I recollected Cassius encouraging me in Antioch.

Maybe, for my mother, Livia, and Armida, I was so unfit and naughty, but still, I was worthy for those whose opinion was valuable to me.

"I'd better die than let you down," I said to both women, and unrolled the scroll.

The author of the scripture, using Vulgar Latin, wished to warn the people of the Roman provinces of the quickly spreading cult of Mithras, and its aims and means.

"I could guarantee this book's veracity." Said Rachel, putting her hand on her chest. "For it was written by a man who was with them; who saw and heard it all."

She was still talking, when Actaeon and Orla came along.

"Where have you been?" I asked the secretary. "You've missed everything."

"I've been preparing this delightful breakfast." The Greek smiled confusedly, and placed a wide silver tray on the desk. "Eggs stuffed with cheese, olives, and mushrooms, and fish baked in wine… "

"Great." I smiled back, and referred to them all. "Help yourself, friends."

"Domina," Orla spoke in a thin voice. "Dominus Lucius is home."

"Let's go to my room then." I shrugged.

"Sorry, my dear, but I have to go now." Rachel rose from her chair. "There's a lot of work at the market still waiting for me."

"I understand, your religion does not allow you to share your meals with foreigners," I said.

"Since Jerusalem fell under the influence of liars, our religion hasn't allowed us to think by ourselves." The Jewess shook her head. "But, you know, next time I wouldn't miss a rabbit or pork from your table, Sophia."

The sound of this name made me feel sudden cold and then unbearable heat inside my heart. I looked at Rachel, then at Susannah.

"Bonam fortunam,[175] Highness." The shopkeeper came up to me and went to my ear. "Fatum tuum te vocat."[176]

---

[175] (lat.) Good luck.
[176] (lat.) Your fate is calling you.

Bewildered with her words and the mysterious feeling, I'd been silent for a while. Orla went out to see the guest off, and Actaeon headed to my room with a full tray.

"Shall we?" The nursemaid took me by the elbow. "You must be hungry, Little Owl. You look so pale."

I grabbed the precious scroll; I clumsily left the tablinum. The last thing I was thinking of was food.

"Actaeon!" I shouted through the hallway, ignoring the servants and guards who were passing us by.

The secretary didn't hear me. Carefully, with Hellenic elegance, he was setting the small table, crooning some bucolic song.

"When we're done, we'll write a letter," I referred to him, closing the door.

"I hope it's not for Caesar," Finally he turned around. "Lady Antonia, too, thinks you shouldn't tell him everything you know."

"Who mentioned Caesar?" I waved aside. "I want to write to Callistus."

Actaeon looked at me suspiciously, squinting one eye.

"He is the first to reading all Caesar's letters, and he has access to every single room in Villa Jovis. You should be aware; he is my fellow countryman, but also a thief and a liar."

"Whatever he *was*, he helped me revenge Photice," I said earnestly, as I took my place by the table.

The Greek sighed, and began eating, followed by my nursemaid.

"If he reads the letters of his dominus, does then Tiberius read his?" I murmured with my mouth full.

Actaeon turned to me and whispered, "For that possibility, your grandmother used a secret language. She wrote about the weather, about flowering and harvesting of fruits in the gardens of Augustus, about the flight of birds over the Palatine... So innocent, but wise - no one but Callistus and me could figure out what it was about."

"Great." I smiled. "One problem less. And now, to make it more exciting, Susannah will read to us."

XXXI

The Jewess reluctantly reached out for the scroll.

"A thousand years ago," she began half-loudly, keeping the door in sight. "In the lands of Babylonia, where is the Kingdom of Parthia now situated, there were seven wise-men, called 'the Kings.' Once, they foretold their people the new god coming – young and splendid like the rising Sun; the one to mediate between the God-Creator and the mankind."

"Sounds like a fairy tale," the Greek remarked with irony. "Especially the wise-men called 'the Kings.'"

"Be quiet." I frowned. "For now this is the only explanation we possess."

Actaeon nodded, still in disbelief, and Susannah continued reading.

"The Sumerian name of that deity was Shamash – 'the all-seeing.' Unlike his ancient relatives, Shamash was quite disgusted with the temple's debauchery and bodily pleasures. According to the seven wise-men, the Sun God offered his worshipers the eternal bliss in the afterlife, but, in return, he demanded the complete renouncing of... the human love. Allegedly, Shamash himself was born of the Father-Creator Marduk alone – without a mother. This strange deity considered love the cause of earthly plagues, discord and even wars. The duty of a Babylonian was to live for strengthening the power and influence of the Kingdom; and the marriages were arranged solely for the purpose of the childbirth. Most people embraced the new religion without thinking, for they didn't have to renounce their wealth or other material treasures. The haughty and estranged Babylonians found it easier to live without feelings, so the treacherous wise-men could control them, imposing their own will..."

"What does that remind you of?" I asked the Greek, now looking at the nursemaid with the childish curiosity.

"Incredible!" Actaeon shook his head. "Now, in Rome, everything is the same."

When Babylon was conquered by the Assyrians, their king was fascinated by the Sun-cult, and decided to keep it. The influence of the bizarre god wasn't diminished even when the Persian ruler Cyrus came to power, for he was worshipping his pendant – Mithras. The kings changed, so did the languages and customs, but the people of these lands still venerated the luminary, becoming more and more impassive. The Seven Wise-men had achieved the goal, and their descendants even started spreading their religion far beyond the borders of modern Parthia.

"The question is – who these Wise-men alias the Kings were?" Actaeon thought aloud. "And how did they, along with their deity, get to Mesopotamia?"

"As for Mithras, I know who he is and where he came from. Tell me more about the Seven."

"That author doesn't know their names." Susannah said, looking through the script. "But they are said to descend from the Jewish tribe of Dan, known for the slyness and deceit. The symbol of their kin was the Serpent."

"And the Serpent tempted Eve…" I thoughtfully concluded.

"Tempted who?" Actaeon asked confusedly.

"Pandora," I tried to explain it. "The Jewish Pandora. It's a long story, after all."

"The author speculates that Dan, the father of the tribe, was, by his mother lineage, the descendant of wicked Naomi." Said the nursemaid, and then looked at me. "Do you remember?"

"Of course," I replied. "The daughter or Eve and… Mithras."

"Excuse me, but I don't understand anything!" The Greek got anxious. "These weird names make me shiver."

Susannah tried her hardest to tell him the whole Genesis in short, but that story got the secretary even more upset.

"I've seen a lot of rotten things in my poor life, but if your tales are true, it's better for us all to die." Actaeon sighed, tapping his fingers on the table.

"That's exactly what *they* want us to!" I exclaimed angrily. "To lose our hope and to surrender, to die, and to let the world crumble! Will we help them or stand up and fight them?"

The Greek thought a little, and whispered embarrassedly.

"Fight them."

After I had calmed down, I told Actaeon to continue reading so Susannah could have breakfast, too.

"The Unclean tribe." The Secretary's voice was trembling. *"Out of pride, they rejected the true God and bowed before the Evil spirit. As the punishment, the Highest Lord had destroyed Dan's homeland and scattered his kin around the world. However, the God's foe made Dan astute and reckless, endowing his people with the power of persuasion, so they could mislead other tribes. It was hard to resist the radiant and captivating deity – Shamash, Tammuz, Mithras, Phoebus, Horus, Aton… who promised his worshipers well-being in exchange for their immortal souls. Very few people knew the awful secrets hidden on the dark side of the Sun. Only the priests and the nobility were aware of the price for the glory and power obtained from the demons. While the populace believed in Mithras' virtues, he was fed with the blood of the sacrificed children, the perverted lust, the abused women's tears, and, above all, with lie."*

"That's true – deceit is the greatest weapon of the devil," Susannah explained to us. "What can't be taken by force, can easily be wheedled by sweet lies."

"Quocirca, Sol invictus est,"[177] I concluded. "Who needs the truth when the whole world is used to deception?"

Both of my interlocutors looked at each other and fell silent thoughtfully.

"Cene bene!"[178] I said kindly, as I took the scroll. We hadn't read even a half of the script, but, for that day, it was more than enough.

"Oh, I forgot!" the Greek exclaimed with his mouth full. "Tiberius expects of you to visit the Esquiline military camp."

"The only missing thing!" I laughed. "It's true I was born in a garrison, but I don't know much about military things."

"As far as I'm concerned, you have a friend there," Actaeon went on, wiping his mouth with a small linen napkin.

"Cassius…" I recalled with sudden pain inside. How could I forget about the man who had been here for me every hard moment?

"He's right." Susannah nodded. "For thirty-seven years of my poor life, I haven't seen a man who cared about a woman like the Tribune did for you."

---

[177] (Lat.) That is why the Sun is invincible.
[178] (Lat.) Enjoy your meal!

And what *I* did? Since the Old Wolf engaged me to the Bat by force, I haven't even looked at him, nor did I say a word… I was a fool, too burned with my plans, fears and illusions.

"Well, Callistus can wait," I said to the secretary, as I stood up. "I want you to arrange one meeting for tomorrow."

XXXII

"Although the founders of the solar cult wanted to invite as many people into their hateful world," I was reading to myself on my way to the Esquiline. *"Not everyone has the right to become a fully-fledged Mithraist. Since Dan's descendants have always considered women inferior beings, meant only for childbirth, the access to the mithraeum was open to men alone. Namely, wealthy, healthy, and, preferably, noble men could follow the path of serving the Invincible Sun. With the help of his money and origin, the follower ensured himself progress in the secret hierarchy; and the ability to extend his bloodline was crucial, too. The structure of initiation was divided into the seven grades, which symbolized the stages of the stairway to the Sun. The first degree was called the Raven, the second was the Bridegroom, then went the Soldier, the Lion, the Serpent, the Sun-Runner, and the seventh and the highest was the Father. The Raven is the messenger, the Bridegroom cooks the sacred meal – the flesh of bulls, and the Soldier hands over to Mithras the conquered lands… the great conquerors are advanced to the grade of the Lion, with the ritual washing their hands with pure honey and changing their names; while only the descendants of Dan can be promoted to the next degree and call themselves the Snake. Above them, almost on the top of Mithraic stairway there are seven Sun-Runners or the rulers of great lands, led by the Father – the arch-priest of Mithras and the king of kings, who holds his throne and castle in Mesopotamia."*

"Do you really believe the Jews?" Actaeon looked at me skeptically, sitting next to me in a litter. "How come their god is real and our gods are daemons?"

"When Uprising on the Rhine broke out," I recalled my second year of life, "the father was on the battlefield, and the mother in the tent crying and kneeling before the statue of Juno Populona. She thought that the goddess was angry and abandoned us because of some misdeeds. I didn't get that much, so I was squatting in the corner, trembling with fear. Then, there came Cassius Chaerea, took me in his arms, and said to my mother – 'It's not the gods you should beware of, Agrippina, but the men.'"

"Perhaps, he was right." The Greek sighed, and placed the scroll between the sheets of my codex. "They didn't create us, we created them."

At that moment, the litter stopped, and the porter exclaimed.

"Campus Esquilinus!"

I moved the curtain aside, and squinted in the sun. Actaeon quickly fixed my hood, and jumped down to help me out.

In front of the large gate – porta praetoria, side by side there stood tall guardsmen.

I don't see Cassius, I thought, fastening my palla with a brooch. *He must be angry with me...*

"Don't worry, they don't bite." Actaeon nodded toward the young men. "Lady Antonia used to come here quite often, and made no secret of it."

"I'm not afraid of soldiers." I rolled my eyes. "I've been thinking…"

"He's here, and certainly not angry, Princess." Nothing could be hidden from Actaeon. "Last night, when I mentioned your name to him, he melted with tenderness."

"Don't lie." I elbowed him aside. "How can you know my mind?"

"It's written on your forehead," he answered with a smile of satisfaction. "You're born under the sign of Aries, aren't you?"

"You bet!" He made me smile. "Whimsical, painfully honest, thinking with my heart, because my head is lost forever in the clouds."

"Quis venit? Tessera!"[179] One of the guardsmen stopped us.

Without a word, I showed him the first page of codex, where there were written 'viginti.'[180]

"Ignosce mihi,[181] Princepessa. Salve!" the officer greeted me a bit confusedly.

"Tribune Chaerea has almost finished training the infantry, so he is asking you to wait in the praetorium."

"Bene."[182]

The gate of wood and stone was opened with the creaking sound, and one of the soldiers took us inside.

"What does that watchword mean, Actaeon?" I whispered in the secretary's ear.

---

[179] (lat.) Watchword!
[180] (lat.) Twenty.
[181] (lat.) Excuse me.
[182] (Lat.) Alright.

"I don't know, Princess." The Greek shrugged. "The tribune made it up."

The guardsman showed us a large area with benches, a wall drinking fountain and a sundial. I sat down on a roughly cut bench with a backrest and looked up. Recruits in heavy metal armor were marching along the main street – Via Principalis, led by severe centurions. From the cavalry section I could hear a loud horse growl and hoof thud. At the piercing sound of a trumpet, announcing the prandium time, Actaeon shuddered and grabbed his ears.

"Ma ton Dia![183] If I had been born in a place like that, I would have gone mad or deaf."

"You haven't seen a garrison during the war." I hugged him. "But don't worry, they don't bite."

The Greek murmured something, and turned his head toward the wall. I took off my hood with my eyes following the soldiers. In the crowd of helmets and arms, I noticed a warrior dressed in a red sagum over a dark-blue tunic. He was marching toward me, looking ahead. I recognized Cassius, and smiled. In contrast to his similarly trained and equipped combatants, he had always radiated gentility and goodness, never suppressed by the difficulties of a soldier's life. He was still far enough for me to see his face, but I could feel his smile – one of my first childhood memories – so I sighed with relief.

"Well, I begin to understand…" Actaeon thought out loud, studying my scroll discreetly, "I think we're done anyway."

I left him to read, and headed to meet Cassius.

"Salve, mea cara[184] Princepessa!" The tribune cheerfully greeted me, then took my hand, and added. "Let's move somewhere we can talk."

Not sure if I greeted him back in excitement, I just followed my friend.

"I came here with Actaeon," I spoke, showing towards the benches, now slowly being filled up with soldiers. "We can't leave him there alone."

"Bring him with us," Chaerea replied. "I am so sorry for his loss…"

---

[183] (anc.gr.) By Zeus!
[184] (lat.) My dear.

"Don't worry, he's already found solace." I smiled ironically. "Now he is mad about my new maid."

"Frankly, I don't understand such people." My friend sighed, and spontaneously squeezed my hand. "I would have never let my woman down."

His words made me feel a huge lump in my throat.

Blessed is the woman you will love, I thought, but didn't dare say.

We left the camp in no hurry, heading to the large altana by the Temple of Minerva Medica.

"Here we can talk in peace."

The Floral altana, as it was called, had two vaults – the stone roof, held by ten columns and an arch or red climbing roses inside the pavilion, which made this place attractive and mysterious on warm September days.

"So now you're the emperor's advisor now, Drusilla?" Cassius asked me with concern and pride, as we took seats on a bench at the pavilion.

"Oh yes, Tiberius had gone insane." I smiled. "This Greek knows more about the Law, economy or military than I do!"

Actaeon, who was sitting on the stairs, quietly giggled, but the tribune gave me an earnest look.

"That duty is indeed dangerous and demanding," he said in a half-whisper. "But I understand why Caesar chose your very self. You are the only woman of a warrior spirit, purest heart and the insight of a Sibyl."[185]

He made me blush again – like on gloomy day six years ago by Goat Lake. I wondered to myself – how did he do that? Why had I always felt that agreeable embarrassment when he was praising me?

"The emperor is waiting for the accurate report on military trainings here in Rome, and on the situation in the provinces."

"By Quirinus![186] The task is worth a praetor!" Cassius exclaimed, and then continued steadily.

---

[185] (lat.) A fortuneteller.
[186] The divine name of Romulus.

"Give me three days, infantula. I'll find out everything you need, add something I already know, and send you the report by Actaeon."

I looked at him with admiration he deserved. "A 'thank you' is too small for what you do for me."

"A 'thank you' is superfluous." Cassius reached out for the flower vault, picked a rose and placed it carefully in my hair.

I touched the flower behind my left ear. Its bright color and breathtaking scent drew in my mind a familiar figure of Sophia, with her hair rose-red. This time she wasn't crying – on the contrary, I heard her laughing like a child.

What do you want from me? I asked inaudibly. *Why are you following me?*

She didn't answer me. Instead, I heard Actaeon's warning coughing. As otium[187] got to the Esquiline, broad Via Labicana started filling up with walkers.

"I have to go." I stood up. "I will no longer keep you here."

"Don't worry about me, Drusilla," Cassius replied. "I'll see you off."

I gave him my hand in response and waved to the Greek from upstairs.

"I am really glad to see you. I thought you were mad at me then," Chaerea said when we got to the camp gate.

"Mad at you? Never in my life!" I might have been too honest.

"I'm sorry for you had to marry Longinus." There was a shade of sadness in his voice. "I wish I could help you."

"That marriage is a dead letter on the paper," I whispered to him. "It will only last as long as Caesar is alive."

Chaerea's gaze had slightly brightened.

"With Macro's help we won't be waiting for too long," he replied in my ear, ready to greet me goodbye.

Suddenly, a strange idea had come to my mind.

"Cassius," I stopped him, as I wrested my codex from Actaeon's hand. "Take it, and write me a report right here."

"This tablet is too small." He smiled, but still, carefully took my notebook.

---

[187] (lat.) The leisure time of the day.

Actaeon made a fearful face, reminding me of a scroll that remained between the covers, but, by look and a slight node, he could find out I did that on purpose.

"Keep that notebook as the apple of the eye." I winked at Cassius, taking a sit in a litter. He replied with a fist over his heart – the salutation of a soldier. It seemed like he was turning back to his duties in the mood.

…Unlike my secretary, who looked quite ill-tempered.

"May I ask you, Highness?" the Greek wondered, as the porters started their march.

"Something like – have I lost my mind?" I tried to joke.

"I wouldn't express it like that," he explained, "but I don't understand why you gave you-know-what to the tribune."

"Because he is reliable and wise," I replied. "I needed his opinion and his advice… I know I acted recklessly, but I just felt I had to leave him vademecum."

"You haven't even read it to the end."

"*You* have."

"Factum est quod factum est," Actaeon sighed. "I hope it won't be stolen from his quarters."

I laughed – that was not possible. Cassius' bold nature seemed intimidating for the better part of the young nobles and the veteran warriors. My father often spoke with admiration of the bloody battles, when his young centurion could easily defeat five large barbarians alone. So, even with the whole camp serving our enemies, no one would dare to sneak into the tribune's quarters.

"Let's now leave the Esquiline, and talk of the Capri." I changed the topic. "We do not have time for secret language, nor for asking Callistus. I'll write to Caesar about what he must be interested in – the crisis – both economic and monetary, for which the Senate blames his very self. The stingy man will die from botheration."

"Photice has always called me naive." The secretary sounded disappointed. "But I must admit, you are far more naive than me."

"You are so boring!" I turned my head to the curtain and moved it aside. "Don't worry; we've already passed the Celio. Just wait a little more, and you will kiss your Gaul again."

"Drusilla." The Greek timidly touched my hand. "I did read the message to the end, and it was horrifying. Caesar is a monster, and your duty as his close advisor is a trap like your late father's last promotion!"

"What?" I exclaimed worriedly.

"He can't wait for you to fail, or to be caught eavesdropping in the Senate. He can't wait for you to…"

"To fall like Germanicus?"

That very moment, the pedisequus slave yelled, "Villa Longini!" Actaeon helped me to my feet.

"And what should I do now, wise man? Jump off the roof of the Bat's house?" I asked irritably.

"No way," the secretary spoke much sharper than he might, "Just think before you do. Consult me. I am neither Socrates, nor Plato, but your grandma always asked me for advice before she got to the new task."

He was right. I did not free him to be a cookman or a mute companion, but to advise me and teach me everything my grandmother knew.

"I am so sorry, filo mu," I said in Greek to cheer him up, "I was so fucking insolent and stubborn."

"We accept an apology – Orla and me," Actaeon said, and finally smiled. "Let's go inside. You need some rest, and then – we'll see what we can do."

XXXIII

AD 33

Three summers later, in early April, Tiberius gave Gaius the honors of a quaestor,[188] and sent him to Misenum to prepare for his wedding to Junia Claudilla. All the Roman officials, as well as the governors of the major provinces, and of course, the members of the imperial family, were invited to the ceremony.

"How do I look in this pallium?"[189] Longinus asked me anxiously, getting ready for the voyage to Misenum. "I have bedeviled the vestiplici, but yet I haven't chosen the right outfit!"

The cloak was loose, just like the better part of his wear. I understood my husband's wish to look a little taller, for I was ashamed of my curves, too.

"I think Greek cloaks are rather for old men, Lucius," I began, willing to help him. "Middle-aged men like you would feel more comfortable wearing the Gallic cucullus."[190]

Longinus rejoiced as a boy. "You are right! I love red color and the Gallic clothing!"

I had no time to tell him 'Non debes'[191] as the jurist sprinted back to the apodyterium.[192]

"He's comic, but he seems to be good-hearted," I said to Susannah, who was thoughtfully choosing dresses for me. "Who would endure three years with me under the same roof?"

"I have endured much more, and I am not complaining." She smiled as she showed me the tunics, stolas and pallas one by one.

---

[188] A public official in Ancient Rome, a position appointed by the emperor to lead the imperial council and respond to petitioners.

[189] A man's large rectangular cloak, especially as worn by Greek philosophical and religious teachers.

[190] An outer hooded mantle with wide, long sleeves.

[191] (lat.) You're welcome.

[192] (lat.) A large dressing room.

"Oh yes, but he is still my husband," I said in a whisper. "Imagine my sister Livilla refusing to share the bed with Vinicius, or just avoiding family gatherings with his relatives! I bet the Consul would complain to Caesar if she ever did… I am afraid to know what Ahenobarbus would do to Agrippina for such disobedience."

"Indeed," Susannah nodded. "Could we finally start dressing, Little Owl?"

"The Owl completely understands the Bat." I came up to the mirror. "I will wear all green.[193] At least I'll have some fun confusing those patrician muzzles."

Susannah tried to encourage me, explaining that there was no need to criticize my looks, but she was suddenly cut in by Orla's shout.

"Domina!" The young Gaul rushed into my room without knocking. "Vae, Domina!"

My heart began to race. "What is it?"

"I was in the atrium to empty the impluvium when…" Orla's voice was trembling. "When the darkness fell at midday."

"Stop frightening the princess!" Susannah rebuked her. "It has been cloudy and gloomy since the dawn broke. The wind has stopped; the rainstorm must be coming."

The young maid, still in a panic, started murmuring about Cernunos[194] and the end of the world. In perplexity, I went out to cavaedium,[195] looked up at the compluvium, and… stopped. The gray-blue sky I had seen that morning suddenly turned black as if night had closed in.

"Defectus solis,"[196] I thought out loud, and yelled to both the women. "Come on, bring more lights! Tell the servants to go downstairs, play and make some noise!"

The maids ran to the kitchen, as I went back to my chambers to calm down.

"It's alright. It has happened before," I said to myself.

Vertigo caught me as I tried to catch my breath. Feeling unstable to walk, I grabbed the bed pole.

---

[193] Green was traditionally the plebeian color, while blue was associated with the Senatorial class.
[194] The Gallic god of the underworld.
[195] Central hall in a Roman house.
[196] (lat.) Solar eclipse. In accordance with the old Roman custom, during the eclipse of the sun, the mob danced and roared, to drive away demons from their homes.

"Actaeon!" I cried out.

"Something bad has happened." A strange premonition had come to my mind. "Very bad."

Fortunately, the secretary was close by.

"Are you alright?" He helped me lean against him. "Do you want me to call a physician?"

I shook my head and hugged him.

"How can you go in such a condition?" The Greek slowly put me to bed. "Misenum is not across the street. They may carry you in a litter to Ostia, but then, you'll still have to travel by sea."

"I wish you would come with me," I told him, when my mind became clear. "Tiberius will be there too. Your advice would have been meaningful to me."

"Do you want the third nursemaid?" He smiled. "I'm sorry, but I thought you ordered me to observe what's going on the Palatine."

"When did I *order* you?" I asked. "What are you talking of, you liar?"

We burst into laughter together, swiftly interrupted by Susannah and Orla.

"We brought the lamps," the nursemaid said, windless. "Longinus wanted to remind you that you leave for Ostia at the fifth hour."

"He's not happy about the noise." the Gaul giggled. "All the Longini can't stand those plebeian customs."

"But they do stand for far worse customs." Actaeon suddenly frowned. "They haven't freed a single slave for centuries."

"Don't worry." I got up and headed for the mirror. "I'll convince the Bat to give me Orla, and you'll marry a freedwoman."

"We'll find someone for Susannah too," Orla, with her eyes rejoiced, said shyly. "My uncle Falcon likes her very much."

"No, thank you," Susannah said, a bit annoyed. "I'm fine."

I looked at the three of them and felt happier. In the light of dozens of lamps, even my reflection in the mirror now seemed lovely and mysterious.

"Well, business before pleasure," the Greek said, nodding towards the clepsydra. "Lady Antonia is waiting for me, so I'll leave you in the care of those two women."

I relaxed and squinted, as the young Gaul started to set my hair. She always said I had gorgeous thick hair, which many Celtic women would envy me for, and the face of a baby girl that needed no cosmetics.

"Your sisters and Claudius will be waiting for you in the harbor," Actaeon whispered in my ear.

"Please be reasonable and ignore the mockery. Stay away from Claudius' slave – he's Parthian, so I don't trust him. And at the celebration, please talk less and smile to everyone. Avoid the bride – these sweet homekeepers often have poisonous tongues. And when it comes to Caesar, have no fear - he'll be nice… this time."

I gave him a slight nod. Some of his pieces of advice were no easy to follow, but unless I did as the Greek said, I would now be dead.

The eclipse followed us to the Tyrrhenian coast until it drowned in the fresh April night. The strongest slaves with torches were marching in front of my litter. Longinus decided to ride, to avoid the further rumors of his infirmity. All the entourage of ours followed his horse, pretty aware that it was me who persuaded their dominus to empty the stable for their comfort.

"You're late," said Agrippina when I left my litter to greet the relatives.

"Good morning to you, Agrippina." I smiled, trying to remember when and where I heard a similar response.

My older sister gave me a cold and haughty look, but due to the presence of Ahenobarbus, she gave up further conversation. Livilla, who recently gave birth to a long-expected son, welcomed me with an almost sincere grin. Uncle Claudius, with a grimace, spoke of Grandmother being ill again.

"Is she feeling worse now?" I asked with a heavy heart.

"So-so," he replied, "Ch-ch-changeable."

"What you mean?" I wondered.

"For people of her age, the return of any illness can be fatal," Narcissus suddenly spoke, looking at me with his narrow black eyes as if he explored me.

"What did this vulture say?" I asked my uncle, still in a reserved manner but ignoring Actaeon's warning.

A little weary, like a philosopher, Claudius began explaining Narcissus' words, mentioning death, which made no difference between the nobles and the beggars.

"Podex perfectus es!"[197] I spoke out to his face, and nodded to the maids to follow me toward the dock. "I cannot recognize him! All his life he's been attached to Grandma, and now, he easily talks of the worse!" My words were full of fury.

Susannah gave me a warm hug and asked me to calm down and not to draw attention.

Orla took my hand and whispered something unexpected: "Do not let them scare you, Domina. If you can't keep calm, show them your pride, anger, or even wickedness – but not your fear. Fear means defeat, for it surrenders you right to the hands of enemy – without a battle. Your Old Caesar knew it how to advantage of the fear, so he broke Vercingetorix[198] with an army twice as small as Gallic."

"You're right," I answered. "Even wild animals do not attack bestiarii[199] until they smell our human trepidation."

I thought over my petite maid's words as I entered the ship. Its captain, one of Licinius' former assistants, took me to my room, which happened to be larger and more spacious than my sisters'.

"Looks like my great-uncle had a Fury nightmare once again. First he wants me to die, and next he sheds crocodile's tears and raises me to Etna."[200]

Insomnia had always bothered me when I changed beds. Unlike Susannah and Orla, snoring by my left and right, I couldn't even take a nap. The thoughts kept seething in my head – about what I saw and heard – today, three years ago, and since I'd known myself. At the third watch, when the scariest mares lurked in the night, something odd got me out of the bed. That time it was not fever, nor thirst, but a sudden wish to leave a room alone.

I need some air, I thought, moving like a sleepwalker, trying to reach for the door. I put the palla over my nightgown, lit a tiny lamp, and got to the board.

The sailors will be thunderstruck, I smiled, but there was no one there. I looked up to the sky – it was starless. The calm sea and dead silence around me felt like something

---

[197] (lat.) What a moron!

[198] A king and chieftain of the Arverni tribe; he united the Gauls in a revolt against Roman forces during the last phase of Julius Caesar's Gallic Wars.

[199] (lat.) or venatores – gladiators, who went into combat with beasts.

[200] An active stratovolcano on the east coast of modern Sicily, where, according to Roman mythology, the residence of the gods was.

I had already experienced. I rubbed my eyes, as I saw an eerie shape at the forecastle, where captain Fulvius was now supposed to be.

"What the…?" I spoke, as the figure leaned carelessly over the mast.

"Bonum vesperum,[201] my Princess!" I recognized a somber voice of the Claudius' servant. "Better said – bonum mane."[202]

"What are you doing here? And where is everyone?" I asked, pretending I was not upset.

"Ask yourself first – what are *you* doing here in the dead of the night?" he answered boldly and started stepping to me slowly.

"Narcissus, by all the gods, what is it?" I raised my voice, hoping that the guardsmen could hear me, but that didn't happen. I lifted the lamp to see his face more sharply.

The Parthian was smiling cunningly.

"Do you really think my name is Narcissus?" the dark-skinned slave went on, ignoring my question. "No, it isn't. That's what your uncle called me, for he failed to pronounce my name correctly."

"You are getting boring. If you were my slave, I'd get you beaten." I grinned, almost ready to leave.

"The truth is that I'm no one's slave." The young man sounded like a teacher, trying to explain the rule to a dumb child. "I was born as Parysatis – the illegitimate son of King Artaban and the priestess of Nabataea."

Startled by this bizarre statement, I turned around to listen.

"I bet there are two questions in your woman's head right now, eating it from inside – how did I manage to hide my origins, and did I spy you then in Curia Hostilia?… Aren't there, Princess?"

"What do *you* know about a woman's head?" I yawned, still smiling. "Can you read my mind?"

He paused, somewhat distracted by my calm response, and burst into an effeminate laughter.

---

[201] (lat.) Good evening.
[202] (lat.) Good morning.

"In a certain way, the two of us are much alike," he chuckled out false-friendly. "Primo, we know something. Secundo, we think we are something, but nobody takes us seriously. A bastard and unwanted kin. Bad, isn't it? But, tertio, if we were normal, who knows what would happen to us."

"Good talk, but you are wrong again," I replied earnestly. "We are entirely different. Anyway, thank you for a bedtime story. I am sleepy now, so pardon me."

Narcissus waved aside and came up very close to whisper in my ear.

"I'm not the enemy, Your Highness. So I'm giving you advice – give up before it is too late. The one you want to fight with is stronger. He destroys everyone getting in his way. The world belongs to him."

"You wish," I rolled my eyes. It was the time to overwhelm him with my question. "Why does Mithras hate women? Is he afraid of the weaker sex?"

"You wish!" His chubby lips twisted sardonically. "Women are an easy prey for him to hate. Since Eve or Mashyana, struck by Mithras' light, became his lover, none of her daughters could resist the charms of Sol Invictus… Well, some ugly, foolish spinsters, guarded by our foe, Adonai, do not count."

For anyone who knew by heart what was in Rachel's scroll, it was so easy to relate some things… and to find out that there was something Narcissus would rather hide.

"And, what about *the very first one*?" I asked carelessly, as if talking of the next free games at Circus Maximus. "What was her name?"

The Parthian fell back. He looked like he was stunned and now regretting he had gone too far.

"You know about Layla…" he went on indignantly. "A witless maiden who refused to be a wife, a mother, and left Adam alone in the Garden of Eden… She, who uttered the forbidden name of Adonai, and got her punishment… The one who dwells for centuries alone, looking for daydreams…" Then, his voice became fearfully rough.

"When our noble Mithras wanted to have mercy on a poor woman and to soothe her in the endless light, insolent Layla gave him names and drove away."

"So there was a woman who resisted him?" I blinked.

"And our Lord Mithras cursed her," the narrator finished slowly. "She was damned to hatred of the human race forever… Though, Adonai changed his mind and let her live again to find someone alike, I personally doubt that our Lord and his keen servants let it happen."

Now I smiled sincerely, for I was glad to know the other side of Lilith's story – to complete my knowledge. *She left Adam, looking for true love*, I thought, observing Narcissus, who looked confused by my good mood. *All she wanted was to love and to be loved, and Adam didn't care for anything but her obedience and children.*

"What's so funny?" Narcissus observed me too.

"I really enjoyed your story, Narci… Parysatis," I spoke thoughtfully, "but now I have to go. I really need some sleep."

"I hope, you learned the moral," he said to my back, while I was heading to my room.

"I always do," I whispered. "I know more than you imagine."

With the last word on my lips, I woke up in my bed.

XXXIV

It was the first day of the week – dies Solis, and the sun was really shining when we arrived in Misenum. At Portus Julius – a harbor in the Gulf of Naples, built by my mother's father, Admiral Agrippa, the servants and guards from Caesar's summerhouse had been waiting to welcome the ruler's nephew and great-nieces.

"They look scared," my husband noticed, in a lawyer's voice, observing the imperial escort.

"No wonder." I sighed. "Divi filius[203] is here."

"Do not you see?" Ahenobarbus roared, pushing forward to be first to pass. "Something was breaking rocks and pulling up trees with the roots."

"I think it's an earthquake," Vinicius concluded, pointing up at the trail of the accident.

"And that has happened recently," Longinus went on. "The Vigiles haven't got the shore in order yet."

I hope Gaius is fine, I thought, looking up for the famous summer residence.

"How come we didn't feel the shake?" My elder sister raised her thick eyebrow. "It must have echoed all the way to Rome."

"For we were at the sea, you fool!" Ahenobarbus shouted. "The damn ship always rocks."

Agrippina fell silent, and both of my brothers-in-law continued with the morning talk of the repurchase bride along the dock.

"How are you feeling?" Longinus asked me, as my sisters followed their husbands.

"Believe it or not – great." I smiled. "And what about you?"

"Well, I can't complain," he said. "I just feel weird to be the bridesman at the age of thirty-nine."

---

[203] (lat.) "Divine son" – a title much used by the emperor.

Thank gods I'm not a bridesmaid, I thought, remembering Actaeon's words about Junia Claudilla. *'If I had to tie a knot of Hercules[204] around her waist, I would be tempted to strangle her.'*

"Salve, my Princess! Consul!" We were greeted by two lightly dressed young men. "The emperor expressed a special wish for his youngest grandniece to stay in the palace during the celebration."

"Drusilla alone?!" I heard Agrippina's outcry in the crowd. "And what about us?"

"The other members of the ruler's family will be housed in Villa Vipsania – the second largest domus on the Misenum foreshore," the nomenclator replied in a sweet voice. "Once the residence of Admiral Agrippa."

"Clear." Livilla broke her natural stillness. "We are invited to the insula for sailors."

"F-f-fellow, what has h-h-happened here? And when?" Claudius turned to one of the Vigiles.

"Tandem Veneris,[205] aedile, we were struck by an earthquake at ninth hour," the watchman replied readily. "Fortunately, with no victims, so the emperor forbade us to raise the alarm."

"Take care, Drusilla." Longinus mildly touched my hand. "I'm going to have rest before the feast."

I need some rest as well, I thought, but then I noticed dark Parthian eyes watching me as if my nightdream was oracular.

"Tonight, you are invited to the emperor's convivium." The slender nomenclator suddenly appeared in front of me. "After the supper, all the women are awaited at the bride's to help her with the wedding preparations."

"Great." I tried my hardest not to sound cynical. "Now, get these bags and show me to my chambers."

The spindly man frowned haughtily and nodded to porters to take care of my dress bags.

---

[204] The most important part of the Roman wedding dress was a belt, tied around her waist in the "knot of Hercules" as Hercules was considered the guardian of wedded life.
[205] (lat.) Last Friday.

"Come with me, Your Highness," he said, capriciously enough for his position, and led me through the boardwalk to the palace.

"You are honored to stay in the house where Caesar wishes to… become a god!" the servant went on proudly, as I followed him through the narrow cypress alley.

Climbing the stairs of white marble, I tried to suppress my thoughts of the wedding and tried to focus on a conversation with Tiberius. In comparison to the dark and richly decorated Villa Jovis, Caesar's summer residence seemed more than modest. As I walked through the nymphaeum with the only bronze sculpture of Neptune, I wondered what made the emperor abandon the big castle for a dollhouse by the noisy harbor.

"And where do all the servants, guardsmen and goldfishes[206] live?" I joked.

The nomenclator answered nothing, but his weary and disdainful look had been enough.

Poor thing, I thought. *Who knows what he had done to you, so you became a moron.*

"Baldwin, are you deaf or mute?" I heard a mild Greek accent from the peristyle. "The princess asked you something, so take pains to answer!"

"Callistus!" I recognized my friend immediately, and my mood improved.

The Greek, just like a secretary should, emerged from the tablinum.

"My heroine!" he reached out and hugged me. "Hairos de!"[207]

"I don't know how I did survive those years." I opened my arms in astonishment. "But here I am!"

Squeezing my hand in admiration, Callistus turned to the nomenclator and shouted, "If you don't want to talk, you fool, get out!"

Baldwin fell back, casting another hateful glance at me.

"The German." Callistus rolled his eyes. "He was a hostage of Prince Castor, Caesar's late son. When they besieged his village, the boy barely knew how to use a sword, so he began to cry and beg our men to spare his life."

"A Roman soldier would have chosen death rather than shame." I frowned, imagining this scene.

---

[206] Tiberius was believed to be a pool orgy lover, so he called his multiple favorites that way.
[207] (anc.gr.) Long time no see!

"Like any normal man," my friend agreed, and then covered his mouth to answer my question. "The emperor is very bad. He can barely walk, eat, and when it's time to sleep, he dwells in the garden like a lemur.[208] Suddenly, he sent away his favorites, freed a large number of the slaves, and moved here to Campania. The palace you are in, which I call a pigeonhole, is only for the trusted servants and, of course, Sutorius Macro."

"The most trusted one." I muffled my laugh. "Why he had invited me to live with him?"

"He didn't tell me." The man shrugged. "But do not worry; he stopped killing too."

"You wish." I waved aside. "He will be playing wicked games until he dies."

"Here you are, Princess." Callistus opened the door to my room, "Get ready for the supper with the emperor tonight. Please, just be nice and leave your worries to your Callistus."

"*My* Callistus," I chuckled. "Have you forgotten I'm a married woman?"

"Just like Aphrodite." The secretary raised his hands theatrically. "Married by force to a cross-eyed Hephaestus, you sometimes find relief in the arms of handsome Adonis, but you truly love brave Ares."

"That's enough, Apollo," I spoke, taken aback by such a metaphor. "You've messed it up. Hephaestus was not goggle, but lame, and the part with Adonis and Ares was kind of… the other way round."

"For Aphrodite – yes indeed, but not for Julia Drusilla." He waved his pointer finger left and right. "A liar can't be fooled so easily."

"You are exaggerating things," I tried to reassure him, but in vain.

"Do not be afraid, I'll keep your secret," Callistus said sincerely. "However, so much of attachment between siblings always seems suspicious. But the things are different with Cassius Chaerea. Caesar hates him, for he envies him his character and courage. As for me, I respect him a lot – after all, Hellenic blood flows in his veins!"

"Hellenic?!" I awed. "Wasn't Cassius' mother born Hispanic?"

---

[208] A mythical demon.

"Yes, she was," he nodded, "but the tribune's father was of the Chaereas – the old lineage of the warriors from Athênai. By the way, his agnomen means 'joy.'"

"Oh." I smiled, reflecting upon that. "Another reason for me to love Greeks… So, if his father was also a peregrine, he must have been an extraordinary warrior to be appointed equestrian[209] by Augustus."

Callistus wasn't listening. "I have to go," he said. "Tiberius will wake up soon. I'll call your nursemaids to help you get comfortable."

"A new room, again," I sighed as I sat on the bed. "Anyway, I don't think I will get a sleep a night before this wedding."

Susannah rushed to fill my wardrobe with the clothes and Orla hurried to the kitchen to prepare a meal.

"When the holidays are over, I will send the little one home with the Bat," I thought aloud, taking off my stola. "She isn't safe here."

"You are right," the Jewess nodded. "I can serve you all alone."

"No need for that," I said. "Great-uncle will lend me some slave boys."

Done with unpacking, Susannah sat next to me to massage my tired back. Now it hurt constantly.

"What did that gossip in the menswear tell you?" she asked, referring to the Greek.

"A lot of things." I smiled. "About Tiberius' disease, the nomenclator's cowardice, Greek ancestors of Cassius… And even about me and Gaius – you know what I mean. But yet the funniest part was…"

"Me excusa,[210] mea Principessa!" I was interrupted by a deep male voice, followed by heavy knocking on the door.

"Quid est?"[211] I spoke out angrily, not recognizing Anicetus, the large janitor.

"Your second cousin came to visit you," the Cypriot replied confusedly. "She's waiting in the atrium."

"What are you babbling?" I got up reluctantly and walked toward the door.

---

[209] In ancient Rome – a knight, originally a member of the cavalry.
[210] (lat.) Excuse me.
[211] (lat.) What is it?

Anicetus smiled widely and gestured to a pretty red-haired girl sitting on a guest bench.

She looks familiar... I thought.

"Drusilla!" the guest noticed me and went on cheerfully, "Long time, no see!"

These eyes, so honest, a bit wild, gave her identity away. She was my kin, blood of Antonii – like Grandma, Queen Selena and myself.

"You must be Messalina!" I rejoiced, and hurried to embrace her.

That was she – the daughter of the Senator Valerius Barbatus and my arrogant aunt Domitia. The future Roman Empress... and the mother of my niece and nephew.

XXXV

Caesar appeared at the pre-wedding feast just in time, as the guests filled the triclinium, lit with hundreds oil lamps and candles. Dressed in a casual toga over a long white robe, sickly thin and exhausted, Tiberius took a sit on a couch, straight opposite to mine.

"Ave, Noblissime!" The greetings came from all sides. "Ave, Dive!"

"Avete et salvete," the host replied in a weak voice.

Callistus discreetly signaled to the slaves to serve the appetizers. Soon, the spacious dinner room was drowning in the rare aromas of smoked cheese, mulled Samos wine and Egyptian spices.

The emperor looked at his plate of venison bone broth, and exchanged a few words of the legal part of the ceremony with Longinus. The disease, which was now slowly taking life out of his body, seemed to take away his hatred, too… It seemed so.

These torments I would never wish even to you, my father's murderer, I thought, trying a piece of mushroom pie. Food carriers and cup-bearers were twisting and turning around each guest, offering more drinks and delicacies – so great in number that it could feed the whole Suburra.[212] To Caesar's left, there stood the stone-faced praegustator, ready to taste the first bite of his dominus' dish.

"Do you remember, great-uncle," Caesar suddenly addressed Gaius. "When we had such dinner altogether last?"

Caligula got the ambiguous message, and swallowed a lump.

"Yes, my Emperor," he answered thoughtfully, avoiding our father's name. "It was the celebration of the Roman victory over the Germans… fifteen years ago."

"Sixteen, to be precise," I entered their conversation.

Caligula turned pale with fear, our sisters and brothers-in-law stopped eating, and Claudius chocked on a piece of meat.

---

[212] In ancient Roman times – a crowded lower-class area that was also notorious as a pleasure district.

"You're right, child." Tiberius grinned, showing his dark, rotten teeth. "You have a better memory than your brother."

"I wouldn't quite agree with that," I said in a nice tone. "Zaleukos, our teacher, claimed the opposite. I remember the year of your triumph mostly because of the wonderful sight of my father and Gaius riding a chariot."

The old man nodded approvingly, but his eyes became blurred – with anger, or pain, or even both.

"I remember, Caesar, how my father used to tell me about the triumph of Augustus." Longinus spoke all of a sudden, trying to save the situation. "He mentioned jewels, beautiful captives, arena games and feasts from dusk till dawn, but I am sure these scenes were pretty pale, compared to *your* victory."

Tiberius had always been weak on his flattery… at least, he seemed so. When my husband finished praising him, the host started laughing. As he took a bite, the guests could finally breathe out… for a while.

"I spent a whole lot of money on the triumph of thankless Germanicus!" Caesar exclaimed, looking at me and expecting me to confront him. "And now, I have emptied the fiscus, so that his son, and my great-nephew and heir, can have a worthy wedding… "

"I'd rather spit on your muzzle like I did on your lord Mithras'," I said in my heart. "I know you want it, you son of a whore, but I am not a fool to let you kill me… not today."

The rest of the dinner was spent in a relatively peaceful atmosphere. The talk was mostly about my brother's upcoming married life and the beginning of his quaestorship. In the other side of the triclinium, two young men were playing harp and tibia. The melody was graceful, but sorrowful.

Finally, the host thanked to the guests for their visit, and, clinging to Callistus' hand, left the dining room.

"I'm so happy to se you, Drusilla!" Gaius hugged me when we got alone in the chamber. "I missed you so much."

"I missed you even more," I replied sadly. "But it won't change anything, will it?"

"This night, I'll spend here in the palace," he whispered excitedly, waiting for me to react. "That will be our night."

I nodded and kissed him on the mouth. Gaius kissed me back – like a gentle and experienced lover, suppressing my reluctance with his passion.

"This marriage is a necessary evil," he continued, moving the strap of my stola down my shoulder. "Nothing is going to change between us."

He was not lying; he believed in what he said. I knew he loved me, and I felt the same about him. Ready to forget where we were and what could happen if anyone saw us, I reached out to untie a belt of his tunica, but suddenly, I felt unprecedented fear and stopped.

"I think this is not a good idea." I stepped aside and fixed my robe. "I was invited to Claudilla's spinster night."

"You're right." My brother sighed. "It's better for you to show up."

Then, to my own astonishment, I wished to leave the room as soon as possible.

I refuse to be another woman of Caligula. I interpreted this unforeseen rejection in my mind. *Nobody will humiliate my love.*

My brother, with a premonition of my sudden change, hurried to close his arms around me.

"We will see each other soon, I promise. And, when I become the emperor, I will divorce that girl to marry you."

"You know, you can't," I replied with a bitter smile. "The laws of Pompilius are unchangeable."

"I'll order Macro to let me know when you come back," Caligula went on as if he hadn't heard me, "and we'll sleep together."

That morning, these words could have inflamed all of my senses, but that night, a new, unknown part of my self opposed them.

Is it me? I wondered in my mind, and winced. *Or is it she who doesn't fear Tiberius, Vespasian, nor Mithras himself?*

"Are you alright, sister?" Gaius slightly touched my forehead. "Are you tired?"

"I am!" I shouted helplessly, and headed for the door. "Don't look for me… please!"

As Caligula, upset with my behavior, was trying to figure out my reason, I was already rushing through the corridor towards my chambers.

"Heus, puella,[213] where are you hurrying to?" A mild voice had stopped me, before I bumped into Callistus.

"Don't ask." I tried to fix my messy hair. "I need some rest and… silence."

"Doleo,[214] Princepessa." The Greek took my hand. "Caesar is waiting for you in his tablinum."

"Oh, good," I replied cynically. "I'd rather go to Hades than to Claudilla's spinster night."

"He doesn't look angry or bitter." Callistus nodded toward the door of the office. "On the contrary, the Wolf is in a good mood, and even joking with the servants."

"Haven't you studied him so far?" I sighed. "He's only happy when planning a new atrocity."

The secretary gave me an omniscient look. "You better hurry up. I hear the prince looking for you in the nymphaeum."

"Ball' eis korakas!"[215] I whispered, and I knocked three times.

"Veni, cara neptis!"[216] the old man spoke out hoarsely.

As I entered a half-dark and messy room, I felt much sickness and demureness in the air. Tiberius was reclining in a wide soft chair at his desk, worn out and pale, but with the same mocking look from the Capri.

"Sit down." He gestured to the secretary chair.

I did as he said, putting a likeable smile on my face.

"I often wonder," he continued thoughtfully, tapping his long fingers on the desk, "why haven't I punished such a stubborn and incorrigible person yet?"

"The will of the gods," I replied in a humorous manner.

"They do not care about us," he responded. "I didn't worship them even in my childhood."

"Not even one god?" I couldn't help myself.

---

[213] (lat.) Hey, girl.

[214] (lat.) I'm sorry.

[215] (anc.gr.) Go to hell! (Literally: throw yourself to the ravens).

[216] (lat.) Come in, dear grandniece!

Caesar's sly gaze became leery and furious. "I didn't invite you to talk of damn deities!" he shouted, slamming his fist on the desk. "Your behavior is so immature and insolent, but now I have to tolerate it, because you are useful to me as a fucking advisor!"

I realized that I had gone too far, and silently ordered myself to shut up. "Ignosce mihi, Imperator."

"Well, that's better," Tiberius croaked. "Now listen up carefully, and only answer when I ask you."

I nodded and looked at him.

"I am very pleased with your service, grandniece." He rose up, slightly clinging to the back of his chair. I wanted to follow him, according to the courtly custom, but he gestured not to stand up. "I didn't get such detailed and timely reports even from Antonia," he went on, breathing harder. "Now I know all I needed, so I wouldn't endanger you anymore…"

I thought Caesar was informed of what I had been hiding from him, and squinted, ready for the judgment. However, he straightened his thin back, looked at me bitterly, and started a completely different topic.

"Forty years ago, I could fight like a lion; twenty years ago, I was able to crush gladiators in the circus, and today? My age and illness made a ruin of me, a living dead!"

I found myself having a pity on him in my heart but I didn't show it. "You look good, Caesar." I'd forgotten that I might not speak without question.

"Liar!" Tiberius pointed at me with his twisted finger. "You think I cannot see my body decaying and rotting? Leave that flattering for fools like your Longinus, and now listen to my order!"

There fell silence for a while in the tablinum. The emperor took five heavy steps towards the bookshelf, pulled out a bundle of bronze keys from under a scroll, and hurled it to me.

"You will stay here in the palace until my death," he continued in a softer, more earnest tone. "You will get everything that is proper to a woman of your status, even the freedoms of a Vestal virgin. All I expect from you in return, Drusilla, is your devotion and willingness to alleviate the last days of my life."

I looked at him in disbelief, twirling thick keys in my hands. Despite my clumsiness, I grabbed them just at once. Receiving freedoms of a Vestal virgin would entitle me to the things that other women, even noble ladies, might not even dream of. A place of honor at all the public games, freedom of movement in my own chariot, testifying without oath, and even the right to release a convict sentenced to death… All those privileges would help me achieve my goals.

"Rome is waiting for me to pass on sooner rather than later." Tiberius squinted. "People, for whose welfare I have given up my happiness, now hate and despise me. They call me a murderer and a lecher, the worst one in history."

"Augustus was the worst… for me." I couldn't restrain myself again, and I was honest.

"Good." The old man smiled. "It is because of Cleopatra, right?"

"…And Anthony, my great-grandfather," I replied.

Tiberius began to cough, loud and hard. "You still believe in love, Drusilla?"

"Yes, I do… my Emperor."

"To your detriment," he said, irritated, and, clinging to the chairs and columns, went back to the desk with a trembling step. "In this empire, lovers always get a raw deal."

"Every rule has an exception, Caesar," I said firmly. "My grandmother and your brother, Drusus –"

"Drusus died on the battlefield," he interrupted me. "He left a thirty-year-old widow with three children. You must be a fool to call that happiness."

"They loved each other," I reminded him. "They did not divorce."

"Tace!"[217] the old man roared, his eyes almost red with anger. "I am not looking for a nanny to make up some fairy tales, but a serious and trustworthy person who will see about I would not end up infamously as Old Caesar, but to breathe my last quiet and painlessly, when the time comes. And at that hour, I don't want to be alone!"

"As you command," I answered. "Still, I don't know what to tell my husband, to whom you married me off three years ago."

Tiberius, already tired of talking, burst into Homeric laughter.

---

[217] (lat.) Shut up!

"If you want to lie," he giggled, patting himself on the knee. "You better learn to do it right. I know the nature of your marriage to Longinus, for I had been through the same with Caesaris,[218] but at least I didn't hide how much I hated her. Besides, I know you were seen with Cassius Chaerea, and I've heard a rumor you're in love with your own brother."

"Caesar, that's not true!" I shook my head in denial.

"Of course, it is not," he continued ironically. "I remember your reports concerning all the military camps. Not even the Praetorian prefect has such information!"

There was no point to keep on justifying myself. "Cassius is not guilty," I said hastily. "I asked for help."

"I like your adroitness." Tiberius cheered up completely. "And I hope you'll keep on using it, serving your emperor."

I nodded and sighed with relief.

"That's all so far, Drusilla." The old man stood up, clapping his hands twice to call the slaves. "Enjoy the celebration. You're already late for the spinster night."

I left the room wondering what kind of a game this man was playing, and what would happen next to me and my dear people.

"Looks, you are more in luck than any other member of your family." Callistus winked, letting me know he was eavesdropping on what had been happening in the tablinum.

I look at the bundle of keys I received from the emperor.

"I don't understand why he did this…"

"The will of the gods." Callistus shrugged. "Now, better go to get some sleep, so as not to scare capricious Tyche[219] off."

"Fuck Tyche and Fortuna, too!" I laughed nervously. "I don't know how long this imperial mercy will last, but I swear I'll make good use of it."

"I have no doubt, Your Highness." The Greek half-embraced me and escorted me to my room.

That night, I slept like a baby.

---

[218] Julia the Elder, daughter of Augustus.

[219] The presiding Greek tutelary deity who governed the fortune and prosperity of a city, its destiny. Roman equivalent: Fortuna).

XXXVI

"Long live our Emperor Tiberius!"

"Long live our Prince Caligula!"

"Feliciter!"[220]

The long wedding cortege made its way from the Temple of Jove to the new house of the newlyweds, followed by the vivas of the cheerful crowd. From both sides of the road, women and children of Misenum threw coins and grain to the litter, wishing happiness and wellbeing to the future family. The prince and his wife were sitting in a lavish lectica, signed with a golden eagle on its velarium. Tiberius was riding in a chariot far in the head of the parade. Callistus carefully held him by one hand, and by the other he was held by his newly adopted daughter, Julia Drusilla.

"What do you think of the bride, Callistus?" the emperor asked, breathing heavily.

"I didn't see her face under the orange veil, my lord, but I am pretty sure the girl's a beauty."

"She is scrawny." Caesar squinted against the sun. "Besides, she's boring and arrogant like her mother. Gaius is going to hate her, but how could I help him? No prince may choose his bride."

"And those who tried wasted their time," I said half-loudly, looking toward the imperial gardens where the servants, as diligent as ants, set up the tables for the feast.

"You're a fast learner, child," my great-uncle nodded. "I finally hear you talking like a big girl."

Callistus winked at me discreetly. It was really hard to play pretend like I was cold and cynical, but now I had to learn.

The feasting lasted until late into the night. First, the actors of the Theater of Pompey entertained the guests with famous scenes from the history – from the wedding of Aeneas and Lavinia to the Triumph of Augustus on the Actium. After them came the

---

[220] (lat.) May they [the newlyweds] live happily forever!

gladiators, ready to wrestle to the death, and, by the end of the treat, half-naked dancers showed their skills, showering the newlyweds with fresh rose petals.

"Now the bridesmen will take the bride," Messalina turned to me and whispered, when the emperor, by custom, left the celebration. "They will carry her over the threshold of her husband's house, where she wounds the door posts with bands of wool and anoints the door with oil and fat."

"Luckily, I avoided that madness," I replied, observing Junia and Gaius, somewhat worried. "I better hurry to congratulate them, before they're gone performing their marital duties."

My second cousin smiled and left to join the rest of bridesmaids in decorating the marriage bed in the cubiculum.

"I wish you an abundance of harmony, prosperity and... children." I gave my brother a warm hug, putting a wedding-appropriate smile on my face.

"We will do our best," the bridegroom joked, and wrapped his arms around Junia's waist. The young wife shyly buried her doll face against his shoulder.

"Prince," the stout matron from the bridal family said to Gaius, "now it's time to light the torch of Talassus!"[221]

He nodded and, with little jitters, took the symbol of marital happiness, and walked toward the exuberant women.

"So, we are sisters now?" I turned to Junia Claudilla, willing to embrace her, too.

"Not really," she said arrogantly and stepped aside. "We are sisters *by law*."

"Look," I replied confusedly, reaching out to take her hand, "it would be better if we stay in good relations, Junia."

The girl came closer and, gently lowering my hand, whispered scornfully. "Don't bother, Drusilla. I know everything about you and Caligula, and I won't let you destroy our marriage."

"You're so young," I smiled, barely managing to stay stone-cold. "I'll teach you something. For you, my brother Gaius is not 'little boots,' but Prince. I recommend you refer to me as 'Princess' too."

---

[221] A Roman god of marriage ceremonies.

"And you're so dumb," Junia's mouth went slightly askew, "I am not afraid of you at all. My father is a close friend of the emperor, and your late father was his enemy."

"My father lived as a hero, fought as a hero, and died as a hero," I retorted, as I noticed Silanus trying to devour the whole lamb ham. "Your father lives like a swine, sits in the Senate like a swine, and one day, when Tiberius gets bored with him, he'll end up on a skewer – like a swine."

Junia's freckled face turned crimson and swollen with rage.

"You…!" she let out in a shaky voice, clenching her fists.

"Enjoy yourself, Claudilla," I turned my back with a sardonic smile, and headed for my litter.

"Do you want to greet your kinsmen first, Domina?" Anicetus spoke, straightening his back. For his impressive height, strength and loyalty, I asked Tiberius to let him serve me as my carrier and guardian of the quarters, and he granted it.

"Oh, I have, believe me," I replied reluctantly. "I'm tired."

"You don't want to sing epithalamium?"[222] The Cypriot made a joke to cheer me up. "There's one I know by heart." He sang in Greek: "To yasemin stin porta su, yasemin mu…"

"I prefer roses," I stopped him, smiling reluctantly.

"I will remember," Anicetus nodded, and with the help of the other porter, lifted the litter. "When you are marrying the one you love, I'll sing about roses."

"And Callistus will dance zeibekiko,"[223] I muttered, resting my head on my knees. "Carry me home and don't make me laugh."

When I returned to the palace, I found Susannah and Orla, dressed and exhausted, sleeping across my bed. The room was shining clean and tidy – all my clothes, washed and dried, were lined up in a wardrobe, and all the books and scrolls were carefully packed on the shelves above the desk.

You fools, I thought, covering them with a blanket. *Who told you to do it all at once?*

Susannah, probably hearing my steps in a half-dream, turned on her back, and snorted loudly. Orla, curled up like a kitten, dreamed quietly and carelessly.

---

[222] A Greek-Roman song or poem celebrating a marriage.
[223] The oldest known Greek folk dance.

What now? I smiled. *Alright, I'll sleep in a chair. You both deserve to rest like ladies at least once in a lifetime.*

I lit two lamps with an effort, then reached out to the bookshelf and chose one of the scrolls – sent to me by Rachel and translated literally into Latin by my nursemaid.

Canticum canticorum,[224] I read to myself, for the God knows how long. *The poem of King Solomon in his original form.* I loved this book because of its sincerity and glorification of the true and undamaged love soaked in these whimsical verses. The author admired the faithfulness of beautiful Shulammite, who rejected the king's advances for her chosen one.

I am my beloved's, and my beloved is mine:
He crowns my head with a wreath of lilies,
Awesome as an army with banners…
In him dwells my joy, and his wisdom lives in me…

I read it almost to the end and dropped the scroll as I fell asleep.

"Mighty waters cannot quench love; rivers cannot sweep it away," the mild, familiar voice of a woman spoke into my dream, *"for love is strong as death; its flashes are flashes of fire, the very flame of the Lord."*

As I felt my head slumping against the desk, I woke up and rubbed my eyes. There was no one beside me. I turned around – Orla and Susannah were still asleep. At the other end of the desk, I noticed a dried rose, half-covered with a piece of parchment.

Cassius… My memories returned me to the altana on the Esquiline. *How are you doing now?* I wondered, taking the flower in my hand. Its fragile petals had retained some color and the velvety scent of that fall.

I found myself wanting to see him, but not like before – asking him for help or his opinion on what he had read in my codex. I found myself longing for his voice and his bottomless gray eyes, so kind and bright. I remembered how gently and manly he held my hand and took me in his arms… This time, I felt something odd, beyond friendship or gratitude.

What if these Greek babblers are right? I thought, surprised by this new feeling. *I guess I'm really in love with Cassius.*

---

[224] (lat.) Song of Songs.

My heart was not responding – it was madly pounding, driving my sleep and weariness away. My mind was recalling each and every time I saw him, starting from the Abitarvium... There was a lone girl following the young centurion, pulling him by the lacerna and repeating sadly: "Play with me, Chaerea, play with me…"

He always played with me. Hungry and tired, sometimes mocked by the soldiers, and admonished by my father – his commander – still, he dedicated every moment of his short rest to his 'infantula.' I lived these days over again – Antioch, the Goat Lake, Capri and Flower altana… For that moment, all I had was only Cassius.

"I love him, and he loves me too," I let out with a joyful smile and wet eyes.

A footfall on the stairs woke the nursemaids up. I hurriedly took the scroll, put the rose inside, and pushed it carefully under the soft pile of books.

"What's going on?" Susannah jumped out of bed. "Vey, we were sleeping like a log!"

"Princess!" Callistus called out from the prothyron, and Anicetus banged on the door like a Cyclops.

"Oh, Domina," Orla, still sleepy, murmured. "When did you come back?"

"It's alright, I was reading." I calmed her down, and let the men in.

"Sorry we woke you up," Anicetus began, but the secretary interrupted him.

"Caesar calls you, Highness – straight away."

My legs grew numb from sitting. With Susannah's help, I rose and freshened myself up with some cold water from the washing bowl.

"What does he want?" I asked the secretary.

"He's not well – the wounds became inflamed," he answered anxiously.

"What does the doctor say?" I remembered a grayish physician who was trying to save already-dying Photice.

"Which one?" The Greek smiled bitterly.

"If you meant Lisidas from the Capri, he has long since ended up as bait for predatory fish. Chariklos, a man, who healed hundreds, faced the death no less cruel."

"Why on Earth did he kill them?" I asked in perplexity.

"There is no cure for the venereal disease," Callistus shrugged, pulling my hand to hurry me, "and death is usually slow and agonizing."

"Who would like to hear such condemnation?" his companion interjected, as his kit clanked in the half-dark.

"I think I know why he invited me." I sighed and knocked on his door thrice.

"Be careful, Princess," Anicetus whispered, "When he is in severe pain, he usually throws things around."

"O veni, futue te ipsum!"[225] Caesar shouted from inside.

"I go with you." The secretary took me by the hand. "Now he is dangerous like Chimera."

I opened the door and felt an unbearable stench. Irksome and stagnant heat was spreading from the room. The dirty rags and bowls of ointments and other remedies were scattered on the floor. Two young, terrified-to-death slaves were twisting and turning around Caesar's bed – one clumsily applying some white balm on the old, damaged body, and the other covering the wounds with bandages.

"Amateurs! Deceivers!" Tiberius roared, referring to the medics. "They promised to cure me within one fucking moon! I gave them everything they wished – gold, freedom, land, and they have ruined me!"

"Oh, Caesar…" I said sympathetically.

"I know there is no cure," he went on with his voice trembling. "One way or another, I will die. I'm only looking for a remedy to ease this awful pain!"

"What can I do for you?" I asked, barely standing on my feet with shock and tiredness.

"Just go to Rome and find me a physician," he replied. "Even if it may take your fucking life."

The slaves looked at me sadly, the way a passerby looks at the one convicted to bad death. Adroit Callistus was close to tears.

"Certe,"[226] I nodded, trying not to think about the consequences. "Volo."[227]

"Domine," Callistus said timidly, "may I accompany Her Highness on this journey?"

---

[225] (lat.) Come the fuck in!
[226] (lat.) Of course.
[227] (lat.) I will.

"Fuge in malam crucem!"[228] Caesar grabbed an amphora and threw at the Greek. "Your service is like getting milk from a he-goat!"

Fortunately, he missed. Callistus' step encouraged me.

"When should I leave, my Emperor?" I asked.

"As soon as possible," Tiberius replied. "At dawn. You will have ten days and a letter of permission to go anywhere, even to the sanctuary of Silvanus.[229] Unless you find a medic, or a cure, you will end up like those Greek fools. And your brother," he grinned odiously through the onset of pain, "will have to let Gemellus take the throne."

I realized that Gaius' life depended on me, and my body started panging. Unable to say a single word, I nodded like a mute.

"As you order, the Exalted One." The secretary bowed to him, and pulled me out of the room, as I was torpid.

"What did Caesar say?" Anicetus was waiting in the corridor.

"We're done." The secretary sighed. "Neither Hippocrates[230] nor Asclepius[231] himself would help him."

The giant looked at me with sympathy, ready to lend his helping hand.

"Whatever happens," he said earnestly, "I'll stand by you, Your Highness."

I exchanged glances with them both. With such sincere and incorruptible companions, I could be able to reach for the shores of Acheron.[232]

"Anicetus," I said, I lifting myself up on my toes to pat the guardsman on the shoulder, "from now on, you are free. And you," I turned to Callistus. "Stop panicking like my Actaeon, and help me get ready for going."

"Unless you are friends with Asclepius…" He muttered with said irony.

---

[228] (lat.) Go to hell! (literally – go to the bad cross)

[229] A Roman tutelary deity of woods and fields, worshipped by men only.

[230] A Greek physician of the Age of Pericles (Classical Greece) who is considered one of the most outstanding figures in the history of medicine.

[231] A god of medicine in ancient Greek religion and mythology.

[232] In ancient Greek mythology, one of the five rivers of the underworld.

"I'm friends with someone better," I answered, remembering Rachel. "One merchant who seems to know everything."

"If we succeed," Callistus' eyes turned bright with hope, "would you ask Caesar to give me... a manumission?"[233]

"No, I will sell you to the brothel for the double sestertius instead," I joked, and stroked his curly hair. My friends shook with laughter.

"You are still vulgar like a soldier." Callistus sighed and turned to the cubiculum. "Vale, mi Caesar, morituri te salutant."[234]

---

[233] The act of releasing from slavery.
[234] (lat.) Goodbye, my Caesar, those who are about to die salute you.

XXXVII

When a small merchant ship sailed into Ostia, it started raining. Lack of sleep and the sudden weather change made my headache and my knees shake as heavily as if I was an old woman or a drinker. That morning caught me sitting on a deck bench, wrapped in Anicetus' cloak with my head leaning on Susannah's shoulder.

"Why didn't we wait for the bigger ship, Domina?" Orla asked sadly, offering me a small lagena of water. "This raft was a torture for you!"

"For my brother's future, I would not detest even the oar of Charon," I returned with my lips numb.

"If you don't rest, you will fall ill," Callistus added. "Let us take you to your grandma for a while."

"We've talked about it before." I shook my head. "When we're in Rome, Orla and Susannah will stay at Villa Claudiana, and the three of us will keep up to the market."

"Rachel is not almighty, Little Owl," Susannah spoke to me with gentleness. "Antipas' father, King Herod, died of exactly the same malady. No doctor could calm down his suffering."

"Tacete!" I exclaimed, barely getting to my feet. "There is no rest for me until I find the cure for Caesar. Dixi!"[235]

The maids silently went to a lower chamber for my travel bags. Callistus and Anicetus took me under both hands to help me disembark.

Like every market day, that Sunday was extremely busy. Merchants from all over the Empire were swarming around in the harbor. Their slaves were cautiously carrying motley pottery, rich cloth and precious stones to the carts, while vendors and craftsmen were arguing about trading places and prices.

"Find two litters," I asked Callistus, struggling with pain. "Maybe I'll take a sleep along the way."

The Greek nodded and disappeared into the tumult right away.

---

[235] (lat.) I have said all that I had to say and thus the argument is settled.

That morning, standing on my feet was heavier for me than marching. Anicetus reached out to take me to his arms, but I didn't allow him. When they finally carried a litter, I immediately fell asleep.

"Forum Romanum!"

When the voice of the carrier roused me, I was feeling better. Noticing my smile, Callistus sighed in relief. "Great is Hypnos!"

I replied with an ironic look.

"Princess, don't," the secretary said as he shook his head. "Who knows, perhaps they really exist."

Basilica Aemilia, the largest trading pavilion in Rome, looked like an anthill. On the south wing of the building, across the entrance, Rachel kept a visibly small store. However, small as it was, it was possible to buy and order anything a heart could wish – from cheap dishes to lavish textiles.

"Vey, Princess!" She noticed me. "What are you doing in the market at noon?"

"Please, be quiet." I hugged her. "I do not want to be recognized."

"Looks like someone started putting our plan into action?" Rachel winked at me as she showed me to the store – into a room that was divided from the counter with a wide sheet of Greek linen.

"I'm working on it," I replied confusedly. "But…"

"You are not doing well." The Jewess read me like an open book. "You need my help, don't you?"

"The good news is that the emperor adopted me," I whispered. "He gave me the keys to the palace and all freedoms of a Vestal virgin, so I guess now it will be much easier for me…"

Rachel was delighted. "So you outsmarted the old womanhater! A great start!"

"I'm looking for the cure for him," I finally explained. "Caesar is ill… with a bad disease for which there is no cure. Unless I do it in ten days, me and my brother will be killed."

"That is no good," the Jewess frowned. "But have no fear – I know who can help you."

I spread my arms to give her a big hug, but Rachel warned me.

"This man has been hiding in a basement on the Suburra for years, secretly healing people, mostly the poor and peregrines, from all the ailments – from phthisis to those bad ones. He doesn't take money; he just loves to cure. Nobody knows his name, so they call him the Cretan – because of his accent and crow-black hair."

"Why is he hiding?" I wondered. "Medicine is legal."

"I'll tell you," she whispered, "if you swear by your life, you will tell no one."

"I swear," I said readily.

The merchant looked at me, still a bit apprehensively, and, wrapping herself up in a palla, went on. "About a month ago, I came to the Cretan's to look for a cure for my swollen feet. He mixed me a balm of some herbs in no time, so I could walk like a girl. That day he was drunk like a fish, and, knowing my benevolence, he confessed to me…" She paused before continuing to tell the Cretan's story. "'I've always wanted to be a physician,' he told me. 'As a kid, on my native Crete, I often watched my grandfather gathering herbs, cooking balms and decoctions, and helped him. Alas, my influential father wanted me to be a soldier, so I went to Rome to join the legions of Germanicus.'"

I shivered as I heard that.

"How old is that Cretan?" I asked Rachel.

"I don't know," she shrugged. "With that long, untidy beard, he looks like he's in his fifties."

I tried to recall my father's companions in Magna Germania, but none of those soldiers, at least the remarkable ones, could resemble a Greek with the healing abilities.

"I bet you don't know him." Rachel shook her head. "It's been twenty and two years since he deserted."

"Did what?" I was stunned. It was the greatest shame for a Roman soldier to leave the battlefield. Deserters were punished by beheading, with no rights to be buried or mourned.

"An army hut!" Rachel grimaced. "The man escaped, for he refused to join the plot against your father, the commander."

"Tiberius!" I assumed. "He's always hated Father."

"And his son, Prince Castor," she continued. "As he heard about the riots and uprisings within the Rhine legions, he bribed Arminius and planned the Cherusci rebellion."

"Irrumator!"[236] I exclaimed. "Aunt Livilla was right poisoning him!"

The merchant pressed her index finger to her lips. When I fell silent, she went on. "Well, in some battle, Germanicus almost got murdered. The Germans attacked from the rear, and the only one soldier reacted in time."

"It was Cassius," I nodded, recalling the story.

"Cassius or not, he managed to repudiate all the barbarian scum, but one young heathen struck him –"

"I know where," I stopped her. "What does this have to do with the Cretan?"

"That man was there, too," the Jewess said. "His knowledge of the military medicine saved Cassius."

"Wait." I thought back to the Goat Lake. "A medic… from the Crete… Alcaeus!"

She goggled at me.

"Yes," her voice got quieter, "he told me his name in the end."

Thus, by the game of fate, Tiberius' life depended on a man who once refused to join his stratagem.

"And how do I find him?" I wondered.

"I'll explain you, but it won't be easy. Alcaeus is a deserter, and you are a princess. If they recognize him, they will kill you both."

"I have no choice." I sighed. "I need to see that man."

Rachel took a stylus, an ink bottle, and a piece of parchment from under the counter and outlined the way to Alcaeus' hiding place.

"Don't take the mishpahah,"[237] she said earnestly, referring to Anicetus and Callistus. "You'll scare him off and draw excessive attention."

I nodded and hugged her.

"God help you, birdie." Rachel kissed me on the forehead. "Go now."

---

[236] (lat.) Bastard!

[237] (hebr.; fig.) An extended family.

Leaving the store, I thought of Adonai – the Jewish god, but instead of profane thoughts or denial, I felt sudden peace within my heart.

He does exist, though. I looked up to the cloudless blue. *Someone must have created this world – the wildlife, the solar eclipse, and us, people… If Mithras is his foe, that god is good.*

My friends were waiting downstairs.

"Did she help you?" Callistus rubbed his eyes sleepily.

"Yes," I returned with a smile. "I have to go to Suburra – alone."

"You cannot," he protested. "Are you mad?"

"It's dangerous," Anicetus came up, closing the passageway. "We'll go together."

"If I take you, I will lose my chance," I said, going around him. "You will wait for me in Villa Claudiana."

"Ou!"[238] Callistus stood in front of me. "Suburra is a fertile spot for thugs and whores! This man is a deserter, he can kill you."

"Has anyone else but you heard our conversation?" I asked angrily.

"Certainly not." He calmed me down. "Only your Callistus has rabbit ears."

"To me, Alcaeus is not a deserter," I whispered. "But a man who saved Cassius. His escape was not a treachery, but an act of loyalty to his commander."

The secretary shrugged and pulled his companion by his robe to move aside.

"As you say, Princess. We will go to Lady Antonia."

"Epaino."[239] I pushed him gently with my elbow. "I gave you enough money to buy horses. You are not beggars to walk."

As the servants headed down the Via Nova, I noticed a free litter by the Temple of Cloacina.[240]

"Take me to Suburra!" I called out to the porters.

One of them, blonde-haired like a barbarian, came out with a mocking grin.

---

[238] (anc.gr.) No!

[239] (anc.gr.) Great!

[240] A goddess who presided over the Cloaca Maxima ("Greatest Drain"), the main trunk of the system of sewers in Rome.

"Doleo, baby girl, we only serve the upper class."

I realized that I had purposely put on Susannah's penula to look as unpretentious as possible. After I'd looked around to make sure nobody else was listening, I threw it away.

"Up from myself is only Caesar."

As the porters looked at me in astonishment, I took a pouch of aureuses out of my pocket and hurled it at the fair-haired man.

"Oh, Princess!" he exclaimed confusedly, gaping at the coins. "Please, forgive me! We will carry you to the Suburra, wait as long as you desire to stay, and take you back to the Carinae."

"I don't live there anymore." I smiled. "You'll take me to the Palatine."

"Wherever you wish, Your Highness…" said the other porter. "Agrippina?"

"Non." I took a comfortable sit inside a litter. "You have one more try."

"You're not Livilla," spoke the third. "I often see her on the square enjoying Seneca's orations."

"You're the youngest!" the blonde man concluded. "Julia Drusilla!"

"I am," I yawned, leaning against the pillow. "In my current life."

XXXVIII

"Suburra! Porta Argiletana!"

I opened my eyes. The blonde man stared at me over his shoulder.

"I wonder what Your Highness came do in this havoc."

I waved aside, and jumped out of the litter. Along the clivus Suburranus – a dirty and bumpy suburban street, stood long insulas lined up in a crooked row. Motley clothes were drying on the balconies, with the odors of cooking and cries of children spreading around.

"Wait for me here," I told the porters, and clumsily headed towards the highest and noisiest insula, half-shadowed by a large pine.

"Watch your foot, Princess."

Too preoccupied with the upcoming meeting with Alcaeus, I returned to the path with a curse, and… stepped into a big puddle of mud. "Deodamnatus!" I exclaimed, shaking my foot like a cat. The carriers began to giggle, and a passerby – a dumpy old woman, a bit hunched from carrying a heavy basket, spoke to me.

"Do you need help, child?"

Her kind and trustful eyes reminded me of Antonia. *This woman is old and sickly like my grandma… and she has no slaves to help her with the basket.*

"I'm looking for the Cretan… a physician," I replied, as I crumpled Rachel's drawing. "They told me he lives somewhere near."

"I'm just going to visit him," she nodded toward her hamper. "I'm bringing him some fruit and vegetables from my garden. He does not take money for him help, but people must eat something. This man saved half of Suburra from bad fevers."

"Can I carry it?" I asked her sympathetically, reaching out for a full basket. The old woman, pretty tired of long hiking and her own weight, gladly allowed me.

"Thank you, darling. I barely managed to do it from the Esquiline."

An old straw handle, sharp and rugged, scratched my palm. I tossed the basket over my shoulder as if nothing had happened and hid my hand behind my back.

"You are gentle like silk," the stranger noticed, "and you came here in a litter. You must be a noblewoman."

I didn't want to lie to her. The woman gave me an astonished look, and a slight bow. "Your Highness... I'm honored... I am Alfidia, a merchant."

"Great," I smiled. "I have a merchant friend. The rest of my companions are freedmen."

The old woman tapped me on my back and opened the wooden door of the insula.

"Here we are, Princess. Watch the stairs."

Through the cold, barely lit common corridor full of logs and dirty bowls, we slowly went down to the basement.

"Who is it?" I heard a male voice, hoarse with wine.

"It's me, Alfidia," my new acquaintance said. "And you must be drinking again."

"What I am doing is my business," Alcaeus retorted. "I hear by the steps that you're not coming alone."

"You have a patient." Alfidia led me into a room with an earthen floor and moldy walls. "Please, be nice."

Alcaeus, a middle-aged man with a sloppy look, sat at a desk full of herbs of multiple colors, bowls and scrolls, covered with writing. Behind him stood tiny furniture – a cane bed, a stove with surgical instruments on its slab, and a bookshelf.

"Don't say a word." The Cretan glanced at me. "You have a constant back pain; I can see it by the way you walk. With my miraculous bath salt, you will forget –"

"Easy, Celsus!"[241] the merchant admonished him, as she placed a basket on his bed. "Your guest is a noblewoman from the Palatine."

Alcaeus gave me a longer look, full of suspicion and curiosity, and said, "The daughter of Germanicus."

"How do you know?" I wondered. "Is it written on my forehead?"

"You look like Lady Julia Antonia," he answered, reaching out for a lagena with wine, "as if she was your mother."

---

[241] A Roman encyclopedist, known for his extant medical work, De Medicina, which is believed to be the only surviving section of a much larger encyclopedia.

"Benigne," I smiled, and came up closer to shake hands with him, according to the Greek tradition.

"Julia Drusilla… Longini."

The Cretan sighed, then took another sip, and gave me a slight bow.

"Have a sit, Your Highness. Feel like home."

"Excuse me, I must leave you now, Alfidia spoke hastily, and pointed at the basket. "Enjoy yourself, son."

The physician waved aside, full of displeasure with the sudden visitor. As the old woman was already by the door, I rushed to her and offered two small bags of gold.

"One is for you. Don't even try to protest. The other is for Rachel from Basilica Emilia."

"I know her," she said, astounded. "She is always cheerful and hardworking as a bee."

"I owe her more, but she's not taking an assarius,"[242] I smiled, "and now she has no choice."

"May all the gods bless you." The old woman hugged me and hurried out.

I turned to the Cretan.

"I know who you are. I need your help."

"They sold me, didn't they?" The man smiled bitterly. "They tattled around like two hens –"

"There is no better doctor in the whole Empire than you are," I interrupted him. "You saved your associate, Cassius Chaerea."

The man emptied his lagena, threw it on the bed, then shook the crumbs off his clothes, and said, "Yes, I remember him… Who else could fight like Hercules age eighteen? If the damn Germans had a fair fight, that shit would not have happened… They intentionally let some cock attack your father… The commander didn't even notice, and Chaerea rushed to save him, while the German bastard gave him a forbidden strike…"

---

[242] A bronze, and later copper, coin used during the Roman Republic and Roman Empire.

I shuddered and squinted, imagining the way I'd kill the scoundrel who hurt Cassius.

"Fortunately, the young jackass was a bit cross-eyed," he went on, as he read my sight. "In short, the wound was not that fatal… even, in extent, to his love life."

"To what extent?" I asked him, regardless of decorum for a Roman lady.

"I studied military injuries in the Greek handbooks. In most cases, such a wound causes infertility, but doesn't make the wounded sexless."

His words gave me relief… in an extent.

"But yet you didn't come to talk about Chaerea, did you?" His voice suddenly lost warmness.

"My life is in danger," I whispered.

Alcaeus shook his tousled head and shoved a backless chair for me to sit.

"What hurts?"

"It is about… the malady of Venus." I swallowed a lump. "It's Caesar."

"No, that's impossible." The Cretan laughed, as he got sober in an instant. "You're not asking me to cure him, are you?"

I raised my head to hide my eyes, already full of tears.

"I have no choice. If I don't find the cure, Tiberius will kill me and my brother."

"Ma ton kuna!" he exclaimed in a raucous voice, throwing the basket on the floor. "I am a deserter, Lady! Do you understand what you demand of me?"

I couldn't help myself weeping.

"Please, Alcaeus…" I murmured in Greek, tired and desperate. "Do it for the memory of Father… Your commander."

The Cretan came up and leaned over me, squatted in his chair.

"Euge! I will do my job, and let them punish me. But yet," he nodded at the hamper on the floor, "I'm sorry for those people. Who will help them when I'm gone?"

"You will not die, I promise." I stood up, wiping away my tears. "If someone recognize you, I will use my Vestal freedoms to absolve you of your guilt."

The Greek looked at me softer with a thankful bow, and moved aside shamefacedly.

"I... haven't had a bath for a long time. Excuse me, Princess, if I stink."

"Far less than Macro." I laughed nervously. "That one stinks like he was born of Cloacina."

"I heard, he's been promoted," he recalled, and started packing the dried herbs to the small patched bags. "But, who cares about Macro? Nature has given us the cure to all the ailments. If you have this," Alcaeus gestured at the table. "You are wealthier than Caesar."

"We'll put it all into the litter," I said, carefully picking the medical tools from the stove. "We ourselves will walk. Can you walk to the Palatine?"

"Are you joking, young lady?" The man laughed. "I used to be a soldier! The question is, how can *you* make your way to there in such condition?"

"I will have to," I replied, barely moving through the room. "To save my brother."

Alcaeus rummaged through the bunch of freshly picked plants, pulled out a long root of pungent smell, and spoke.

"Consider him already saved."

In the vestibule of Villa Claudiana, two fellow countrymen and secretaries – Actaeon and Callistus – had a heated debate about Alexander the Great.

"You wish," Callistus frowned. "I've read hundreds of stories about him! The king was not a stoic, but epicurean! He enjoyed good food, books, women, even, sometimes, men..."

"Shame on you!" Actaeon cried. "How dare you objurgate are a man of godly virtues! In the war time, he was sleeping in the poorest tent, sharing his bread and wine with all the soldiers, like they were his brothers! And his only love was the Bactrian princess..."

"Airy-fairy!" the imperial slave mocked. "Beside Roxana, he had other wives, dozens of favorites and some hetaeras!"

"Hairete!"[243] I smiled from the doorstep, and the two of them, finally noticing that I was coming, ran to meet me.

"We were just talking," Callistus was blushing.

---

[243] (anc.gr.) Hello!

"Yes, I heard it," I replied, taking Actaeon by the hand. "I think you both are right."

"You did it, Princess!" the freedman rejoiced, as Alcaeus followed me inside.

"Friends, meet the –" I began to introduce the medic, but he interrupted me.

"Call me the Cretan."

"Yet another Greek!" Callistus bowed to greet him. "As our late Photiki would have said."

"Take our guest to the bathroom," I ordered the secretary. "And ask Orla for some better clothes for him."

"With pleasure," he returned vigorously, leading the medic toward the peristyle. "I'm glad you're fine, Your Highness!"

"How is Grandma?" I turned to Actaeon.

"She's been talking about you all the time." He sighed. "She'll be delighted if you spend a few days here."

With all my heart I wanted to embrace Antonia, but I could barely stand straight from tiredness and worry, and, instead of long-awaited rest, I thought of Caesar's moans and pains.

"I'm going back tomorrow. Caesar might be an old wolf, but he is ill and he relies on me."

Actaeon gave me a respectful nod.

"And now," I smiled, "you'll cook me something edible. I'm hungry like an Old Wolf's daughter."

XXXIX

The dawn was rising over Misenum. The sleepy night was slowly fading into the dark sea, dragging a gray train of mist across the sandy shore. The song of crickets, quite and mysterious, were changing into wild and cheerful voices of the seagulls.

I was waiting for the morning on the terrace, surrounded by the ivory reliefs and lush, motley flowers. As I put aside the unread scroll, I curled my tired legs on the sitting place, wishing I could get lost in the noise of sea waves.

I was waiting for the morning and the news from the imperial cubicle…

"Haire!"

I turned around. Callistus, as always came around silently.

"How's the Wolf?" I wondered, moving up so he could sit by me.

"Good." The Greek smiled. "Sleeping like a lamb. The Cretan in the real warlock."

I could feel the stone fell off my heart, as heavy as the world itself.

"What did he give him?"

"He made a third of pythos[244] of some kind of balm with the smell so strong, that I had to ventilate the room." He told, gesticulating lively. "Then, he told the slaves to change the bedclothes, and treated Caesar to some bitter drink, that lessened the pain, so he could fall asleep."

"So he didn't throw small amphorae at him?" I stretched and tossed my cotton palla over my shoulder.

"Never," My friend chuckled. "He was nice and listened to his medic."

"If only he knew who his physician is…" I sighed. "One day, he will find out…"

"For now, he's happy," Callistus concluded. "The Cretan even said there is hope for the complete recovery."

I wondered in my heart what would have happened if Tiberius was healed. Caligula's fate wasn't stable as long as our cousin Gemellus was here. It was hard to believe that our foster-father would feel something noble like the gratitude, and let us be.

---

[244] A Greek (Minoan Cretan) bowl or vase.

"Macro seems to play a double game," I remembered the Praetorian commander. "What's he waiting for? Why not kill… "

"Princess!" Callistus squeezed my hand slightly. "I know, you're not yourself with tiredness and worries about Prince… I know, your heart is reckless like a wildfire, but, please, don't forget where you reside."

"You're right." I tapped him on his hand. "What should I do?"

The cunning smile rose on his delicate, clean-shaven face.

"Didn't you open your gift, Princess?"

I looked at the scroll I found on my desk last night, mistaken for one of the Jewish books, Susannah converted for me.

"Felix Dies Natalis!"[245] the Greek sang cheerfully. "Don't ask me where I found it, and be careful where you leave it."

"Epaino, filo mu." I kissed him on the cheek. "Even *I* have forgotten."

"Twenty years…" he said dreamily. "The best age for a woman."

"You are not old either," I replied.

"For men, it's different," he smiled. "We, Greeks, are at the full strength in our forties."

I waved aside, unrolled the parchment book, embellished with a wide red ribbon, and began to read in Greek.

"Alexander and the Unclean Nation."

"I know about your researching," the secretary whispered, moving up closer. "So does Caesar."

"What?!" I cried out. "Did *you* tell him?"

"No, not me." He shook his head. "Thrasyllus, namely the Sun Priest, had a vision shortly before you arrived to the Capri. The old fool claimed, that, at the sacrifice, he saw Mithras himself, demanding of us all to do away with Libitina who dared to declare war to his children."

I looked back on the day of my infamous betrothal, and I heard unpleasant voice of the astrologer, warning Tiberius about the Death, who was his guest now.

---

[245] (lat.) Happy Birthday!

"Why did Thrasyllus kill himself?" I asked him quietly.

"Our Caesar, for an unknown reason, did not let them hurt you. The astrologer considered that the treason to their god, and cut his veins."

I shivered, wondering, why my great-uncle spared me. Was it really because of the behoof I gave him, spying on his fellow Mithraists?

"Well, maybe the Old Wolf is sick and tired of what he is," I thought aloud. "He should be scared of something or… he is repenting."

"He?! I don't believe it," Callistus retorted. "I would say, there is another Power, even higher than the god he worships… It has saved you, Princess."

"Adonai," I said without thinking. "The Creator."

The secretary smiled at me with curiosity.

"Opa-opa! Someone is converting to a new religion, or it just seems so?"

"Not yet," I answered. "But, to me, this god seems most convincing… different from other deities."

"He also worshipped Him," Callistus touched the manuscript, as he raised to his feet. "King Alexander."

That news did not surprise me. I had read about Alexander's pilgrimage to Jerusalem – the only place he entered as a friend, but not a conqueror. The Jewish ruler and the priests, yet intolerant to foreigners, admired the King's bravery, and recognized in him the Messenger of God. They blessed him for his wisdom and good deeds, and Alexander wished to bow to their god, Adonai. It was said, that the great king will only bend his knee to the most powerful deity… Of course, that gesture was disliked by Mithras.

"So he killed the Macedonian…" I went on, gathering the facts. "His evil children did… in Babylon, the capital of lies and wickedness. King Alexander conquered the whole world, but failed to save it from the poison of the Sun god…"

"Study it," Callistus interrupted me. "And you'll find out how to keep up the King's struggle."

"Me?!" I smiled, imitating lifting of the sword. "Do I look like Hippolyta[246] to you?"

---

[246] In Classical Greek mythology – the Amazonian queen, the daughter of the god of war.

Callistus smiled slightly, and said earnestly.

"This war is not about the sword, Your Highness. Your weapon is a quill, and your shield is a book."

I looked at him thoughtfully, recalling my childish attempts to write a Greek-like drama, and sighed deeply.

"No one cares about my stupid scribbling."

"You are wrong," Callistus retorted sharply. "I read all your notes. You are extremely talented."

"How dare you rummage in my room?" I exclaimed angrily. "You thief!"

"It's called – the Imperial secretary." He retorted. "It's my duty".

Sometimes, by nights, in the light of a small lamp, I wrote short poems and noted my thoughts – about Gaius, Cassius or recently read books. These notes, so naïve and chaotic, I wanted to keep to myself, and never in my life expected someone else to read them.

"Singnomin ehe,"[247] he went on, making a sad face. "Aren't you doing the same thing as the Imperial advisor?"

"Yes, I am." I nodded, giving up my anger. "We are both spies in the Old Wolf's service. As for my writings, I should thank you for the compliment, although I personally doubt its objectivity."

The Greek rolled his eyes tiredly and turned away to leave.

"I thought Zaleukos didn't die in vain."

My teacher's name shook me like a cold wave.

"He was my father," he said by the door. "Together we were taken from the Lesbos, when your sister Livilla was born. Lord Germanicus chose Zaleukos to be your brothers' teacher, while I was sent to the Capri."

"Come back!" I begged him, bewildered.

The Greek heard me.

"I didn't know that," I explained, following him. "I am sorry, Callistus."

---

[247] (anc.gr.) I am sorry.

"And I am not," he answered. "In my homeland, we were slaves of the Roman beast, who cut my pregnant mother on my eyes."

I felt the sudden vertigo, and turned to my still warm bench. The tears had overflowed me.

"You know what *they* can do to us." He finished, reaching out to me. "Calm down. There is no use in crying."

I fixed his disobedient black curls, and opened my new book.

"With God's help," I read in myself. *"The King defeated the violent Darius and ruled in the Mesopotamia. As he built the biggest empire in the world, the son of Philip and Olympia went around the whole plain, down to the Sun-sea. There he met unclean and ugly people – the descendants of the Serpent..."*

"I'll tell the boys to bring you breakfast," Callistus said hastily. "The cook made a delicious..."

"I will do it," I decided, grabbing him by the edge of his toga, "I will write a drama to unveil our enemies. It's time to tell the truth about what they are and what they do for centuries."

"Aristos!"[248] Callistus clapped his hands with joy. "Latreuo se!"[249]

"I'll gather all the necessary facts," I said, already focused on the goal. "I'll call for the allies to ask them for advice. It seems that art and war are fated to make love, aren't they?"

"Now you get it." The Greek winked at me. "So, I don't know which goddess can compare to you. You are not insensitive like *Pallas*, nor foolish like *Cypris*."

"Perhaps, I'm Libitina?" I giggled, reaching out to him with fingers outstretched. "A tough girl from the Esquiline."

Callistus, with enthusiasm of an actor, expressed some fearful trembling, and replied, "Sooner or later, the Old Wolf will die, so you would go to the Esquiline."

As I got the message, I cheered up and sent him for my breakfast.

---

[248] (anc.gr.) Well done!
[249] (anc.gr.) I adore you!

However, I did not manage to finish my meal. Ill-tempered Baldwin entered without knocking, murmuring, "Caesar is expecting you in the throne room, Your Highness."

I changed into a clean stola and stood before him – neat and smiling, just as it was appropriate for the stepdaughter of the emperor. Despite Callistus' prognosis, the Old Wolf looked better, acting like he was immortal.

"Optime factum, neptis!"[250] he spoke out from his gilded seat, raised beneath a huge blind arcade. "Pains are fading, wounds are healing... So, I wonder which gods help you find that wizard."

"Does it matter?" I replied with a well-rehearsed smile. "It only matters that you're getting well, my emperor."

"Ask me for anything you wish," Tiberius went on even more vigorously. "Of course, do not be insolent."

I thought about marriage with Chaerea – real marriage, and lifelong protection for Caligula, but at one moment I remember what I promised to my friend.

"I beg you to free Callistus," I answered.

Caesar burst out laughing like a madman, followed by the guards behind his back.

"Oh, if you want it so, *you* let him go." He smiled. "I'm giving you my secretary for your birthday."

---

[250] (lat.) Well done!

XL

AD 36

"When the king saw the uncleanness of the Serpent tribe, he felt disgusted. Namely, they ate all kinds of unclean animals, dead flesh, aborted and premature babies. And they did not bury their dead, but ate them, too... The hero feared they could plunder the entire earth, so he prayed to Adonai, then gathered them all together, and banished all the way to the edge of the North...

As Alexander praised the God again, Adonai heard his prayer, and commanded the two huge bergs to coalesce into an endless wall... And the king made the giant gate of divine steel, which couldn't be broken down even with iron nor melted with fire. As the vile people knew magic of the Ancient Serpent, God made the gate resistant even to their charms. Thus, none of them could break out and escape.

Alas, the Macedonian didn't know that, in the East, dispersed throughout many countries, there remained the number of their kinsmen — children of the Serpent's daughter. Their father gave them power to bring the king down, to destroy his lineage, and to rule the world... And at the end of time, these evil rulers will invent the way to tear down the wall, so the Unclean nation will be free to break into the Holy Land."

As I finished reading the legend I had learnt almost by heart, I put the scroll aside and stretched on the bed of wool and feather.

When we know who the foe is, I thought in a half-sleep, *And what his strategy is, we'll find out how to... beat him.*

"Or die trying," the familiar voice rang inside my head, like on the night of Gaius' wedding. I rose up and shook my head to drive the sleep away, recalling my peculiar behavior since age nine.

"Am I mad?" I questioned my reflection in the mirror. "There's another voice within me, and when I am talking, I don't think, just speak my mind..." This time, looking at the image in the polished glass – my features blurred due to my nearsightedness – I didn't feel dissatisfied with my appearance. On the contrary, I stared at my reflection as if she enchanted me. A pale face, framed in copper-red hair finally made me feel peculiarly beautiful.

"Quisnam sum?"[251] I went on talking to the mirror, and, as I squinted slightly, noticed in my eyes a scarlet flash, more fervent than wildfire.

"Impossibile est!"[252] I whispered, too surprised to notice Susannah entering.

"Quid est impossibile, ulula?"[253] she asked, inadvertently scaring me.

"Why don't you knock?" I shouted, covering myself in a warm blanket.

"Da mihi veniam,"[254] the nursemaid said, embarrassed. "There's a woman waiting in the vestibule. She's asking for the emperor's reception."

"What's a woman?" I pondered. Like any advisor, I knew the schedule of the client and guest visits a couple of months in advance.

"Judging from her accent and attire, she is my fellow countrywoman." Susannah went on, no less surprised than me.

"The Jewess travels alone to Campania to see Tiberius…" I shook my head in disbelief. "Absurd!"

"Anicetus mentioned a fellow who escorted her to the gate, and ran away, scared of the guardsmen," she remembered, smiling.

"Male cowardice is not a wonder," I waved aside and got out of bed. "The question is – why didn't any of those roosters notify me?"

"I don't know." Susannah shrugged. "But I have noticed that her language is not vulgar… In our homeland, only noblewomen and famosae[255] get that proper education."

"Well, a noblewoman wouldn't have come to Caesar without an invitation or announcement, and definitely better be escorted," I concluded, taking off my nightgown. "As for courtesans, everyone knows that my great-uncle prefers men…"

The nursemaid, trying to restrain her laughter, helped me put my festal stola on, and started combing me.

"Just make a ponytail," I hurried her. "I've never seen a real prostitute."

---

[251] (lat.) Who am I?
[252] (lat.) This is impossible!
[253] (lat.) What is impossible, Little Owl?
[254] (lat.) Forgive me.
[255] (lat.) Courtesans.

Crossing the atrium, I noticed Stella, a sinewy officer of the Praetorians, one of the followers of Macro.

"Arruntius," I called him by the nomen gentile,[256] "I heard we have an uninvited guest."

"Aye, Princess," he replied and stood still. "I've just headed to the peristyle to let you know."

"What took you so long, officer?" I frowned. "As far as I'm concerned, this woman has been waiting for a while."

Stella looked at me with his lips twisted and eyebrows moved closer together and spoke. "The Guard had to question who she is, where she comes from, and for what reason."

"So? What have you found out?" I asked, walking through the prothyron, trying to hear voices from the vestibule.

"Her name is Mary; she came right from Jerusalem," Stella replied with a wry smile. "She wants to stand before Caesar to sew Pontius Pilate, the governor of Judea."

Though for a barely emotional Stella this visit seemed rather bizarre, I was feeling the same tremor I experienced during the solar eclipse.

"It's her right," I said without thinking, making the guardsman even more confused.

The foreigner I found on the janitor's bench was nothing like a courtesan, nor a rich woman. She was dressed very modestly – a thick himation[257] over a long blue chiton,[258] her head covered with a travelling hood. In her hands, she was holding a braided basket, covered with a colorful kerchief.

Five guardsmen were surrounding her like an army edging round the spoils of war. One by one, they mocked her, asking why she's not afraid of them. The woman silently observed them with her wise dark eyes.

"What's going on here?" I spoke out.

---

[256] A name designating a Roman citizen as a member of a particular gens; a gentile name.
[257] A Greek-fashion mantle or wrap.
[258] A simple tunic garment of lighter linen.

The guard fell silent, until their tribune, Arrecinus Clemens, said self-confidently, "This Jewess," he gestured to the stranger, "dared to come to the palace without invitation, seeking the Exalted One's reception."

"I know that." I stopped him with my hand raised. "Who let you treat his clients like you're a barbarian?"

"Your Highness," Clemens said, confused, "it's my duty as the bodyguard –"

"Silentium!" I interrupted him. "Where's Macro?"

The tribune goggled up his catlike eyes and pushed Aquila with his elbow.

"He has one this morning with the prince," the centurion reported nervously. "In some government affairs."

"I see," I stopped him queasily. "Macro is taking the heir to the throne to some brothel."

As the guardsmen didn't deny it, I addressed to Susannah, still waiting at the entrance door.

"Please, take our guest to the tablinum. *I* will receive her."

The nursemaid asked the foreigner to join her to the atrium.

"What are you doing, Princess?" Clemens' face got red. "What if that woman is a spy or… witch? She's carrying a basket full of eggs!"

"Don't worry, Clemens." I smiled. "No one can recognize a spy better than another spy. And as for witches… You are not an old Suburran woman to believe in them, aren't you?"

The officer gave me an obstinate look, while the other four Praetorians barely abstained from laughter.

"Now, everyone go back on duty," I said calmly and hurried to the tablinum.

"Shlom lekh,"[259] I greeted the stranger. "I am Julia Drusilla, daughter of the emperor. I hope your journey has been peaceful."

"Pax tibi, Princepessa," she replied politely, with a graceful bow. "My name is Mary bat Simon. I am a native of Galilean Magdala, though residing in my brother's house

---

[259] (aram.) Peace be upon you.

in Bethany. My journey was no easy, but, thanks God, I'm here to see a person favorable to the populace and foreigners."

I was stunned. She talked of me like someone who had known me, and the way she looked was even more astonishing. Her beauty matched young women of my sisters' age, but her eyes reflected the experience and profundity of an old woman.

"Please, have a sit." I offered her a bench, reserved for the important guests, promptly recalling latest lectures on foreign policy Callistus gave me.

"Let's talk about the purpose of your visit," I went on. "Pontius Pilate has been performing his duty for a longer period than any other governor alive. This means, that both the people and the emperor approve his service. There have been no complaints against him in the province, nor beyond it. What are you accusing him of, Magdalene?"[260]

"Your Highness, everything you say is true." Mary replied. "Lord Governor once was an honest man; he treated all the citizens equally fair, disregarding their status and origins. Still, about three years ago, on the third day of the month you call *aprilis*, Pontius Pilate, persuaded by Herod Antipas and the High priest of Judea, condemned to death an innocent man."

Susannah winced, as she heard Antipas' name.

"It's a serious accusation," I replied, quite stunned. "Why would Pilate, a prominent procurator, fall under the influence of vassal officials and violate Ius Romanorum?"[261]

Mary sighed heavily and embraced her basket, like a child hugging a toy.

"Oh, Princess... Just as a crime profanes the holiest of lands, malice and greed had turned *the chosen ones* into butchers and traitors."

Sadness in her voice was intertwined with faith and hope as well, so desperately screaming through her very being. I recalled another woman of such fervent and unbroken spirit – Rachel. In that state of mixed emotions, I could almost hear the merchant's voice.

---

[260] Mary's epithet Magdalene means that she came from Magdala, a fishing town on the western shore of the Sea of Galilee. Peregrines of Rome were often given an agnomen of their birthplace.
[261] (lat.) Roman Law.

"Since Jerusalem has fallen under the influence of liars, we are not allowed to think at all."

"The Serpent tribe!" I recalled in my mind. "They put to death a man who dared to rebel against their ruler, Mithras!"

"Mary," I asked the guest kindly. "Tell me more about the convict."

The woman smiled slightly and spoke in a gentle tone.

"He healed the sick, raised the dead, cleansed those with leprosy, and drove out demons... Many are His miracles to turn His people to the Truth of God, but we have been unworthy of salvation..."

I caught myself listening to that woman enthusiastically. She was so bold to cross the Mediterranean, to fight the injustice they inflict on her spiritual teacher named Jesus.

"He talked of faithfulness and generosity," Mary went on, with the exalted confidence. "He taught us all the virtues that glorify God, and make a man himself much happier and nobler. The Jews followed Jesus, as they saw in Him the God embodied... Foreigners loved him too, for He has healed a lot of heathens. Only the haughty Judean priests, blinded by envy, wished Him dead... By the lies and slander, they succeed to turn our people against Jesus. So the Jews themselves turned back on their Savior and let Pilate crucify Him."

Terrified by the ungratefulness of Mary's fellow countrymen, I asked her for the names of the main culprits.

"Caiaphas the High priest, and Hananus, his father-in-law," Magdalene replied.

"And Antipas?" Susannah interjected. "I mean the Galilean and Perean tetrarch."

"He gladly supported them." The guest shrugged. "The crimes were no strange to him. A year earlier, for his own fun, Antipas sent to death Yoḥanan, a great preacher and a prophet."

"That's not possible!" the nursemaid objected. "He would never kill... "

"Susannah!" I spoke out sternly. "Don't you have some work in the culina?"[262]

She left quietly, and I started analyzing Mary's words thoughtfully.

---

[262] (lat.) A kitchen.

"The punishment of death requires a big guilt." I sighed, leaning against the back of Caesar's chair. My head was aching with tension.

"Three of them," Mary went on. "They accused Jesus before Pilate of blasphemy and disrespect for Caesar."

"I'm not a jurist," I said, rubbing my temples. "But my husband, Consul-suffect, sometimes read the Code of Law even at dinner, so I, nolens volens, learned some useful things, too. Primo, a public insult of the Imperial Majesty requires the judgment of Tiberius himself, but not the governor or client ruler."

"Are you alright, Your Highness?" she suddenly asked, noticing my anxiety.

"I will be." I shook my head.

Magdalene put her basket on the floor, and came up to my chair.

"May I?"

I nodded confusedly, and, as I closed my eyes I sensed her soft, warm palm on my forehead. Mild shivers went through my body, and I felt relaxed as if I was dreaming.

"Do you believe that He, who descended from Heaven," I heard Mary's voice. "And gave His life for us – would heal you, too?"

I opened my eyes and looked at her closely. The young preacher radiated so much kindness, that it was no hard to trust her.

"I believe!" I spoke without thinking.

In a flash, my ache and tiredness completely faded. Amazed, I jumped to my feet slightly, and finally free from any discomfort, I clapped my hands with joy.

"Faith and good deeds," she explained to me. "That is all that God expects of us."

"For many people it's too much." I sighed, recalling some of my acquaintances. "It seems, the World has consciously chosen evil."

In Mary's glance, so pure and lucid, I could read the answer.

"You are not with the many."

That feeling was more than enough to make all my doubts disappear without a trace, but that was not the end of the surprises.

"Our God neither hates, nor humiliates women," Discerning Magdalene went on. "He loves all people equally, and he is always ready to forgive and save all those, who praise Him."

She was once married to a nobleman, a kinsman of Queen Malthace.[263] This marriage was unhappy, for her husband deceived and abused his young wife. One day, he even threw her out of the house, claiming she was useless and infertile. Desperation, cold and hunger let Mary astray, turning a young virtuous girl to a courtesan. Her evil husband, wishing to destroy her, called the relatives and priests to judge her.

"They wanted to stone me – as a harlot, an adulteress," she told me. "But Jesus did not let them harm me. He reminded wicked men their own misdeeds, so they were too ashamed to throw the stone, and left. I was forgiven, so I knelt before the Savior asking him to let me follow Him."

While I was still listening to her story, determined to help Mary, she removed the kerchief from the basket. What I saw inside were… chicken eggs, arranged in a circle and red like blood.

"Jesus has risen!" Magdalene smiled, gesturing toward the deep red. "Death is dead!"

I took the egg to have a better look, and recollected the solar eclipse, and the earthquake, and even my nightdream.

"When did you say they had Him executed?" I asked distraughtly. "How?"

Her answer was obvious – on Friday, the third day of April, the year seven hundred and eighty-sixth.[264] Everything I saw and heard – then and now – was neither set of circumstanced, nor fraud. The guilt of Pilate, Antipas and the clergy was beyond my doubt, for they chose for Jesus the worst punishment called crucifixion. By our Law, that kind of death was intended for murderers.

"Callistus!" I exclaimed with double clasp, forgetting that he was no longer a slave, not even Caesar's favorite.

Instead of Callistus I saw Helicon. A well-educated and bashful Egyptian was appointed as the Imperial secretary on the day my friend was freed.

"We have an important guest," I addressed the secretary. "She is noble, so is the purpose of her visit. I want you to introduce her to Caesar at tomorrow's salutatio."

Helicon looked at Mary suspiciously.

---

[263] King Herod's fourth wife and mother of his favorite son Antipas.
[264] The ancient Romans counted the time since the founding of Rome. This is about the 33rd year before new era

"Pontius Pilate misused his position," I explained. "He prejudged an innocent man, and hushed it up."

The Egyptian with his eyes wide in astonishment wondered if I was serious.

"I wouldn't make a joke about the death penalty," I said sharply. "Especially not with Caesar."

"Please, forgive me, Princess." Helicon spoke nervously. "I'll report to Divus straight away."

"No rush." I stopped him and turned to the guest. "Lady Mary has traveled half the world, and it would be appropriate to take our guest to the guest chambers."

"As you say," the secretary nodded, still a bit uncertain, as Magdalene thanked me for the concern.

"And then," I recalled Mary's companion. "Send the guards to the port to find the other guest, who seems to have got lost… What is his name?"

"David, a merchant." Magdalene smiled. "He helped me sail here safe."

By the will of Adonai, or, as many would say, by set of circumstances, it was David, who secretly spread the truth about our enemies together with Rachel.

XLI

Magdalene's lawsuit against Pilate was satisfied… generally. After he'd heard the whole story without any question or skepticism, Tiberius thanked the "young lady" for a "useful report" and promised that justice would be served with the culprits punished.

"I gave the arrest warrant of Pontius Pilate as well as both Pharisee[265] dogs." The emperor told me at dinner. "Iustitia regnorum fundamentum.[266] Nullum crimen, nulla poena sine lege.[267] If I was to crucify all fools who call themselves gods or high kings, whole of the Senate would be hanged."

"Verum est,"[268] I smiled. "And what about Antipas? What will be with him?"

Tiberius replied indignantly.

"Nothing."

"May I ask – why?" I gave him a rehearsed cute smile.

Caesar sighed ill-temperedly, signaling to servants to leave the triclinium.

"Do you remember your first task, Drusilla?"

I strained. He meant my eavesdropping in Curia.

"You were prudent enough to hide some things from me," Tiberius went on, uttering word by word. "You have your own advisors, just like Cleopatra, but you keep on asking foolish questions."

This time, my rebel inner voice was silent. I thought that justifying my own self would make me weak, and flattery would make me cowardly.

"At last you stop butting me," he said ironically. "There's a hope for you, my dear."

With a smiling nod, I put my empty plate away just like the old man did a while ago. The next thing he questioned me was rather unexpected.

---

[265] The members of an ancient Jewish sect, distinguished by strict observance of the traditional and written law, and commonly held to have pretensions to superior sanctity.

[266] (lat.) Justice is the foundation of the rule.

[267] (lat.) One cannot be punished for doing something that is not prohibited by Law.

[268] (lat.) It's true.

"Do you know, cara neptis, who is the true ruler of the world?"

"Alea jacta est."[269] I remembered a saying of Julius Caesar and answered sincerely. "The night, when Piso killed my father, I would say – it's you, my Emperor. However, the day in the Senate changed my mind."

Tiberius, by a habit, made an angry face, but then, with respect to my honesty, he nodded.

"Since the world began," he explained firmly, with a note of disappointment. "Everything is in the hands of Mithras' sons – the ancestors of Artabanus."

"They would like us to think so, in fact." I couldn't help correcting him. "That miserable race achieved their power by deceit."

"I've heard that story before," the old man laughed. "From your new friend from Galilee. Please spare me Jewish tales of the good god and the evil one."

"Da mihi veniam." I put his favorite sweet smile back to my face.

"But, as you noticed," he went on. "My influence in Rome is limited. Our Empire, just like every major realm, except of Parthia, is ruled by shadow leaders."

The ominous pact between Rome and Parthia was made back in the time of the Old Caesar – behind his back. Aware that the noble warlord would never accept the bloody cult of Mithras, Parthian king Mithridates decided to bribe his young heir. Octavian, already yearning for more power, instantly agreed to worship Mithras and to murder his right-minded uncle. With the help of the Parthians there was a true spectacle arranged around the ruler's fall. Octavian successfully performed the role of a bereaved nephew and a righteous avenger.

"The dictator was not killed by Brutus," Tiberius said, quite appalled by his own frankness. "Longinus, Decimus, and Brutus were just pawns, who did the dirty work and then got victimized as culprits."

"The history we know is a fraud." I thought out loud, reviving in my mind last days with Zaleukos.

"Possibly maybe." The emperor reached for a glass of wine, despite Alcaeus' recommendations. "Vespasian and Sabinus don't tire to spread the cult of Mithras, to

---

[269] (lat.) The die is cast. Here: There is no going back.

control as many men as possible. They use the myth of the Roman supremacy and all the tosh our people want to hear and to believe in."

Vespasian… Neither Antonia, nor Callistus knew why exactly that thickset, balding tribune had been chosen as a deputy of Artabanus. Well, the answer Caesar gave me was quite logical.

"The damn Flavians, whose name means "gold" in some barbarian language," My great-uncle raised his goblet grimly. "Are some far descendants of the damn Mesopotamian ruling dynasty. The Kings of Parthia believe they are the offspring of Mithras himself, and share their power only with their relatives in blood – like, for example, there were Seleucids and Ptolemeians."[270]

"Were they shadow rulers, too?" I asked, familiar with Hellenic history since childhood.

"The Diadochi?" Tiberius sneered. "They deceitfully killed their king, Alexander, by dragging him to a whirlpool of debauchery, wine, and gamble."

"Cleopatra was a Ptolemeian," I recalled. "Even so she rebelled against her own kin to protect the Egyptians… I mean, not all the rulers were obedient to the evil."

"There is a bad black sheep in every herd," Caesar replied with a slight tone of a narrator. "And, a good, white crow in every flock. A black sheep infestates whole of her drove, a shepherd and, sometimes, a wolf; while a poor white crow is doomed to be thrown out or pecked to death by other birds. The same is with us, people, cara neptis, so I chose the easier path."

Such frankness tempted me to give him everything the tyrants didn't deserve at all – a pity, understanding and… forgiveness.

"The Herodians are even closer kin to Artabanus than the Flavians," he spoke apathetically, gesturing for more wine. "If I dare to raise my hand against Antipas, Parthians will come for us and level Rome to the damn ground."

"Your Majesty," I asked him, stunned by his unprecedented honesty. "Why are you telling me all that?"

Tiberius unclasped his toga, scratching the healing wounds on his neck and chest.

---

[270] The Diadochi (Ptolemy, Seleucus and Antigonus) were the rival generals, families, and friends of Alexander the Great who fought for control over his empire after his death.

"I don't regret a thing I did, nor would I like to be a better person, but… I must admit, I hate these eastern faggots more than your sick Antonian temper."

"Caesar," I sighed heavily. "I really appreciate… "

"I know." He interrupted me. "You are as good as gold, and I won't be the bastard who will do away with you. Moreover," I could hear a harsh tone in his voice. "I'll keep you safe as long as I'm alive, but only if you grow up and quit playing Cleopatra!"

"I don't regret a thing I did," I echoed the emperor's words in response. "Nor would I like to be a better person."

Caesar rolled his eyes and desperately waved aside.

"Get out."

I left the dining room with mere relief, and headed outside for some fresh air.

With relief, I exited the dining room and headed outside for some fresh air. In the atrium I met Alcaeus, Callistus and merchant David.

"Are you alive?" The freedman asked me with a smile.

"I hope so," I said wittily. "He babbled me like I was a young man."

"Don't trust Tiberius," he warned me with an index finger, "The wolf changes his coat…"

"But not its nature." I finished the famous proverb and addressed to all the three. "What was the talk about?"

"There is news." Callistus suddenly got earnest. "Junia Claudilla is expecting a young prince. Next month, on his birthday, the heir is arranging a feast for the family."

"I'm glad," I smiled. "I hope, the little shrew will finally leave me alone."

"She will." The Cretan joined the conversation, like he was familiar with 'enemies-in-law' relations. "Now she's happy, so she'll brood her eggs quietly."

Everyone, even the shamefaced Jew, burst into giggles.

"You're good." I tapped him on the shoulder, and, as I noticed some disturbance in his glance, I asked.

"How are you, fellow?"

"Princess," David spoke, "Magdalene sailed back at dawn."

"I wish her a safe trip," I replied, a little sad that I didn't manage to see her off properly. "And you? You're keeping up to Rome, aren't you?"

"I would like to…" He looked at me worriedly. "But I can't… It's dangerous."

"They are hunting poor David for the secret writings," Callistus explained to me in a whisper. "Everywhere."

"That sounds familiar to me," Alcaeus sighed. "Fortunately, I am safe beside Her Highness."

I came up to the merchant and took his hand to let him know I was his friend.

"What a person would I be not to give shelter to a Rachel's friend?"

Alcaeus and Callistus nodded approvingly, pulling a Jew by the sleeves to calm him down.

"I can be your servant, if you wish." He bowed to me gratefully.

"Don't worry," I straightened his back slightly. "I'll find a suitable job for you."

"Now we are an army," Callistus concluded, looking at me slyly. "Still, with all due respect, Your Highness, we need a commander… of a stronger gender."

His allusion made my cheeks blush.

"I agree," I smiled confusedly, looking up at the wall. "I think I should visit my Grandma… Let's say, when my brother's birthday feast is over."

"Princess," the Cretan brought me back to reality, pointing toward the hall. "There is something else you should know."

Pleasant chills in my body suddenly gave way to anxiety, as I heard Baldwin's repellent voice from the tablinum.

"The German…" Alcaeus whispered through his teeth. "I recognized him."

XLII

"I've been looking round him for three years." The physician clenched his fists. "I asked myself why his muzzle seems so familiar."

I didn't need an explanation to get what he meant.

"Are you sure?" I looked at him, feeling anger closing in.

Alcaeus nodded in agreement.

"He's got old, learned some Latin, dressed himself like a pornos,[271] but still acts like a savage cad."

A German viper, who meanly wounded my beloved man with a stroke, lawless even for his fellow barbarians, ended up in a palace instead of a ditch he deserved.

"Callistus," I half-turned to my friend, barely holding back my irritation. "Take David to the guest room, and bring me Anicetus."

"What are you up to, Princess?" he asked worriedly.

Without a word, I gave him a vexed look I learned from Tiberius, and Callistus rushed to the peristyle, pulling the muddled Jew by the hand.

Meanwhile, still arguing with my servants, the nomenclator walked out of the study, poking his snub nose into a client list.

"By Loki!"[272] He muttered with an effeminate move. "There're no greater morons than the Greeks!"

"Fuck you and all your gods!" I thought out loud.

The German didn't notice me, and walked on to the nymphaeum, growling into his beard about the Achaean laziness.

"I understand what you might feel, Your Highness." Alcaeus leaned over me. "I can kill him for you, if you wish."

"Not you," I replied. "I can't put you at risk. We have Callistus to trap the rascal, and Anicetus to slay him."

---

[271] (anc.gr.) A male prostitute.

[272] A wily trickster god of Germanic mythology.

"It's not their first time, is it?" The physician recollected what I told him of the tragedy on the Capri. "If the dog who killed a cookmaid was thrown off a cliff, I am afraid to guess what awaits the German nit."

"I'm not a savage, filo mu." I shook my head. "Yet, I will watch him dying."

Alcaeus smiled at me amazed, and said quietly, "Only a moron could marry such a woman to a weakling in a white toga."

The moment wasn't right for joking, but I laughed.

"De facto I am separated from Longinus, though lawfully I still share his name."

"The Law is made to be broken." The physician winked. "You know what I mean."

"My Grandma would agree with you," I said, waiting for the sound of footsteps. "There's a thing beyond the laws and rules."

"As my namesake, Alcaeus of Mytilene, once said,"[273] he went on thoughtfully. "The gods are powerless before true love."

"It conquers all," I recalled the next passage of his poem, dedicated to Sappho.[274] "Fear, fate and death itself."

Callistus and Anicetus didn't tarry.

"If you want to know what I think, Princess," the curly-haired man grunted, as he stood before me. "Now is not the right time…"

I coughed impatiently. Callistus looked desperately at the guardsman, but it didn't help him.

"Use your charm," I ordered him. "Make him walk with you to Piscina Mirabilis.[275] At this time those chambers are empty, and no one will hear him."

"It's going to be even harder than with Asinius," he warned me. "Baldwin may be a barbarian, but he's no fool."

"If he doesn't go willingly," I turned my eyes to the Cypriot, "shut his maw, and get him there by force. I will surprise him in the place."

The guardsman never disputed my orders.

---

[273] The most famous Greek lyric poet who is credited with inventing the Alcaic stanza.

[274] An Archaic Greek poet from the island of Lesbos.

[275] A Roman freshwater reservoir built by Emperor Augustus.

"And what will I do, Princess?" Alcaeus spoke. "At least I could scout."

"We're not playing war," I smiled. "It's just a rat hunt."

"Go to Caesar," Callistus recommended him. "You better not seem suspicious to him, if we fail."

"The German is the one to fail." The physician replied, as he went. "I already hear Thanatos cleaning his feathers."

The entrance to the Piscina was always guarded by one of the Vigiles, while the aquarii[276] visited the inner chamber every morning to remove sludge and to observe the water level.

A guardsman, seemingly just a trainee, measured me with a tiredly curious boyish look.

"What do you want?" I advanced him. "A watchword?"

"Well…" He said confusedly. "That won't be bad, my lady."

"Is that enough?" I took out of my handbag the timeless permit from Tiberius, which enables me to enter any building.

The young Vigile became petrified as he saw the imperial seal and my title.

"Today it's me to take care of a cistern," I spoke firmly and persuasively. "Go, get some rest, but don't tell anyone you saw me. Understood?"

He nodded, thoughtfully and addle-headedly, and opened the door.

"This way, Your Highness. Do you want me to escort you to the drinking fountain?"

I shook my head. As I made sure the Vigile left the place, I went down the wide stairs, somewhat slippery and cracked.

I am really lucky for places like that! I thought, comparing this dark tunnel to the secret corridor in Curia Hostilia.

Downstairs, in a spacious chamber with high columns, there was the famous cistern made of tubes and pipes, used primarily for supplying the Roman fleet with drinking water. Some torches, sharp like spears burned on the walls, alongside round floor lamps. All around me there were arcades of various proportions with reliefs decorating

---

[276] Aqueduct slaves.

wet walls. The pieces of sculptures represented river deities and scenes from our legends. A clepsydra at the faucet showed me that my friends were getting late.

"Ubi es, Calliste?"[277] By Rhea Silvia!" I started losing patience. "Are you dumber than a German rat?"

The disturbance I felt was unbearable. The only sound I heard was the murmur of the water. I sat on a wide slab and supported my chin with my hands. On the wall in front of me I saw a certain deity, looking at me happily.

Rhea Silvia.

"Lupus in fabula,"[278] I smiled, looking at the mother of the legendary founder of Rome. The masterfully sculpted image represented beautiful Rea as a bride, led by both hands by Anion and Tiber, the divine guardians of the rivers, to her husband Mars.

"Excuse me, dear," I addressed her friendly. "I didn't mean to give you names... I really find our gods ridiculous, but you were always somehow... dear to me.

The sculpture goddess smiled as if she understood what I was talking of.

"Felix es,"[279] I sighed. "You fooled your evil uncle, and got married to the one you loved."

Instead of an answer I heard the sound of steps and the nomenclator's grumbling.

"I hope it's about something urgent," Baldwin deprecated. "You Greeks, are resting all day long, and I have lots of things to do!"

"O noli dolere,"[280] Anicetus replied. "We'll be done soon... I mean, you will be done."

The German, already suspecting that had been caught in a trap, started yelling like a jackass.

"What is that? Where have you brought me?"

The Greeks were silent. When the failed warrior saw me, he got startled even more, and made an effort to escape.

---

[277] (lat.) Where are you, Callistus?

[278] (lat. prov.) Speak of the wolf, and he will come.

[279] (lat.) Lucky you!

[280] (lat.) Don't worry.

"Where do you think you're going?" The guardsman grabbed him with one hand. "We've just begun."

"Princess!" Baldwin exclaimed desperately, shaking and twitching. "What have I done wrong?"

"Remember!" I replied, losing my breath with anger. "Remember the day, when they captured you... and pardoned you... Recall!!!"

He did, with his eyes goggling and corners of his mouth quivering as if he was a child.

"I am not guilty!" Once again, he tried to free himself the giant's grip... in vain. "Your... Caesar ordered Prince Arminius to kill your father... "

"This I know," I stopped him with my hand raised. "And you failed."

"A soldier of rare strength defended him," Baldwin returned to the hard battle on the Weser. "He fought our men like Donner..."[281]

"And?" I interrupted him and came up closer. "I'm just wondering – how such a silly peasant came alive from such a bloody battle?"

Baldwin, so naively taking my tone seriously as a sign of sympathy, calmed down, and grew some hubris.

"I admit ... I surprised him a little," he smiled timidly. "Even the Romans laughed... "

As he was talking, I heard every word reverberating in my mind, causing my heart to skip a bit. A though of Cassius' wound, the danger threatening him, made me wish I could tear the poor servant to pieces alive, along with the bastards who laughed at blood and pain.

"So you feel proud?" I asked with disgust. "Proud of your acting like a beast???"

"H-h-highness ..." Baldwin muttered, trying to evoke my compassion. "I did what they told me! I defended my village from the Rom... invaders!"

"You did – what?" I suddenly burst into laughter, so mad that sensitive Callistus shuddered and quietly cursed in Greek.

---

[281] The German god of Thunder, the aggressive extension of the main deity.

"You, Cherusci," I reminded him. "You sold yourselves to Rome – twice! You changed your freedom, land, women and children – for a handful of our money!"

The eyes of the barbarian were full of terror, but not shame.

"Your Caesar is a vicious monster!" he exclaimed, still trying to avoid his fate. "They could have killed me, unless I obeyed!"

"And you feel like a hero," I retorted. "Bloody master of low strikes! A slave, who calls his lord a monster after he raised you from a swamp to a palace!"

"I was young!" he tried once more. "I wanted to survive!"

"Cassius was younger," I replied, barely catching breath. "He also fulfilled orders and commands like all the soldiers, but never in his life – against his honor!"

The scrawny Baldwin, realizing his near death, closed his eyes.

"Am I going to suffer?" he asked helplessly. "I'm scared of pain."

I looked at him, and I didn't notice a shred of repentance in those ice-green eyes. His hubris did not let him kneel and weep, as he once did before the legionnaires. For a moment, he reminded me the first-born daughter of his Prince – my stubborn nurse-maid, Armida.

"Do you, Cherusci, believe in anything... like love?"

The German opened his eyes wide, stunned by my question.

"Of course, we do. For our tribe, Your Highness, children are of paramount importance."

"Then you understand," I finished up. "Why I can't end this otherwise."

The servant nodded speechlessly.

"Anicetus," I whispered to the Cypriot. "Scrag him."

As we walked back across the coast, the three of us were silent. I was feeling bad – it seemed that my childhood illness yet hadn't forgotten me.

I killed two people, I thought, squeezing my companion's hands. *I still have to punish those mockers as well.*

The noise of the sea waves soothed both my conscience and my nausea. The turquoise color of the water got me captivated with its smoothness and beauty, as the summer breeze eased my headache.

"What was my Cassius thinking of?" I asked myself. "While he was standing on the shore of the inhospitable North Sea…"

An inseparable pair of seagulls, my old acquaintances, landed on a bare and spiky rock with a cheerful song. And above, in the bright July sky, two clouds were driven by the wind with almost fanciful speed.

"Sic transit vita mea,"[282] I sighed. "For what it's worth? Those hypocritical honors, or a damn tiara on my head, squeezing it like a foe's hand? All the treasures of this world are meaningless, if I'm alone."

"Your Highness," Anicetus carefully broke my melancholy. "That fellow in the ditch… We should have buried him. What if the Praetorians find him?"

"Sooner or later, they will," Callistus added ill-temperedly. "So Tiberius will get us…"

"Praised?" I smiled. "Who do you think will mourn a traitor's death?"

"True, Princess!" Anicetus nodded. "The barbarian betrayed him."

"Yes and no," Callistus shrugged. It was obvious – my judgment made him scared.

"Well," I embraced him. "Good girls sometimes lie. So do good fellows, don't they?"

---

[282] (lat.) Thus passes my life.

XLIII

My dear Cassius, I started my letter, still doubting between an official, distanced *care* and tender *carissime*.

I hope you're in good health, I wanted to go on, but quickly changed my mind. Of course, he was. For tribune Chaerea, it was not a question.

"It's been three years," I spoke, but I couldn't lift my quill. "It has been six... I guess he's not sitting and waiting for me."

On the desk, behind my inkstand, there were two keepsakes on a small silver tray, which I was guarding distrustfully even from the trusted servants – the rose from the Esquiline and Magdalene's egg.

If you still keep me within, I thought, carefully stroking the dried flower. *Like I keep your rose...*

A curtain of tears made me cover my eyes with my hands. The memories of Chaerea's touch on my cheek and neck were now feeling like dance with an element. Undoubtedly, he was of fire, just like me, but in its higher and creative form – like warmth, *joy*, peace and light.

"I will be yours forever," I whispered, wishing I abandoned everything and left for Rome. "If I could," I addressed him, trying to embrace the void around me. "If I understood!"

I took a sharpened quill and once again dipped it in the ink. I wrote in a flash, deciding not to waste another day, but to embrace the love I felt perhaps since early childhood, once suppressed by the apparent closeness with my brother.

I miss you. I need to see you.

Suddenly I tore the parchment to small pieces and stopped crying. "No, it doesn't work that way. The written word was meant for art. Love needs to speak... and to be spoken to."

As I barely finished talking to myself, I heard Callistus knocking on the door.

"Just at a perfect time," I stood up and quickly tidied my desk. "*Veni!*"

The Greek, dressed in an elegant robe, greeted me cheerfully.

"Freedom becomes you," I remarked, alluding to his dress. "You look like an eques."

"You're dreaming awake of the eques, Your Highness." He smiled at me shyly, as he turned round by the mirror. "I don't even know what to do with all that salary!"

"You deserved every assarius of it," I answered heartily. "Still, I don't know how I should call you now… I mean your duty…"

"Am I not your secretary?" he asked, funnily blinking his amber eyes.

"Actaeon is my secretary," I reminded him. "I left him in Rome to take care of my grandma."

"So, I'm dismissed," he concluded theatrically. "I'll kill myself!"

"Bite your tongue!" I waved aside. "I've just made up a thing for you, Curly."

Callistus raised his head cautiously, and took a few steps on his toes, acting like a dog reaching for a bone.

"It's Gaius' birthday soon," I said through laughter. "I'm not going to have sleepless nights choosing a present for a fellow who already has everything."

"Your Highness, please!" the Greek protested. "Libertus sum!"

"Absolutely," I calmed him down. "But the future Emperor will need a secretary, too."

"And what about the Egyptian?" he frowned, thinking of Helicon.

"Come on," I giggled. "What do they know but stonework and black magic? The best Emperor deserves the best assistant – wise and trustworthy as you are."

"You're right." My friend blushed. "Prince Gaius is honest, brave and smart, but still he lacks some… experience."

"Thank you, Curly." I pulled him to myself and kissed his wide forehead. "And now, a farewell task for you from your matrona."[283]

Callistus raised his brow vivaciously as he noticed a mess on my desk.

"Have you made up your mind?"

"Leave me alone," I pushed him away slightly. ""It's probably too late."

---

[283] A person, who freed a slave, was no longer called his dominus/Domina, but a patronus/matrona.

"It's not!" The freedman shook his head. "I remember the way tribune Chaerea looked at you, and talked to you on the Capri… Love never passes. If it does, it is not love."

"I love him, Callistus!" I exclaimed, lettings my tears go. "And let the whole world hear – I want him!"

"There will be time for that." He hugged me. "You should tell the tribune first."

"No letters," I spoke in a low voice, changed with weeping, "I have to see him."

"So, we are going to Rome?" the Greek guessed, tapping me on the back.

"I can't miss my brother's birthday," I said sadly. "And the emperor won't let me travel either. All I can is to arrange a comfortable sailing for you… both."

"I'll have company?" he asked me curiously.

"Yes. Anicetus." I smiled with effort. "For your safety and…"

The secretary blushed.

"There's nothing you can hide from Libitina."

"Tell the tribune," I continued impatiently, "about how I met Alcaeus, and of my revenge on the German. You may also mention the drama I'm writing, for he knows who our enemies are. Invite him to Misenum, and I'll tell him the rest face-to-face."

"Mi soi meleto,"[284] Callistus winked cheerfully, ready to leave. "I'll better hurry up to my Antaeus."[285]

Actaeon has Orla, I thought, washing my face in front of the mirror. *Callistus has Anicetus, Susannah was married twice… Alcaeus has already 'cured' half of the women in Misenum… Even David doesn't look that innocent… It's only me – alone like a tumbleweed.*

Meanwhile, the 'twice married' and 'not-that-innocent' were heading to my room. As I heard their voices through the hallway, I wiped my slightly swollen face, and asked them to come in.

Still angry with me for Antipas, Susannah silently began setting the table for the prandium, and David showed me the last scroll, which he managed to convey from his homeland.

---

[284] (anc.gr.) Do not worry!

[285] In Greek mythology – a mighty giant and wrestler in Libya.

"The Book of Isaiah!" he whispered excitedly. "No Pharisee corrections."

I looked at him curiously. Since my childhood, books have been my only comfort.

"The only chapter of the Torah, where Lilith is mentioned," the nursemaid explained, cutting a green pie. "Just one concise sentence."

"Kol hakavod!"[286] I praised the merchant. "Shall you read it to me?"

David unfolded the scroll carefully, looking for a needed passage with his long finger.

"It is written here about how the Lord sentenced the unfaithful Edomites."[287] He spoke enthusiastically. "For the injustice they've done to the Israelis, the 'red people' are forever deprived of their peace and doomed to evanescence…"

"Come on," Susannah interrupted him, taking the book. "Who cares about Edom? Listen… The fratricides share their doom with demons, as their kingdoms turn into sand…"

"While even Lilith will find peace in the barren land, where the God let her dwell." The merchant calmly finished the line, remembering it.

These words ran through me like a thunderbolt.

"What?" I asked quietly.

"From all the prophetic epistles – before and after," David went on thoughtfully. "This one was surely rewritten by the Pharisees on the behest of the Herodians."

"I suppose, not to Lilith's advantage." I rubbed my eyelids, to wipe away the strange feeling away.

"I'm not a literate," David nodded, taking back the scroll. "But I do know the Law and the epistles better than any rabbi. What I see with the naked eye is the fact that God's judgment on Lilith will be much more merciful that on the Edomites."

"What does it mean – the barren land?" I thought out loud. "A city in the desert like Palmyra or Petra?"

"Prophets speak in metaphors." Rachel's neighbor shrugged his shoulders.

Susannah called me to have prandium… in a wrong time.

"Later," I waved aside, preoccupied with the prophecy. "I am not hungry."

---

[286] (hebr.) All honor!
[287] The descendants of Esau who often battled the Jewish nation.

The nursemaid muttered something in her language, looking angrily at David.

"Let him be!" I said irritably. "Stop taking out your anger on the innocent."

The woman reluctantly apologized and fell silent. I reluctantly took a bite from a thinnest pie slice. The words of Lilith's fate kept on echoing in my mind.

"I'll search for more in all the books, Your Highness," the merchant promised me. "I'll stay awake all night to help you."

"Only God knows the answer to your question, I afraid." Susannah said dispassionately. "We can only speculate."

Well, she was right... in her own way. Unwillingly, she gave me an idea.

"David," I smiled and took another bite. "Would you like to be a priest?"

The Jew got astonished.

"I want you to teach me your faith." I explained. "And I want to know more of your God's descent on earth."

"Oh... Princess," he mumbled. "It would have been honor to me, but I cannot be a rabbi."

"The priest must be a Levite," Susannah expounded. "A man of the genus Leviticus, either elected by the Sanhedrin, or appointed by the King."

"I know what your priests and rulers are." I retorted with irony. "Is there a commandment they haven't yet broken?"

My friends exchanged some hesitating glances.

"If they can break the Law for the sake of the evil," I went on. "So can we – for the goodness' sake."

"There is some logic," David shrugged.

"Good!" I hugged both of them and turned to the woman. "I'll eat your pie if we make peace."

The nursemaid laughed, and slightly clasped my bottom.

"That's how I punished my sons," she sighed, remembering her family. "My naughty baby boys... I hate Antipas – he is guilty of that all!"

Feeling her pain, I leaned my head on her shoulder and whispered.

"If we have to violate the Law... I will bring your children back to you."

XLIV

The 31st of July 36 was gloomy and chilly enough. From the daybreak, the dark sky had been twitching in labors, trying to pluck out of its vast body a saving downpour.

"Why today?" I wondered, coming down the stairs. The gold-edged festive dress seemed so unpleasantly tight, and the pearl diadem – too out of place and heavy. As I got to the litter with effort, I ordered my new carriers to help me take a seat immediately. Four unfriendly Thracians to take care of all my going outs were a gift from Gaius… and his wife.

"How are you feeling, Princess?" Alcaeus asked me with concern, lifting the curtain.

"My joints hurt," I replied. "And when I take a look… it seems like I'm watching with somebody else's eyes."

"Drink this to the bottom," he gave me a glass of a scented decoction. "It's bittersweet, but you'll feel better shortly."

A sip of the hot liquid made me cough.

"You're such a child, Your Highness." The Greek laughed. "No wonder why you still have a nursemaid."

"I had two of them once," I smiled back. "But, one of them betrayed me."

"Arminius' bastard girl?" the Cretan guessed, scratching his neatly cut nape.

"Callistus has a long tongue." I made a link. "Who knows, what he is gossiping around on the Esquiline now?"

Alcaeus got earnest as I didn't answer.

"Why don't you let Susannah go with you? Just in case… "

"There is no need." I patted him on his hairy arm. "Go back to Caesar. He's been too complaining about vertigo this morning."

One of the Thracians shouted something in his language, and the litter moved.

"They'll vilify me anyway," I took a comfortable position, squeezing a small present in my hand – a sardonyx cameo. "Flocci non faccio!"

The house of my brother and the only daughter of Junius Silanus was sinking in floral wreaths and colorful ribbons. One by one there came in horsemen, carts and litters from all sides. By the entrance, beside severe guardsmen, cheerful slave girls served the guests with fruit and pastries.

"Ave, Princess!" A young black girl greeted me, barely holding an overfull tray. "Domina has baked those sweets for you!"

They told the same to every guest. I casted a look at the overripe fruit and stale gingerbreads.

I wouldn't try it, even if you paid me, I thought, entering the atrium.

The hostess, already in her advanced pregnancy, was welcoming the visitors in front of a tall statue of Juno Caprotina.[288] Her sixteen-year-old oblong face was smiling greasily at everyone, but deep-set eyes, forever in high dudgeon, were observing them with envy.

"Stay far away from Silania,"[289] Actaeon warned in my head. *"That wench has a nature of an asp."*

I straightened my back. Luckily, the cure began to work.

Junia Claudilla noticed me and wished me a reluctant welcome.

"Congratulationes tibi ago, Junia,"[290] I smiled, nodding at her belly.

"My spouse and I were expecting the Consul to join you," she said, proudly stroking her stomach. "Looks like our dear brother-in-law is not feeling well... is he?"

I was prepared for such questions.

"By the will of Caesar, my marriage to Lucius Longinus has come to an end."

"Sane."[291] The young woman shrugged, lowering her eyes toward the jewelry bag. "You made a gift for your brother? How considerate of you!"

"I don't have *that* talent," I caught the sarcastic note in her voice. "But I am friends with the best goldsmith."

---

[288] Goddess Juno as the fertilizer and protectress of pregnant women.
[289] The daughter of Silanus.
[290] (lat.) I congratulate you.
[291] (lat.) Of course.

"Quod felix es, negare non possumus."[292] She looked snobbishly proud of herself, intentionally using the first-person plural. "Please, make yourself comfortable in the triclinium, Your Highness."

In the corridor, filled with some odd perfume, I got aware that Ziraxis, my pedisequus and porter, wasn't following me for some reason.

He must be chattering with other slaves, I thought, driving the sudden creeps away. *He didn't understand me and stayed out.*

A housekeeper woman helped me get to the big hall.

"This way, Your Highness." She addressed me with strong eastern accent. "The prince is keeping for you locus consularis."[293]

The feast had not begun yet. Six musicians in gilded wigs were greeting the guests with a joyful tune. By the sounds of the Egyptian sistrum, fife and lute, a couple of terpsichoreans, lithe and enthralling like two wildcats, started their dance.

"Is that Julia Drusilla?" I heard whisperings among the women. "She has grown thin! Is she sick?"

"She wears Vipsania's diadem!" The matrons talked in displeasure. "It is said that Caesar fulfills all her wishes."

I chuckled at the last phrase and, duly greeting them, took a place next to the host. Caligula, handsome like the Kouros of Samos, welcomed me with a happy smile.

"Mea sororcula!"[294] He rose from his couch and kissed me hello.

"We're neighbors, but we see each other once in years." I hugged him back, ignoring all those disapproving looks.

"We'll change it soon," he whispered, and half-turned to Macro, who was watching over him. "Just waiting for a better moment."

"I know what *he* is waiting for," I frowned. "But we will steal a march on him."

"Let him be… now." My brother slightly interrupted me, helping me take a sit. "Tonight we'll speak of agreeable things."

---

[292] (lat.) The fact that you are lucky we cannot deny.

[293] A seat, intended for the most important guest, usually next to the host.

[294] (lat.) Little sister.

"O, felix Dies Natalis!" I gave him one more kiss on the cheek, and, laughing at my own mooniness, handed him the gift. "Tibi!"[295]

Gaius, like a child, opened a pouch immediately, and took the cameo out, placing it carefully to his palm.

"It's gorgeous!" he admired, gazing at two profiles on a sardonyx relief. "Are that we?"

"Of course," I replied. "A craftsman who made it once served our great-grandfather."

"I'll wear it all the time." The prince pulled a cameo to his chest. "And never take it off."

Soon the dinner hall was filled with guests, the tables with fine meals, and the goblets with vintage wine, smelling like saffron and honey. Then began the toasts with inevitable wishes for the unborn baby to be male, and to be followed by siblings. Junia Claudilla was returning compliments with seeming modesty, mostly lowering her eyes silently. Her mother Appia, on the contrary, used every opportunity to praise her daughter's domestic abilities.

"Powerful statesmen, skilled at law and rhetoric," Appia spoke out, raising her head in a jovial manner. "And their ladies, watching over children and the hearth, are indeed the bedrock of the Empire."

"Don't forget about the warriors, my dear," reminded her Domitia, the praetor's daughter. "Who would guard the Roman borders and conquer the new lands for us?"

"Yes, you are right." Junia's mother nodded hesitantly. "Though, I must admit, I don't like soldiers. Look at their univiras,[296] with those noses constantly in books, and unmannerly children!"

The insult, mostly referred to the Antonii, I couldn't pass over.

"De gustibus non disputandum est,"[297] I spoke, startling the better part of the guests. "What is *vir*, if cannot defend his own family? What is *femina* if she's illiterate?"

First there was silence… until Corbulo supported me.

---

[295] (lat.) For you.
[296] Univira (lat.) – a woman who only married one man.
[297] (lat. prov.) There is no disputing of tastes

"I think so, too," said the young tribune from a prominent aristocratic family. "The patroness of our city is Minerva – a goddess of wisdom and war."

"I worship all the gods," Appia frowned. "But Jove forbid a Roman mother has a daughter-in-law like Minerva!"

Corbulo laughed out loud, confusing all the noblemen, almost like me a while ago.

"That's enough, woman!" Silanus exclaimed, grabbing a dozen of linen napkins to wipe his oily lips. "You cluck like a hen all the time!"

Marcus Vinicius, Livilla's husband and a good conciliator, started an ever-burning topic of tax collection, gladly adopted by other men.

"Are you bored?" Gaius asked, as the feast began to turn into carousing.

"Very much, if you don't mind." I yawned, nodding at my plate, half-empty. "That is the most annoying part."

"Mater Familias[298] avoids unhealthy foods," he explained with some irony. "I've got accustomed to the boiled and unsalted."

"Feels like I'm in a shed," I whispered. "A roost to my left," I pointed towards Appia, Domitia and our distant relative, gossipy Scipiona. "And a piggery to my right." I glanced at the drunken senators.

My brother chuckled, covering her mouth with her hand.

"It's only the tribune," I went on. "That I can talk to without effort."

"No wonder," Gaius replied. "Corbulo is my friend. I met him in Rome during my first sitting in the Senate, and he helped me a lot. "

"I didn't see him at Hostilia that day." I recalled. "So there are chances he's no Mithraist yet."

"Corbulo?! Never in life!" he giggled, hugging me around my waist unnoticed. "May I steal you for a while, Your Highness?"

There was just warmth, not lust in his touch. I glanced towards Claudilla cautiously, but didn't see her among the guests.

"She must be gone to have some rest," Caligula concluded.

I gave him my hand with a smile.

---

[298] (lat.) A mother of the household.

The wide nymphaeum, much like a smaller temple, had a lot of frescos, nacre mosaics and statues bathed in fountains. One of the sculptures, in the shape of a girl sitting on an overgrown stone, reminded me my first years in Germania.

"I finally have something of my own." My brother said contentedly. "And of my taste."

"Your home is fabulous," I got amazed with his gentility, too far from Caesar's obscenity or Antonia's love for the orient.

"Wait to see what my palace will be!" His blue eyes flashed. "I'm already making plans for my future reign."

"Tell me." I carefully fixed a golden clasp on his robe. "You know, I'm your ardent supporter."

Caligula embraced me and welcomed to sit on a bench.

"Look at the stars, little sister." He raised his head up to the open midnight sky. "There is a myriad of them, and each of them is different."

That night the lights on the dark blue dome were shining brighter than the tripod torches.

"Just like us, people," Gaius went on zestfully. "The Romans and those from the provinces… All over the world… Everyone has his own story and goal, something to live for… We believe, we love in our own ways… Isn't it marvelous, my dear?"

I nodded in agreement, observing his gaze and movements.

"August and those above him wanted to destroy all the diversity." He moved his eyebrows down and closer together. "Now Tiberius does the same, for gray and faceless masses are much easier to control. And I," My brother looked at me. "I will give back to our people everything the fiend took away from them – their temples, rights and freedoms."

"What about the fiend?" I asked, thrilled with his courage and determination.

"Oh Drusilla," Gaius smiled. "You're the daughter of a warlord, and you don't know what we do to enemies?"

"The forces are not equal," I sighed, "But it's a certain defeat to give up."

As I made sure nobody was eavesdropping, I shared with him my plans about the future drama, inspired with the legend of Alexander and the Serpent Tribe.

"Well done, girl!" Gaius praised me. "That is the solution! I will do my best to gain trust and support from the people of Rome, and you will show them who is secretly controlling them! And even the whole Senate stands with Vespasian, yet he won't be able to defeat the whole of Rome."

"We must be good with strangers too," I followed the flow of his thoughts. "We need reliable allies in case we get attacked by Parthians."

"The first thing I will do as Caesar is giving autonomy to Achaia, Macedonia and Cyprus," Gaius promised. "I must thank Callistus and his tall friend for saving me from going mad on the Capri."

"Speaking of Callistus," I recollected. "He should be your secretary. You wouldn't find a better counselor even in Sericum."[299]

Caligula nodded, as he pulled his forehead to mine.

"So you'll be a father," I smiled. "And I… I'll be an aunt."

"I'm still in disbelief," he shrugged. "But I feel happy."

"Have you managed to love her?" I asked, as I noticed a familiar shade in his voice.

Caligula giggled and shook his head hard.

"Claudilla?! She is much alike old Livia!"

I thought about how disgusting were marriages of convenience and thanked almighty Adonai for my union with Longinus not being consumed.

"I'm in love." Gaius suddenly opened his heart. "I've been mad about the certain girl for over a year."

The joyful expression of my face gave him relief.

"I'm glad you understand me, dear."

"More than anyone alive," I sighed, hugging him clumsily like when we were kids.

Caligula, a bit taken aback, moved slightly aside, trying to catch my sight.

"Little sister?"

I could barely hide the truth from anyone, especially my brother, who was only nine months older than me.

"Chaerea, right?" He turned his head toward a murmuring fountain. "I know…"

---

[299] Modern-day China.

The bitterness in his voice almost gave me a guilty conscience… and tears which he could never handle.

"Don't cry," he stroked my head. "I guess that's good news."

I nodded, hiding my wet eyes on his chest.

"Does he know?" Caligula asked favorably.

"I invited him to Misenum," I replied, "But, I'm afraid I've waited for too long."

"It's never too late for the true love." He tapped me on the nose. "That's what our Grandma told me when I visited her last."

"How is she now?" I recalled about her illness.

"Still mad as a hare," Gaius smiled. "But, she does like my paramour!"

I ultimately asked for her name.

"Messalina."

In my mind, I went back on the day my red-haired cousin came to visit me. She reconciled the aesthetic valerian grace and fatally passionate nature of the Antonii; and her viewpoint of a family was very similar to Gaius'.

"She'll make you happy," I concluded. "More than I would…"

The prince touched my lips tenderly.

"Hushhh! Drusilla, you are the best… sister."

Lost in this touching moment, we didn't notice Macro came along.

"Your Highness." His deep voice surprised us. "I've been reported that the emperor is feeling bad, and asking for Lady Drusilla."

"I'd better hurry," I embraced Caligula goodbye. "He's going mad when he has pains."

"And… Prince," the prefect added. "The guests want to see you."

"Sometimes I hate being a prince," Gaius frowned, heading back to the dining hall.

Disturbed, I quickly walked out to vestibulum. The 'lost' Ziraxis stood by the gate, staring at me in a strange way as his fellow countrymen were fixing the litter.

What does he want? I thought, startled by the shady seriousness of my new servant.

Ziraxis courtly gave me his hand, and my bad premonition subsided.

To my detriment.

XLV

Outside – drop by drop, the rain started to fall.

"What the hell?" I thought out loud. "The sky was clear enough to see the stars."

Night rain was cold and unpleasant.

"Come on!" I shouted to the weary porters. "I have a canopy… you'll get soaking wet."

The Thracians hesitatingly lifted me up and made a few uncertain steps.

"Fool," I whispered to myself, "Who in the world would trust barbarians?"

"Drusilla!" I suddenly heard my sister's-in-law voice, this time surprisingly sweet, behind me.

I made the porters halt, and headed to meet her – against the rain.

"Junia? Why aren't you sleeping?" I asked, putting on hood.

"We told each other ugly things," she said nicely. "Still, I cannot let you go in such nasty weather."

"Thanks for your concern," I spoke, startled. "Still, I have to go, for Caesar is waiting for me."

The face of the young hostess suddenly became despondent. "Come back, just for a moment… Please."

The last word, her condition, and that sorrowful gaze made me follow her plea.

"Abeamus!"[300] I turned to the servants, feeling the rain turning into a downpour. The four Thracians stepped after me.

"Since I've been expecting, I'm feeling a constant hot flash," she complained to me, taking my hand. "Even when it's cold outside, I'm finding some relief down in the cellar."

"What does your medic say?" I asked, going downstairs.

---

[300] (lat.) Let's go!

"A medic?!" she asked ironically, clinging for the banister. "For a woman of my age, it is a shame to have a medic!"

Here we go again... I thought, as I got the allusion. *People never change.*

When we came down, Claudilla ordered three of my porters – Lycurgus, Finneas and Iras – to watch the door to the underground chamber.

"How does she know their names?" I startled, and finally realized that I had just been trapped.

"All that is funny, but I really have to go," I tried to make a joke. "Thank you for hospitality."

"No, sister dear." She shook her head. "You won't leave this place alive."

The Thracians made a live wall, and Ziraxis slowly headed toward me.

"Don't even think of that!" I shouted, trying not to show fear. "I am Tiberius' fosterling!"

Caligula's wife laughed aloud. "Are you? As you act like a hoyden who insults other people and destroys families!"

"You're overstating things," I replied, pushing Ziraxis aside. "But for the sake of my brother's child, I promise you I will forget what happened here."

"Of course, you will." My sister-in-law grinned. "As soon as you drink some water from the Lethe.[301] Ziraxis," she rebuked my slave, "what are you looking at? Kill her!"

The Thracian quickly removed his belt and approached me, muttering something through his teeth. My blood got freezing. The idea of fighting a court gladiator[302] seemed absurd to me.

"What are you going to tell Gaius?" I asked her, feeling the flood tide of tears ready to set out.

"I've thought it out," Junia replied. "It will look like a suicide... Your heart was broken by news of Caligula's lover."

---

[301] (gr.myth.) One of the five rivers of the underworld of Hades, whose waters cause drinkers to forget their past.

[302] Slaves, who, unlike ordinary gladiators, did not fight in the arena, but at feasts, entertaining the high guests.

Ziraxis grabbed me with one hand, making sure he's not leaving bruises as traces of struggle, and threw his belt around my neck with the other hand.

"Wait," Junia suddenly stopped him, and looked me in the eye. "Maybe I'll spare you though… If you kneel before me, begging for mercy."

Lost in tears, I could feel my knees dragging me down to the floor. Barely hearing my own voice, I mumbled what my sister-in-law wanted to hear.

"Behold a princess!" she giggled, being followed by the servants. "Tell us, what's it like to kneel before an offspring of 'an optimati pig'?"

I tried to get up, thinking about what I would do to that ferocious youngster after she gave birth, but the porter pulled me hard to the cold wall again.

"You don't deserve to live," Claudilla said, and ordered to the traitor, "Do away with her!"

I don't know how I managed to raise my strangled voice, but just a moment before the barbarian threw his belt again, I screamed.

I do not know how or why, but before the executioner pulled on his belt again, I reached for it.

"Cassiiii…!"

"Shut her up!" Claudilla fretted.

The leather belt started to choke me. A dark purple started lingering before me, as my mouth grew dumb.

I killed two men, I thought, losing myself. *What goes around comes around.*

"No!" I heard a kind, sonorous female voice breaking through darkness. "Fight, my child! Cassius needs you!"

I saw her face, just for an instant, and in the gentle and mature, motherly beauty, I recognized a woman I had never met – Annea Helvilla.

It took me the last ounce of my strength to kick the Thracian in his stomach. Bewildered, he bent in half with pain, losing the belt.

"She lives!" Claudilla shouted angrily.

"I do," I coughed, and kicked Ziraxis once again, knocking him down. "I do indeed!"

I hadn't wasted a single moment, kicking him and beating with his own wide belt, until the Thracian lost his conscience.

"You had it coming, bastard!"

"She's a witch!" Claudilla shuddered, and addressed the other slaves, "Put her down or I'll kill you all!"

The porters stepped to me, but quickly stopped, as one of them heard footsteps and voices above, calling me.

"Princess! Where are you?"

I recognized the anguished cry of Callistus, followed by Anicetus' heavy steps.

"I'm in the cellar!" I exclaimed, rubbing my sore neck. "You hurry up!"

The porters glared at Junia Claudilla and shook heads. Yet, she didn't want to accept her defeat, so she attacked me herself.

"Die, you piece of carrion!"

I tried to move her aside, in order not to harm the unborn child, but that small, wicked woman grasped my hair, pulling it furiously.

"Hold on, Your Highness!" Anicetus roared somewhere close.

The next thing I heard was the sound of a fight, but I couldn't see it out of severe pain, caused by my sister-in-law as she scratched me like an animal.

"No, tribune, she's pregnant!" Callistus was finally with me.

"Take your hands off me, you beast!" my tormentor suddenly yelled, letting me go. "I am…"

"A mad woman," Cassius was here as well. His voice, so dear to me, could pacify the pain. "Luckily for you, I never raise my hand to women, pregnant ones especially."

As I moved my tousled hair aside and wiped blood and tears from my face, I saw three of them – Chaerea, Callistus and Anicetus – standing by me, four lifeless bodies on the floor, and my sister-in-law trembling in the corner.

"You're hurt!" The tribune hugged me. "Can you walk?"

"Better than him," I smiled, nodding toward dead Ziraxis.

"I'll find the Cretan!" Callistus exclaimed.

"And I'll warn the prince!" Anicetus followed him.

I looked at Junia, hugging her stomach and groaning desperately where they left her.

"Don't," I stopped the servants. "I can't find it in me to tell Gaius."

"But Your Highness!" Callistus protested. "She wanted to kill you!"

"Well, she's not the only one," I answered wittily, and asked him if anyone saw them coming.

"I doubt it," Anicetus said. "We're headed here straight from the port. We knew you're at the feast, so we wanted to surprise you."

"You succeeded," I kissed all three of them.

The guardsmen, who greeted them by the gates of Villa Germanici,[303] were so much occupied with gambling, that they asked for neither a watchword, nor an invitation letter.

"I should be lucky," I smiled, and turned to my sister-in-law. "Go your own way, Junia. I won't give away what you did."

In the courtyard, still soggy with rain, I gestured to Lupus, the centurion to come up.

"Go down to clean the cellar immediately. If someone asks you something, you don't know what happened."

"Yes, my lady!" Lupus sounded like drunken. "How else can I help, Your Highness?"

"I'm alright," I said, twisting and turning a broken diadem in my hands. "Just been practicing some self-defense… a little."

Lupus turned around to see my slaves, and, realizing they were dead, nodded in understanding and asked if I need other porters.

"Take that ruin away." I pointed to the litter, completely saturated with rainwater. "We'll walk to the palace."

---

[303] Caligula's house in Misenum, as he kept his father's agnomen.

XLVI

David lit two long candles of white wax and ritually covered his eyes with his hands, chanting a quiet prayer.

"Let me put a headscarf on your head," Susannah whispered behind my back. "Shabbat is a sacred day, and you should cover yourself."

"Leave me alone," I replied almost silently, turning my gaze toward Cassius, who was sitting next to me.

"Tonight," David began excitedly, "we are celebrating Holy Shabbat. It's the time we exercise our prayer and freedom from everyday labor. This tiny treat," he gestured toward the braided bread, some mushy legume, stuffed baked fish and an amphora of wine. "It symbolizes the Genesis – the creation of the world, and the Exodus from Egypt – the end of slavery and the rise of the Jewish people…"

"Da mihi veniam," Alcaeus said tiredly from across the table. "Do we Greeks also have to listen to this?"

"Speak for yourself," Anicetus growled. "I find this story interesting."

"So do I," Callistus added earnestly.

"With all respect for the Hellenic culture, your religion is false, like any other heathen cult."

"Your Highness," Alcaeus started, confused, "how can you be so sure that Abraham's descendants tell the truth?"

"Friends, it's no good to argue on this day," Susannah interrupted him.

"I'm sorry for this Greek theater, David." I sighed. "I heard you don't invite strangers for dinner, and now I know why."

The newly appointed rabbi smiled, and started laughing, inviting us to join him.

"Of all the religions," I went on disputing with the medic, "the right one is the one that gives us answers for the hardest questions and guides us on crossroads."

The medic's gaze was no longer annoyed, but now interested.

"Only Adonai can defeat Mithras," I concluded, approved by my guests. "Those who believe in Creator overcome the servants of Creation."

David raised his hands with wide sleeves.

"Shabbat shalom!" he exclaimed, breaking the ritual bread. "Susannah, pour us some wine!"

The nursemaid, recalling her native customs, hastily filled seven glasses of Nabataean wine; and Anicetus, out of his customs, chugged the drink and broke it on the floor.

"Oooooopa!"

"Even in the Iliad, you can't find such a bunch." Cassius winked at me.

"Nor in the whole of Torah." I smiled, delighted with his closeness.

After two hours of sharing meals and cheerful talks, the rabbi thanked to all the guests with a slight bow.

"The law, I obey," he said. "The faith I follow has nothing to do with the fraud of the Pharisees and the Herodians. Their hands are stained with the blood of the innocent and most expensive ink, with which they rewrite the God's word."

"I know what conspiracies are," the stubborn Alcaeus spoke again. "One of them made me a deserter. I have seen an uncle who set two armies on his cousin, a fake war and well-played triumph, but I still don't understand the purpose of distorting history."

"At the head of each of conspiracy, my friend, there's always Mithras," David explained patiently. "He wants to portray God as a cruel and greedy ruler, in order to lead astray as many people as he can."

"But, can you prove it?" The physician asked, still doubtful. "Is there any evidence?"

The Jew fell silent for a while, recalling something bittersweet, and then replied.

"When Adonai descended on earth and preached in the Temple, He made me so inspired that I wished to become His disciple. And Him, He looked at me with all the goodness of the universe and asked, if I could give up my wealth for Torah…"

"And what did you do?" Cassius asked him, impressed by the story.

"I… went away," David confessed with teary eyes. "Out of vanity, I gave up our Savior."

That man's sincerity made everyone, even Alcaeus, feel confidence and compassion.

"But one day," he went calmly, "I met Magdalene, His closest disciple, and I got a second chance to serve Him."

"I believe you, flamen,"[304] Anicetus said kindly, and then joked, "Although, I am still hungry…"

We all burst out laughing.

"By your permission, Princess, we'll continue to the kitchen," Callistus said, pushing seamlessly Alcaeus with his elbow.

"Me too." The medic stood up hurriedly. "Caesar asked me for some sleeping drink."

Susannah, out of a habit, reached out to clean the table, but Callistus pulled her out in the corridor.

"Don't you forget, today is Shabbat! We are resting!" In a moment, I heard his merry voice in prothyron. "By Athena, I like your religion, David!"

So Cassius and I were finally alone in my chambers.

"My big mad family." I smiled, nodding toward the closed door.

Chaerea caught my look, and the abyss of his gray-blue eyes swallowed me.

"I read the text in your codex attentively the very same day," he recalled. "At the Esquiline, I have heard very little about Mithras, mostly about his noble worshippers."

By my dreamy face, he understood I was no capable to talk about serious things that moment. As he read me like an open book, he looked back at two half-burned candles.

"The Jewish faith is interesting," Cassius smiled. "Even for a combatant like me, it seems convincingly enough for all its logic and simplicity."

"That faith helped me find out who I am," I replied honestly, and… opened my heart ultimately. "When a man finally finds his true self, he will find the one Adonai made for him."

Cassius took my hand and pressed it to his lips.

---

[304] A priest in Ancient Rome.

"Sic erit," I heard my favorite poem.

"Haeserunt tenues in corde sagittae,

et possessa ferus pectora versat Amor…"[305]

From the very sound of his manly voice I shuddered, and took his both hands, covering his palms with kisses.

"Cedimus," I continued the stanza.

an subitum luctando accendimus ignem?

cedamus: leve fit, quod bene fertur, onus."[306]

Torrid in longing and mad after years of waiting, our lips met in the sweetness of mutual love.

"We have been separated by time, origins and the duty," he whispered as he lowered my stola, caressing my shoulder like a sculptor, who enjoys every carved line. "But I've always known that one day you will be mine."

"Forever yours, Cassi Chaerea." I repeated his name like inebriated – the only name on earth I loved. "My savior… double savior."

The tribune stopped abruptly.

"Triple," he sighed, returning memories. "To be precise."

As I felt sudden disturbance, I reached out to embrace him, asking with a glance what he was talking of.

"One April afternoon, I got the most amazing birthday present," he said, reliving the events.

"I met a little girl who made my life meaningful."

I closed my eyes listening to him, so I could imagine that picture as vivid as possible.

That Tuesday the garrison was trapped with freezing rain. Awaiting the Germanicus' army from a long campaign, my mother got preterm labor.

---

[305] (lat.) Thus it will be: the slender arrows stick in the heart,

And savage Love turns the occupied heart. (Ovid, "Amores").

[306] (lat.) Do we surrender, or do we inflame the sudden fire by struggling?

Let's surrender: the burden becomes light which is borne well. (Ibid.)

"Delivery at the seventh month is a punishment of gods," Said Gudrun, a German midwife, watering a half-conscious Agrippina with some barbaric drink from a goatskin. "The Fire Father hates intemperance!"

The youngest centurion, Cassius Chaerea, was staying in the camp to guard the governor's family.

"I heard your mother's screams from inside," I could feel his horror. "The witch forced her Lady to curse both the baby and her father; and your exhausted mother repeated the spells."

After six hours of fiery tortures a baby was born – little and weak, like a newborn kitten. Outside the door, Chaerea exhaled with relief.

"A girl!" Gudrun yelled with disgust.

"So ugly!" Agrippina moaned disappointedly. "Looks like Antonia!"

"She's barely breathing," Midwife frowned. "I doubt she survives."

"Better for her," Agrippina replied. "I didn't want that child."

"In my sea land, we swaddle such babies in a clean linen sheet and leave it alone in a room, so Loki can take it away." Old Gudrun half-whispered.

To Cassius' horror, Agrippina left me there to die.

"Whatever you heard, centurion," she warned him, as she left the cubicle. "Forget it immediately!"

Chaerea saw my mother off with a look of contempt, and as he got alone in the corridor, hurried to the baby.

"You were lying on the bed, wrapped in a robe, and crying quietly with cold and hunger. I slowly took you in my arms, trying to warm those little hands and feet." He went on, as he gently stroked my palm. "It seemed to me like your blue eyes were smiling to me, and I recognized my happiness in you."

Despite the order, Cassius took me to the barracks, where they kept hostage Germanic women. In a dark cell, one of the barbarians, who spoke Vulgar Latin, showed him to a sad towheaded woman, who had lost her infant lately.

"Freda will feed the little Roman." The captive nodded. "You be good with her, she loves the kid."

For a moment, Chaerea left behind both – war and duty, and knelt before a grieving woman, asking in a rather poor Cherusci dialect to suckle me.

So, in the teeth of the atrocious midwife predictions, I survived that spring, and welcomed my father back smiling.

"As he found out the truth, the Commander got Gudrun flogged to death, and never visited your mother in her room again."

"And Freda?" I let the tears go. "What happened to her?"

Cassius wiped my wet cheeks.

"Germanicus sent for a better wet nurse for you soon. When she arrived in the garrison, poor Freda jumped off the rampart."

That night I finally slept next to my sweetheart. I cried my old self out on his shoulder. Considerable for my feelings, Chaerea didn't ask me for a farther closeness.

"I'm so happy to look at you like that, Drusilla," I could almost hear him in my sleep. "I lived in hope that you love me too."

"How didn't I know we were born on the same day?" Half-awake, I was smiling. "Why didn't we celebrate your birthday?"

"We were at war, and I'm a soldier." He spoke earnestly. "The only day that counts for a soldier is the day of triumph… or his fall."

XLVII

"Salve, mea aethra siderea!"[307] Cassius greeted me as I opened my eyes.

The lamps were lit, the room was tidy, and carefully prepared breakfast awaited us on a small table.

"When did you get up – before or after Susannah?" I asked, stretching on the bed.

"She almost caught me dressing," he smiled. "Your nursemaid nicely offered me to have a breakfast – three times now, but I was waiting for you to wake up."

"I'm not an early bird," I explained somewhat shyly. "I go to bed late, so…"

"I don't mind," Chaerea helped me get up. "I always woke my mama up… She was pretty much of a child, even in her forties."

As I heard of Annea Helvilla, I wished I could tell him about our strange encounter between the worlds and the mysterious power that woman awakened in me…

"Requiescat in pace,"[308] I uttered instead. "I believe she was pulchra res creata."[309]

"Helvilla loved me, but she loved my father most" he said. "She couldn't live without him… so she did not."

"Do you miss her?" I asked, embracing him.

Cassius nodded.

"She was dying with a smile, as she was going to meet Marcus soon… She forbade me to cry, and promised me I wouldn't be alone… but next to someone, meant for me."

"She was so right." I kissed the tiny wrinkles on his forehead. "We both have lost our parents, but we'll never lose each other."

"This, I would not survive." Cassius took me in his arms. "It's time to wash your face and dress you up. I must admit, I am as hungry as a horse."

"I'll do it by myself." I smiled. "But I adore you taking care of me."

---

[307] (lat.) Good morning, my starlight!
[308] (lat.) May she rest in peace.
[309] (lat.) A wonderful creature.

"A man who doesn't care about his better half is a moron," he replied earnestly. "A woman who pretends she doesn't need some care is even worse."

At noon we took a walk along the forum. The main market square of Misenum was half smaller and less developed than the one of the capital city. Modeled on the Athenian agora, it was shaped an accurate square, surrounded by pavilion porches, with the large altar for Mercury in the middle. Like in any other port city, sailors made the better part of the customers, bargaining and joking salty all the way. Suntanned agricolae[310] and talkative artisans were arranging motley items on their counters merrily, convincing passers-by that "Caesar himself" bought their goods.

"Speaking of Caesar, I hope he truly doesn't mind my presence here," Chaerea thought aloud.

"Callistus convinced him," I replied contently. "I don't know how exactly, but the Old Wolf didn't mind."

"The curly boy is dangerous," the tribune laughed. "When I told him that I may not leave the castrum without praetor's permit, he just showed me another one, sealed by the emperor."

"Cinaedus,"[311] I waved aside. "A useful one though."

By the entrance of basilica where they sold jewelry, an old but perky goldsmith waved to us, as he recognized me.

"Princess!"

"This is Dion." I introduced him to my betrothed one. "There's no better jeweler in the Empire. He made a birthday gift for Caligula."

"And you must be tribune Chaerea." The old Greek addressed my companion. "I made an equestrian ring for your father, Marcus Cassius. There was no braver and more loyal warrior in the entire army of Augustus."

"Thank you, for your kind words, craftsman." The tribune was moved. "May he rest in Elysium, as the Greeks say."

"He, too, was Greek!" the grey-haired artisan said proudly. "A son of Cassii by mother, but by father he was the true Hellen. I swear if he leaded the legions instead

---

[310] (lat.) Farmers.
[311] (lat.) A pederast.

of that coward Quinctilius Varus,[312] we would have beaten the hell out of the Germans!"

"Don't exaggerate it." Cassius smiled bitterly. "Marcus was just a primus pilus.[313] Unlike Tiberius, Augustus did not gift high ranks."

"Augustus was a jackass," Dion whispered, giggling. "All the Greeks hated him; let him rot in the depths of Tartarus! So, Little Princess," he then turned to me. "Did our royal birthday boy like my cameo?"

"Gaius was amazed," I said. "He promised not to take it off."

The Peregrine[314] nodded contentedly, and Cassius, gesturing toward the counter, asked him if he had anything for "the most beautiful woman in the world."

"You bet!" The old Greek took a slip to his workshop, and brought a small velvet box with amethyst earrings and a silver ring inside.

"This kind of precious stones," he pointed to the earrings. "Was a dare for Cleopatra herself! And that…" Dion carefully took a thin ring to his hand. "Is a symbol of eternal love. I used a special kind of silver to create it."

Cassius looked at me, ready to purchase the jewelry set.

"Do you like it?"

All the Dion's goods looked elegant and unique, but the ones he offered us were sparkling in the sun like empyrean ornaments.

"How much do you want for them, Dion?" I asked the Greek, as I didn't want to put my man in some uncomfortable situation.

"Don't even think!" Chaerea threatened me jokingly. "I'll give you that jewels even by the price of all my possessions!"

"Long live the love!" Dion rejoiced, handing him a box. "A gift from old Dion to his best customers!"

I kissed Cassius, ignoring the curious crowd around us, and then turned to the goldsmith.

---

[312] A Roman general, generally remembered for having lost three Roman legions when ambushed by Germanic tribes led by Arminius in the Battle of the Teutoburg Forest, whereupon he took his own life.

[313] A senior centurion of the first cohort in a Roman legion.

[314] A freeborn foreigner.

"One day," I said in Greek. "We'll order a wedding ring here."

As we greeted our friend goodbye, we turned toward a rotunda to rest. Surprisingly, there was no one inside, so we took a seat on the semicircular bench by the fountain.

"How are you feeling, infantula? We have walked this city through." Cassius stroked my hair.

With him around me, I forgot about my illness. The only thing that actually bothered me that moment was thirst.

"Come, let's drink from a fountain," I stroked him back, and pulled him by his toga.

We washed each other's faces and drank cold fresh water from each other's hands… and then reunited in a kiss, unable to separate again.

"Oh, Princess," the tribune laughed. "You've hardly left your litter until recently, and now you march along Misenum and drink from a city fountain… Have I spoiled you that much?"

"No," I replied, gently wiping his forehead, "you mended me. And now, you have to marry me," I joked. "If you don't want me to be stoned, as I'm a Jewess now."

Cassius readily opened the box, and gently put an engagement token on my ring finger.

"Whoever dares to think of hurting you will have to face me first." He spoke out earnestly and asked me the question he had heard on the Goat Lake twelve years ago.

"Yes!" replied Drusilla… and Sophia. "Ad infinitum."[315]

We didn't care what cynical Tiberius would tell us. At that moment, the marble rotunda was the only world we knew, and we were its only inhabitants.

"At the Esquiline, I've always been considered a hardcore bachelor." My betrothed laughed. "They talk of me like I'm a lover of easy relations…" He went on embarrassed, as he helped me put my earrings in. "But I was waiting for you all the way – to grow up and love me back."

What I fool I was, I thought. *How could I chase chimeras, when I had my happiness here, at my fingertips?*

---

[315] (lat.) Forever.

We decided to go back to the palace by the longest path – along the Imperial gardens, follow by the rustle of the leaves and the birds singing. Hand in hand and side by side, we walked through the green arcades, leaving behind all the duties, words, and thoughts, and the whole world.

"They called her – Phantom Queen…" Straight off, we heard an elegant female voice with a Gaelic accent.

During the Old Caesar's dictatorship, the Gardens of Misenum belonged to the free Gauls, who accepted the new rule, moving to smaller Roman cities. In the time of harsh Augustus, who loathed peregrines, most of the Gauls were forced to leave the city, and the beautiful gardens became the property of the emperor's stepson – Tiberius.

Curious, we accelerated step, and as we walked out to the meadow, we saw the old Gaul, sitting on the grass surrounded by happy children.

"Morrigan is a skilled warrior," the woman went on, as she hadn't yet notice us. "But at the same time, the goddess of arts."

"Salud!" I greeted the stranger in her language. "Can we, too, listen to your fairy tale?"

"Degemer mat." The Gaul stood up, welcoming us. "I am Fedlimid, the manageress of Lady Ennia. By my days-off, I come here to the gardens as a storyteller for those kids."

Among the rosy-cheeked listeners, I noticed both the poorly dressed plebeian children, and the neatly combed nobles in small togas.

"It doesn't make a difference to me where each of them comes from," Fedlimid said, gesturing to us to join the circle. "I love them all equally."

"This I approve." Cassius nodded as he sat on a wide log. "I, too, as a child shared a nursemaid and a wet nurse with her sons."

"I'm not their nursemaid, knight." Fedlimid, like a foreigner, took his words literally. "My sons are grown up men; they lead now proper lives in the city of Rome, and never ask for their mother. First, I met those little Greeks," she showed towards two lovely brothers of tousled brown hair. "They were wandering around the market, crying with hunger, for the landlord didn't want to pay their mother wage."

"Who's the landlord?" I jumped to my feet, imagining the awful picture. "If he still let them starve, I will sue him at Caesar's!"

The younger boy gasped in astonishment, as his older brother humbly asked.

"Do you know Caesar, my Lady?"

All the children lifted up their eyes to me.

"I'm Julia Drusilla, his grand-niece," I said, and pointed to my companion. "And this is tribune Cassius Chaerea."

"I've guessed, that you are a patrician," Fedlimid replied. "Your speech, robe and attire revealed you. Well, I certainly fed the boys and made up some tale about the winged people. As I was telling, little Petronius heard us…"

"I really liked it." She was interrupted by the blue-eyed boy, sitting next to the Greeks. "My teachers are so boring, and the Grandma Gaul knows hundreds of legends!"

As they befriended Fedlimid, Petronius and the two brothers – Nestor and Melanthios brought to the gardens more children, eager for stories with a happy ending.

"For now, we meet here secretly," Fedlimid sighed. "No parent approves his offspring playing with a lower-class kid. I don't even know if I'm allowed to stay here… Still, I'm so attached to the toddlers, as if they were mine."

"You have my permission," I smiled, crouching between the brothers like a six-year-old. "I can easily solve the rest, too, if you tell me the story about the warrior goddess."

The Gaul smiled back at me, then fell silent for a while, as if she was listening to something in the distance, and began mysteriously.

"Morrigan is real. She lives in the Aquitaine forests. By day, she aids brave soldiers in fierce battles, and by night she turns into an owl to search for her loved one…"

"Who is her loved one?" asked the thin perky girl.

"No one knows." Fedlimid went on quietly, "For her wisdom and exceptional beauty, Morrigan was proposed to by all the mighty kings and deities. However, none of them could win her heart.

"One of the kings, cunning Nuadu, disguised himself as a shepherd, thinking that the goddess loved simplicity and virtue. He took her to the hut, offering hot bread and fresh milk. 'Oh, my king,' said Morrigan, as she knew who was hiding under tiny clothes. 'Your resourcefulness is worth the praise, but look at me! I am a goddess; I'm not made for cooking and tending cows. But, if you beat me in a single combat, I will think about it.' Nuadu was enthralled, so he accepted the duel with a godly warrior… and lost his head.

"The next admirer who was keen to marry Morrigan, was wealthy king Dagda. As he'd heard what happened to Nuadu, Dagda stood before the goddess in his full splendor, offering her all his riches – to the last coin. Morrigan thanked him for his generosity, yet rejected the proposal. She had magic powers to create herself as many treasures as she wanted. Since Dagda didn't want to leave without a fight, he followed his predecessor.

"The third king, Cuchulain, worshipped his dame like a goddess of arts, so he brought her a harp, celebrating her beauty in songs. Morrigan thanked him as well, but she didn't accept his proposal. 'Fine arts are for women. You, men, should perform on a battlefield.' These were her words. Alas, Cuchulain wasn't artful enough with a sword, so he fell.

"So," the Gaul finished her tale, "Morrigan, with the beauty of a maiden, kindness of a mother, wisdom of a sage, is still alone, still seeking for a knight to tame her heart."

Impressed by the story as greatly as the children, I could see the similarity between the heroine and… me, Sophia.

This is a decent portrayal, I thought, as I thanked the old woman. *Much better than Lamia or Hecate.*

"Will she ever find her hero?" asked the boy next to Petronius.

Fedlimid fell thoughtful, and I, guided on by the mystical part of my soul, looked at Chaerea, and answered. "I think she found him."

The dark-haired Greek girl raised her hand. "But, how did she know he was the one?"

Cassius had the answer.

"Her man was no king, but a soldier," he said. "He didn't offer Morrigan a star from heavens, nor did he boast of his talents, but he gave her his ardent heart…"

"Was there a combat?" little Nestor asked wittily.

"The true man never fights a lady," Cassius replied, embracing me. "He keeps her as the apple of his eye."

"And she keeps him," I finished.

The little listeners burst into applause.

"Please, visit us again." Fedlimid smiled. "Now they adore you more than me."

"Unfortunately, we are very busy." I sighed, and, as I took my little money bag and handed it to Nestor. "Share it fairly, and buy whatever you like."

While the children gazed excitedly at golden coins, Fedlimid hugged me from behind, and whispered.

"Whoever is divided by death, will be once reunited by life… in eternity."

I didn't understand her… then.

XLVIII

By the palace gates, we faced a horrifying sight. Servants, dressed in black were lamenting over someone recently deceased in a manner they grieve for a member of the imperial family.

Oh please, not grandmother, I thought, but cries of sorrow gave away the dead person's young age.

"Oh dove of ours! Hope of our land!" the maids wailed. "Vae nobis!"[316]

"Junia Claudilla died at childbirth this morning," Helicon explained in a tearfully deep voice. "The baby did not survive either."

I pressed my palms to my eyes. I didn't wish her anything bad, but even, for the sake of my nephew, I was willing to forgive her the attack.

"Caesar has declared mourning," the Egyptian went on. "And canceled all the receptions till the end of the month."

"Due to the warm weather," Pallas, the steward, spoke with his lips trembling, "the funeral will be held tomorrow."

I recalled my brother talking about how much he wanted children, and I clenched my fists in pain. As I was trying not to cry in front of claves, I felt vertigo taking hold of me.

"Call the Cretan," I ordered a slave boy in the atrium. "I'm going to be sick."

The young servant hurried along the corridor, and Cassius, without a second thought, raised me up.

"You were walking hungry in the heat," Alcaeus noted strictly, examining me. "They say, amantes sunt amentes,[317] but in your condition it can be dangerous."

"You're not going out without a litter anymore," Cassius said, helping me lie down. "I'll beg the emperor to let me take you home, to the Esquiline."

---

[316] (lat.) Woe to us!
[317] (lat.) Lovers are mad.

"Oh, I'll beseech him to do so," I sighed, lowering my head to his lap. "I can no longer endure captivity."

Alcaeus shook his head as he was making me a saving potion.

"Alas, Your Highness, you will have to."

I looked up to the man who dared to wake me up from the dream in my lover's embrace.

"Emperor is desperate for the death of the baby," the Greek expounded. "Every ruler cares about the heir and his offspring."

"Why, should I be a victim?" I asked him wearily. "Don't I have the right to be happy?"

"You do and you will," Alcaeus handed me a glass of mixture. "When the Old Wolf dies. For now, he needs you here, especially on the days of mourning."

I took the potion inadvertently. This time it tasted sour. I turned to the wall, and bent my legs toward my stomach.

"Let her rest," the medic whispered to Chaerea. "I will shake the sisters[318] in the kitchen to quit moaning and to make some dinner for Her Highness."

Cassius leaned over me.

"Do not worry," he uttered gently, but yet earnestly, and kissed my ring finger. "No one can separate Morrigan from her knight."

"If I was Morrigan," I said hoarsely, staring at the wall, "I would fuck them up unmercifully."

"And you will." The Greek smiled. "But, you know, both – love and war – demand a perfect time."

He always made me laugh.

"I know you have to go back to Rome," I said to Cassius, a bit cheered up. "There are new riots in the provinces, so they need new recruits."

"That's right, my love." He hugged me. "I train them for combat… and for certain death at the Parthian border."

---

[318] Ancient Greek slang name for pederasts.

"Bow to Mithras and Artabanus – and become a hero, or welcome to the slaughterhouse." The medic, too, recalled his military past. "From the old guard, there were just Corbulo, your Cassius and I, who somehow managed to avoid the division."

Thanks God, I thought, as I, again, became aware of what was going on – in Rome, and in the world, and all around us.

"You are right," I said. "No time for the rest yet."

When Cassius was already in the prothyron, and the physician turned to follow him, I asked, "Why do us, women, die in childbirth?"

The Cretan looked at me, a bit confused.

"Age is the reason in most cases, Princess. It may happen that a very young body cannot bear delivery, or the natural health of a mother is poor, and her baby is large… If you ask me about your sister-in-law, I suppose her… women's parts were not mature enough for labors."

I nodded in understanding, and decided aloud, "I'll have some rest and continue my writings."

"Good girl." He winked at me as he was leaving. "Don't worry about the things which are not threatening you anyway. Enjoy your love."

It took me a while to rest my spine before I went back to my drama. The medication seemed to be working, and my aim was too serious to waste a minute more. I took the scroll Callistus gave me, and unrolled it.

"On the other end of the earth plain," wrote the unknown storyteller. *"In the lands of eternal summer, Alexander met the people of dark skin, short height and easy-going nature. They were heathens and worshipped idols, the most fervently – the goddess Huitaca and her husband Chaquen. Huitaca, who was believed to turn into an eagle-owl, gave her people all kinds of arts, while Chaquen protected them in wars. The southerners welcomed the great king warmly and, as they heard of his feats, bowed to him and begged to save them from the Serpent's children. The odd enemies were predicted to come from the very edge of the firmament, attacking the good-natured hosts. Even the high priest was trembling in fear by the vision of them breaking down into their settlements…"*

In one breath, I set the stage directions, thinking over the main character's line. What could a warlord and a king, who had recently followed Adonai, reply to the heathens?

"*ALEXANDER:*" I wrote, analyzing his character. He was wise enough not to offend the hosts, nor to behave like a superior being.

"*O brothers!*" I began his speech, unwillingly recalling the dispute of the secretaries about the hero's modesty. "*Why do you ask me, a mortal man, to protect you from demons? Don't you have your powerful deities to give you wisdom and power to win?*"

HIGH PRIEST:

For thirty nights, I have prayed to the Immortal Dyad, until I dreamed what they revealed me. Those ones beyond the sea, like you and us are just creations – the erring children of the Great Spirit – the sole ruler of destiny.

ALEXANDER:

Even the idols cannot speak against the Truth. There is no gods before Adonai; only He can help you.

HIGH PRIEST:

You will do as He wills to protect us.

ALEXANDER:

Why me?

HIGH PRIEST:

In the same dream I was told that you are coming as His envoy.

As I finished the line, I put my pen back to the ink bottle, and took a scroll to read the legend once again.

"It's fascinating," I noticed. "The gods of these barbarians remind me Morrigan and her Knight... Or does it only seem so?"

As it often happened, thoughts of mine were interrupted by a knock.

"Your Highness, it's me, Helicon." The secretary entered. "Caesar calls you to dine with him now."

"Just in time." I smiled, quickly hiding my scrolls and writing supplies to the bookshelf. I indeed was very hungry, and Tiberius so providentially shared my taste for some unhealthy food.

"Tell Susannah to find me the black dress I wore at Photice's funeral.

In the triclinium, Tiberius was sitting at the table, grudgingly scooping something with a spoon over his plate.

"Cene bene, Caesar," I greeted him, embarrassed. "Me paenitet, tarda sum."[319]

"Rem nihil morare."[320] The emperor waved aside. "You excuse me, for being rude to you the last time we had dinner."

I opened my eyes wide, as I could barely believe my ears. Realizing that the ruler was actually waiting for the answer, I accepted the apology.

"Please, have a sit," he spoke ill-temperedly. "I've lost my appetite today."

He didn't lie. The death of an unborn baby, an imperial great-grandson seemed to take away his wickedness, leaving him only wormwood.

"The death of this innocent creature is a punishment for me." He sighed. "For the misdeeds of Augustus, and Livia, and my own, too… the gods decided to exterminate our lineage."

I took a few bites, murmuring something about how impossible is to stay flawless in this cruel world.

"I see, you haven't given up on that love," the old man changed the subject. "Have you?"

I looked him in the eye, already ready to repeat these words at the Forum, in the Senate, and before Artabanus himself.

"Neither have I now, nor shall I ever."

Again, Tiberius surprised me, as he suddenly stood up and gave me a half-bow.

"I really admire you, girl. No one alive has a dash of your courage, Drusilla."

"Cassius shares my feelings." I, too, rose up from my chair, due to the courtesy. "He is ready to wait for whenever it takes."

The emperor raised his right hand to silence me.

"I don't mind about your marriage, neptis."

It was obvious that the order about my espousal to Longinus came out of the Senate, from Vespasian and Sabin. The satrap of Artabanus would never allow "Layla" to bond with someone beyond their cult. Undoubtedly, the enemies knew who I was… but still had no idea of what I was planning.

---

[319] (lat.) Sorry, I'm late.
[320] (lat.) Nevermind.

"I approve your engagement." The ruler went on, as the slaves left the hall. "And I will allocate funds for the wedding ... Still," he raised his index finger. "I demand of you to keep it secret."

"Cassius must back to Rome tomorrow," I replied, as my heart started galloping.

"Hurry up then." Tiberius fixed his crown. "Fuck the mourning. Who knows much time is left for me."

Still hungry, I filled my mouth with stuffed turkey, wiped it with a crumpled napkin and ran out to the corridor.

"David!" I exclaimed, pushing two guardsmen away.

I found the Jew at the desk in the library.

"Guess what?" I smiled at him. "After all, Caesar approved my engagement to Cassius!"

The rabbi jumped to his feet merrily, pointing to the pile of scrolls.

"Elohim gadol,[321] Princess! I've just been reading about preparations for kidushin[322] and nisuin.[323] We will have a lot of work to do…"

"We have no time for that," I cautioned him. "Cassius is needed in Rome."

The Jew sighed and looked down sadly.

"We can't prepare a wedding overnight, Your Highness. Remember, the tribune is a pagan, and for an adult male, the process of converting to our faith is long and… not very convenient."

"How long would that take?" I asked, trying not to think of something he called 'not very convenient.'

"Well, first, the high priest – that is me – must acquaint the convert with the wisdom of the Talmud and the Torah," David explained earnestly. "Then, he must relinquish the false gods; undergo the circumcision and ritual bathing in mikveh."

I put myself down to a chair, rubbing my temples.

"And?"

---

[321] (hebr.) Great is God!
[322] (hebr.) Engagement.
[323] (hebr.) Wedding.

My friend gave me a sympathetic glance.

"Since you two have committed fornication, lying with other people, you will have to fast for forty days…"

"No way!" I exclaimed. "With all the dutiful respect, isn't true love above the law?"

"Oh, Princess…" He wiped sweat from his forehead. "Who am I to advise you? I myself, shouldn't have become a priest unmarried!"

I suddenly recalled the story of Ruth, the young pagan widow, who fell in love with the reputable Jewish landowner Boaz. As Susannah told, in order to avoid force marriage to another, wise Ruth walked into Boaz's tent to be his wife or maid. Despite the rules and customs, that marriage was approved by the elders, and even God Himself blessed it, for their grandson was the famous king and prophet David.

"What about Ruth and Boaz?" I asked him anxiously. "Did they also have to go through hell and deep blue sea to be together?"

"Please, Your Highness, use the proper words," the young man spoke bewilderedly. "You're mentioning the righteous people."

"What about King David and Bathsheba?" I went on, barely listening to him. "Wasn't their love adultery? What about Esther, marrying the pagan king? What on earth makes them better than Cassius Chaerea and me?"

"My namesake paid dearly for his love to Bathsheba." The priest shrugged. "Their firstborn son died…"

"God punished him for murder, not for love," I waved aside, remembering the story well. "The infant died, for David sent Bathsheba's husband to the eye of war to see him dead!"

"You're right," my friend reluctantly agreed, gesturing toward the books again. "For what is worth a loveless marriage?"

"Oh, David," I came up to him and hugged him. "Haven't we already been suffering and waiting for too long?"

He patted me by my hand.

"Do you remember the name I gave you at conversion?"

"Chokmah." I smiled, as I recalled that happy day.

"And, do you know its meaning?" he went on a little more cheerfully.

I shook my head.

"Sophia, Wisdom," the young man replied. "The night before the ceremony, that name visited me in a dream."

I squinted thoughtfully, letting my heart decide for me.

"Oh," David nodded toward the clepsydra. "My workday is over." I helped him make the desk, rolling the scrolls and putting them back to the shelves.

When we finished, I hurried to my chambers. Susannah was worriedly waiting for her 'Little Owl.'

"Find me a clean underdress," I asked her, ignoring her questions. "Better the new one."

The nursemaid, probably thinking I was sleepy, asked me whether I planned to take a bath first.

"Definitely," I replied. "Ask them to prepare thermae for me."

"I'm afraid, you'll have to wait, my dear." The Jewess lowered her eyes like she was embarrassed. "Tribune Chaerea wished to take a bath before he leaves."

The bright reflection in my mirror smiled.

"Oh, great." I snatched a thin violet tunic from her hands. "Get some rest. You are free for tonight."

XLIX

AD 37

"Militat omnis amans, et habet sua castra Cupido..."[324] Cassius started his letter, quoting incomparable Ovid.

I took a piece of parchment closer to my face, wishing I could feel the smell of my beloved mixed with the aroma of frigidarium.[325]

"What are you doing to me?" I asked his broad and wide handwriting, as I leaned against the cold wall, finding salvation in my memories.

"Amata mea,"[326] I heard him whispering, as our bodies merged into one. *"I've been longing for you ever since I was aware of myself..."*

That night, two hearts were beating in the same fast-paced rhythm, and two breaths combining into single sound of pleasure. I could still see our naked souls embracing even more ardently than our bodies, feeling even greater bliss...

"Lilith is fire," my memories intertwined with a forgotten text. *"You cannot rule a flame, but you can conquer it."*

"Verum est." I opened my eyes, awakened by the downpour on the terrace. Somewhere deep inside myself, hidden from everyone, even Gaius, there had been a stronger part of me, discovered only by one man.

Cassius Chaerea.

"You marched uninvited into the secret harbor of my pride," I wrote to him a month after he left. *"You broke down the doors of my doubt and loneliness the way you crashed by the gates of the enemy camp. You walked unharmed through the flames of my heart without trying to douse it, for we were both made of the same blaze..."*

---

[324] (lat.) Every lover makes war, and Cupid has his own. (Ovid, Amores, 1.9.1).
[325] (lat.) A cold room in an ancient Roman bath.
[326] (lat.) My love.

It was March AD 37. That whimsical month, once dedicated by King Pompilius to the deity of war, was believed to bring around big changes. Statesmen used its changeable weather for starting military campaigns to take their enemies aback.

That spring, with the help of Susannah and David, I was preparing for the first Purim[327] in my 'Jewish' life.

"By the holiday's eve, we send gifts to our relatives, friends, and share alms," the priest taught me. "Women prepare a rich table with sweets, men read the Megillah[328] at the synagogue, and children make noise and sing songs."

"My sons adored that holiday," Susannah recalled sadly, making cookie dough. "No one in Tiberias[329] knew how to bake such tasty cakes as your nanny did."

That March, Gaius returned to the capital city, where, as the quaestor, he was to take part in the political and civil life of Rome. At my request, Caesar allowed Macro to follow the prince for his safety. However, my brother didn't care about the senators and their malicious plans, but he was happy to depart so he could reunite with Messalina.

"If you are so enthusiastic," I said to him ashore, "make sure your servants visit Rachel, Cassius and our grandma with my gifts."

"Antonia will die from laughter when she hears you've become Jewish," Gaius replied cheerfully. "And that Chaerea, too…"

"You better… take care," I jokingly threatened him. "And pass my greetings to your sweetheart."

"I will marry her," he spoke aloud, stepping on board. "We will have many, many children!"

It was March, AD 37. The night was falling on Sinus Cumanus[330] like a black scarf. Wet with rain, I was watching from the terrace the misty seashore intermittently by the sharp lightning and the small blinking lighthouse.

---

[327] A Jewish festival held in spring to commemorate the defeat of Haman's plot to massacre the Jews as recorded in the book of Esther.

[328] "The Scroll of Esther" is a firsthand account of the events of Purim, written by the Queen Esther herself.

[329] An Israeli city on the western shore of the Sea of Galilee. Established around 20 CE, it was named in honour of the second emperor of the Roman Empire, Tiberius.

[330] The modern-day Gulf of Naples.

"*Militat omnis amans, et habet sua castra Cupido…*" I repeated the poet's words, and lowered my palms to the cold plate of the balustrade.

"*Quid facis,*[331] Princepessa?" Callistus rushed to the patio. "The sky has opened, and the thunder is hitting like a hammer!"

"*Valeo,*" I said, ultimately feeling the unsavory coldness of rain. "I was born in the nasty weather."

"*Mecum veni!*"[332] The Greek pulled me into the chamber. "The Wolf calls for you."

"He's really boring." I rolled my eyes. "What does he want now at the dead of night?"

The secretary took off his cloak and wrapped me in it like a doll, gesturing me not to ask, but to hurry.

I tied my hair in a quick bun and headed for the peristyle, giving names to the Furies, who often visited Caesar by nights.

"Come in and close the door behind you." I heard his voice coming from the bedroom.

I found Tiberius lying in his bed under its heavy canopy, with his gaze restless.

"What's wrong, great-uncle?" I asked without a notion of the reason.

"Sit by me," he whispered earnestly. "Now take a listen and don't interrupt me. Time is running out."

I looked at him. The emperor looked neither pale, nor sick.

"The sixteenth…" He let a sigh out. "The death day of Romulus, Pompilius and Old Caesar is dawning."

I was startled, catching something sinister, for all those rulers died violently.

"The equinox is here," Tiberius went on. "The time when those Mesopotamian bastards honored Mithras' return from the Underworld."

"So they sacrifice an inappropriate ruler," I uttered, recalling.

Tiberius nodded.

---

[331] (lat.) What are you doing?
[332] (lat.) Come with me!

"You heard it yourself," he said bitterly. "Each new emperor receives from Artabanus a certain number of years – to prove his allegiance to Mithras. And if he fails, he's being sacrificed."

Caligula had gotten four years.

"As Augustus vouched for me, damn Pater honored me with twenty-two." The old man sighed. "So far, I've failed him twice, and it's enough to fuck me up."

Tiberius was so flustered that his usual cough could choke him.

"At the behest of these monsters, I lied, I destroyed foreign sanctuaries, stole from the poor, killed my own kinsmen…"

He had left me speechless.

"I bowed to the Sun and kissed Artabanus' robe, believing it could make me more powerful than Augustus… I lost the ones I loved and everything that made me human…"

Until one day, Tiberius' loyal service suddenly collapsed… for love.

"Seven years ago, they ordered me to kill 'Lamia and her Knight,'" Tiberius recalled, not hiding his sincere remorse. "But, when I met you and Chaerea, all I could have done was separate you."

"It didn't work," Sophia laughed in me, while Julia Drusilla was upset and silent.

"I was stunned by my own decision," he went on in a barely audible voice. "All of a sudden, I looked at myself and all around me with new eyes, and for the first time, I refused obedience to Mithras."

Wet clothes, lack of sleep, and shocking new facts aroused shivers in my weak body.

"Take a cover," Caesar handed me a blanket. "Warm yourself."

I wrapped myself in it without my then-disgust.

"When was the second time?"

"Just… yesterday," he answered, glancing down at the clepsydra. "I refused to send tribune Chaerea to the Parthian frontier."

My mouth quivered, and the painful tide of tears pressed my forehead.

"Oh, Caesar!" I groped for his hand in the half-dark. "They will…"

"No, they will not." He grinned, throwing a pillow to my lap. "You will."

Out of sympathy and gratitude, I burst into weeping.

"Don't whine, Drusilla!" the old man exclaimed. "It is better to die swiftly and painlessly now than to be skinned by motherfuckers later."

I nodded and lifted the pillow.

"Don't worry about the guardsmen." He patted me on the hand. "The Cretan will confirm my death as natural."

"What about Gaius?" I murmured, squinting.

"You mean, Gaius Julius Caesar?" He smiled for the last time. "I bet he will give bloody hell to Artabanus. And so will you, by gods! Four years would be enough to finish up your drama, Libitina."

PART II
...IN BELLO PERIBIS[333]

I

"Our baby! Our star!" the masses hailed, as Caligula was entering Rome. "To the Tiber with Tiberius!"

The motley mobs, like lava, spilled onto the streets of the capital. Such admiration and euphoria about the new reign was known to neither the Old Caesar, nor to Alexander himself.

"I accept the powers of the principate as conferred by the Senate," Gaius said solemnly at the Forum, as the parade was over. "I'm not promising you the moon and the sky, but from now on, my life as the emperor I dedicate to you, people of Rome!"

There were large crowd applause and singing of triumphant songs, just like the day Germanicus was welcomed as the victor.

"Mark Antony and Cleopatra opened the granaries of Egypt for the hungry," he continued. "And so am I, Gaius Julius Caesar Germanicus, now opening the public treasury for people!"

We both knew that mentioning state enemies and spending millions of silver sesterces to fight the poverty would provoke senatorial wreath, but we didn't care. We had pure intentions and... four years.

To honor his predecessor's demise, Gaius arranged pompous games at the Taurus amphitheater, which was the invention of the late emperor. The audience of all the

---

[333] *Ibis redibis nunquam in bello peribis* (lat.) *"you will go you will return never in war will you perish"*. The phrase is thought to have been uttered to a general consulting the oracle about his fate in an upcoming battle. The sentence is crafted in a way that without punctuation, it can be interpreted in two significantly different ways.

ages and classes were blessing the young Caesar for hilariously low entering prices and the large variety of events.

The bloody gladiator fights turned into spectacles of the strongest and most skilled warriors from every province. As for the theatrical performances, my brother introduced 'The Oresteia,'[334] 'Alcestis'[335] and 'Lysistrata'[336] to plebeians. All the minority religions were legally recognized, making the grateful peregrines sacrifice thousands of animals for the sake of new ruler's prosperity.

"A citizen has the right to believe in whatever he wants, on the condition that the law is never violated." With these words my brother took the curule seat of the Hostilia.

The senators reluctantly accepted the new laws. Vespasian observed his emperor with a sly smile, deeming that the solar cult, under different masks, had already settled down to all the temples. Artabanus' deputy couldn't suspect that right then, the first synagogue, devoid of the hostile influence, was being built on the Esquiline by the old cemetery.

"The pillars of the temple must be straight and undecorated," David repeated to the busy workers. "The door hinges should be made in the shape of a hyssop herb."

"Look at that easy rider!" Rachel laughed, as she was painting the round window. "What would you do without me, friend?"

Well, David finally gathered some courage to return her blissfully.

"If Her Highness allows, you will be my Rabbanit[337] soon."

On the other side of the hill, once dedicated to the goddess Libitina, soldiers were enjoying bonuses under the new, loyal warlord Corbulo. On Cassius' advice, Caesar

---

[334] A trilogy of Greek tragedies written by Aeschylus, concerning the mythological hero Orestes and his deeds.

[335] An Athenian tragedy by the ancient Greek playwright Euripides, which tells the story of a Greek queen, who agreed to die instead of her doomed husband.

[336] An ancient Greek comedy by Aristophanes, originally performed in classical Athens, which was a comic account of a woman's extraordinary mission to end the Peloponnesian War between Greek city states by denying all the men of the land any sex, which was the only thing they truly and deeply desired.

[337] (hebr.) The title used for the wife of a rabbi.

appointed a new governor to rebellious Germania. Lentulus Gaetulicus was rather mediocre at war, but skilled at diplomacy, moreover grandmothered by a Germanic woman from Rhaetia.[338]

"When you're surrounded by the enemies," Caligula reasoned. "The silliest thing would be starting a war. You can gain victory in peace if you are cautious and you have a right ally. The right ally may not be good, but smart enough to be useful for us, and enough of a fool not to expose our game."

The same tactics he used, promoting Claudius to the title of the censor, and naming the stout senator Aemilius Lepidus the proconsul. As we knew that Vespasian used our uncle to spy on the young Caesar, Gaius offered fearful Claudius to play a double-spy. To get a kind of loyalty from Lepidus, my brother promised him the hand of Agrippina.

The next step was closing the Gates of Janus.[339]

"For such a great empire, every new war would be a waste of men, time and resources. I will work for peace in our provinces and strengthen all the borders," he explained before the councilors.

Throughout Italia began the upbuilding of ports, aqueducts and bridges. Gaius didn't spare the wealth Tiberius had been accumulated aimlessly. To the plebeian rapture and senatorial resentment, he reduced the taxes, abolished those convicted by Tiberius, and restored dilapidated houses on Suburra.

"I'm so proud of you, Caesar," Antonia praised him, listening to happy shouts from her terrace. "I wish your parents could welcome this moment."

Our executed family was not forgotten either. In the company of two young women, once betrothed to late Nero and Drusus, Gaius sailed to Pandataria to bring the ashes of our mother and brothers to bury them worthily in the Mausoleum of Augustus. As a tribute to our father, he ordered to erect a golden memorial plaque in the Temple of Mars.

---

[338] A province of the Roman Empire; modern-day Switzerland.

[339] The double doors of the temple, called the gates of war; for the temple always stood open in time of war, but was closed when peace had come.

Macro and already-put-aside Ennia tried to regain Caligula's attention by boring flattery and denouncing some less important renegades. They were replied with a lucid, mysterious gaze and bewildering smile.

"I was the first to stand by you, my Caesar," the prefect reminded him. "I've always believed in you reviving Rome."

"As far as I'm concerned, you were the third," Gaius explained. "My sister was the first, almost immediately joined by Cassius Chaerea."

Macro stared at him astonished, wondering how come a woman, or a man beyond their cult, could be considered the ruler's allies.

"Remember, on the day of Father's triumph, you told me I was going to ride an imperial chariot?" My brother returned to the year 17. "And I promised you the title of Augusta."

"The only woman to carry that title was Livia." I smiled, imagining the outrage in Senate.

"I'll strip her of that name posthumously." He chuckled, recollecting my conflict with the late dowager empress. "After all, I'm making you my equal."

I didn't care about the titles and the privileges. Sitting next to Gaius in the throne room of the palace, once called Domus Tiberiana, I was thinking about all the obstacles and pitfalls of our way.

The way we chose. The way that chose us.

II

My twenty-fourth birthday was full of surprises – mostly unpleasant ones.

Toward the morning, Susannah woke me up with her face as pale as a ghost's.

"Yom hu'ledet sameah, Little Owl!" She murmured, pointing to a big garland of colorful flowers above my desk.

"Toda!" I sat up, and rubbed my eyes. "Are you a rooster to wake me at dawn?"

"Your cousin Messalina arrived." The nursemaid said. "She didn't tell me what's the matter, but she's all in tears."

"If my brother hurt her," I got up, and headed to the washing bowl. "I'll tear his kingly ears off!"

Changing my dress, I turned to the balcony. How many times by then I had already changed my room? Now, as the emperor's sister, I lived in the palace. My spacious chambers were once built for Julia Caesaris, the infamous daughter of Augustus.

I hope Vipsania's jewelry and Julia's chambers won't bring me bad luck. I thought, as I hurried downstairs.

Both of Tiberius' former wives ended up dying. Vipsania, the only love of my great-uncle, was divorced from him by force, and soon remarried to a senator she'd barely known. As for unfaithful Julia, her banishment, bad illnesses and lonesome death had already become the basis of the scary tales told by plebeian children by the fire.

The kinswoman was waiting in the atrium, dejected and bored by my caring maids trying to wipe her tears, sit her down and give her some water to drink.

"Leave us alone!" I ordered the slave girls, and took Messalina to the peristyle.

"Caligula… Caesar…" she wept in my hug. "He wants to marry me… to Claudius!"

That news shook me harder than an ice bath.

"Caesar must be joking, right?" Susannah asked hopefully.

My brother couldn't have been that lunatic. His mind and mood had tendency to change, but this bizarre outburst must certainly had had a serious reason.

"It's been decreed… by the Imperial order." The favorite sighed heavily.

"Don't worry, I will handle it." I fixed her wild red curls. "Wait for me here, and listen to Susannah."

"I am pregnant!" Messalina's moan followed me to the throne room.

"I want to see my brother!" I announced the guardsmen by the door.

"Caesar is busy, Your Highness," one of them dissuaded readily. "He does not wish to be visited now."

"I'm not a client, you idiot!" I exclaimed. "Get off my way, or I'll call Anicetus."

As they hear about the Cypriot, whose height and fist strength could frighten even haughty Macro, the praetorians exchanged glances, and opened the door.

Caligula sat on the throne, surrounded by advisers, studying the state documents in detail. Traces of insomnia on his young face announced some trouble.

"What the hell is going on?" I heard my own anxious voice echoing in the room.

My brother looked at me, astonished.

"Shouldn't you be sleeping?"

"That is not funny," I replied, barely refraining myself from a quarrel. "Would you please explain why you are marrying your pregnant favorite to Uncle Claudius?"

"Leave us." Gaius half-turned to the prefect. "We'll discuss that matter later."

Macro obeyed with an ill-tempered face.

"You too, Helicon," he said to the Egyptian. "And you, Protogenes." The gray-haired steward, once a loyal servant of our father, also left the hall.

Now there were only three of us – my brother, Callistus and me.

"Drusilla." Gaius looked at me, annoyed. "What do you think you're doing?"

"I'd like to ask you the same thing," I responded in the same tone. "I was sure you loved that woman even more than me –"

"I love her more than you imagine!" Gaius interrupted me, as he stood up. "That's why I want to keep her safe."

"Safe?!" I laughed nervously. "Next to that sleazebag?"

Caesar nodded to the secretary to continue.

"By the patriline, Messalina belongs to gens Valerii, the distant kin to the Flavii," the Greek explained. "Since her very birth, she had been promised to a follower of Mithras, or…"

"Don't even mention it," I whispered angrily. "Why Claudius?"

"Because I want to save her from the real marriage!" Gaius shouted. "Are you both too foolish to figure it out?"

"What about the baby?" I was still in doubt. "What if this dog doesn't acknowledge it? What if he blackmails her for that lie?"

The Greek replied again, reminding me of the infamous conversation between Vespasian and my uncle at the Curia. Despite his strong desire to become an insider of the Sun-cult, he still did not fulfill the crucial requirement – fathering a child. His only daughter Antonilla was widely suspected to be born of her mother's adultery.

"Who would be faithful to him after all?" Callistus giggled and went on earnestly. "Aware of that, our Caesar made a bargain with your uncle, due to which the cripple fool gets what he wants, but only formally. So, misogynist Claudius was glad to take the terms."

"Do you think Vespasian will believe it?" I looked up to Caesar.

"That depends on Messalina," he said. "On her willingness to play the role in public until we defeat Vespasian and Artabanus."

"I will try my hardest to convince her," I promised. "But if only that fool dares to touch her, I will kill him, and throw his body to the dogs!"

"Ecce Augusta!"[340] Callistus rolled his eyes, smiling embarrassedly. "I have been teaching her good manners for seven years, but…"

"Skase bre malaka!"[341] I called out, and then thought aloud, "At least I got away with it this time."

While I was still speaking, I noticed the worried gaze of the secretary, and the uneasy look of Gaius. In a moment, they exchanged those glances and then turned to me.

---

[340] (lat.) Behold the Exalted one!
[341] (anc.gr.) Shut up, you fool!

"Is there anything else I should know?" I asked, still soberly, but with a bitter premonition.

First, my brother wanted to entrust this news to Callistus, but as he noticed pain and horror on my face, he came up slowly and embraced me.

"Help me, little sister," he spoke to my ear. "It turned out harder than I thought."

Drusilla wished to run away, to disappear, to die... but Sophia, with her head high, gathered some strength, calmed down and asked him for the name.

Well, Aemilius Lepidus sounded too nauseous.

"As you know, I promised him Agrippina for wife," he said honestly." She and her husband have hated each other since they first met. Still, after ten years of barren marriage, our sister finally conceived. Most likely, Ahenobarbus is the father."

"What about Livilla?" I uttered indignantly. "Her marriage is, too, a calamity."

"She has a son," he reminded me. "The only successor of the house Vinicii. I can't find it in me to separate a child from his father... or mother."

"So you're separating me from Cassius?" I couldn't hold back tears. "Everyone wanted it this way: our mother, Tiberius, goddamn Vespasian, and even you!"

"Don't worry, Your Highness," the 'all-seeing' secretary tried to comfort me. "Lepidus doesn't care about your money, but your status."

"He is not the Bat." I shook my head in doubt. "He is young, ambitious, and a Mithraist. I bet he plans to have children."

"I know how you feel, and I'm not mad at you," my brother said. "But do you think I'd let him hurt you?"

In despair, I had forgotten that Lepidus was a widower with a daughter.

"So I'll have to move to Carinae again?" I rolled my eyes.

Caligula, close to the edge of patience, turned away to the huge fresco above the throne.

"You are staying in the palace, Princess," Callistus explained. "Your relationship with tribune Chaerea should be kept in secrecy."

These conditions weren't strange to me. However, then, I hoped Gaius would change everything as soon as he became the emperor. Unfortunately, it was still too early for the miracles.

"Now is not the time for us to act like capricious children," he concluded, as he took a big scroll and opened it quickly. "Do you know what the Sibylline Prophecy says?"

I shrugged my shoulders with somewhat ill-tempered curiosity.

"Yet only *the true child* of Alexander can defeat the Parthians," he read aloud, adding. "I will need allies for that."

First of all, you will need true faith, I thought. *Without God's blessing, all the kingdoms turn to sand.*

"I will marry Lepidus," I spoke, startling myself. "If you promise me to follow my advice when the time comes."

"Everything you want, my dear." Caligula rejoiced. "After the ceremony, we will go to Cumae. The Sibyl had a special prophecy for every ruler."

I nodded emotionlessly, thinking of Messalina, who was still unaware of our plan. Our poor kinswoman was expecting salvation from the one who couldn't even save herself from an unwanted marriage.

"Sophia is always a scapegoat,"[342] I complained to David after some uneasy efforts to comfort my cousin. "I'm engaged to Cassius, but I will have to share a wedding table with another man."

"Ratzon Hashem,"[343] he sighed, as he touched my forehead for blessing. "Our father Abraham gave his own wife, beautiful Sarah, to Pharaoh's harem, thus saving them both from Egyptian wickedness."

"I know that story." I smiled. "Pharaoh couldn't touch her, for Adonai watched over her."

"He will watch over you, too," the rabbi assured me, raising his index finger. "Cadent a latere tuo mille et decem milia a dextris tuis ad te autem non adpropinquabit…"[344]

---

[342] (in the Bible) a goat sent into the wilderness after the Jewish chief priest had symbolically laid the sins of the people upon it (Lev. 16). Commonly – a person who is blamed for the wrongdoings, mistakes, or faults of others, especially for reasons of expediency.

[343] (hebr.) The will of God.

[344] (lat.) A thousand shall fall at thy side, and ten thousand at thy right hand: but it shall not come nigh thee (Psalm 90 (91):7).

"...Verumtamen oculis tuis considerabis et retributionem peccatorum videbis,"[345] I went on with the psalm, the very first prayer I learned.

"Vey, Princess!" David recalled. "Rabbanit and I prepared a birthday gift for you!"

"Good boy," I finally cheered up, as he was groping on his bookshelves with his robe funnily rustling. "Even Caesar has forgotten."

"Here you are!" He handed me a silver pendant on a chain with inscription in Hebrew. "Don't ask me where I got it, but I'm damned if it is not the real abracadabra!"

I allowed him to put the present around my neck, and slowly came up to the mirror.

"The practice of women wearing a protective amulet with Lilith's name," he pointed to the inscription. "It's denying the official myth."

I gratefully kissed the rabbi on his bearded cheek, making him blush.

"You've brightened my mood," I explained somewhat shyly.

"Diluculum,"[346] he nodded toward the large, mechanized clepsydra.

I wished him goodnight and hurried to my chambers to change my clothes and put some makeup on.

Cassius was waiting for me in the garden, holding a carved box with the letter Δ on its lid – a trading emblem of Dion from Misenum.

"Caesar granted me promotion to the Praetorian Guard," he said brightly, giving me a present. "I will serve Caesar in the same rank, protecting his family."

All I wished in that moment was to hide myself in his arms from the rest of the world forever.

"Let's go inside," I whispered. "We deserve a proper celebration."

---

[345] (lat.) But thou shalt consider with thy eyes: and shalt see the reward of the wicked (Psalm 90 (91):8).

[346] (lat.) the evening time, "the fourth watch" – the end of the working day for wage earners and freedmen (6 PM).

III

Lepidus personally asked the emperor's for the wedding celebration to be held at Lapis Niger – the shrine, where, as the legend said, they buried Romulus.

"The house Aemilia is the one of the great antiquity," he interpreted his choice before Caligula. "I would like to pay tribute to my ancestor-triumvir,[347] and to all the statesmen of my family."

Gaius agreed inadvertently, immediately recognizing in that bizarre gesture the handwriting of the Mithraists.

"Festivity at someone's resting place," he said to me in secret. "They are turning every act into profanity."

That one is going to surprise us even more, I thought, watching the clumsy groom parading through the Forum proudly, with his head artificially curled and his belly stuck out over his toga. *Yet we won't remain indebted.*

"You are prettier than they say," Lepidus dared to whisper in my ear at the midst of the wedding feast. "Now I feel sorry that our union is fictive."

"Did you know Marcus, the youngest son of the consul Asinius?" I asked my husband, imitating his disgusting dirty-flirty tone.

"Of course I did!" Lepidus gave me a wide smile, as he rubbed his cheek, already red with wine. "He was my friend."

"Do you know what happened to him on the Capri?" I went on cheerfully, handing him another glass of wine.

The imperial brother-in-law raised his eyebrows confusedly.

"He… fell out of favor," he muttered. "With Tiberius."

I shook my head in negation and moved to sit closer to him, as he did a while ago.

"No, dear. *I* killed the bastard."

---

[347] Marcus Aemilius Lepidus – a Roman statesman who formed the Second Triumvirate alongside Octavian and Mark Antony during the final years of the Roman Republic.

First, Lepidus thought it was a joke and started laughing, but as our eyes met, he fell silent and swallowed a lump.

"Refer to me that way again," I spoke through my teeth. "And I will skin you like a hare."[348]

His round face turned pale in terror, but I still had something more to tell him.

"I am not afraid of your masters," I whisper. "*They* are scared of me."

Consul Lepidus spent the rest of the dinner in silence, hidden at the opposite end of the big table. Gaius swiftly occupied the empty bridegroom's couch.

"Those idiots will always gossip," he explained, referring to bewildered guests. "We'd better let them talk about incest than endanger our loved ones."

"Yes, Caesar," I embraced him, discreetly removing the new ring and replacing in with the one I got from Cassius. "Ludi Incipiant!"[349]

That summer, rainbow days of joy were ceased by dusky sorrow as Actaeon brought me the worst news of my life.

"Lady Antonia is dying. She is calling you to bid farewell."

I knew it would happen. Alcaeus had been staying at Villa Claudiana for a month, desperately trying to cure her.

"It's a rare disease, Your Highness," the medic informed me in a letter, not separating from the patient. *"Hippocrates once said it was coming from the East. The cause is unknown, it is not contagious. In its early stages, it is impossible to notice and incurable afterwards."*

From the East,[350] I thought, suppressing tears and anger. *The cradle of sin and plague.*

Grandmother didn't take her illness seriously, nor was she afraid of death.

"Mors expectat,"[351] she replied with a smile when I was begging her to take care of her health. "Filius caninis!"[352]

---

[348] The name Lepidus was derived from the Latin word "lepus" – a hare.
[349] (lat.) Let the games begin!
[350] The Romans called "The East" mainly unconquered territories of Mesopotamia.
[351] (lat.) Death comes for us all.
[352] (lat.) Son of a bitch! (the word "death" is masculine in Latin).

It was extremely hard for me, but I did not allow myself to cry. Antonia deserved to leave in peace. At her wish, Cassius followed me to her dying bed.

"Come, children." The old woman, weak and decrepit with pain, gave us a loving look. "It seems to me like I see my father Mark and stepmother Cleo."

I tried to suppress laughter, ineffectually.

"I resemble Mark Antony only with my military dress," the tribune said. "But, anyway, I thank you for the compliment, my Lady."

"I look like Cleopatra even less," I stroked Grandmother's hair. "She was the goddess of beauty."

"Venus herself," the matron nodded, sinking into memories and visions. "Venus never leads to victory."

"The noble triumvir has always been my role model and will always be a symbol of the Roman strength," the tribune told her. "Only the one who is not remembered is really defeated and dead."

Antonia replied with a slight smile, then grabbed his hand, and whispered.

"They are lying, Cassius. Augustus knew that the Roman fleet had no chance against the Egyptian, and he would have been defeated at the Actium, unless he called Parthian king for help."

Chaerea didn't look surprised. I had told him everything I heard from Zaleukos, and, many years later, from Tiberius, and he had believed me unconditionally.

"Selene, she saw it with her own eyes," Grandmother went on in a shaking voice. "When Father realized they were surrounded by the enemies, he took his dagger and took Cleopatra's life, not to let her suffer in the hands of the bloodthirsty Parthians…"

Losing her breath with the efforts, she looked at me sadly.

"Don't speak, if it's hard for you, Grandma," I whispered. "I love you."

The tribune, startled by the desperate decision of the triumvir, fell silent.

"The queen was not a coward," said the matron with her last ounce of strength. "She would never have committed suicide, nor would have my father."

When Cleopatra was dead, Mark Antony embraced their weeping daughter for the last time, and then stepped outside to face his death heroically.

"What happened to your brothers, lady?" Cassius remembered Cleopatra's sons.

"Caesarion," Antonia went on through silent tears. "Alexander... Ptolemy... even Antyllus,[353] who had never been to Egypt... One by one, the bastards murdered all the sons of Cleopatra and my father."

Leaning over her, I kissed her gently on the pale cheek.

"Venus never leads to victory." She looked up to the ceiling absently.

It was the time for us to part. Alcaeus hurried to Antonia, and Cassius embraced me.

"A-anat!" the old woman moaned, calling her maid. The Egyptian rushed to the matron, carrying the rich leather-clad box.

"Princess," the servant spoke to me, handing a box. "According to the will of Lady Julia Antonia, all of her movable property, including slaves, is now yours."

Antonia nodded approvingly and went back to her memories... forever.

Alcaeus touched the matron's forehead to close her eyes.

"Cassius," he whispered sadly. "Take Her Highness out of this room."

"I-ui em hotep." I said goodbye to Grandma in the language of the Pharaohs, and took Chaerea by the hand to leave the chambers.

On my way outside, I passed over Claudius, pouring crocodile tears in the middle of the atrium. I was impatient to see the last gift from Antonia, so I opened the box.

Right on the testament scroll there laid a wooden statuette of a young woman with a spear in her hand.

"Rhea Silvia," Chaerea recognized it, and added surprisingly, "I thought Lady Antonia did not believe in gods."

"She didn't," I sighed. "Mother of Rome was not a goddess." Then I took a statuette and pressed it to my chest. "My dearest memory."

"She looks like you." The tribune tried to cheer me up.

"I don't think so." I waved aside. "They call me Libitina."

"It seems that you don't know the legend well," Chaerea smiled as he pointed to Rhea's small spear. "After saving her from the cold river, Mars took his bride to Etna,

---

[353] The eldest child of Mark Antony by his third wife, Fulvia.

and bestowed on her two godly names – Bellona, 'the one worth the war,' and Libitina, 'the liberatress.'"

I felt embarrassed to have missed such a beautiful legend.

"I know a lot of the Esquiline stories," Cassius went on, gesturing to the slaves to open the front door. "Helvilla loved them very much."

"Now she is welcoming my grandma… to a better place," I spoke, as I felt my soul burning with terrible thoughts. "What if Tiberius was infected with his bad disease intentionally, and my grandma fell a victim to some evil sorcery?" I whispered helplessly.

"I do not know," my lover replied gently. "But I know what Lady Julia Antonia would have advised you now." His voice and touch could always calm me down. "First, get some rest and gather strength," he finished quietly, "so you can justify her expectations."

He was right. I tapped the wooden princess on her spear and said, "Together, we will justify them."

IV

In the imperial tablinum, the workday began before the daybreak. The huge responsibility, duty and fear dragged the young emperor into the depths of insomnia, opening the door to bitterness and anguish.

"What do you think of my coins?" he asked me, turning new pieces of precious metals on the table.

The reverses of the golden coinage were decorated with the profiles of our parents – Agrippina and Germanicus, as well as the great ancestors – Mark Antony and the Old Caesar. The silver bits were dedicated to me and the sisters, while the coppers represented our brothers.

"Dion is good at his work," Caligula concluded, handing me a silver coin. "As for these two trollops, they should thank me for calling them sisters."

On the back of the shining sesterce I saw three goddesses with cornucopias.

"Concordia,"[354] Gaius pointed to the character above our older sister's name. "Protectress of the senatorial class."

"You bet!" I laughed, almost forgetting the true purpose of my visit. "Such a role becomes her."

"Securitas,"[355] he showed another godly figure, leaning on a column. "Patroness of the equites."

"That's not funny," I said earnestly. "I thought, we were keeping my relationships a secret."

"And, Fortuna," Caesar described the third deity. "The guardian of the plebeians."

"I don't think Livilla will like it," I sighed. "Nor will our brother-in-law."

"Vinicii are nothing, but conceited Sicilian plebs." He waved aside. "Now, turn the coin over."

---

[354] A Roman goddess who embodies agreement in marriage and society.
[355] A goddess of security and stability, especially the security of the Roman Empire.

"Handsome like the Northern star." I looked at his profile, depicted on the obverse – with his laurel wreath and aureole of his titles. "But, unfortunately, not so good."

"What?" Gaius frowned, as he grabbed the coin back. "Why?"

"What was the reason for your absence from the grandma's funeral?" I changed the tone and conversation topic.

The young man stood up with an angry look.

"The emperor's reasons are undiscussable."

"Even for his co-ruler?" I reminded him.

"My bad," he said with bitter irony, and headed for the door. "I'm sorry; I have more important things to do right now."

"If you leave this room," I stood in his way, "I swear by Grandma's shadow, you'll regret it!"

"Sister," he rolled his eyes dejectedly, "you're getting boring."

It depends, I thought, this time not offended.

Caligula silently nodded toward the resting couches. Suppressing anger, I followed him.

"I honored Antonia with the title of Augusta." He explains to me, rubbing his eyes, wet with weariness.

"She sacrificed it all for us," I said down-heartedly. "Even her life! The whole of Rome attended her funeral, only her kingly grandson didn't move his ass off the terrace!"

He wasn't listening, just pulled me closer to him. His gentle face finally expressed compassion.

"I didn't enjoy it," he said into my ear. "That was a part of the plan."

I looked at him bewilderedly.

"Macro advised me to confuse the senators with stories about me poisoning her."

"Stories of you – what?!" I shouted terrified. "You must be crazy to follow the rascal's advice and help them spread the rumors they will hate you for!"

He interrupted me, reminding me of the blind love Romans felt for Augustus and his conflict with then-young Antonia about her father. "Mark Antony was the state enemy," Gaius went on. "Grandmother didn't hide, she was his ardent follower."

"So, you're an Augustan now," I guessed.

Caligula gave me a weary, dry-lipped grin, and turned to the batch of coins on the desk. It took him a while to find an aureus with Augustus' profile and toss it to me.

"You want to fraud a fraudster, right?" I smiled, as I caught it.

"Just like you," he noted, yawning. "Don't you?"

"It's so… artful," I replied. "But, please, next time be kind to ask me for advice… or consult Callistus."

My brother nodded carelessly and uttered, fading to his thoughts.

"Our glory, people's love… it is like morning mist. It comes and goes; it can be sold and bought… We shouldn't care for it, and never should believe in it."

Verum est, I thought. *The crowd worships the kings, silently watches them fall, and in the end blesses the assassins. The populace threw flowers at the feet of the Old Caesar at his triumph, and cursed him bad after his death. The people of Jerusalem, bribed and deceived by the dishonorable priests, demanded from the pagan judge to crucify the God in human's body, once venerated by them all.*

"That's how the wheel of history is turning," the young emperor concluded. "But we shouldn't give up, Little Sister."

"No way," I replied. "If we can't stop the wheel, we will try to make him turn toward ourselves."

"I'll be good with the good," he explained, slightly nodding to the door. "And with the others…" Gaius clenched his fist. "Oderint, dum metuant!"[356]

The alleged murder of Antonia as the last opponent to optimates could be seen as the new emperor's desire to approach the senators, as well as an eerie warning to the mobs.

"What about our loyal praetorian prefect?" I asked, barely calming myself down. "He must be wanting something in return… for his advice."

"You won't believe it," Caesar laughed. "As he heard that the Senate forces me to get married, Macro offers me his Ennia for wife."

"Don't even think of that," I looked at the gold coin in my hand and flipped it. It fell tails, letting Augustus kiss the floor.

---

[356] (lat.) Let them hate [me] as long as they fear [me].

"If you can't marry the one that you love, you should at least find someone who won't stick a knife in your back."

"You know, I granted Piso and his bride-to-be the ultimate return from Rhodes?" My brother changed the topic. "They will get married in Rome, by my will."

"What is the reason of your mercy on the son of the damn poisoner?" I wondered suspiciously.

Caesar's smile, just like his plan, was worth Tiberius himself.

"They say that young Piso, called Proculus, is totally obsessed with his betrothed one… and the girl is rumored to be the most beautiful on Rhodes."

"You want to abduct someone else's wife?" I got earnest. "Like Antipas?"

"Like Augustus," he said calmly. "Or like Romulus."[357]

It was a shrewd, but clever move. A bloodless revenge on the only descendant of the man who killed our father was meant to confuse both – our enemies and their spies.

"Two birds with one stone," I agreed. "Should we care about the affections of our enemies?"

"I doubt they know what true affections are." Caligula was pleased with my support. "Oh, by the way, I ordered Cassius to move to the palace tonight. The tribune of two cohorts of my bodyguards belongs in here, next to his Caesar."

"You are the best brother on earth!" I gave him a tight hug.

"I'll finally get some good sleep." He stretched on a couch, and then winked at me. "Unlike you, sister dear."

Despite my mourning, I laughed. Grandmother loved 'male jokes,' and she would certainly reply with some salty ones, too. And, above all, she loved to see me smiling.

Meanwhile, the heavy footsteps were heard from downstairs. Protogenes took dozens of laborers to our atrium.

"I'm rearranging our entrance hall… a little," the young emperor explained. "The palace will be joined with the temple of Castor and Pollux."[358]

---

[357] According to the Roman legend, Romulus organized the famous "Kidnapping of the Sabine Women" to increase the population of his kingdom.

[358] The twin semi-god brothers in Greek and Roman mythology, known together as the Dioscuri.

V

Caligula's marriage to Cornelia Orestilla had lasted for one week.

"The role of the empress implies the complete commitment to her husband, his household and the people of Rome," he said publicly. "It requires the proper upbringing and education. Unfortunately, Lady Orestilla wasn't ready for the challenges royal life brings."

The Rhodesian had no reason to complain. This rather unlovely dame of solid curls, small breasts and wide hips left the Palatine quietly, with a marriage prohibition, but a large severance pay as well.

"What now?" I asked my brother when the story of humiliated Piso Proculus echoed through Italia. "The Senate must be choosing you a new consort."

"I've made my own choice, dear," Gaius replied calmly. "Now it's time to bang another finger flick."

The autumn festival of Armilustrium welcomed to the city of Rome all the governors of all the provinces. The guests were to take part in the ritual purification of the weapons. Among the first ones to arrive was Publius Regulus, the gray-haired deputy of Macedonia and Achaea. His young wife, Lollia Paulina, followed him in a carriage.

"Old Regulus incites the Greeks against Caesar," Callistus notified me. "But what I heard of that young thing is even more disgusting. She is said to be bibulous, and to have made a fortune sleeping with her own grandfather."

"Really disgusting," I replied, observing the arriving guests from the terrace. Regulus was clumsily getting out of the carriage with the help of two servants. Lollia Paulina, adorned with precious stones like the tiara of King Darius, walked lazily behind her husband, stealthily glancing at the soldiers. "Keep an eye on them."

The solemn ceremony began in the sanctuary on the bank of the Tiber, where the twelve Salii – dancing priests of Mars – were keeping the Ancilla[359] as the symbol of the Roman power.

---

[359] The sacred golden shield, believed to be a gift from Mars to Numa Pompilius.

"I want peace all over the Empire," he said as the custom demanded. "But the ones who dare to strike us, we have swords sharp, armors unbreakable, and warriors strong and fearless!"

The soldiers shouted in support for the ruler, while the senators nodded disgruntledly.

"Publius," Caligula turned to Regulus. "As far as I'm concerned, your work is worth the praise... so is your wife."

"It is my honor to serve you, Caesar," the former senator and consul said. "As for this woman," he looked down to Paulina. "She's not worth the attention of Your Majesty."

The emperor burst into laughter. "After the ceremony, I invite you all to Circus Maximus," he addressed the senators and senior officers. "As for you, Publius, and your *majestic* wife, I want you both to join me in my lodge during the games."

Regulus blushed excitedly and started burbling of his hard work in Athens, mentioning the stubbornness and laziness of the Athenians.

"Not now, my friend." Gaius patted him on the shoulder, keeping the dangerous smile on. "Enjoy the parade, not to anger Mars and Bellona."

"Well, Bellona is already angry," I whispered, disgusted by the governor's behavior.

Caligula, noticing my gaze, pushed Macro aside, and came up to me.

"You're still ignoring my advices." I half-smiled, grabbing him by the arm.

"Sister, please," he said. "You better get used to *my way*. There are more pleasant and effecting things than slaughter."

"You want to mix business with pleasure?" I asked, nodding toward our beautified guest.

"Thus I can pull the wool over senators' eyes," he said quietly. "And to win some time."

Caligula's earnestness and self-confidence gave me relief.

"By the way," he recalled before the procession set off along the Aventine, "After the wedding, we go to Cumae[360] – just me and you, some servants and Praetorians."

---

[360] A Greek colony located near modern-day Naples.

"Would you believe a witch?" I smiled.

"According to the custom," he replied, "Libri Sibyllini[361] have a prophecy for every ruler."

The debate was over. Caesar stood the chariot, announcing the beginning of the parade, and reached out to me. I almost physically felt familiar curiously judging glances on the back of my head, and joined my brother, whispering to him.

"Iugula!"[362]

---

[361] (lat.) The Sibylline Books – a collection of oracular utterances, set out in Greek hexameters.
[362] (lat.) Kill! (the ceremonial crowd shouts when they wanted a gladiator to die.)

VI

While travelling to Cumae, I was reading Actaeon's report. For the sake of my safety, Caligula decided that my secretary would do the eavesdropping in Curia, accompanied by two trusted Praetorians.

"*May the God of your faith keep you save on that journey, Your Highness,*" my friend wrote. "*The Latins may talk this and that, but Cumae is the most Greek town in Italia, just like my native Caesarea in the Mauri kingdom…*"

I smiled. I missed his gentle soul and faithful friendship in Misenum.

"If he show off his intelligence than be sure the serpent's lair is quite… for now," Susannah spoke, curling her feet up like a cat on my seat.

"Actaeon always speaks hexameters," I sighed, folding my legs to free more space for her to sit. "I must admit, this carriage is more comfortable way to travel than a ship."

The Jewess sat straight and, rubbing her numb feet with one hand, reached for the lagena of some hot healing drink Alcaeus made for me.

"*At last the optimates concurred with the populares,*" the Greek wrote. "*As they consider Caesar mad and dangerous, they want to use it their behoof.*"

Such a scenario was our goal indeed. However, that was just a prologue.

"*While the senators were prattling about Caesar's marriages to married matrons, his public benevolence, and the rumored poisoning of Lady Julia Antonia, Vespasian sat still with a grin of a faun, until Asprenas mentioned you…*"

"Who the hell is Asprenas?" I wondered aloud.

"Whoever he is, do not mention the devil." Susannah reproached me, handing a lagena.

"Ah yes, the nephew of Quinctilius Varus." I recalled, pushing her hand aside rashly. "A traitor, who let our soldiers, and my lover's father, fall in Teutoburg forest."

"What's going on?" The nursemaid asked worriedly.

"Nothing out of the ordinary," I replied – more to myself, and turning to the bulkhead, kept on reading.

"As he heard that Caesar caused your name in the loyalty oath, the Flavian flew into such a rage, that I shuddered in horror."

The words written on a piece of parchment slowly turned into pictures. Now I could imagine the whole scene as if I was, too, present at the sitting.

"What? The damn woman for co-ruler?!" Vespasian roared, overturning the tripod table. "How come we haven't broken her so far?"

"For a moment," my friend wrote. *"It seemed to me, that his round face lengthened, and I swear, his neck became motile and sinewy as if he was a serpent."*

Just like Actaeon, I shivered, and gestured for medicine. My secretary had a lush imagination of an untried poet, but he never would have lied to me.

The Curia sank into anguish and fear. Only Sabinus dared to address his brother, touching him by the shoulder.

"We'll handle it, *magistrate*."

Vespasian cooled down, making a quiet growling sound.

"And what do our *brothers* suggest?" Sabinus rose up from his seat, stepping toward the senators' benches. "What shall we do about Drusilla, recently proclaimed a goddess and the Mother of Rome by her mentally ill brother?"

"The plebs love her," a councilor called Rufus spoke. "As they love Caligula. And they are guarded by thousands of the loyal Praetorians."

"Loyal my ass!" Sabinus laughed, coming up closer. "As far as I know, Macro took an oath to Sol Invictus as the Raven, his messenger."

"O noble Titus," Vitellius interfered. "Macro's influence got visibly diminished as the tribune Chaerea joined the Guard."

"Tace!" Vespasian raised his voice again like a fire-breathing dragon. "As if that was not enough for me to put up with three hundreds of fools, unable to kill a female, now that idiot mentions a critter, created at a woman's request!"

"You are right, o Sun-Runner." I almost heard the familiar, serpent-charming voice of Asiaticus. "Drusilla is our enemy, and only fools forgive their enemies. That woman has today, and certainly she will, but wouldn't it be wiser to destroy her brother first?"

The senators supported him – quietly and cautiously, gazing at the magistrate.

"Caligula has got four years," Sabinus replied ill-temperedly. "By our Pater's resolution, with the permission…" then he stopped abruptly like he didn't want to mention someone's name. "For now, it is impossible."

"For a fraternity member," Asprenas responded. "But the prohibition works for members, not for apprentices."

"That's smart," Sabinus nodded, as he changed glances with Vespasian. "Do you know a wretch who hates him as we do?"

"Of course." Asprenas smiled, "But I would rather speak of that on Friday in Mithraeum. As I've heard this bitchy princess has a spy on every corner."

That was the end of Actaeon's report. Scared to death, he hurried to run out along with Lupus and Stella.

"I'm sorry, Your Highness," he finished the letter. "I had to stay alive to convey what I learned."

Just in time, the coachman exclaimed – "Cumæ!" – and stopped the horses.

"Susannah, Susannah!" I shook the sleepy Jewess. "Help me to get out!"

The nursemaid, moaning from an uncomfortable nap, wrapped me in peplum and jumped out of the carriage.

"Brother!" I exclaimed, as my feet touched the Cumaean ground.

Aquila, the centurion, quickly dismounted and escorted me to the emperor's carriage.

"What's going on?" Cassius rushed to me. "Are you alright?"

"Bad news, my love," I replied, looking for Gaius. "I should have read this before we left Rome."

"Drusilla," Caesar finally got out of the coach. "Look at those beautiful woods… and the hills, and the lake!"

I looked around. It was a nice October afternoon. The gentle zephyr was playing with the tops of thick conifer-trees. The majestic green-blue pines had risen around the Cave of the Sibyl like a wall.

"They plan to kill us," I whispered to Gaius, squeezing his hand nervously.

"That's not news to me." He smiled, removing my hand gently. "There's no reason to spoil my impression of this fairy glade."

"The bastards knew they've been eavesdropped," I said, as I stood on his way. "Actaeon can no longer…"

"That was logical." My brother stopped me angrily. "Please, tell me something I don't know yet."

"Macro is with them." I tried to drive away the awful picture of the things which could have happened. "The scoundrel you entrusted Rome and pregnant Messalina to!"

The young man sighed, trying his hardest to keep calm.

"Rome won't collapse within a week, nor do I think they give a damn about Claudius' child."

I looked at him heavy-heartedly.

"The last thing Actaeon heard was that our future murdered is chosen from outside their society."

"Like who?" he asked, not taking my words seriously.

I shrugged, and Gaius headed to the cave.

"Cassius," he turned to the tribune, "I'm going inside. Line the guard up by the entrance, the carriages, and along the road toward the settlement."

"Faciam ita ut iubes!"[363] Chaerea tapped himself on the chest readily.

"Will you go there alone?" I asked, casting a worried glance at the stone gate of the cave.

"The Sibyl receives rulers only," Aquila reminded me. "That is the rule."

"Fuck the rule!" I thought aloud, followed with the laughter of Praetorians.

"Dimitto!"[364] Cassius shouted at them. "Ordenem servate![365] Moveo!"[366]

"What are you giggling at?" My brother turned around. "That is your watchword for tonight."

Now it was me who burst out laughing.

---

[363] (lat.) As you command!
[364] (lat.) Dismissed!
[365] (lat.) Keep your position!
[366] (lat.) March!

"When we're done," he pointed his finger up to the hilltop town. "We'll spend the night at Villa Gracchi.[367] Tomorrow morning, at the square, I'll talk to the locals about the upbuilding of new houses and restoration of the bridges."

---

[367] Tiberius Sempronius Gracchus was a Roman politician of the 2nd century BC. He served two consulships and was awarded two triumphs. As a soldier, he defended Cumae in the Second Punic War.

VII

Still upset, I accompanied him to the entrance arch of a strange, sarcophagus-like frame. The Sibyl, like the mythical Pythia, was a priestess of Phoebus, born with the gift of divination. This role demanded of a chosen one to devote herself entirely to serving her god and conveying his sacred messages to the Book of fates. Only the ruler and the High priest of Phoebus were allowed to visit the Sibyl. When an old priestess died, the flamen came to Cumae to choose her successor. Rulers visited the Sibyl to ask for the future of Rome, and she greeted them sitting on her tripod chair with a book, older than King Numa, on her lap.

"Mighty Aeneas will vanquish ingenious Dido,"[368] Said the priestess to Magistrate Gracchus, when the First Punic War was about to flare.

"Venus never leads to victory." This was her prophecy to the Old Caesar, after he returned from Alexandria. *"Cybele will swallow her, but then, one day, there will arrive the one to win against Cybele."*

Nevertheless, there were rulers, who refused to seek the advice of the priestess even in the times of war and crisis. Augustus and his successor Tiberius declared their reluctance to reveal the godly secrets. Or, perhaps, they were simply afraid to hear something unpleasant, as they could identify their lords from Parthia with cruel and sly Cybele, goddess of the East.

Gaius entered the cave with no fear.

"Pagan prophets are possessed by demons," Susannah reproached me. "Their words come from hell."

"What should I have done?" I sighed, crossing my arms on the chest. "My brother is as stubborn, as our father was."

"You're not meek either." Her warm smile mad me smile too. "But there are those who love it."

---

[368] Dido was the legendary founder and first queen of the Phoenician city-state of Carthage, located in modern Tunisia.

Here, on the paved roadway, strewn with gravel and stone, the tribune performed some defense exercises with the guardsmen for the case of a sudden attack.

"Gladius et scutum parati!"[369] Cassius ordered. "Reconde!"[370]

Staring at my lover, I no longer heard Susannah's grumbling. So handsome and young-looking, with his wide back and manly strength, he was the only one to quench my fears and worries. As he read my inner message, the tribune turned his head and nodded to me warmly.

"Susannah," I pulled the Jewess by her stola. "I am hungry."

The nursemaid obediently headed to my carriage.

"I don't want cold meal." I stopped her. "Buy us fresh buns or a pie in the settlement."

The woman's tar-black eyes widened.

"You're not going through the woods alone," I explained to her, pointing to the youngest guardsman. "Priscus will take you up there."

The white-haired fellow stepped out, and the Jewess smiled embarrassedly as she perceived my intentions.

"Cassius," I called the tribune, coming up to him. "I can barely feel my feet after the ride. It would be nice to take a walk to the forest."

"What are they doing – Caesar and the Sibyl now?" We heard a burst of muffled laughter in the guard as Cassius and I hid behind the imperial carriage.

"Fools," Chaerea shook his head, and then asked carefully. "What did Actaeon hear in the Senate?"

"It seems that Vespasian is not a human anymore," I whispered anxiously, recalling what I would rather have forgotten then. "Mithras possessed him, and rules the Empire."

"Felix."[371] Cassius embraced me. "I am ready to fight even Mithras himself to protect you... and Caesar."

---

[369] (lat.) Raise your sword and shield!

[370] (lat.) Sword and shield down!

[371] (lat.) [My] happiness.

"They will choose the assassin from the mobs." I signed. "The followers of Mithras may not touch Caligula until the four years of his reign are over."

"I'll put that plebeian rat easily," Cassius said, as he touched my lips with the tips of his fingers. "Don't worry."

The fervor of his touch ran through my body, obsessing my mind. I felt a flood of nasty thoughts crashing against the cliff of his love like a wreck broken by Symplegades.[372]

"Remove the armor and unclasp those fittings." I grabbed my lover by the collar of his cloak, pulling him gently to the carriage.

"Want to capture me?" He leaned forward and laid hold of me. "You better surrender, young lady!"

The perception of my being flared up like a tree, struck by lightning. In that blazing glow there was no time, no space, just Cassius and me indulging in each other…

"Tribune!" Aquila's voice from somewhere near was so amiss now.

"By Quirinus!" Cassius exclaimed as he quickly fixed his tunic and paludamentum,[373] and got out of the coach. "What's happening?"

The bizarre noise made me look outside. The scene I saw made me more startled than Actaeon's report. By the cave there stood ten women, dressed like Vestal virgins with long tousled hair and savage eyes.

"Who are you, ladies, and what are you looking for in here?" The tribune asked them without greeting, noticing the turmoil in the guard.

"We are the helper priestesses of Phoebus," the dark-skinned Cumaean said haughtily, and yelled. "By what right, you soldier, desecrate our holy grove?"

"I am the tribune of the Praetorian guard," Chaerea replied. "I see nothing irreverent in protecting the emperor during his visit to Sybil."

The laughter of the dark-haired woman made me feel chilly sweet on my back.

"The emperor's a grain of dust to the almighty Phoebus!" One of her companions spoke, rocking back and forth as if she was drunk. "He is the only ruler of the world!"

---

[372] A pair of mythical rocks at the Bosporus that clashed together whenever a vessel went through.
[373] A Roman cloak, worn by high-ranking military officers.

I squinted to see her face better. The witch stared at Cassius with furious eyes like a predator, ready to attack a venator.[374]

"You nasty mortals!" the third woman shouted, spinning around like a balladine.[375] "Slaves to small desires! Do you know that one word from Phoebus is enough to turn you into dust?"

Before he answered, I took on my peplum and went out to the meadow. All ten women turned around and saw me.

"Stay back, Princess." Aquila warned me. "These peasants are dangerous."

"Damned be, Lamia!" the dark-skinned uttered through her teeth, as she pointed to me. The others headed toward me with obvious intentions. "We'll tear you apart!"

Cassius stood in front of me and ordered to the guardsmen.

"Impetus!"[376]

At first, the Praetorians, unwilling to hurt the weaker, tried only to immobilize the women, but the Cumaens fought astonishingly hard, making inhuman noises.

"Do not let them scare you, Domina." I suddenly remembered Orla's sincere advice.

"That won't help," David's voice in my head interrupted her. *"When a demon attacks, just remember Michael the Archangel. The bravest warrior of God, he did not tell the devil – I will beat you, but may Adonai rebuke you!"*

Meanwhile, right before my eyes, one of the witches easily knocked down two soldiers.

"May Adonai rebuke you!" I shouted, so loud that I felt pain in my temples.

The women fell back all at once and dropped breathless under the Praetorian spathas.

"Fuck Phoebus!" Aquila spat, as he kicked the overgrown stone. "I know the killing thing, but, man, those Temple Amazons were far too much for me."

Cassius wiped the blood off his sword blade with the dead woman's dress and embraced me. "Why did the dark one acted like she knew you?"

---

[374] A gladiator specialized in wild animal hunts in the arena.

[375] An ancient eastern dancer in a temple.

[376] (lat.) Attack!

"Well, her master knows me... well," I whispered in his ear, "Phoebus, Mithras, Loki – these are all the names of the same daemon."

"Why did she call you – Lamia?" He looked at me earnestly.

Hiding the name of my soul from the one who ruled my heart wouldn't make any sense. "Because she was Greek," I replied. "A Jewess would refer to me as – Lilith."

His grey eyes expressed astonishment, concern, but also trust. "The Egyptians believe in soul travel," he spoke, holstering his sword.

"But not every soul has that gift," I explained, quoting David's words. "Only the chosen ones."

"Wait," the centurion interrupted us, showing toward the cave. "If those sibyl helpers were true harpies, imagine what the beldam is like!"

"Caligula!" I shouted fearfully and rushed inside the cave.

The tribune followed me, hastily ordering the guard to do the same.

"Gaius! Where are you?" I screamed as I was running through the tunnel, paying no attention to big spider webs and a colony of bats that had been awoken by the torch light.

"Down in the chamber! Why?" I heard him answer, and my heart stopped galloping.

The chamber of the prophesies was shadowy and spacious. By the hearthstone with a bluish flame, I saw a woman in a red hooded chiton sitting on a tripod.

"Yet you have come..." the Sibyl addressed me in a raspy voice, as her eyes flashed in the dark.

My brother was sitting right there at her feet, breathing some intoxicating fumes from the gap in the earthen floor. "What are you doing here?" he asked me absentmindedly.

"Take Caesar outside," I ordered Chaerea. "Now!"

The Sibyl rapidly jumped to her feet.

"You think you're stronger, don't you?" She grinned at me mockingly.

Five of the guardsmen took my brother by both arms to take him away, while the rest of them surrounded the hostess.

"What does that mean?" Caesar protested. "Let me go!"

The Praetorians had no dilemma whom to obey at the moment. Chaerea stood by me as always, ready to defend.

"Can you do anything yourself?" the prophetess went on, followed by sinister echo. "Shall you kill me now and take a curse on your pitiful soul?"

I turned around reflexively and noticed a spear leaning against the wall. Without a second thought, I took it. It was heavy, somewhat rusty and cold, but I raised it.

"None of us can really do anything *alone*," I said to her, as I came closer. "And *your* curse is too familiar to me to be afraid of it."

Struck down and mortally wounded, the Sibyl wheezed out her last prophecy.

"Brother-in-law… will kill… the emperor."

That was the true, infamous end of the Cumaean oracle.

VIII

A mild but eventful autumn was followed by a long, exceptionally cold winter. It was the time of arranging the Saturnalia – the first winter festival for Gaius as an emperor, and for me as a hostess of the fair. As per tradition, almost all my servants got their week off, so I was preparing to go out to the Forum alone.

"What on earth are you wearing, Princess?" Callistus said, startled when he saw my cloak made of wool and thick leather.

"The Gallic way of handling winter." I turned around twice. "If you like it, I'll ask Orla to sew something for you, too."

"No, thank you." The Greek frowned. "Don't tell me you are going to the Forum dressed like a spoil of war!"

"How vulgar you are," I replied with a smile.

"Guess who my role model is," he giggled back, as he glanced at the pile of gifts for children. "Oh, I like those workations!"

"For double pay, right?" I asked ironically, squinting one eye in Tiberius' manner.

"Do I look German or Gaul to you?" Callistus looked at me earnestly, a bit offended. "All I do it for is you, Your Highness. Those endless duties are not for your health."

"Oh, Curl!" I fixed his perfumed hair, slightly pushing with my elbow. "Pame,[377] bre malaka!"

The crowd of children at the Temple of Saturn greeted me with joyful shouts and throwing up their handkerchiefs.

"Ave, Augusta!" they singed me welcome, somewhat out of tune. "Io, Saturnalia!"

Among their little faces, rosy with cold weather and thin cloaks I noticed an old friend of mine, Petronius.

"What are you doing here, Misenian?" I asked a fair-haired boy surrounded by his lower-class friends.

---

[377] (anc.gr.) Let's go!

"My father has become a member of the Senate recently," Petronius smiled. "So, we all moved to the capital, to the Carinae."

"I guess you often see my relatives there, don't you?" I hugged him.

"Just the proconsul, Marcus Vinicius," he said a bit sourly. "Lucia, my younger sister, is already betrothed to his old brother."

"Will you help me with the gifts?" I winked at him.

"That's why I came." The boy cheered up and proudly pointed at the bag by the stairs. "I brought my old clothes and toys!"

I gestured to a couple of fat flamens, ordering to set tables in the hall. Gladdened children ran upstairs to the hypostyle hall.

"Callistus," I addressed the secretary, "you will share coins and sweets, and you, filo mu," I turned to Anicetus. "Will bring up bags with clothes."

"And me, Princess?" Petronius caught me by the stola like a toddler.

"You can share books," I said, taking him by the hand, "and help me dress the youngest children up."

Halfway outside, the secretary turned around and spoke.

"I really admire you, girl. You care about brats a whole lot more than their parents do."

"I love them like my own." I answered honestly. "Next spring I'll raise a public reading room and a playroom on the Capitolium."

"Eugepae!" Petronius clapped his hands. "I'll bring my books and make new friends!"

"Don't you have friends among the young patricians?" Anicetus asked in surprise.

"No, they don't understand me." The boy shrugged. "All they are interested in is becoming senators like their fathers. And I…" he whispered, "I dream of being a writer."

"Sounds familiar." I sighed and looked him in the eyes. "Never give up on your dreams, Petronius. I'm sure one day your book will be read all over the world."

The boy, moved by my words, embraced me and climbed onto my lap.

"Eho!" I laughed. "Someone wants to be a baby once again?"

"I'm playing Romulus, and you are Rhea Silvia." He giggled.

"Heu, corculum!"[378] I kissed him on the cheek and let him aside. "I wish…"

Anicetus caught up my thoughts and kicked the front door to interrupt them.

"Let the party begin!"

Two lively brothers, Nestor and Melanthios, had also moved to the city of Rome, for their mother now was a charwoman to Petronius' father.

"Imagine, Your Highness," the little Greek said, playing with a ball, "the day after our meeting, the Praetorians came to our old lord and beat him hard in front of servants."

"Yeah, he had it coming!" his brother added with his mouth full of sweets.

"And then?" I asked them curiously, acting like I had no clue about what happened next.

"Then the centurion took our mother and us to Petronius!" the elder brother exclaimed playfully.

"I wonder," Callistus asked me suspiciously. "Which god or *goddess* worked that miracle?"

I shrugged and bit an apple that Melanthios had kindly shared with me.

"Did he really eat children?" Chrysothemis, the pretty daughter of some freedman, asked me carefully, pointing to the statue of Saturn.

I looked up. The bearded severe god was threatening us with a stone sickle from his pedestal.

"No, he does not exist." I shook my head. "He's just a doll like that of yours, a big and ugly one."

One of the flamens grimaced angrily, and Chrysothemis pressed a new pretty doll to her chest, rocking it like a baby.

"All you women are the same," Callistus joked, waving aside in the effeminate manner. As I gave him a reproachful look, he added sheepishly. "Except you, Princess."

As the deadened winter sun was setting, the square plunged into the dark quiver.

"I can't wait to rest," I complained to Callistus, getting to the carriage. "Winter that cold, I witnessed only in Germania."

---

[378] (lat.) Oh my little heart!

"Tomorrow are the chariot races," he reminded me. "We should take care of the treat and the guest list for the feast."

"No sleep for us tonight," I concluded disappointedly. "These races are important to Caligula – because of Incitatus."

White as an alpine peak, Incitatus has shown the incredible agility and racing skills since it was a foal, to admiration of the stablemen and guardsmen. During his fearful stay on the Capri, Gaius became very attached to his horse, and treated him like a friend.

"Have you heard, Princess, what the damn senators talk of that horse?" Anicetus laughed, as he, with efforts, took a seat, between me and the secretary.

"It has a marble stable," I said wearily, pressing my cold hands to his large palms to warm them. "And the gilded manger, too."

"There's more," Callistus sighed. "They never miss the opportunity to denigrate the emperor."

"King Alexander cared about Bucephalus a whole lot more than Gaius does for Incitatus." I yawned. "I hate Roman dumbness."

The carriage stopped abruptly near the palaestra.[379]

"What the hell?" I rolled my eyes.

"Your Highness!" Tribune Clemens moved a curtain aside roughly. "Caesar... He fell ill."

I jerked like I was marked with a branding iron and rushed outside.

"What do you mean?" I exclaimed, gasping cold air.

"This afternoon, he suddenly got fever," he reported. "The Cretan tried to bring it down with vinegar, but Caesar fainted."

"Get me on that mare!" I ordered, not letting him dismount. "Take me to the palace – now!"

My brother called me in delirium.

---

[379] An ancient athletic establishment.

"Just tell me it's not cherry laurel or some other hemlock!"[380] I shook Alcaeus by his shoulder, squeezing Gaius' palm with the other hand.

"It doesn't seem like poisoning to me." The Cretan shook his head. "I took all the measures, but his status hasn't changed... yet."

"Aquila is trying the cookman and the praegustator," Chaerea spoke. "Lupus is questioning servants, and Stella is watching by the gates."

"Have them tortured!" I burst out crying. "Gaius has been in the palace this morning!"

Cassius reach out to calm me down, but I pushed him aside nervously. As I sat on the edge of the bed, I examined my brother's pale face.

"Do you hear me, Gaius?" I stroked his cheek. "It's me, Drusilla."

"If I don't... come back..." he muttered half-consciously. "You are my successor... and Claudius... a regent."

"Yeah, you wish," I replied sternly. "You must fight! You must get well – for Messalina and your baby."

Caligula nodded weakly and gave in to a troublous sleep.

"Do you have some medicine?" I turned to the Cretan.

"I've tried everything," he answered firmly like a soldier. "I'll be here until he's back or I will kill myself, Your Highness."

"You must save him." I looked the medic in the eyes. "Whatever it may take."

As I dried the sweat off my brother's forehead, I could feel the fever reveling inside of him. Unable to kiss it away, I hardly resisted my cry.

"Princess!" Overwrought Callistus ran to cubiculum. "It's... Lady Messalina..."

My look could give away my almost hysterical state.

"She suffers a lot," he said timidly. "She's begging to let her see Caesar."

"No way!" I stood up. "In her condition, it is dangerous."

"Solace her, Your Highness," the freedman went on. "Only you can do that. Gods forbid..."

---

[380] Ancient poisons.

I ran past him like a shooting star, but on my way to atrium I met another favorite, a former one.

Ennia.

"Princess dear!" she prated, fluttering her painted eyelashes.

"Who invited you?" I wreaked all my anger on her.

Startled Ennia began to justify herself – not too convincing, as she talked chaotically of her loyalty to Caesar, wickedness of her own husband and dumbness of her steward Fedlimid.

"Where is your husband?" I asked suspiciously. "Shouldn't he be investigating now?"

"Macro is..." Her red lips shuddered open. "Caesar ordered him to examine aerarium and fiscus!"

Suddenly anger in me mingled with terror. The duty of the Praetorian prefect indeed included tax collection and sequestration, but the access to the treasuries was the exclusive right of the censor, Claudius.

"How dare you lie to me?" I grabbed her hand, adorned with serpent-like bracelets, and called out to the guardsmen.

"Please, Your Highness!" Ennia moaned, kneeling down. "I beseech you by the gods, have mercy!"

"I don't give a damn about your gods," I replied. "Nor have I mercy for traitors."

Cassius was the first to hear me, followed by Priscus and Clemens.

"Shall we arrest her?" The novice asked flustered.

"Princess!" The woman tried to hug my feet. "I swear by Father's shadow, I am not guilty! Macro got me into these intrigues, he threatened me with death!"

I looked her in the face - it was all red and blue with smeared cosmetics.

"You seduced my brother," I recalled, kicking her like a mangy dog. "You laughed at my family sentenced to death... You've been spying on us all, and maybe...

"You laughed at the deaths of my loved ones ... Stalking all of us, and maybe... "

"O, Augusta!" She growled like a wounded female-bear. "If you have mercy, I'll reveal all Macro's secrets! I'll be your own spy..."

"Shut up," I gestured her to stop. "I'm not Caligula to swallow your sweet lies. Clemens!" I turned to the tribune. "Take her to ergastulum!"

The officer unscrupulously grabbed the woman's hair and pulled her out.

"Cassius," I said to my betrothed. "Come back to Caesar. You, Alcaeus and Callistus should watch over him all the time."

"What shall we do about Macro?" he asked worriedly.

"Centurion will arrest him, and Claudius too," I said quietly.

"Stella is busy, my dear," Chaerea reminded me. "Aquila and Lupus as well."

"He will do it," I nodded to Priscus.

"But, Your Highness, I'm a common guardsman!" the young man said surprisedly.

"You've been promoted," Cassius explained. "Can you bring culprits yourself?"

"I like his enthusiasm." I looked at the fair-haired youth. "As Seneca once said – no matter what you do, but how you do it."

The newly promoted centurion proudly pointed his finger at the scorpion on his armor, showing his readiness to kill for the ruler's security.

"Oh, yes," I said. "You will replace that ugly emblem with the one of a lion."

IX

"May I?" Alcaeus knocked on the door of the tablinum.

"You bet!" I moved aside a small chest with important scrolls. "I couldn't close my eyes."

Unwashed for some days and exhausted, the medic came up to the desk.

"I've found out the reason of Caesar's disease," he said comfortingly. "It's common cold, a nasty one though."

"How is he now?" I whispered in a sleeplessly hoarse voice.

Alcaeus had a sit on a round backless chair.

"He will be fine," he encouraged me. "Caesar is young and hearty – he'll get over this."

I thanked God. However, it was still a mystery how could Caligula get a cold in a well-heated palace? My brother has always been vigorous, even as a toddler at the Rhine, when winters were cold enough to freeze the freshwater and make birds drop stiff from icy trees.

"The weather is extremely bad," I thought out loud. "Caligula was tired, as the better part of our slaves were resting… But wasn't there someone to throw a warm cloak over him and make him some mulled wine?"

The Cretan rolled his eyes.

"You talk about him as if he is a child!"

"All good people are eternal children." I put my elbows on the desk and rested my face on my palm.

"You should rest, Princess," he said earnestly. "Consider this a recommendation from a medic."

I raised my head and nodded to a bunch of the government documents.

"I have a lot of work to do."

"Do as you wish," Alcaeus shrugged. "But, to your knowledge, if you, too, fall ill, I'll run away from Rome."

"Are you threatening me?" I squinted with one eye and yawned.

As the Cretan was making up some joking response, Callistus stormed into the office without knocking.

"We know who the culprit is!" he exclaimed. "And who got Caesar to that state!"

"So, he confessed?" I asked, referring to the prefect.

"No, Princess, Macro died under torture. His wife gave his secrets away."

The first task of a newcomer as the messenger of Mithras was to kill the emperor without a weapon, combat, poison or shedding his blood. As Caligula had been complaining of insomnia, the crafty prefect secretly advised him "a little unpleasant" remedy, allegedly once used by his Gallic ancestors.

"Just hop in a cold bath, sip a hard drink, and go outside for a breath of fresh air," the prefect recommended. "And you'll sleep like a log, Caesar."

Gaius did exactly what he was advised, and in an hour, he got fever.

"Excuse me, Princess," the physician interrupted us – still sympathetically, but a little angry too. "I can't believe how naive Caesar is!"

"Oh shut up," I frowned at him. "Why you, a medic, didn't you cure him from insomnia?"

"Well, it's an ailment of the psyche." He shrugged. "Caesar or not, a man should overcome his fears and worries by himself."

"Go back to him," I ordered. "You annoy me."

"All the servants are found innocent," Callistus said as Alcaeus left. "We shouldn't have tortured them, Princess."

"Pay damages to everyone." I sighed. "We had to do what we have done."

The secretary caught my sight and quietly asked me about Ennia's fate.

Callistus looked down at me and quietly asked me about Annie's fate.

"Leave her in the dungeon," I decided. "My brother will judge her."

"Ennia is an accomplice. She deserves to die." the Greek reminded me.

"It's up to your Caesar," I said it again. "His lovers are not my concern."

Callistus silently turned aside to look for some unwritten sheets of parchment in the bookcase. As I noticed a trace of wormwood on his face, I reassessed my solutions, and asked him.

"What would Zaleukos say now if he still was alive?"

The secretary turned around with a warmer look.

"He would be proud of his Little Owl." He smiled. "There's only one thing he could have advise you."

I straightened my back and raised my head.

"When you stand against the evil, do not fight it with its own weapon. A soldier, who repeats the moves of his enemy, is meant to lose."

"Yes, vengeance is contagious," I agreed. "It destroys the avenger himself more than his foe."

"Oh, by the way." Callistus fixed his disobedient curls. "Ennia begs you to have pity on her children."

"Certainly, I will," I said, startled. "Does she consider me a butcher?"

Callistus shook his head.

"She fears the punishment for the atrocities which Macro made to the children of Sejanus."

I opened my tearfully tired eyes wide. I remembered the day when Tiberius sentenced Sejanus to death, but there's nothing I knew about the offspring of the former prefect.

"Macro and Sejanus were a lot alike," the Greek explained. "This sort of people once they are promoted high, can level to the ground everyone standing on his way. Such beasts fear neither kings, nor gods, Your Highness."

Tiberius, manipulated by Sejanus, starved to death my barely grown brothers, but Macro dared to raise his hand on a nine-year-old girl. The youngest daughter of Sejanus was killed in the most despicable way.

"Like Photice," Callistus ended the story, sparing me the ferocious details. I took a flask of cold water from the desk and pressed it to my forehead, hot with anxiety.

"Send Macro's children to Ennia's mother," I spoke word by word, barely able to think. "If that's all, you may go."

Callistus shifted from one foot to the other, hesitating.

"I beg your pardon, Princess. The worst news is still ahead."

"Claudius, right?" I guess, taking a sip of water straight from the flask.

"Your uncle confessed under pressure that he was, too involved in the robbery of both treasuries and spreading false news about the emperor," the Greek said cautiously.

I finally stood up and headed toward him with my legs heavy like two boulders.

The extent of the theft was one hundred million silver sesterces.

"Damage is almost irreparable, Your Highness." Callistus covered his eyes with his hands.

The senators made up a crafty plan for the fall of Caligula. The prefect's task was to kill without a trace, and Claudius was to open the treasuries for the robbery, sharing false news about Caligula's unreasonable expenses, as well as his imminent death.

"The guard arrested Claudius' lover, too," Callistus added, holding me by the elbow, as I was almost ready to collapse. "The Parthian."

"A bastard son of Artabanus." I remembered aloud my dream on a ship.

"Sorry?" the Greek startled.

"Nothing." I waved aside. "I had a nightmare."

"Narcissus is sure of their success," he sighed. "He even dared to encourage his master and offend the guardsmen."

I took a deep breath and gestured to my friend to take me out of the room.

"We need a miracle, Your Highness," Callistus murmured in Greek. "Or we all will end up like my father… or yours."

I raised my trembling hand, and with my last ounce of strength, I cuffed him on the nape.

"Stop that Andromache's cry or I'll kill you!"

The Greek shook his head and gave me a shockingly intimidated.

"Guards!" Echoed through the prothyron. Callistus all went pale and shuddered like a child.

"Oh calm down!" I hugged him roughly. "I'm not Livia to beat my servants just for being dumb!"

Priscus and Stella had never been late.

"Listen now," I addressed the praetorians, as I felt the onslaught of dizziness. "Station the guardsmen all over the Palatine, especially by the gates of the palace. Bring the whole Viminal if it's necessary…"

"Princess," Callistus plucked up some courage. "Aerarium is almost empty, soldiers can raise a rebellion."

"Do not worry," I addressed the centurions. "I'll pay you from my savings. Caesar will soon get well and make the senators return all the money they stole."

"Yes, Princess!" Stella raised his fist to salute, but suddenly turned to his companion.

"Your Highness," the young guardsman spoke shyly. "There's a misunderstanding."

I nodded to let him report.

"I know you promoted me to the rank of centurion," Priscus explained with his blue eyes wide open. "I am honored, but I don't know how I should perform my duties as I have no people to form a centuria."

I smiled, tapped Stella on his chest, and asked the young man.

"What do you think of his *centum*?"

All three of them exchanged suspicious glances.

"Oh, you fools!" I raised my hands like a flamen. "If Priscus gets Stella's centuria, this means that Stella is promoted to the rank of tribune."

"Well... it is honor to me." Stella coughed. "But which cohort am I about to command?"

"The Palatine cohort, you idiot!" I exclaimed, leaning against the pillar.

"Nescio quid dicis[381]..." The older guardsman swallowed a lump in his throat. "I must inform tribune Chaerea first."

"Of course you must." I laughed anxiously. "He's your prefect now."

"A woman commands the Praetorian guard!" Callistus clapped his hands, regaining his good humor. "Vespasian will die of rage."

"He will indeed." I winked at him. "Sooner or later."

After that, I followed the Cretan's advice.

---

[381] (lat.) I don't know what to say.

X

My fragile sleep was invaded by nightmares, threatening to tear my whole being apart. A bad dream, as sheer as my reality, took me to my chambers in Misenum. In my hands, I was holding a quill and a piece of rich parchment.

"Write it down!" The otherworldly voice came from above like thunder. "Let them know!"

I reached out for an ink bottle to dip a thin quill, but couldn't find one.

"Fortunately, all the company is down there in Mithraeum," I heard Callistus' words, now spoken in a different, low hissing voice. *"Celebrating the death day of the first woman – Layla."*

I wanted to run away, but I felt motionless. Those eerie whispers, resembling snake sounds, could reach me from all sides.

"The summer solstice… A woman is sacrificed." A ghostly thing was burbling tensely. *"Abduction, violence, blood… Mithras has come to revenge on the rebellious first woman."*

I tried to cover my ears, but the shrill grew louder.

"The Spring Equinox." I felt a cold breath on my shoulder and neck. *"Our dear lord's return from the Kingdom of Shadows… The fall of a disobedient king."*

"A female child for the Autumn Equinox…" The whisper behind my back turned into throat singing. *"A male child for the Midwinter."*

I finally noticed my ink bottle on the floor and reached out for it, but my hand was too limp.

"Do you know…?" The invisible creature leaned heavily upon my back. *"Myths are the spirits' prophecies of what shall happen."*

Numb with fear, I couldn't say a word. The only thing that came to my mind was a prayer.

"Deus in adiutorium meum intende," I remembered David chanting beside Caesar's bed. *"Domine ad adiuvandum me festina!"*[382]

---

[382] (lat.) Make haste, O God, to deliver me; make haste to help me, O Lord. (Psalm 70:1).

These words dispelled the ghosts faster than Aquilon dispersed the autumn leaves.

"Hush, dear, I am here!" My lover's gentle voice awoke me.

"Cassius!" I wrapped my arms around his neck in the darkness.

"It was a dream," he whispered, soothing me with kisses. "It is over now."

My heart craved for love, commanding the body to give in. However, the macabre voices still occupied my head. For the first time, I resisted his embrace.

"I'm not feeling well." I moved aside, and lifted up to sit.

"What did you see?" Cassius asked, worried.

I asked myself, how many innocent people were killed in Mithras' bloody feasts? How many children were sacrificed? The thought of little human beings brought me back to my recent conversation with Callistus.

"Macro brutally murdered Strabonia, the young daughter of Sejanus," I uttered with a shiver. Cassius wrapped me in a warm blanket.

"Tell me," I turned to him, "when exactly Sejanus and his family were killed?"

"Seven years ago," Cassius said. "At the end of the seventh month."[383]

"The equinox," I said, startled. "She was sacrificed."

Cassius stood up and lit a lamp to see my face.

"Is that all real?"

"In this world," I replied, "the worst things have been real since the very beginning."

The oil lamp shaped as a Corinthian amphora lit the turquoise clepsydra. It was the third watch of the night.

"Photice was killed in the Midsummer," I thought out loud. "Tiberius foresaw his death at the Spring Equinox."

"I don't know exactly how many people they have," Chaerea reasoned. "Still, we can count on six hundred Praetorians and the entire Corbulo legion."

"Less than a half, my love." I sighed. "Vespasian and Sabin are watching for new naive heads, and the trainees got quickly taken in by their lies."

---

[383] September was originally the seventh of ten months on the ancient Roman calendar that began with March.

"High ranks, wealth, power," Cassius said thoughtfully. "Every rattlebrain dreams of having that all."

"And every rattlebrain consider himself clever." I added, sharing a blanket with him.

"Do you know what's even worse than a rattle brain?" My lover hugged me. "It's a rattle heart." I hugged him back clumsily, and he went on, "We are the happiest two beings in the world."

"We are indeed," I nodded, still haunted by daemons of my sleep. "Howsoever, we must save innocent people... and children."

Cassius wiped the sweat from his forehead and whispered in my ear, "It's only left for us to start a civil war."

"Not now." I shook my head. "I haven't finished my stage play."

Owing to the circumstances, I only managed to write one third of the story I planned. Besides, I ran out of facts. A risky decision had come in a minute.

"I have to find a way to enter the Mithraeum."

"No way, dear!" The prefect stepped back, putting on his tunic. "Don't even think of that!"

"Are you commanding *me*?" I got a little angry. "Aren't I your princess?"

"You're my wife de facto," he replied, and glanced at the clepsydra. "I must go. The new guards need some help on patrol."

I felt helpless, sleepy and torpid.

"You're right, love." I slowly got back on the back. "But I am Sophia! No matter how he tries, Mithras can't fool me."

Cassius silently fastened his cloak and bent down to take his boots.

"You don't believe me, do you?" I thought out loud, feeling lost.

"You are the only person I believe." He turned around. "Mithras can't fool you indeed, but his people can kill you."

"You're right all the way." I banged my head against a linen pillow. "You must teach me some fighting moves, Cassius!"

"Calm down, Rea Silvia." The prefect smiled. "You better have some sleep. We will discuss that later."

"I miss you already." His look endeared me.

"We'll make it up." Cassius winked. "You cannot hide from me even at Vestals."

"You tell me things like that and order me to sleep," I chuckled. "Oh, by the way," I got up and handed him his helmet. "You look great in your new uniform."

Suddenly a woman screamed somewhere in the western wing of the palace. "A-a-a-ah!"

"Messalina!" I recognized her voice immediately and hurried to get dressed. Cassius disappeared into the prothyron.

"Cohort, alarm! To your feet! Accelera!" It echoed through the peristyle.

In the half-dark I could barely manage to find my stola and palla.

"Susannah!" I called desperately, before I could remember she was resting in the insula for servants.

"Anat is here, Your Highness." The Egyptian hurried to my room. "It seems that Lady Messalina is in labor."

I felt unrest that the baby was arriving early.

"Dress me up and make me a high ponytail," I hurled my clothes to the woman. "I am not the prefect to equip myself before you light an oil lamp!"

Always earnest and reticent, Anat could now hardly resist laughter.

"Call Alcaeus!" I shouted to the guardsmen at the prothyron. "And light more torches!"

Anat stumbled on the stairs and stuck to me not to fall.

"You let a man deliver a baby?" I asked her with an angry look.

"Should I go for a midwife?" she asked me confusedly.

"The labor is premature," I said. "Messalina needs a medic, not some loquacious witch. Ten midwives couldn't manage to save Junia Claudilla and her child."

Callistus met us by the chambers of the favorite.

"The Lady is about to deliver!" The Greek grabbed his head. "Ah le-le-le!"

"Find the Cretan!" I moved him aside to pass.

"I'm afraid he cannot come." The secretary shook his head. "Caesar is still weak."

We found Messalina in the middle of the room, bent in half with pain.

"Hold onto me," I gently took her by the hand. "You better lay down, dear."

The woman nodded and jerked, squeezing my palm.

"You'll be alright, my dear." I stroked her head. "You are delivering a baby prince."

With the next moan, her waters broke right on the nacre floor. Anat start singing something in Egyptian, more lingering than Messalina's groans.

"Stop howling like a dog!" I pulled her by the hair. "Bring me hot water and clean linen cloth – now!"

Messalina, sweaty and pale, rose up on her elbows.

"Princess," she uttered. "Please, help me, Drusilla."

With my hands trembling, I tore the skirt of her long dress and helped her spread her legs. From the excruciating sight, my head started spinning and I felt my stomach hitting my throat.

"I am the midwife and she who does not bear." Suddenly, almost familiar words were drawn before my eyes. *"I am the solace of your labor pains…"*

Messalina's scream brought me back to reality.

"Breathe deeply, dear!" I encouraged her. "Don't strain yourself! Just push!"

Exhausted, the woman scratched my arm all over like a wild cat.

"I see the head!" Anat exclaimed joyfully. I exhaled deeply.

The imperial favorite brought into the world a little girl.

"Who gave her such beautiful eyes?" I asked, delighted. "When Gaius sees her, he'll get well at once."

"We need to separate them." Anat pointed to the naval cord, still bonding the child and her mother.

"Cover her with something," I replied, and I turned to the door. "Cassius!"

"What are you doing?" Messalina looked at me bewildered.

Cassius was near to guard us.

"Pull out your dagger," I said to him. "Cut the tube, but very carefully."

The prefect did that job with the precision of a jeweler, and Anat took the baby to bathe and to swaddle her.

"Due to the custom, Caesar gives the name to every newborn baby of the family," the young mother recalled. "But, in such circumstances, this right belongs to you, Drusilla."

Before I analyzed her words, my little niece started crying.

"Octavia is crying for Mark Antony," I smiled and kissed the baby on the cheek.

"You know, Lady Octavia was our mutual ancestor," Messalina noticed.

"Then," I gently took the infant in my arms, "welcome, my dear Claudia Octavia!"

"Congratulations, ladies!" Callistus peeped through the door. "We have good news from the Carinae, too."

"Vespasian died?" I joked, handing the baby back to Anat.

"Unfortunately, no." The secretary sighed. "Your sister, Lady Agrippina, too, has given birth. It is a boy."

I looked at Cassius, and gave myself a while to think.

"I'll call him Nero," I decided. "After his grandfather."

XI

AD 38

The circus performance began with the wild hunt of venatores fighting predators.

"Call the Senate for tomorrow," Gaius addressed Uncle Claudius. "We'll have an extraordinary sitting."

"Are you sh-sure, Dive?" The disgraced old man asked apprehensively. "I mean, you've just overcame the d-d-disease."

Caligula's sharp look stopped him at once.

"Diseases – I am yet to overcome."

"But, Your Majesty," Claudius muttered bewilderedly. "We're having f-f-festi now... "

"I'm wondering," Caligula said thoughtfully, observing the performance. "How dare you argue with me?

"N-n-never in my life!" The censor shook his head and half-bowed to his nephew. "Your wish is my command."

Disgusted, Gaius moved aside a little.

"Do you see those lions?" He pointed to the hungry beasts, roaring at the tamers. "Thank the gods that you're my father's brother, otherwise I would feed you to them!"

"God of the g-g-gods!" The old man turned pale and flopped down to the bench.

My brother looked at me – as always sitting at his right hand.

"I'm too merciful."

I smiled and handed him a small silver tray with nuts in honey.

The bloody game with animals was followed by the breathtaking dance of the acrobats.

"Where did you find that marvel, sister?" He gestured to the dancers.

Three young Egyptian men in wide colorful trousers were performing composite and risky movements, accompanied by a girl with a colored-glass necklace, walking fearlessly on a thin rope.

"The kinsmen of my Anat," I replied, a little proudly. "They didn't want to take but a sesterce for that wondrous performance."

Caesar got earnest.

"You will get your money back tomorrow," he whispered. "So will my people."

I didn't want to discourage him with my doubts, so I just fixed his toga picta.[384]

"I know how," Gaius assured me with a cunning smile. "Tonight, at the feast, I'm preparing a surprise for our enemies."

The senators were watching us from their soft benches with a canopy in a half-bewildered, half-malevolent manner.

"Caesar," Callistus peeked from behind the Imperial lodge. "Everything is ready for tonight's… festivity."

Caligula, with a satisfied face, leaned back in his showy sit and put a handful of sweets in his mouth.

"We begin after the race."

At dusk, by the gates of the palace, the cashier greeted our foppish and vain guests – Uncle Claudius.

"Welcome to O-o-olympus, sirs!" The censor, dressed like the blacksmith Hephaestus, clumsily made a profound reverence.

"What is the matter with you, censor?" The noblemen asked, one by one, in confusion. "Are we back to Circus Maximus?"

"The entrance costs are one thousand s-s-sesterces." Claudius blushed with both fear and embarrassment. "Your absence would be c-c-considered as an offence against the dignity of Caesar."

First, the patricians burst out laughing and insulting him, but when they noticed a row of the praetorians behind the censor's hunched back, they hurried to take out their pouches.

"Get out of my way, you buffoon!" Sabinus exclaimed, trying to save face. "Seems like your nephew went completely out of his mind."

Claudius jerked aside, ready to give in, when Cassius Chaerea came along.

---

[384] An imperial cloak dyed solid purple, decorated with imagery in gold thread, and worn over a similarly-decorated tunica.

"How dare you, tribune, raise your voice to the censor?" The prefect asked him in a tone, appropriate to a warlord. Stella and Clemens, equipped to start the war, followed his every step.

"A thousands silver sesterces." Stella reminded the senators, as he pulled a money box out of the censor's hands.

Sabinus turned to his older brother, already boiling with fury.

"It served us right," Vespasian uttered through his teeth. "As we gave the things over to a cunt like Macro!" Then he reluctantly counted his money, and grunted, "I need my change back!"

The throne room was sinking in flowers, and filled with the delicate smell of sandalwood. Dozens of maids, dressed like the Graces and the Muses, were heartily serving the guests with various sweet drinks and appetizers.

"Would you like to try some peacock escalope, my lord?" The half-naked Greekess smiled to consul Galba.

"That wine has traveled all along the Incense Route." The narrow-eyed brunette sat nimbly on Asprenas.

"Try some seafood with pearls dissolved in vinegar," the slim Gaul crooned to Asiaticus.

Listening to the harp song, sensual and pure as snow, the patricians were wondering what was the reason of the feast that sumptuous… and where actually was the host?

Caligula had been two hours late. Lollia Paulina and Livilla gazed at Cassius interrogatively, but the prefect didn't hurry to reply.

"His Imperial Majesty, Gaius Julius Caesar," Helicon finally announced his dominus arriving.

The guests stood up and… got astonished with the sight. Caligula, wearing a tunic of fine silk with an artificial beard and a thick wig, rode into the room on horseback.

"Get down on your knees before Zeus, the king of the gods!" Callistus shouted, as he hit the floor with the copper wand.

The senators, his wives and other officials knelt down on the marble, calling out "Ave!"

Callistus helped the host dismount, and Gaius carelessly raised his hand to greet them back.

"Avete."

Enraged with his first defeat, Vespasian insensibly tried to straighten at least one leg, but Stella with a well-trained movement brought him down again. However, this wasn't the greatest humiliation for the Mithraists.

"Diva Augusta Julia Drusilla, the Mother of Rome!" the Egyptian exclaimed with a smile, gesturing to Callistus to open the door before me.

My tiara and long dress were exactly the same as those worn by wooden Rhea Silvia. In my right hand I held the spear from the Sibylline Cave, now sharpened and polished.

There was everything – goggling, clenching fists under-the-table, bitterness, curiosity and even whispering: "O futuo! "

"Salvete." I smiled amiably and took my usual seat beside Gaius.

"Cene bene." Caesar signaled to continue with convivium and… slowly removed his tunic.

"What is that for?" I asked him half-loudly, as most of the guests chocked on wine.

"I'm Zeus!" He gave me a white-teethed smile. "I need to show my torso."

"You have shown too much." I shook my head as I leaned my spear against the column. "Please, don't catch a cold again."

Caligula straightened his back and looked at Vespasian.

"Tribune!"

The self-proclaimed magistrate stood up quickly, swallowing a large bite nervously.

"I heard of a Parthian custom of kissing a king's hands and feet. Is it really so?" the emperor asked cheerfully.

"Aye, Caesar," Vespasian nodded. "It is."

"I see," Gaius smiled, as he turned to Sabinus. "Better kiss the feet of your own ruler than to a strange one, right?"

"Of course, Your Majesty." The younger Flavian was good at acting.

"I like your wife," Caligula went on, and winked at a woman sitting next to the tribune. "O Nymphidia! Come to the lap of god, my lovely mortal!"

Nymphidia, a woman over thirty and a mother of three children, was indeed a pulchrous woman. With a grace of a butterfly, she moved through the room at my brother's desire.

"Tonight," Gaius grabbed her around the slim waist. "You'll share a bed with Zeus."

The senators, surrounded by the guardsmen, could only stare at him, looking upset.

"I hope you're good in bed." Caligula addressed the woman with Tiberius-like grin. "Your friend Saturnina has made no impression on me."

Asiaticus no longer looked self-confident or easy-going. As his wife was mentioned, the eloquent senator now wished the earth could open up and swallow him. Saturnina, the seemingly chaste matron, covered her face with pale hands.

"Why are you doing this, Zeus?" I wondered, openly contented by our enemies' humiliation. "Aren't you happy with Hera?"

"I do not tolerate injustice," he replied, playing his role like a skillful Greek actor. "When these *cinaedi* ignore their wives, fucking each other for the sake of Sol Invictus, someone has to comfort the poor ladies."

Nymphidia chuckled in a foolishly unbridled manner, as my brother stroked her by the neck.

"How graceful this neck is," Gaius spoke amusedly. "Imagine, one my word would be enough for it to be cut from that body."

"Please, brother," I stopped him. "Don't cut the wrong neck."

"As for Hera," Caesar suddenly remembered of his wife, Lollia Paulina. "Make sure she gets her severance pay and send her far away – as soon as possible."

"How are you going to explain it to your people?" I wondered.

"First, she didn't give me children," Gaius shrugged his shoulders. "How a woman who drinks harder than Alcaeus could bear anything at all?"

"You're right, the lightning-slinger." I supported him, as I was hoping he would finally get married to the mother of his daughter.

"Now, I'm going back to the Olympus." The young man rose up, pulling Nymphidia to follow him. "Enjoy your meal, my dear mortals."

The noblemen stood up to greet him readily.

"No, you won't kiss my feet." He smiled as he headed outside. "Tomorrow at the sitting we'll discuss the robbery of both treasuries."

The senators no longer just looked awkward, but now horrified. It was still too early and risky for us to attack, but yet the right time to intimidate and stab them to their weakest spot – their pride.

In the doorway, Caesar turned around.

"See you tomorrow," he reminded the patricians, and nodded toward Cassius. "I'll bring him with me."

Cassius, dressed in a new prefect's uniform, wearing a bronze helmet and armed with a spatha, looked boldly and magnificently like the god of war.

"We're leaving too." I came up to my man and took him by the hand. "The party's over."

XII

"Ma'oz Tzur Yeshu'ati, lekha na'eh leshabe'ah...!"[385] David sang, as he lighted the eight candle in a big menorah.

David sang, lighting the eighth lamp on the grand menorah.

"Now we can enjoy ourselves." Susannah whispered to me, smiling. "Congratulations on your first Hanukkah,[386] Princess!"

That day, in keeping with tradition, I'd been fasting with my friends from dusk till dawn, watching nimble Rachel baking donuts, walnut pastries and, of course, her 'very Jewish' fish with mushroom stuffing.

"I want to try a bit of all the victuals, they smell so wonderful!" I said to the Rabbanit impatiently.

Rachel filled my plate with lavish helpings, as her husband finished the prayer, and invited us to take our seats.

"When the Lord needs our sacrifice," David said cordially. "When He asks us to reject a certain thing, He offers something more and better in return."

"He never demands of us more than we are able to give up," Susannah added.

That evening, we were joined by Antipas' brother-in-law – Prince Agrippa, who grew up in my grandmother's house. For his loyalty and goodness, Gaius freed him from the status of a hostage and a protégé, but now proclaimed him the successor of the tetrarch.

"Tell us, my Prince, what do you know about this holiday?" Rachel addressed him merrily.

"Hanukkah is a day of freedom and the light." Agrippa showed the eight-candle candelabrum. "On that day, many years ago, the brave priest Yehuda HaMakabi rebelled against the pagan king, destroyed his idols and lit the candles in our Temple once again."

---

[385] (hebr.) My Refuge, my Rock of Salvation! 'Tis pleasant to sing Your praises.

[386] A Jewish festival commemorating the rededication of the Second Temple in Jerusalem at the time of the Maccabean Revolt against the Seleucid Empire. It is also known as the Festival of Lights.

"Well done!" David exclaimed. "Thanks God, you weren't led astray by Romans or your kinsmen."

"I believe in God," Agrippa said, inspired by the history. "And I believe that He left heaven and came down to earth."

"Keep what you know a secret," I sighed, warning him. "As long as Antipas rules your homeland, it belongs to Mithras."

At the mention of the evil name, Susannah jerked and murmured a protection spell.

"Speaking of foreign idols," David suddenly got earnest. "It's a sin for the faithful to take part in pagan rituals."

Yes, it was me he was reproaching. Even Roman beggars knew how… picturesque Caligula's recent feast was.

"I am a member of the ruling family," I explained myself even-mindedly. "Did Esther change traditions in the court of the Persian King?"

"My Lady Wisdom always has answers for everything." The rabbi sighed. "But how can we resist the evil spirits if we keep on doing what they want us to?"

I took a bigger sip of wine and grabbed my head.

"Alright," I asked the four of them. "What do you advise me to do?"

"At first, you must persuade your brother to turn to Adonai," David replied, wiping his beard. "To settle down beside the woman who bore him a child…"

"You too, Your Highness, should get married," Rachel interrupted him. "To Prefect Chaerea. Do you really care what they might say?"

"Stay away from sinners," Susannah took her turn. "Callistus and his… friend," she bit her lip in disgust, "They are doing a terrible thing."

"I am refraining from giving advises," Agrippa said kindly. "I can imagine how you feel, Your Highness."

"That's my boy!" I pointed at him thankfully and finished my donut voraciously.

"Lupus in fabula," the nursemaid recognized the voices in the peristyle. "Sodom and Gomorrah are here."

"Watch your mouth, Susannah," I reprimanded her. "Your Galilee is no better."

The woman turned her head down-heartedly, as Rachel imperceptibly cuddled her back to comfort.

"Venite!" I called my friends to join us.

Callistus and Anicetus looked a little lost and frightened, too. It wasn't hard to guess what kind of news they were to tell me.

"I have to go." I got up from the table. "Keep on having fun."

"If you need some help," Agrippa whispered worriedly. "I'll be in here Rome until next nones."

"I'll be alright." I patted him on the back thankfully and went out to the fauces.[387]

"Shall we begin with the bad news, or with the worse?" the secretary asked me.

"From the worst one," I replied, showing them to the tablinum.

Callistus took a seat and pulled a tiny scroll out of his tunic.

"I was snooping around in the guest chambers yesterday," he said half-loudly, glancing at the door from time to time. "Your cousin Gemellus was staying there…"

"He found a letter that the little fellow wouldn't like to be discovered." The Cypriot interrupted him.

There was the time, when Gemellus, as the offspring of the only son of Tiberius Caesar, had better chances to become an heir than my brother did. However, when the love affair of my aunt Livilla and Sejanus came to light, the throne was lost for my cousin forever. After the death of his mother, Gemellus was raised by senator Sisenna, known as the friend of the Flavians.

"Now that your cousin came of age, the senators consider him a future, favorable ruler," Callistus explained. "And the young man feels flattered."

I took a parchment scroll from his hands carefully. It was the draft of my kinsman's letter to his foster-father, senator Sisenna.

"I am ready to prove my allegiance to Lord Mithras," I read, barely believing my own eyes. "And to defeat his enemies."

---

[387] (lat.) Narrow entryway.

"Tu quoque, Brute?"[388] I sighed, as I recalled him as a baby in my mother's lap. "Go on." I turned to the secretary, tearing the ominous letter to pieces.

"After Macro's fall, the senators have chosen more assassins, yet unknown for us."

I recollected the last prophecy of the Cumaean Sibyl.

"Gaius should keep an eye on his brothers-in-law." I leaned against the back of my soft chair.

"No chance," Callistus spoke with little hope. "Actaeon heard with his own ears – the rotter who should kill the emperor would not be Mithraist."

Besides, Ahenobarbus, Vinicius and Longinus, were sent to the eastern provinces. Lepidus, my "forgotten" current husband was still here, but he was too much of a coward even to attack a dog, afraid of being bitten.

"Gemellus won't be an assassin either," Callistus continued worriedly. "The letter you were quick to tear apart tells of his swift initiation… It's tonight."

Tonight… It was the Winter Solstice. Realizing that was like being attacked by the beast.

"An innocent child will be sacrificed!" I jerked. "I must prevent it!"

Callistus gestured to me to speak quieter, and to Anicetus to watch by the door.

"Tiberius knew that one day you would seek to enter the Mithraeum." He squinted mysteriously.

"Where is the serpent's lair?" I asked him anxiously. "What if the bastards caught Corbulo's son or… Petronius?!"

"I could have reminded you how dangerous it is." The secretary came up to the bookcase, pulling out a dusty map from underneath. "But you would hardly listen."

The old map was the secret plan of the City of Rome. The keeper of the chambers looked down sadly, crossing his big arms on his chest.

"Aren't we friends, Your Highness?" He spoke in a deep voice, expecting me to let them escort me.

"You are the best friends ever," I said mildly. "Together we're the army, but… "

---

[388] (lat.) 'You as well, Brutus?' were reportedly last words, spoken by the Roman dictator Julius Caesar, at the moment of his assassination, to his supposed friend Marcus Brutus, upon recognizing him as one of the assassins.

"This is your battle, Princess," Callistus concluded. "The time of Sophia."

I wiped the dust off the map and pointed at the round square in its center.

"The Forum, isn't it?"

The secretary nodded.

"Look east," he whispered, as he showed toward the Gardens of Peace – an abandoned and rarely visited park on the Palatine outskirts.

"Cybele's grotto, I guess." I looked at the thick black spot in the middle of the park. "By the dried lake."

"Cybele, Aphrodite, Ishtar – all of those are shades of the same bastard," Anicetus said knowingly, surprising even Callistus. "He likes to turn into women, I guess."

"To hell with Mithras!" I grabbed the parchment with the map and glanced at the clepsydra. "I only have an hour until midnight."

"It is not that easy, Princess." Callistus fixed his dark curls. "The entrance to the grotto is guarded by a dozen of armed soldiers – from inside, so it's a trap."

"But there's a back entrance, too, right?" My finger stopped at a small point under the Staircase of Caucus. "Faustulus'[389] hut!"

Anicetus clapped his hands.

"Did Ariadne learn from you?"

"Come on, get serious!" Callistus pushed him with the elbow. "Better give her advice how to fight a pack of Minotaurs unarmed!"

That was indeed a problem, but I had no time to jitter over it. Immediately, my gaze stopped at Caesar's bust. Right next to it there was my spear, as if waiting for me.

"Why not?" I grabbed it and ran to the prothyron. "Fortuna audaces iuvat!"[390]

---

[389] Faustulus was the shepherd who found the infants Romulus and Remus, who were being suckled by a she-wolf on the Palatine Hill.
[390] (lat.) Fortune favors the brave.

XIII

Between ala[391] and vestibulum, Priscus was keeping his watch along with another young guardsman.

"Your Highness?!" The tow-haired soldier showed surprise. "Where are you going at the dead of night – alone?"

I rolled my eyes.

"Let's say, I'm going for a walk."

Priscus touched the head of my spear cautiously.

"For a walk – with this?"

"If you tell anyone, especially the Prefect what you saw," I whispered sharply. "I will stick that spear into your ass!"

The young centurion reluctantly saluted in agreement, and his companion asked me excitedly.

"Shall I find you a litter or escort you, Princess?"

His noble face profile and melodious Attic accent gave away his origin.

"Onoma soi ti estin?"[392] I looked at him curiously.

"Sophonius Tigellinus." The young man smiled. "Ek Atenai erkhomai."[393]

"Se gignoskon hairo,[394] Tigelline," I said kindly. "May your service in the Praetorian Guard be successful."

"Thank you, Princess." Tigellinus nodded, embarrassed, as he fixed his helmet.

"By Mars, why wasn't I born Greek?" Priscus sighed deeply.

Now it was the perfect moment for me to sneak out.

"Valete!" I covered my head with the hood and disappeared – before they both could blink.

---

[391] A wing room at the atrium.

[392] (anc.gr.) What is your name?

[393] (anc.gr.) I am from Athens.

[394] (anc.gr.) Nice to meet you.

I went down the stairs, which once belong to the Temple of Castor and Pollux, followed by indifferent glances of the other guardsmen. When Cassius was not here to supervise them, the praetorians indulged in gambling, their usual night-time amusement. They knew well, that I often closed my eyes to their weaknesses. Unlike the typical Roman matronas, I was aware of my own imperfection, and didn't demand flawlessness of those in my service. Well, there was another reason, too. My tolerance was thanked with their loyalty and deep appreciation.

In the light of the big, almost full moon, I saw the shining silver ornaments of my carriage and new litter. Tiredness and fasting made my kneels shake up, but I decided firmly not to risk another life.

"*Dominus reget me et nihil mihi deerit,*"[395] I spoke, accelerating my steps. The wintry streets were empty. My daytime peplum could hardly protect from December wind, and the long spear in my hand felt too heavy to carry.

"*Nam et si ambulavero in medio umbrae mortis non timebo mala quoniam tu mecum es virga tua et baculus tuus ipsa me consolata sunt.*"[396] I went on, as I left behind Villa Claudiana. That uneasy foggy night, even my uncle's dogs felt too lazy to bark. Panting out winter smoke, I ran through the gloomy Field of Mars.

"Go ahead, Sophia," I whispered with my lips numb. "Save the child or die trying."

Finally, the milky moonlight took me to the hut where Romulus and Remus spent their childhood. The ramshackle roof and the walls, covered with frozen ivy smelled like hopelessness and rotten leaves. I concentrated on another prayer, opened the door and step into darkness.

"*Quoniam in me speravit et liberabo eum, protegam eum quia cognovit nomen meum,*" [397] I whispered, as I felt the tiny stairs under my feet. As I stuck out my spear ahead, I cautiously moved downstairs, sticking to the earthen wall with the free hand.

---

[395] (lat.) The Lord guideth me, and nothing is wanting to me (Ps. 22:2).

[396] (lat.) Even though I walk through the darkest valley, I will fear no evil, for you are with me; your rod and your staff, they comfort me. (Ps. 22:4).

[397] (lat.) "Because he loves me," says the Lord, "I will rescue him; I will protect him, for he acknowledges my name. (Ps. 91:14)

"Clamabit ad me et exaudiam eum; cum ipso sum in tribulatione eripiam eum et clarificabo eum."[398] The bizarre blind spearman went ahead, warmed by the faith in Adonai alone. *"Longitudine dierum replebo eum et ostendam illi salutare meum."*[399]

As I uttered the last word, I felt some solid ground beneath my feet. I strained my ears, and heard male voices, followed by a long, loud, piercing cry of a child.

"Petronius!" I shouted in horror, and moved forward as fast as I could. My spear hit the door, opening it.

In a large, rectangular chamber I found the better part of the senators, all dressed in black with Phrygian caps[400] on their heads and shameless smiles on their faces. The flaming torches on the tripod emitted eerie greenish light in front of the image of Mithras. In the middle of the wicked sanctuary stood a stone altar with a naked boy on it, tied hand and foot. Vespasian was leaning over him with a dagger in his hand.

"May Adonai rebuke you!" I exclaimed, stopping the bloody ritual at the last minute. "Hold on, baby!" I addressed Petronius. I'll get you out of here!"

"A woman in Mithraeum!" Sabinus became enraged, as other senators spun around in confusion.

"How did she find out?" Asiaticus looked at Vespasian bewilderedly.

"Kill her!" Lepidus raised his voice.

I lifted up my weapon, moving in a zigzag manner like Leonidas[401] before the endless Persian army. In my eyes, the enemies couldn't see fear, but defiance. The crowd was ready to tear me apart, but I was ready to defend myself.

"Manete!"[402] The 'Sun-Runner' gestured to the men to stop, pursing his dry lips into a grin. "You!" He pointed at me, beckoning. "Come closer."

"Leave the child first!" I said, not moving. "Damn ventriloquist!"

---

[398] (lat.) He will call upon me, and I will answer him; I will be with him in trouble, I will deliver him and honor him (Ps. 91:15).

[399] (lat.) With long life will I satisfy him and show him my salvation (Ps. 92:16).

[400] A soft conical cap with the apex bent over.

[401] A warrior king of the Greek city-state of Sparta, who led the allied Greek forces to a last stand at the Battle of Thermopylae; while attempting to defend the pass from the invading Persian army; he entered myth as the leader of the 300 Spartans.

[402] (lat.) Wait!

Petronius, cold on the altar, started coughing.

"Now, untie him!" I brought the head of my long spear closer to Vespasian's chest.

Then, for a while, his hazel eyes turned blood red, and his short, wrinkled neck suddenly stretched and straightened.

Actaeon didn't lie, I thought. *They are no longer human.*

The magistrate barely tamed his inner demon, and gestured to Vitellius to take the boy off the altar.

"Nomen est omen,[403] Layla."[404] He curled his lips. "You've always been as silly as night... and as ugly, too."

I put my spear down, and stepped cautiously toward him.

"Why are you doing this, my Lord?" Sabinus yelled. "Will you allow a woman defile our mystery?"

His brother said nothing. I carefully took Petronius in my arms, wrapping him in my peplum hurriedly.

"She saw us; she will speak at the Forum!" Vitellius shouted, and the others joined him, making the fierce noise.

"We need to kill them both," Sabinus interjected, as he moved toward the door, to block it. "I will not let her destroy us!"

Vespasian shook his head like a disappointed teacher and cursed out the God's name.

"He will not save you." The magistrate looked at me. "He doesn't care about the sinners."

"Whoever is not against Him, is for Him," I replied, hugging Petronius, and with an effort made my way to the door. "And who's against Him, woe to him!"

"Your brother has already threatened us." Asiaticus waved aside and stepped to Sabinus. "He confiscated our property!"

"I do not have the time to talk who actually robbed whom," I said reluctantly, and shook my spear in front of him. "Get out of my way!"

---

[403] (lat.) The name is a sign.
[404] (hebr.) Night.

The haughty laughs echoed all over the grotto.

"Drusilla!" Suddenly I recognized my cousin's voice.

I turned around. Gemellus, dressed in dark like all his "brothers", spoke to me condescendingly.

"Come to your senses, sister, bow to Mithras!"

"Futuere, traditor!"[405] I threw to his pale face, as if I spat in it.

The senators reacted with the worst curses over me and all my dead.

"Enough!" Vespasian uttered through his teeth, as he took his dagger back to the holster. "The game is getting boring, so I'll change the rules."

Sabinus tried to interfere, but the magistrate reprimanded him, and opened the front door to let the guardsmen in.

"The way is free – for now." He grinned at me. "I give you half an hour to get out of here. If you succeed, praise Adonai, if not… you will end up like Edith, the Lot's wife."

I realized that there was a trap to follow, so I hurried up to leave the grotto, bending under the weight of a spear and a nine-year-old child.

"I must be heavy, Princess," Petronius moaned. "Please, let me go by myself!"

"Just be quiet!" I whispered, losing my breath. "I'd rather toss this pagan beanbag!"

"This is the spear of Alexander," someone called inside my head. *"Whoever possesses it, has power over the Unclean nation."*

"I choose – life!" I thought aloud, leaving the weapon in the dark.

Finally we left the cave. I looked around. From there, the shortest way to the Palatine… lay across the Tiber.

"Well, at least I can swim." I judged. "Still, the water is icy… But yet, in this place the damn river is the narrowest."

Free at last, the boy smiled weakly, falling into the exhausted sleep.

"No, no, corculum, wake up!" I touched his shoulder. "We must cross the river now. I need your help."

"I want to sleep," he murmured. "I want back to my flowers… and butterflies…"

---

[405] (lat.) Fuck you, traitor!

"Petronius!" I shook him. "If we don't get to the palace, they will kill us!"

The fear woke him up from the feverish dream.

"Listen up," I slowly put him down on a shore, and knelt. "Hold on to my back like a baby turtle, and do not let go!"

Petronius nodded and did as I said.

"When I start swimming, you just flounder with your feet." I tried encouraging him. "You're a man, you can withstand it!"

The water was chilly enough to take my strength away. Terrible cramps attacked my feet like predatory fish. Petronius went yelling out of horror.

"Adonai!" I called out desperately. "Save this child!"

"Hey, Victor!" I suddenly heard a male voice from the other bank. "There's someone in the river!"

"It's a woman with a child!" Another man responded, as he raised a torch. "I am jumping for them!"

"Hold on, the help is coming!" I said to Petronius, and we both started floundering to stay afloat.

One of the two young Vigiles quickly swam to us, and grabbed the boy.

"I got him," the man said, clenching his teeth, and turned to his companion. "Help the lady, Justus!"

"Take us somewhere," I said to the Vigile who saved me, barely believing that we'd reached the shore. "We are in trouble."

"Oh, I see," Justus replied half-loudly. "Our mother lives nearby."

"But first," Victor said earnestly. "You tell me who you are."

"I'm Julia Drusilla," I uttered, trying to stay conscious as long as possible. "And this is little Gaius Petronius," I pointed at the crying boy.

"Oh goodness!" Victor got bewildered. "All of our unit has been searching for him from early morning!"

"My parents didn't know they took me!" the boy wept, almost choking with cold air and tears.

I remember myself barely holding to Justus' horse, and a misty street of the Esquiline... a house looking like a Jewish hut... and a good-natured face of a woman, who opened the door for us.

"Your Highness?!" The hostess somehow recognized me. "What is the matter with you?"

"Help the child," I whispered, clinging to her so I wouldn't collapse. Victor took Petronius inside, and Justus cautiously locked the door.

"God is merciful." The woman kindly reassured me. "Photice will take care of you."

I smiled, repeating the name that was dear to me.

Of course, that was a completely different Photice.

XIV

The next thing I saw were clay walls, patched up at the corners, but still looking neat. Then, there were a sideboard and door curtains. I found myself lying in a tiny bed of wood and straw, wrapped in a warm sheepskin blanket. My little hero was still dreaming next to me, hugging a soft pillow.

"Toda lecha Elohim," I whispered, as I kissed him on his forehead. It seemed like a bad fever passed us by, but my stealthy and annoying headache woke up together with me.

"I'm here, corculum." I covered Petronius as if he was a baby and got up slowly. The old spasms attacked my legs again, making me bow in pain.

"Your Highness!" Photice suddenly came in, moving long curtains aside. "Why don't you call me?" She reached out to me, as I stuck to her hand, greasy of kneading dough.

"I didn't want to wake him up," I nodded at the boy.

"While you were still sleeping, he's been up, eating hot soup." The hostess smiled, and showed me to the kitchen.

I was moved to tears, and I kissed her on the rounded swarthy cheek.

"Thank you, Photice… for everything."

"Non debes," she smiled. "Everything happens by God's will."

I settled down on a wooden bench with a backrest.

"Where are you from?" I wondered. "You talk like a Jewess, but your name is Greek."

Photice covered my back with some kind of wrap, and went on cooking.

"I am a Samaritan."

"And what about your sons?" I was a little curious. Foreigners were rarely allowed to join the Imperial police.

"Their father is a Roman citizen." The woman sighed as if she was embarrassed. "He named them in Roman fashion and brought them to Cohortes urbanae."

"I see," I smiled. "Your husband must be a personage."

"Calvisius is not my husband." She smiled bitterly and handed me a leather bottle of water. "Here, refresh yourself."

The water was cold and tasted… marvelous. To my big surprise, just a few sips of it could take away the headache.

"*He* gave it to me," Photice whispered mystically.

"Who, Calvisius?" At first, I couldn't understand.

The hostess shook her head.

"That one who tastes His water will never get thirsty again."

Astonished, I fell silent, watching Photice cooking skillfully by the round stove. This woman had known Jesus, the incarnation of Adonai, and, like Mary Magdalene, was chosen to be his disciple and preach the undefiled Truth in farther lands. She seemed to have found in me a like-minded person and, maybe, even somehow found out who I was.

"I've never been married," she said suddenly, taking the fresh bread out of the oven with a black poker. "Samaritan girls are raised more free-mindedly than the Jewesses. We can inherit a house or gain some other wealth on our own, without a custodian."

Her late father, a well-to-do merchant and cattle breeder was a dear guest at the court of Queen Malthace, who was herself a Samaritan from Shechem. Malthace was known as the only wife of Herod with her own treasury, made of the savings she made long before she had been married.

"Wealth gives you power and freedom," the queen once said to little Photice. "Our fathers raise us to sell to the strangers as if we were cattle, and our husbands are free to put us aside when they're bored. So, better be smart and start making your own money while you're still young and agile, and you'll rule your destiny."

Sharp-witted Malthace with her sharp tongue, all jeweled with jasper, became a role model for a callow girl. When Fotis came to a legal age, she decided to go trading with her father, and very soon became even more thriving than her old parent.

"Other merchants called me – a 'man's head,'" she laughed, recalling, and treated me to her bread. "I've traveled all over Asia, and earned a property yet in my twenties."

Modeled on the queen, who got married in her thirties, Fotis didn't hurry up to settle down. Unlike another merchant woman – Rachel, the Samaritan lived lavishly.

"I was afraid of love," she explained, embarrassed. "I didn't want to be attached to someone, didn't want to care for anyone, but my own children and myself."

The longest relationship she had was with Calvisius, a Roman soldier, who used to serve in Shechem as a centurion.

"He loved me and wanted me for a wife." Photice went on regretfully. "I gave him two sons, but my pride and my greed drove him away forever."

Years went by. Victor and Justus grew into men and joined the army. Photice left alone in her big house. A barren summer, followed by the reforms of the new governor, led to a crisis in her region. Once rampant woman, she had to sell her costly possessions to survive, and then, to ask her neighbors for a loan.

"Even then, in misery and hunger, I was too proud to repent," she recalled. "I was comforting myself with my notion of freedom and my illusion of independence."

One day, a rich neighbor sent Photice to fetch him a hydria[406] of water from Jacob's well.[407] As she filled her bucket, she sat on a slap to catch her breath. Weary with the heat of noon, she looked around in despair, but there was no one... until the young Jew appeared out of nowhere.

"Give me a drink," he asked. "I've traveled a long way."

"How is it that you, a Jew, ask a drink of me, a woman of Samaria?" Photice wondered. "Doesn't your faith forbid you sharing things in common with foreigners?"

"There are no foreigners for God," the young man replied cordially. "If you knew who is asking you for a drink, you would have asked him to give you the living water."

That very moment, Photice realized she felt no longer tired and hungry.

"Sir," she begged Him, irradiated by the divine power. "Give me that water, so I would never be thirsty again."

"Go, call your husband, and come back." Jesus replied.

Photice, all at once, became aware of her sins, and lowered her eyes.

"I have no husband."

Yet he wasn't here to judge her.

---

[406] An ancient water-carrying vessel.

[407] A deep well constructed from rock that has been associated in religious tradition with the biblical patriarch Jacob.

"God created a man and a woman to love and to become one." He reminded her graciously. "To be a husband and a wife, and with this love to serve Him, giving an example for their children."

Photice became speechless, as she perceived the truth about her vain and selfish life. While she believed that wealth could bring her happiness, she really knew nothing of true happiness.

"Do not despair," Jesus comforted her. "If someone feels in himself that he is not meant for earthly love, he may lead a quiet life of prayer, fasting and preaching the Love of God."

And so, the arrogant Samaritan woman was chosen to become one of His messengers, like Mary Magdalene and Rabbi David. I wish I could hear more of her story, but we were interrupted by Cassius and Petronius' father Mannius arriving.

"Your Highness, I owe you my life!" The senator gestured excitedly. "You've saved my son, my firstborn baby!"

I pulled my hand out of his wet palm, not to let him kiss it.

"This woman and her sons helped me a lot." I showed toward the hostess.

Mannius got earnest and nodded restrainedly. I bet it was easy to find a black cat in the dark than a patrician favorable to foreigners.

"I'm going for my boy." The man hurried to cubiculum. "I will get him the best guardsman."

"The best guardsman is already taken," I said wittily, hugging Chaerea. "Will you please forgive me?"

Cassius pulled me close, and kissed me – first with a glance, and then with his lips.

"I went out of my mind, looking for you." He whispered feelingly. "But I am proud of you, dear."

"Are you thirsty, Prefect?" Photice interrupted us, as she handed Cassius the same skin bottle I had drunk from.

He thanked and drank it all.

"Well done!" The hostess smiled at him. "Now, everything is in the right place."

We exchanged glances, hardly understanding what she meant.

"Tomorrow, I am leaving to Mauretania." She changed the subject. "I am needed there."

A little sad, I asked her if we see her again soon, and her answer got me overwhelmed.

"I'll be back, my Princess." Photice said, joining my hand with Cassius'. "I will teach the Truth to your daughter and your daughter's daughter."

XV

The heavy stomping of praetorian boots and the gentle rustle of the slave girls' gowns portended the fourth watch.

"Time for patrolling," Cassius stroked my naked shoulder.

I grabbed his hand and asked him melancholically.

"When was the last time we had breakfast together?"

"In Misenum, I guess." The prefect sighed and put on his under tunic in one motion. I moved aside to the edge of the bed and dropped my feet into the small pantofles.

"What is your favorite meal?"

"Buccellato, larido et posca,"[408] he replied with irony.

"Oh really?" I laughed. "I thought, my brother spoilt all of you like the Capitoline Geese."[409]

My lover smiled, a little startled.

"You want to cook for me?"

"With a little help of Actaeon," I said honestly. "I've always ran from household chores like a bat out of hell."

The prefect fell thoughtful, and went on in a higher voice, imitating his late mother, Annea Helvilla.

"Come on, girl! If we enjoyed the cook room smell, we would have married some agricolae!"

Holding back laughter out of respect to her memory, I thought out loud, "I wish I knew her. She would be the one I had called – mama."

Cassius, already fully dressed and equipped, turned around.

---

[408] (lat.) Hard biscuits, smoked meat and watered down wine vinegar – a usual army diet in the times of the Late Roman republic.

[409] According to the legend, the quacking of the temple geese awakened Roman soldiers, when the Gauls suddenly attacked in the night.

"You should see my aunt Polyxena," he said, moved with my words. "She is the real Omphale."[410]

"What a lovely name!" I was amazed. "She is the namesake of King Alexander's mother and the Trojan princess!"

"Tell her that," Cassius recommended. "She will adore you."

As the prefect left my chambers, Actaeon appeared by the door.

"Hippiaine!"[411] He waved his hand like a child.

"Are you bringing me some breakfast?" I asked as I washed my face. "Lately I've been waking up hungry."

"Hunger caused by love." The secretary lifted up his eyebrow. "Paleness of a sleepless night."

"Shut up, Homer," I hid my face behind the mirror waggishly. "Cinaedi have spoiled you."

The Greek, with a smile, handed me my comb and explained.

"I've got up early to bake you a placenta,[412] but on my way to the kitchen I met Caesar. He is expecting you for breakfast in the viridarium."[413]

"So you are idling now," I winked, tying my hair in a ponytail. "As for my brother, he will have to wait until I have a bath."

"Quidquid vis."[414] Actaeon came up closer with my turquoise morning dress. "What a nice robe!"

"They were it in Armenia," I said. "Since Callistus controls my wardrobe, I finally like what I see in the mirror."

"Hairo."[415] The Greek smiled. "Shall I call Orla to help you get dressed?"

---

[410] Omphale was a queen of Greek mythology, but Omphale was not a queen of Greece, for she was the ruler of Lydia. She comes to the fore in Greek mythology when she buys Heracles as a slave for three silver talents, a not insignificant sum of money. Mistress and slave though would become lovers, and Omphale would become the second wife of Heracles.

[411] (anc.gr.) Good morning!

[412] A dish from ancient Greece and Rome consisting of many dough layers interspersed with a mixture of cheese and honey and flavored with bay leaves, baked and then covered in honey.

[413] A pleasure-garden.

[414] (lat.) As you wish.

[415] (anc.gr.) I'm glad.

I fell thoughtful for a moment, realizing that I hadn't joined Caligula for meal for even longer than I had with Chaerea. As soon as he got well, my brother fully devoted himself to government affairs, while I kept on writing my dramatic dare.

"Noli sollicitus esse." I tapped him on his nose. "I can do it myself."

Bathed in spring sunlight, the garth smelled like fresh irises. Caligula was reclining at the head of the table, made of ivory and palm tree, while the guest couch on the atrium side was occupied by Messalina, their daughter and her nursemaid.

"In the very nick of time." He gave me a gleeful look. "We have already eaten everything."

"Paradoxos." I shrugged my shoulders. "No soldier's woman rises with the lark."

"Our mother did," Caligula remembered. "Seemed like Agrippina never slept at all."

"Such were the times," I sighed. "No easy for us either."

As baby Octavia noticed me, she gave me a sweet smile.

"Animula[416] mea." I kissed my niece on her forehead. "Pulchrissima es."[417]

"Every inch of Caesar, isn't she?" Messalina blurted out of happiness.

I looked closer to the baby and her father. Octavia had his dark blue eyes, a bit cunning and slanting. Everything upon her face, except for the snub Valerian nose, looked reminiscent of Gaius – long eyelashes, tender mouth, thick hair…

"Verum est," I replied. "She looks… imperial."

My brother suddenly got earnest and straightened his back. "Fedlimid, take my daughter to sleep," he said to the Gaul woman.

The nursemaid bowed to him. The former manageress of Macro's stead and a storyteller now enjoyed the privileges of an imperial nursemaid. Alongside Fedlimid, another dignified old woman joined our household. Alfidia from the Esquiline was pleased to be our chief cookmaid.

"Here you are, Your Highness." She appeared under the arcade of olive trees with a placenta, hot and crispy. "I would never leave you hungry!"

---

[416] (lat.) Sweetheart.

[417] (lat.) You are the most beautiful.

Two lively, lovely maids helped the old woman hand over a tray with a pie and a pelice[418] of autumn fig wine to the table. Anat, somber as Sphinx, picked up the dirty dishes readily.

"You may go now," Caesar said passionlessly. "All of you."

His favorite greeted him with a meek smile, and quietly returned to the palace. I noted admiringly that Messalina's had beauty flourished after she gave birth.

"Bene tibi!"[419] Caligula toasted, ignoring my kind observation.

As I raised my glass, I saw familiar fascination of some new idea in his eyes, combined with the perpetual desire to be praised.

"What are you up to this time, Dive?" I asked cheerfully.

"Sit by my side." He nodded, moving aside the hem of his long robe, resembling a trabea,[420] but of the color of saffron. "I've got something to show you."

"Something I've not seen before, I hope." I smiled, resting my head on his shoulder.

Gaius giggled, as he pulled three drawings out of the tablecloth. I recognized a map of the Vatican hill, surrounded by our late mother's lush gardens.

"I decided to build a hippodrome." He tapped on a circular object by the hilltop. "Exciting, isn't it?"

I estimated the requirements for this venture and let out an astonished whistle.

"You'll need a lot of manpower," I answered. "And money."

"The senatorial gold was enough to pay back all the debts and fill the public treasury," Gaius explained. "I have some shortchange left as well, so I can spend it as I wish."

"This shortchange will cost us dearly, I'm afraid," I sighed. "You've stripped them to the bone."

Caesar turned the sheet of parchment and pointed at his drawing of an Egyptian-like obelisk.

"That's not what you think, sister dear." He laughed like a child. "It's a sunray."

---

[418] Ancient Apulian amphora.
[419] (lat.) To your health!
[420] A ceremonial dress, formed like a mantle.

"So damn witty." I rolled my eyes. "Just to your knowledge, that monolith symbolizes Mithras."

Caesar nodded like he was aware.

"Exactly." He raised the sketch with a pleased look. "I will make fun of them."

Under the picture I could read 'Ioh,' 'Heliopolis,'[421] 'Red granite,' 'Bridge,' and 'Ships.'

"What is he doing here?" I wondered, as I noticed my slave's name.

"The Egyptian's a good architect," he said, taking another sheet of parchment. "This man alone is able to embody my idea."

On the draft there was a floating pontoon bridge across the Bay of Baiae, which was long enough to reach the port of Puteoli. The unusual undertaking needed twenty ships to line up from the Baiae resort.

"It can rival the one built by Xerxes,[422] can't it?" he asked proudly.

"What for?" I looked at him skeptically, finally reaching for a slice of pie.

"Remember Thrasyllus' prophecy?" He squinted with his face dead earnest. "Like, I had a chance to rule as much as to be riding across Baiae?"

I nodded, indulging in a mouthful of still hot and fragrant meal.

"I'll show them I'm nobody's Fool," he toasted for the second time. "Panem et circenses[423] for people, sister!"

"If you say so." I smiled enthusiastically. In fact, Caligula's ideas, seemingly insane, were had a well-conceived, right-minded bottom, spiced with humor.

"During the inquisition, before he breathed his last," he went on nonchalantly. "Our cousin Gemellus acknowledged that Vespasian planned to build a stone amphitheater right above the mithraeum – to turn their human sacrifices into performance."

Fortunately, due to sudden financial losses, the senators had to give up on the morbid idea… for quite a long time yet.

---

[421] A major city of ancient Egypt, now located in Ayn Shams, a northeastern suburb of Cairo.

[422] A similar bridge was constructed in 480 BC during the second Persian invasion of Greece upon the order of King Xerxes I for the purpose of the Persian army to traverse the Hellespont (the present day Dardanelles) from Asia into Thrace.

[423] (lat.) "Bread and circuses" – a metonymic phrase referring to superficial appeasement.

"Their biggest problem is Adonis and his followers." Caligula continued knowingly.

"Adonai." I corrected him. "You, too, should finally consider joining them."

"The senators?!" the young man joked, as if he hadn't understood me. "Not at all. I wouldn't like to change a thing about my life."

A big mistake, I thought, turning the draft to take a look at the third drawing.

"No!" Gaius grabbed a piece of parchment from my hands. "It's nobody's business… for now."

I opened my eyes wide; trying to sense what he made up to crown it all.

"A little present," he whispered mysteriously, uttering word by word. "A wedding present for my sister."

I felt my heart galloping in my chest, as my head went spinning of excitement. Caesar smiled and waved aside.

"You have my permission to marry Chaerea," he said decisively, and kissed me on the cheek. "Congratulation, praefectess."

"But, what shall we do about Lepidus?" I asked with effort.

"Never mind," he replied. "Leave it to me."

I kissed him back, and whirled on the spot.

"All in due time, Drusilla." He stood up abruptly. "Don't ask me questions, or I'll change my mind."

XVI

Protogenes stopped by the door to the dungeon.

"Are you sure, Princess?" he asked apathetically. "That sight is not for your sensibility."

"Don't worry, I won't die," I replied calmly. "Open it."

The warden lifted the torch and released the bloody odor off the ergastulum. I shuddered as I noticed a curled body in the darker corner.

"Narcissus?" I called uncertainly.

"His very self." I heard the voice of Superbus, a former gladiator, now known as the "soft-hearted executioner". "The others are already dead."

As he found out about the abduction of Petronius and my adventures in the grotto, Caesar immediately gave the order to arrest the closest servants of the senators, some insignificant Mithraists like Sisenna, and our prodigal cousin Gemellus.

"There'll be no use of slaughtering the senators," Callistus gave him advice, appalled with the moaning of the arrestees. "They are only afraid of Artabanus, so they will not take the lid off their doings. Yet, the slaves are easy to psych out."

Unfortunately, he was wrong. One by one, the woesome men were dying under tortures with the name of Sol Invictus on their swollen lips.

"Our Lord brings the light… and freedom," Vespasian's slave wheezed. "*You are dust and unto dust shall you return.*"

The minor senators defied the executioners with the same words, while the real culprits still held their sessions, acting like they did not care.

"Unless we are one step ahead of them," My brother thought aloud. "We are left to watch those bastards stupefying our people and taking young lives."

Almost desperate, I remembered Claudius' favorite and asked the guardsmen to arrest him, too.

"Your Highness," the Greek warned me, "don't forget whose blood runs through his veins."

My decision indeed was more than risky. However, I did not want him dead, on the contrary…

"Well, Cleopatra belonged *to Ptolemaioi*, but she rebelled against the kin in order to protect her people." I recalled my conversation with Tiberius.

"Ab igne ignem."[424] Callistus pursed her lips disapprovingly.

"Do you gamble?" I asked him, aware that he stealthily 'robbed the Praetorians.

"I…I do actually," he said, embarrassed. "Sometimes."

"So you should know the price of a good game." I winked at him. "It's time to figure out why they put him on the Palatine."

It had been three months since then.

"By your order, the boy wasn't tortured… much." Protogenes explained. "But he remained as silent as the dead."

I touched the iron grate of the cell, calling the prisoner again. The gray silhouette showed no signs of life.

"Is he dead?" I looked at the Superbus.

"No, I don't think so." The jailer shook his head.

I came up closer, stepping on the dirt and bloodstains. Squeamishly, I lifted up the hem of my peplum, and squatted next to the Parthian.

"Parysatis," I tapped him on the shoulder, as I thought aloud. "Who on earth gave you a female name?"

The servant jerked, and so did I. My nightmare on the ship on the eve of what you call *Sabbatus Sanctum* turned out to be prophetic… partially.

"P-Princess…" He turned his dirty and bruised face to me. "A custom… from the evil eye."

"Help me," I addressed him half-loudly. "And I'll forgive you everything."

In the eyes of the swarthy prisoner I could no longer find arrogance. Now it seemed like the demonic bantling from my nightmare wasn't real. All I could see beside me was just a foreign boy, hungry and hurt.

"I can't…" He said tearfully. "They… they will burn me alive."

---

[424] (lat.) As you sow, so shall you reap.

Another look to the depths of his dark, terrified pupils was enough to witness his sincerity.

"Look, I am Layla," I whispered in his ear. "I will protect you."

Barely sane from everything he suffered, Narcissus just leaned his forehead against my chest.

It's not all blood, I thought. The son of Artabanus, the descendant of the demoness Naamah, he still didn't radiate depravity like Livia, Ennia or Armida. *It's about the spirit.*

I stood up and reach out to help him rise up. Narcissus, with efforts, followed me.

"Are you in pain?" I took him by the elbow.

He nodded. I felt guilty, but suppressed this feeling with compassion to the innocent victims of Mithras.

"Take him to the thermae," I told to the old warden. "Then, make sure the cookmaids give him dinner, and ask the Cretan to examine him."

Protogenes fulfilled the order hesitatingly. As soon as Narcissus got well, he asked for the reception at my tablinum.

His story began twenty-seven years ago in Petra, the biggest town of wild Nabataea. The local tribes lived mostly from trading and robbery, worshipping deities Yaghūth and Suwāʿ.

"Yaghūth is the god of war," the slave man told me with jitters. "He longs for the conquests, and is able to turn into a lion, horse or eagle. His wife Suwāʿ is a goddess made of fire, and she carries wisdom. In the days of drought they are believed to ride across the desert to create oases…

"One day, as he was travelling along the Incense Route with his great entourage, Artabanus saw a priestess, dancing at the square in honor of her gods.

"When he found out that the girl was of the far Achaemenid[425] descent, the king wished to have her in his harem," Narcissus went on, "but very soon, my mother understood what she committed to, and escaped to the Sinai desert, carrying me in her womb.

---

[425] An ancient Persian ruling dynasty.

"Making her hard way to safety, young Pyrallis met the caravan of merchants. She offered them her jewels in exchange for some food and a camel. The nomads let her join them first to Palmyra, then to Italy.

"In Rome, a foreign woman with no money, nor a protector, is sentenced to a lupanar." My interlocutor smiled bitterly. "Although, Pyrallis managed to become the biggest bawd on the Esquiline, so here I am – a favorite of 'Uncle Claudius.'"

There was indeed a lot of talk about the strange owner of the military brothel, but Narcissus' mother had always kept her true origin back.

"You played 'Pater' false, and came alive," I noted doubtfully. "How is it possible?"

He tried to smile, but couldn't help crying.

"We are alive, but we lost everything," he said. "Our will, our conscience, our honor… They spared our lives, because they needed fornication in the army, and a spy on the Palatine…"

"You're no longer a spy," I interrupted him, wiping his eyes with my fingertips. "You are nobody's mole, not even mine."

"Then… who am I?" Narcissus asked bewilderedly.

"If you promise to be honest," I replied, "we can be friends."

The young man sighed in relief and reached out to shake my hand.

"Now tell me," I moved his hand aside, as I stepped back. "What do they plan next?"

"You said I'm not a spy, Your Highness." He laughed timidly. "Didn't you?"

"It's up to you, Parysatis," I answered calmly. "To be honest for the honest, or to rat on the liars."

"I see you are really Layla," he stated in a more spirited manner. "But what if your uncle just gave me away? I'm still a part of his household."

"If he dares to try," I reassured him, "I will tear his heart out with my hands."

"Layla, Layla!" Narcissus grabbed his head jokingly. "Is it true what they say about you?"

"Ubi fumus, ibi ignis."[426] I reached out to him, returning a handshake.

---

[426] (lat.) Where there's smoke, there's fire.

XVII

"Everyone wants you dead, Your Highness," Narcissus said in plain Latin. "My… father, heads of the ruling families and the entire Roman Senate…"

The night after a hard conversation I spent writing, as I saw my lover off into the loathly night watch.

"A comedy of manners," I said to the mirror, thinking simultaneously of the script and my experience in Curia Hostilia. "Quid ergo?"[427]

Such exited thoughts were easy to put down on paper, changing into acts, scenes and figures.

"Lamia's annoying you, huh?" I giggled, completing the act. "I've just begun annoying you."

Artabanus had been trying to do away with me for a long time – in all the human and demonic ways, but every time his actions met resistance. Spies and assassins fell back at the last moment, plagued with bad diseases; even Pater himself suffered panic attacks, which he couldn't control by the magic.

"Lost in trepidation, our senators reluctantly decided to ask women for help." Narcissus recalled. "Ten witches came from farther lands, but none of them brought news they liked to hear."

The hex from Germania casted her runes on the cloth even thrice, asking gods for the way they could beat me.

"During divination she saw Sága," The slave smiled. "Some wisdom deity not to mess with."

The Gaul saw Morrigan in the tree hollow, the Egyptian witnessed the presence of Seshat.[428] Pyrallis could read on the sand just one name – of Suwāʿ, the queen of the Red Sea.

---

[427] (lat.) Now what?
[428] The ancient Egyptian goddess of wisdom and writing.

"There even was a priestess from Muziris,"[429] my interlocutor added. "That one sprinkled ashes on her head, murmuring something of ferocious Kali,[430] who has come to trample on great Shiva."

"It's useless! Useless!" Vespasian raged. "She's alive, doing good, disrupting our plans and laughing like an idiot. Undoubtedly, Drusilla is protected by Adonai, so we can't defeat her!"

"You are wrong," the Parthian king wrote to him. "All murderers, harlots and liars have been handed over to Lord Mithras. Just like the moon that hides her dark side, this woman has a lot on her conscience; but in comparison to you she's not a coward. If it turned to be so hard for my governors to save the world from this plague, do your best to deprive her of desire to live and to fight. Take pains or you will blame yourself unless you manage."

Vespasian's decision was not unpredictable.

"Let her be devoured by fire!" he exclaimed to the senators. "Let us enjoy her torments and her cry! We'll murder all her friends and, in the end, we'll do away with Caesar!"

All the senators stood with their magistrate.

"Longinus, too?" I sighed, looking at Narcissus. "My former husband and, by the emperor's will, the proconsul of Asia."

"Yes, he did," my uncle's slave shrugged his shoulders. "I heard him calling you a sow, playing along about Caesar's death."

That very day, I sent Praetorians to the Carinae – not because of the abuse, but for the things he said about my brother.

"Doleo, Luci." I attached the note. "You will be carried to Ephesus in the Gallic urn."

It was quite late when I put down my pen. The desk was in a mess.

"Pegasus must have been too happy here," Callistus joked each time he saw my writer's chaos.

---

[429] An ancient port in present-day Kerala (India).
[430] A Hindu goddess of war, the destroyer of evil forces.

So he crapped everywhere in here, I thought, opening my wardrobe. *Now it looks like hell.*

That night, I couldn't sleep. I wished to wake my brother up, to talk to him, to ask his advice. Despite all his extravagance, Caligula had always been a good tactician and a judge as well.

"Actaeon." I chose a freedman, who was least busy that day to help me dress, but then I changed my mind. "Sloth is a sin, Drusilla," I spoke to myself. "Let him rest, and find the damn dress by yourself!"

By my door, I found Ioh and Anat keeping watch.

"I'm going downstairs to see Gaius." I waved aside to avoid questions. "You both can go and have some rest."

The Egyptian man fixed his short wig with a bewildered look.

"Yes," I recalled as I pulled him by the sleeve. "You've shown yourself as a great architect, so you'll be freed from other duties from now on."

"Dua Netjer en etj, Nebet-i."[431] Ioh gave me a thankful bow and left the corridor, sleepy and happy.

"Would you like to have supper, Your Highness?" Anat asked helpfully, following me. As a girl, I was fond of late dinners along with Antonia, her first Domina.

"No way," I shook my head, pointing to my waist. "I think I already resemble my grandma."

The maid smiled supportively.

"Your look is a sign of your pure, noble blood." She half-embraced me. "In the Land of Khem, they would have called you heaven-sent."

"I know," I nodded. "Greeks enjoy curved bodies even more… even in Galilee they call a thin girl sick. Only the Romans like barbarian skinniness."

"You even sound like her." The woman sighed as she turned to leave, but suddenly recalled, "That David… priest." Her voice got that usual apathetic shade. "He is complaining all the time about new scholars."

---

[431] (anc.egypt.) Thank to the Gods for you, my Lady!

I rolled my eyes, annoyed. It hadn't been a week since the rabbi asked me for some helpers.

"Really?" I frowned. "What's wrong with Victor and Justus?"

"I guess he doesn't want them to be Vigiles anymore," the Egyptian explained. "A priest should deal with books, not weapons."

"Then remind that hypocrite about the time he spent in the market… or smuggling around." I went on. "Now we should do several jobs at once."

"Oh, men especially," Anat said approvingly. "If we still can call them the stronger gender."

"It depends." I stopped by the Imperial cubiculum. "Good night, Anat."

As the maid left, the guards hurried to open the door. They knew how badly I behaved in a bad mood.

"Little sister?"

Gaius was awake. He sat on a carpet cross-legged, drawing something on a sheet of papyrus.

"You recognize me by my steps?" I smiled.

"No," he replied, before he looked up at me. "It's only you who can enter these chambers without invitation."

"It looks like a hull." I pointed to his sketch. "What is it?"

Gaius hurriedly hid the sheet behind his back.

"Nothing."

I came up and took a seat beside him. Caesar slightly touched the ornaments on the wool rug with his fingertips.

"On this very carpet, the Egyptians smuggled Queen Cleo to the Old Caesar's palace."

The ornate covering indeed looked attractive. The delicate work by an unknown weaver introduced us to the sky-blue Nile, the light green palm alleys, and the golden desert sand.

"She was wrapped here like a mummy," my brother went on. "Her slaves were ordered to dress her as if she was dead, and the eunuchs made rumors about her death."

"What for?" I wondered. I used to think my grandma had told me everything about her stepmother, but it wasn't so.

"There is a saying among them – death is only afraid of the one who's not afraid of it," he spoke earnestly. "When her bad sisters Arsenoe and Berenice unveiled the truth, cunning Cleo had already gained a powerful ally."

It took me a while to think before I noticed a scroll on Caligula's bed. It was a famous book – *"The Gallic Wars"* by the Old Caesar.

"He was the best, wasn't he?" My brother caught my look. "Despite his boldness, the old man knew how to bluff. He and Cleo were two of a kind."

"A useful skill," I replied. My head was in a chaos like my desk and wardrobe... As the legend said, the Chaos was a mother to the Universe... and bright ideas.

"*Iulia Drusilla debet mori,*"[432] I decided. "Quam brevissime."[433]

---

[432] (lat.) Julia Drusilla must die.

[433] (lat.) The sooner the better.

XVIII

"You read my mind." The emperor winked at me shiftily.

"Am I that annoying?" I giggled, jokingly grabbing his ear.

"As annoying as hell," he joked back, and went on more seriously, "Have you heard about Milonia Caesonia?"

A squeamish twitch was my reply. In Rome, you couldn't find a fool who hadn't heard that name. Named after my exemplary great-great-grandmother Atia Caesonia, this woman had nothing in common with her. Well, maybe except for fiery red hair. A turbulent divorce, the result of her adultery, debts and opium addiction, made Caesonia the Younger a synonym for immorality. Her former husband forbade her to see their children, in fear that such a mother could spoil his young daughters. Caesonia's half-brother, Corbulo, publically gave up on his wicked kinswoman. Greedy for money, she was often selling her body – always at high price and only to noblemen. Late in the evenings, she was walking down the Forum with a long dark veil on her head, which she was rumored to wear even during the trysts. Some of them saw mystics in that habit, the others considered it just a desire to hide her age and lack of beauty. Caesonia's lovers themselves sometimes called her a witch, but again remained powerless before her charm.

"Don't tell me you are marrying her." I looked at askance at Gaius.

"It depends," he answered, frowning jokingly.

"Depends – on what?" I asked.

He caressed my head awkwardly like a child playing with a cat. I gently clapped him on his hand.

"You've mentioned death, haven't you?" Caesar reminded me, changing his tone. "Well, Caesonia hasn't left her house for months, because she's ill with leprosy. Only Corbulo and her medic know about it, and they both think she is dying."

"Is there leprosy in Rome?" I flinched. Leprosy was believed to be a plague of prisoners and sailors, never met in the neat patrician houses.

"Corbulo blames her rival – Pyrallis," he explained. "The Nabataean whore was jealous of Caesonia's lovers and their riches. As she was afraid her brothel could grow empty, the old vulture sent her an infected gift."

"She didn't manage to escape from Artabanus," I sighed, recalling the story of Narcissus. "Now she behaves as odiously as the father of her son."

Caligula looked up at me ironically, as he moved to his bed, stretching.

"What I hear from a girl who drove out her nursemaid."

"I'm sorry," I frowned. "If I knew what you would grow into, I'd have let the German whore strangle you in your sleep."

Caligula raised his hands as if begging for mercy. "Come on!" he smiled, "I just wanted to say, everything happens at the perfect time."

"Is this some bad joke?" I took a seat beside him, leaning against the bedpost.

"It is not," he answered calmly.

As I figured out his plan, I was startled and disgusted, but again it was so brilliantly conceived.

"Another lie," I grabbed my head. "How long do I have to take this?"

My brother shrugged his shoulders. "Until your play exposes our enemies and their deeds."

There was no other choice. In order to protect the ones I loved, I had to convince the senators they had defeated me. Drusilla had to use the dying woman's secret to play her own death.

"We will bury Drusilla in a closed sarcophagus," Caligula explained, suppressing a nervous laugh. "Like Grandmother."

"And Caesonia will be the Empress and wear her veil until my play is staged," I guessed.

"Oh, by the way," Caligula recalled, "your death will definitely end your stupid marriage."

"*Drusilla's* death," I uttered thoughtfully. "Not mine."

In Caesar's gaze, I saw in amazement and delight.

"You're playing your part well, Caesonia."

"Oh no," I shook my head as I stood up. "Caesonia will be my *public* role."

Caligula let out a sniffing sound, resembling a trapped hedgehog. "Who are you then?" he asked, yawning aloud.

"I am Sophia," I replied. "Also responding to Lamia, Lilith or Ereshkigal."

XIX

"The summer solstice… A woman is sacrificed." The nightmare echo had been following me since the ides of May. I moved Messalina and Octavia to the palace, and forbade my maids to leave the Palatine for a certain time.

Caesonia greeted me from her bed – recently immobile and lean like a skeleton.

"Why do you need my name… Your Highness?" She looked at me with distress.

"I'm not doing it for my advantage," I said sympathetically. "It is about the others, the people of Rome."

The uglified woman exhaled a muffled laugh and coughed. "Kh-corbulon thinks you are a living genius."

Her irony reflected the jealousy of all the noblemen. Another reason for the senators to hate me was my undisguised favor for the equestrian class. I reached for a glass of water on her bedside table to help her, but the fear of getting infected changed my mind.

"I, too, respect your brother greatly, Milonia," I replied somewhat sharply, aware of her quiet provocation.

"From the Esquiline to the Viminale," she crooned in a trembling but still cynical voice. "We sing to Princepessa – hail!"

"I think you're overstating things," I turned to the mosaic on her wall. "I do have more male friends…"

"Because we, women, are so evil," Caesonia laughed sourly. "We don't hesitate to do anything to get our children fed and help our husbands pay their debts…"

"I am not listening to this," I covered my ears with my hands. "I am not here to insult the sick, nor to get those unreasonable insults. I'm asking of you something you no longer need, and offering you my patronage over your children, and a just punishment for Pyrallis in return."

"It's so easy to spend someone else's money," she uttered with effort. "And to kill your own enemy, too."

I gestured to her that I was willing to leave the room now.

"I agree!" the ill woman exclaimed. "What else is left to do?"

"Gratias ago,"[434] I replied with a jokingly bow. "Aveto."[435]

Milonia Caesonia passed away on the Nones of June – about ten days before Midsummer. At sunset, a number of specially dressed Vigiles carried her dead body in a wooden sarcophagus to the Palatine. Later that night, the heralds and wailers woke up the whole of Rome, bringing the terrible news. Her Imperial Highness Princess Julia Drusilla was dead.

"Diva Augusta passed away of fever," the Cretan announced to the servants. The truth was known only to my freedmen, as well as the Praetorians of the main cohort, Messalina, Corbulo and Petronius.

"The mourning will last for three months," Gaius said at the small council. "I'm closing all the public houses and banning all kinds of merriment in Rome. A golden statue of my sister, as a goddess, will be raised in Curia one of these days."

"Will you give a eulogy?" I wondered, recalling his absence from Grandmother's funeral.

"Not me, Corbulo will." He pointed at the warlord. "You will be farewelled like our father."

"Ha-ha!" I rolled my eyes vexedly. "Yet it's much better than the matron wail over your first wife's pyre."

"Shut up, you lemur." Caesar waved aside. "Now I have to prepare for the role of a grieving brother-lover."

"So you're going to tear your clothes, eat ashes, and grow a beard by Augustalii."[436] I smiled. "Disgusting."

Caligula smiled back a little nervously and raised his eyebrow in a seductive manner.

"After the mourning comes the morning."

---

[434] (lat.) Thank you.

[435] (lat.) I bid you farewell.

[436] The Autumn Festival in Honor of Augustus.

I waved aside and changed the subject. "The worst thing is that I will have to hide inside the palace like a thief," I said to Callistus. "How will I now be able to take care of the children?"

"Caesar shares lots of food and money with the mobs on every festival," Helicon spoke, and gave my brother a gaze full of awe. "Don't you, Domine?"

Caligula glanced alternately at all of us, and shouted.

"Utinam populus Romanus unam cervicem haberet!"[437]

"Oh, divine!" Callistus jumped to his feet, applauding. "Amazingly said!"

I shook my head, a little disappointed. There was a noticeable change in the secretary's behavior... noticeable, but not yet definable. The others hurriedly joined him in the admiration.

"Excuse me please, I'm going to rest in peace." I rose up from my couch. "And to sharpen my teeth for the senators."

However, our enemies were already working the next vicious plan.

---

[437] (lat.) If only all of Rome had just one neck.

XX

One August afternoon, on the wide terrace, hidden in the shade of stone pines and palm trees, three friends played "truth or lies."

"Imagine this," Narcissus began merrily, as he jumped aside to the edge of the couch like a squirrel. "Dominus Claudius has written his will."

Without waiting for continuation, Petronius and I burst out laughing.

"Wait, there's more!" The storyteller raised his index finger. "As he reluctantly paid the jurist," he went on, imitating my uncle's voice and movements, "C-c-claudius made up his mind to leave all of the property to his d-d-d-doggies."

"Verum!" I giggled quietly, in order not to draw attention of the slaves, who didn't know my secret.

"Falsum!" Petronius retorted.

"I am sorry, Princess," Narcissus shrugged. "I lied indeed."

"Eia!" The boy clapped his hands. "It's my turn!"

"Go ahead, corculum," I encouraged him. "You have much bigger imagination than Fedlimid."

"Nota bene," Petronius blushed. "It's not a children story."

"What?" The Parthian and I showed surprise.

"As a future satirist," my young friend explained. "I have to deal with bare life."

"Absolutely." I nodded. "Go on!"

A cunning smile lit up his soft, angelic face.

"Princess," he started a bit hesitatingly. "Your sisters, they have had a competition on the Esquiline…"

I suddenly got earnest – both of them could see it in my look.

"In the midst of mourning?" Narcissus wondered.

"It turns out to be so," the boy said confusedly, revealing himself. "At the Forum… I heard they competed to see who could have more lovers in one night."

I felt my heart stuck in my throat.

"You lie!" my dark-skinned friend exclaimed, trying to calm me down.

I felt a sudden vertigo and grabbed my head. Startled, Narcissus bawled at the boy.

"Look what you've done!"

"No, Your Highness!" Petronius batted his eyes. "I didn't want to scare you… but that's…"

"True!" Callistus walked in without an invitation, as he often did. "Unfortunately."

As I caught my breath, I kissed the boy on his cheek, and asked him to come home.

"You too, Narcissus," the Greek added, not waiting for my approval. "The competition of the princesses has already been followed by all sorts of things."

The next one to break the ban of public gatherings for fun was Seneca, the orator.

"No man is free while he remains a slave of his own body." Seneca spoke from the rostrum. "The greatest power in the world is self-control. The lack of it destroys your soul. Look at the Imperial family! They are a living proof of rowdiness and dissipation."

More and more people, sharing the philosopher's enthusiasm, went out to the Forum to mock Caesar and our sisters.

"We mortals marry out of instinct, and divorce out of reason." He went on, ignoring all the warnings of the Vigiles, "Caesars live by instinct, but marry and divorce by lack of reason."

There was a grain of truth in this indeed… My intuition kept me from reacting in a state of passion.

I met Seneca about ten years ago – in Vinicius' house on the Carinae. Livilla, fascinated by the orator's charisma, often invited him to a dinner. Even pragmatic Agrippina often flipped over his books about the soul travel.

"I was born a knight," he used to tell us. "But, unlike other equites, we Annei serve Athena, not Ares."

Seneca's father, the richest man in Cordoba, was known as a wise, but also an eccentric man. First he drew attention to himself by practicing Greek Stoicism, and then by marrying a Hispana, Helvia Albina.

"A widow with a little daughter," Callistus informed me once. "Some of them say – a trollop with a bastard."

Helvia bore him three sons, and Seneca the Elder adopted her daughter in gratitude.

"The daughter had herself a knight as well." I guessed, as the familiar names were linking with each other. "Annea Helvilla married Marcus Cassius Chaerea."

"Right," the secretary nodded. "Seneca is thus the prefect's uncle. Awkward, isn't it? "

I asked myself why the orator would start bad rumors about Caesar and the women, who hosted him in their houses.

"It's not about morality and honor." The Greek took a seat beside me, crossing his legs. "It's all for money."

This contumelious speech was ordered by Vespasian, as he was sure that my death had weakened the ruler's positions. Aware of the impetuous nature of my brother, he wished for an outcome, where Seneca would be an apple of discord between the emperor and the Praetorian prefect.

"Oh you cynic hypocrites!" I laughed anxiously. "You play wise and modest on the rostrum, but when the crowd is gone, you turn into venal fools…"

Callistus interrupted me with a protesting gesture.

"Seneca is not that evil, Princess. He had been in trouble, so he needed money."

"Did he gamble away his possessions?" I asked in a manner I thought stoics held their speeches.

The Greek shook his head.

"Not every *eques* is a gambler, Princess. Seneca often gives alms to the poor…"

"Callistus!" I moved my index finger up and down and up again. "Be careful with your jokes. You and your Caesar often mock the military rank, but when the storm comes down, you call the guard for help."

The Greek fell embarrassed and silent.

"Good boy." The tension made me lie down on the couch to rest my back. "My brother would have argued for two hours."

My friend's gaze enounced more trouble.

"The Divine has already… reacted," he said hesitantly. "Seneca is put to prison, waiting for the death sentence."

"What about my sisters?" I asked, losing my breath again. There was no chance that Agrippina and Livilla cared about the reputation of our family. They even seemed to like the lies about our brother prostituting them to soldiers.

"Caesar turned a blind eye on the princesses," the Greek went on. "He cannot punish women, especially your mother's daughters."

"Yet he can condemn my husband's uncle!" I got up and headed for the door. "Woe to me! Since I am dead, I am the last to know about everything!"

Callistus blocked my way, as he spread out like a starfish.

"You may not leave the palace without Caesar's permission."

Disturbed by those events and my own helplessness, I grabbed him by the throat.

"Bring me my veil," I spoke quietly. "If I do nothing, your Caesar will fuck the things up like he used to."

"He is… not here." The man wheezed out. "He has left to Campania this morning… escorted by Cassius."

I let him go, and sighed out loud.

"Caligula is mad indeed."

In order to make his grief credible, Gaius decided to go to the countryside, where he could mourn in peace his sister and his lover.

"I give you half an hour to prepare me for the meeting with the old moron." I ordered.

"Do you mean – orator?" Callistus asked worriedly.

"Whatever," I said, pushing him out of the room. "Move-o!"

As the secretary disappeared into the corridor, I felt a strange discomfort in my stomach once again.

Too many pastries, I thought, touching my belly. *Alfidia spoiled me.*

Mild nausea was replaced by a slight flicker – like the dance of a butterfly or a glowworm twinkle.

"Too much stress," I went on, looking through the balustrade. The sun was going down the heavenly stairway, bathing the roofs and treetops in the living gold.

"When life was easy for me?" I smiled bitterly. *"For I'm the one you hated in your counsels… I am she who exists in your fears."*

XXI

Inter canem et lupum[438] the Vigiles brought Seneca – with his hands tied, but hastily bathed and dressed up in clean garments.

"Captivus[439] Lucius Annaeus." Victor announced him.

"Quantum tempus!"[440] I spread my arms jokingly, as I creepily whirled round in circles.

The orator got pale and tripped up on a step of exedra. Justus held him by the elbow, pushing the scared man ahead.

"What are you staring at?" The Vigile laughed. "Have you just seen a ghost?"

"I saw this woman's pyre burning like Ilium."[441] Seneca half-smiled. "Therefore, I'm either dead or mad; and honestly I would prefer the first."

"Untie him." I ordered the guardsmen. "And leave us alone."

The philosopher, yet in complete disbelief, took a seat on a bench.

"I'm alive," I explained earnestly. "The funeral was a just spectacle."

"For whom, Your Highness?" He wrinkled his forehead bewilderedly.

"You know it well." I answered sharply. "Was their money worth this trial?"

Seneca shook his head, crossing his arms on his narrow chest.

"I'm not denying – I was doing something inconsistent with my ideology." He looked me in the eye. "But I still find your brother and your sisters an example of shamelessness and madness."

"Even if you're right," I replied with composure, "all the laws on earth demand the ruler to be honored and respected. You revered both Augustus and Tiberius without a second thought as if you've never heard about their cruelty."

Taken aback by my question, Seneca couldn't find the words to answer.

---

[438] (lat.) At dusk (literally "between a dog and a wolf").

[439] (lat.) An arrestee.

[440] (lat.) Long time no see!

[441] A Roman name for Troy.

"The thinker fell silent," I went on with irony. "Let's try another question. Did Augustus or Tiberius care for the people of Rome like my brother does now?"

"It depends, Princess," said the philosopher. "Some find your brother's policy too peaceful for the Empire."

"Really?" I asked in the same tone. "Such a remark from an eques, whose biggest weapon is his tongue, seems a bit… hypocritical."

Seneca grew thoughtful, leaving me a while to study him. Confusion in his eyes could easily be followed by disdain, but swiftly it gave place to curiosity. Still ready for the riposte, I inadvertently paid attention to his face. Beside that Roman rigor in both posture and spirit, this man inherited his mother's goodliness and the unreal grayness of the eyes. The Iberian sky left its umber gray mark on all three – Seneca, Cassius and Annea Helvilla.

"You will not die," I suddenly changed the subject. "I will have you banished from Italia, but you'll be safe and sound."

"Is it… because of Cassius?" he asked, trying to sound indifferent.

"What?" I goggled at him, trying to hide my own public secret.

Seneca exposed us even long before than I myself could understand how much I loved his nephew.

"I do not believe in pure love or decent women," he said honestly, and raised his index finger. "But I know about exceptions."

I nodded to him thankfully.

"I'm really glad you live, Your Highness," Seneca went on. "You are the second of these two exceptions…"

"I will also let you hold one more oration speech," I interrupted him, "when the mourning is over."

The gray-haired man's face, a little pocky, blushed with glee. He treasured his science as much as I cherished my art.

"Homo sum," I reasoned. "Nihil humani a me alienum puto."[442]

---

[442] (lat.) I am human, and I think nothing human is alien to me.

The quote of Terence, a famous playwright and a Stoic, spoke by a woman was greeted with admiration.

"May I ask you something in return?" I looked at him with solemnly.

Seneca nodded with respect.

"Whatever it may be – I am your servant."

It was not about this old man, but Iberia in his eyes, that I could barely suppress tears.

"Take me to *her* grave."

It's been for years that I longed to visit his sister's resting place, but I didn't want to sadden Cassius.

Alfidia accompanied us to the desolate place, once called Esquiline cemetery.

"My husband and son rest on the other side of the Wall,"[443] she said on the way to the burial ground. "Since that barbarian Augustus destroyed the ancient necropolis, our heroes have been buried like some beggars."

Under the influence of King Mithridates and greedy Livia, my great-grandfather ordered the Vigiles to demolish the Temple of Libitina and to level to the ground old tombs and gravestones. As the emperor desecrated the bones of his ancestors, he planted gardens and erected a portico in honor of Livia instead. The land by the Temple, once called sacred, now was cursed.

"Still, you could bury your dead on the Esquiline though," Seneca explained. "Yet it was too expensive for the populace."

Helvilla was farewelled with dignity by Seneca the Elder and Cassius' paternal uncle Philip. Her crypt with a narrow and tall spire didn't look bleak like Mausoleum of Augustus, but sublime and moving.

"H.S.E.[444] Annea Helvia Chaerea," I read on the dark stone. "Uxor uxorum."[445]

---

[443] The Servian Wall, once constructed as a defensive barrier around the city of Rome; and the border between the Esquiline Hill and the Suburra.
[444] (lat.) Here lies.
[445] (lat.) Wife of wives.

Without a second thought, I knelt before the marble vault and kissed the silver letters of her name. My memories suddenly took me back to Misenum, where Magdalene taught me about Jesus.

"He resurrected, and opened back the door to Heaven to the righteous." I almost heard her gentle voice again, breaking the silence.

"Heathens loved him, too." David's words followed her, echoing through the stone walls… or my mind.

"There are no strangers to God." I felt like hearing Photice, and looked up to the ceiling, searching for the Answer.

"If Your Kingdom is not for brave warriors and faithful wives," I whispered fervently, "then who can enter it?"

Unable to muffle his grief, Seneca wept behind my back. Alfidia carefully touched my shoulder with her chubby hand.

"She's happy now," the old woman whispered to the crying man.

"Mater matrum."[446] I stood up, fixing my veil. "She gave your son a whole lot more than Livia offered Tiberius."

After I helped my cookmaid with two smaller tombs, I asked her.

"Where did you find money for the funerals?"

Alfidia smiled gratefully.

"Tiberius himself was there to help me," she told me thoughtfully. "After all, I'm a kinswoman to Livia… though she had always denied it, calling me a lazy equestrian fool."

Seneca, seemingly regaining humor, suddenly addressed me quietly.

"Si vis amari, ama."[447]

"Sorry?" I turned around wondering.

"It's the beginning of my new oration speech," he winked. "My last oration speech."

---

[446] (lat.) Mother of mothers.

[447] (lat.) If you wish to be loved, love.

XXII

"Looks like someone gained some weight," Callistus remarked, as he put away the tailoring tools. "Go ahead, and you will look like Rachel."

"What should I care?" I laughed. "I am dead anyway."

I planned to welcome Cassius in a new, uncommon dress, yet unfamiliar to any lintearius,[448] vestiarius,[449] or tinctorius[450] I knew.

"Don't listen to him," Orla took a look at the dress sketch. "You'll be awesome."

Callistus nodded to the table with her sewing tools.

"Bone needles, leather, and some pebbles." He rolled his eyes. "Are we in Lugdunum?"[451]

The Gaul didn't bother to answer, and I… felt a sudden sharp ache in my stomach. The recent nausea forced me to sit down.

"Choose a cloth yourself," I turned to Callistus. "And call the Cretan."

The secretary goggled at me anxiously and thrust a random linen sample to the sawyer.

"Paouez,"[452] Orla squinted in suspense, as she came up to me and reached out to my belly. "Mar plij… ?"[453]

I got up and took a freedwoman's hand to press it on the left side of my abdomen.

"Ne gomprenan ket,"[454] she murmured bewilderedly. "It's firm like…"

"What are you, a medic?" Callistus exclaimed.

I gestured to him to be quiet and looked at Orla questioningly.

---

[448] (lat.) A weaver.
[449] (lat.) A seamstress.
[450] (lat.) A dexter.
[451] An important Roman city in Gaul, established on the current site of Lyon.
[452] (bret.) Wait.
[453] (bret.) May I..?
[454] (bret.) I do not understand.

"Princess." The Gaul's face turned pale, and then she blushed. "You're pregnant."

I grabbed her by the elbow, gasping for more air. It darkened in my eyes, and I collapsed unconscious into the secretary's arms.

The two of them, with effort, brought me to Alcaeus' chambers. The physician removed my clothes without scruple and examined my body closely. My condition didn't leave him any doubts.

"Impossible, but true." His voice awakened me. "Her Highness is expecting."

Orla carefully covered me with a long blanket and uttered warm congratulations in her language. Callistus was staring at me silently like Midas startled by the view of his poor daughter turning to a golden statue.

"Elohim gadol!" I heard David's joyful voice behind the folding screen. "His curse can turn a blooming tree into a withered stump, but yet His mercy can plant gardens in the middle of the desert!"

Loud footsteps gave away my other friends, hurrying through the corridor. I hardly could remember Susannah, Actaeon and Anicetus that happy ever before.

"What will I say to Cassius?" I sat up in bed and hugged my knees.

Alcaeus sat beside me, bringing up to me a glass of some clear liquid. "I guess the prefect knows where babies come from," he joked, and then got earnest. "For your good and your child's safety, I forbid you any stressing."

I smiled blissfully, remembering the prophecy of Photice. I never could believe I would be able to become a mother, to conceive a child with Cassius. Right then, as I caressed my swollen belly, I was too excited to remember about Caesonia, who was still going to become an empress.

"What lovely news!" Rachel was already here as well. "Barukh Hashem!"[455]

Too much of that merry noise made me feel nauseous again.

"Tell them to leave." I looked at Callistus. "And to keep quiet."

The secretary saw our friends off in quite a rough manner, and fixed a canopy above my bed.

---

[455] (lat.) Sweet Lord!

"In case you wonder," he smiled cunningly, "which of your sisters won the competition…"

I nodded curiously.

"It's Livilla," he giggled. "Twenty and five soldiers, mostly Greeks."

"Not bad," I giggled back. "What did my other sister say?"

Callistus waved his hand leisurely, as imitating Agrippina.

"This whore's insides must be made of army boots!"

As I had laughed to tears, I asked for his assistance about dressing.

"Please, forgive me what I've said this morning, Princess," the Greek sighed, carefully belting my dress. "You look… blessed."

"Te futueo et caballum tuum!"[456] I said jokingly.

"Who taught you that?" he wondered. "Since the prefect never curses in your presence…"

"I don't even remember." I clasped my silk toga, and fixed the dark veil. "Probably Corbulo or Tigellinus."

"Ah, those Greek warriors." Callistus rolled his eyes dreamily. "Your sisters have good taste in men."

"Good taste indeed," I stroked my belly. "But yet not the sense of measure." As my mood turned better, I felt a little hungry. "Come on, walk to kitchen," I winked at the Greek. "Tell Anat and Alfidia to move it – I'm giving a feast."

"As you wish," the man nodded, confused. "Who are the guests?"

"You," I replied fixing his curls. "*Amici mei, familia mea.*"

---

[456] (lat.) Screw you and the horse you rode in on!

XXIII

Caesar's return to the capital was followed up by the sound of trumpets and exalted shouts.

"Look, baby girl, who's back to us," Messalina cooed on the terrace like a mother dove, as she fondled sleepy Octavia. "And the prefect is riding beside him."

Heaving a blissful sigh, I clasped my amber necklace and put on an unbecomingly red wig. Now she was there – infamous Milonia was grinning to me through the misty veil from the other side of the mirror.

"O my gods! You look exactly like Caesonia!" Messalina clapped her hands. "Her brother will be scared."

"My brother too," I replied discomposedly. The extravagant dress could barely hide my condition.

"They're already in the portico." The woman smiled and hurried outside. "Let's go!"

The servants and the guard paid no attention at me, for their emperor looked even more bizarre than me wearing a courtesan's attire.

"I'm bringing you blessings of Ceres," Gaius greeted everyone, removing a grass-green cloak from his shoulder. "Some annoying duties tore me out of her lap back to this stinky city."

Underneath the plebeian toga, he wore a tight yellow tunic, while his crown was replaced with a wreath of some half-wilted flowers.

"I was curing my grief walking barefoot through the fields and picking fruit," he went on with a sigh. "Accompanied by diligent bucolic women, always willing to give me fresh milk and fulfill all my wishes."

Messalina, helplessly jealous, bit her scarlet lip almost insensibly. I wished I could reprimand him, but the presence of too many people made me only cough.

"Milonia Caesonia." My brother opened his arms wide. "My dear woman!"

I greeted him with a bow, trying to sound like a middle-aged woman whose voice was changed by wine and opium.

"Caesar," Messalina uttered shyly. "Me and my daughter made a gift for you."

He raised his hand to stop her.

"Later. Now I need some rest. "

The servants swiftly lined up in front of the guardsmen, awaiting his orders.

"Callistus," Gaius spoke to the secretary, who was obviously in a better humor. "Tell my uncle to convoke a sitting of the Senate – for tomorrow."

The Greek, having read a new trick on the imperial face, finally let his laughter go and headed to vestibulum.

"Chaerea," Gaius turned abruptly to the prefect. "Do you see the goddess of fertility?"

Muffled laughs and whispers echoed through the atrium. Cassius, without a trace of confusion, readily responded.

"No, I don't, Caesar."

"Of course, you do not," Caesar went on, grabbing my necklace as if it was a dog collar.

"Only us gods can see each other."

Forced to follow him for the sake of the spectacle, I minced to the tablinum.

"What a moron!" My brother waved aside, not turning around. "He was the one to stay away from our fabulous amusement."

I slammed the door shut and pushed Caligula away with all my might.

"Quid agis, futuo?!" I wondered furiously, freeing myself from suffocating veil and jewelry.

My brother twitched, and smiled sourly.

"That's how you welcome me home?"

The unbridled irony enraged me even more. I rushed towards him like a harpy and, as I tore a wreath from his head, began hitting him on the back.

"How dare you, cunt, insult my man?"

"Are you insane?" he yelled, barely breaking loose to hide behind the folding screen. " I didn't mean… That was a part of our plan!"

I inhaled deep and exhaled slow. Caesar peeked out of the cloth.

"That was… disgusting." I sat down on a chair with a slight flop, grabbed my head and started weeping.

Gaius, somewhat cautiously, came up to me and whispered.

"What's going on, little sister?"

Without a word, I pressed his hand to my rounded belly.

"But how?" he asked, astonished. "Are you sure Chaerea is the father?"

"Ede faecam!"[457] I uttered through my teeth. "Not counting that insane affair we had eight years ago, I've never deceived Cassius!"

Caligula embraced me.

"Well, the baby is making things more complicated," he spoke honestly. "But yet, it is great news, isn't it?"

I nodded, a bit tranquilized by his hug, and smiled.

"Now you understand Claudius."

The emperor's return, not marked with black, put the end of the mourning. The sudden pregnancy of fake Caesonia demanded my brother to prepare for his new marriage and the birth of his lawful heir.

"Well done, Chaerea," Gaius laughed, looking to the door. "First he took my sister, then tossed up this child… what next? Perhaps, he'll kill me."

"Don't flatter yourself," I waved aside. "Be patient – two months before Midwinter, at the Palatine Games, we will declare the truth."

"There are three more years until then," he reminded me, a little sullenly. "What if the child is a girl?"

I didn't want to sadden him with the prophecy of the Samaritan.

"It's hard for all of us," I said. "Ma, etiam hoc transibit."[458]

Sick and tired of hiding and waiting, I left my chambers at the third watch of the night, when the better part of servants were already resting. In the colonnade of embellished caryatids, the guardsmen were preparing for their night shift.

"What is the watchword for tonight?" Tigellinus asked Cassius.

---

[457] (lat.) Eat shit!

[458] (lat.) This too shall pass.

"Priapus,"[459] the prefect said composedly.

"Yes, sir," the Greek nodded, seemingly indifferent to my brother's provocations. His fellow guards, however, were far less polite and noble.

"May I ask you something, Cassius?" Clemens stepped forward, encouraged by the mocking grins of his comrades. "What did you do so wrong to get watchwords like that?"

"Excuse me?" I appeared in the portico.

The soldier looked at me as if I struck him dumb, why others fell grave silent.

"Princess…" Clemens murmured. "We… we didn't know you're here."

"Of course you didn't," I imitated his confusion. "All you know is enjoying someone else's stupid jokes."

"Never in my life, Your Highness!" The tribune straightened his back. "I just asked the prefect…"

"For such questions, you'll be standing in this place until the dawn." I notified him. "All of you." I looked at the guard in rotation. "Except for Tigellinus."

"Yes, Your Highness!" the tribune replied.

Cassius observed us with patient and dignity. I greeted him emotionally, and turned to the men one more time.

"I planned to give you back your right of marriage," I spoke in a mild tone. "Prove me you're the knights, not damn agricolae, and I'll remain your friend."

"Thank you, Your Highness!" the soldier to the left of Clemens said embarrassedly.

"Whatever my brother's plan is, you will not be the victim." I whispered to Cassius.

That night, reunited in love, we thought over names for our daughter.

"Her formal name will be Drusilla," I recalled Caligula's decision. "David will give her a Jewish name, too, but I would like to call her something special."

"A Greek name?" My lover smiled. "In honor of her Attic origins."

Moved to tears, I leaned my tired head against his chest, and felt the gentle movement of our child under my heart.

"Acte," I whispered. "Lady Cassia Acte."

---

[459] A Roman god of fertility and manhood.

XXIV

Gnomon[460] in the center of the garden showed meridies.[461] By the gates to hortus,[462] I noticed a shape of Callistus, shaking with laughter.

"So the sitting is over," I thought out loud and put off a scroll with the histories of Xenophon.[463]

"Princess." The secretary's face was crimson and his eyes wet. "Caesar is indeed eccentric, but even I could not imagine what he's able to."

The meeting began with Caligula, solemnly entering the Curia… on a horseback. Vespasian and Sabinus, accustomed to such tricks, had been observing him indifferently… for the first two minutes.

"As soon as he took the curule seat," the Greek went on in a hysterically thin voice, "the Praetorians broke in – almost whole of the Viminal led by Chaerea."

"Nothing new." Yet I could hardly understand the reason for that euphoria. "What did they decree?"

"The Senate has elected a new consul," he giggled unclearly. "Unanimously."

"Who's the lucky man?" I asked without much interest.

"The horse!" Callistus exclaimed. "Officially – with the signatures and the imperial seal featured."

The story was becoming interesting.

"Since you've been sitting in this bestiary," Gaius shouted to the men in the first row. "Eating the bread of robbery and taxes – have you done anything for our people?"

No one, even artful Asiaticus, knew what to answer.

"This horse." Caesar stroked the rich white mane of Incitatus. "It rescued three people during the earthquake in Misenum."

---

[460] An ancient sundial.
[461] (lat.) Noon.
[462] A lesser garden in the nimfeum.
[463] An Athenian historian, philosopher, and soldier.

"Well… that's logical." I smiled.

Looking asquint at the armed guardsmen, the senators adopted two more legal acts.

"From this day on…" The secretary finally could catch his breath. "Prominent soldiers, born commoners or peregrines will be admitted to cavalry service."

"Well done, brother," I praised Caesar. "Sometimes I just admire his cleverness."

In fact, it was me who advised him to straighten the cavalry. The upcoming war with the Mithraists required a big army, formed of capable and committed men.

"And finally," Callistus said. "Caesar declared a God… Himself."

Of course, this decision was, too, signed and sealed.

"Didn't anyone object?" I smiled, imagining my brother's earnest face.

"It's not that easy with a sword above your head," the Greek explained.

For a moment, even Vespasian was afraid there would be massacre. As the formal part of the meeting was over, Gaius abruptly left the hall, followed by Cassius and Claudius.

"What is it going to be now?" my 'widower' Lepidus anxiously asked Tigellinus.

"I don't know what to tell you, Consul," the guardsman replied.

"There will be what *he* wants it to be," Clemens said soberly, threatening Sabinus with his weapon.

After half an hour of waiting in terror, they saw Claudius, limping to the podium, disguised in… the Capitoline Wolf.

"H-h-honorable s-s-senators," the censor spoke timidly. "And you, g-g-guardsmen… "

"What the hell is he doing?" Asprenas plucked up courage to ask Priscus, but the glance of the centurion made him fall silent.

"We are honored to witness the h-h-heavenly dance of our Caesar!" Claudius' head, adorned with a hat, made of the real wolf fur, was nodding nervously. The next scene the spectators saw were Anicetus and Alcaeus, dressed like true Greek actors with the artificial gilded beards.

"The Dance of Mars and Venus," Claudius announced, and slowly waddled backwards, as the medic and the guardsman started singing "To Yasemin."

The next scene Callistus described explained his hysterical laughter, making me twist and turn, too. My brother, the emperor, stepped on the podium, rocking his hips like a drunk whore. He wore a blond-curled wig, a lot of jewelry, and the red bathing suit he took from my room without asking.

"The prefect had the helmet and armor of the Old Caesar on," Callistus smiled. "To the senators' resentment."

The performance was not bad indeed… if to believe my secretary, any theater must have been so envy for such actors. At the closing figure, Mars lifted up his Venus, letting the song sink into the thunderous applause – mannered, by senators, and exultant by the guardsmen.

"I was the choreographer," Callistus added proudly. "As well as the scenographer."

"I could expect it from Caligula," I waved aside. "But Cassius! What was that circus for?"

"First of all, Caesar wants them to believe he's mad," the Greek replied. "And dangerous for anyone who tries to mess with him."

There was another reason for my brother to behave so grotesque. To my freedman's disappointment, Caesar disapproved the senators' perverted preferences, publicly mocking them.

"He's right," I said without hesitation. "The fact that I turn blind eye on my friends cannot change what is right and what's wrong."

"Will we please change the subject, Princess?" Callistus frowned. "I have some better news – your friend Agrippa will be here by winter."

"Perhaps, he wants to express sympathy to Gaius," I supposed. The royal obituaries quickly reached even the farther provinces.

"I guess not." He took a letter from under his tunic. "*Oriens ferbuerit.*"[464]

The governor of Batanaea and Trachonitis wrote that he remained the only eastern deputy, still loyal to Caligula. The others secretly stood with Artabanus.

"Antipas, along with Egyptian prefect Avilius and Antiochus are planning a rebellion, spreading ugly stories about Caesar on the streets of their cities." I read quietly. "They don't want to wait for three more years."

---

[464] (lat.) The East is seething.

Fortunately, the former Roman hostage had an influence on the young Jews, favorable to romanization, while Antiochus, the other protege of ours, was less popular in his Commagene.

"It's not too late to dismiss traitors, and to replace them with trustworthy men." The secretary read my mind.

"Like you?" I joked, as I noticed suspicious note in his tone, yet for the second time.

"No, thank you. I'm not crazy about shaggy stinkers," the Greek said squeamishly – as if I seriously offered him promotion. "Eastern men are terrible in bed, they say."

"Apropos to bed," I thought out loud, wishing for immediate revenge. "It's time to banish Venus from the Esquiline."

"Excuse me?" Callistus goggled at me, as he couldn't understand the metaphor.

"I'm closing down all the brothels near the military camp," I explained briskly. "The taxes on prostitution will be levied all over the Empire, and sexual deviants will be banished…"

"But why?" the secretary wondered, interrupting me. "How can you leave those poor fellows without any consolation?"

"No, I just want those fellows to get married." I tapped him slightly on his chest. "So they can no longer be poor."

XXV

"I appreciate your loyalty and your adherence," Caesar dictated to Callistus a discreet letter for Agrippa. *"I have no doubt about the reliability of your allegations, and I invite you to the celebration of Saturnalia."*

Agrippa's treacherous neighbors also received invitations, but they still had no idea that the upcoming festivity would be the last in their lives.

"First, I will strangle the snake nourished in Antonia's lap," My brother's voice was full of disappointment, not hatred. "False friend Antiochus."

"Have you mentioned execution in Saturnalia?" Helicon and Protogenes wondered in the same voice.

"If we wait for nefesti," Callistus replied on the ruler's behalf. "We can get into trouble."

"Publius[465] the Syriac dog, and Avilius the Hippopotamus," Caligula went on, ignoring their dispute. "You will get what you deserve at Winter games. Whoever has the audacity to pay court to Artabanus should try to tame a tiger or a lion first."

"You know best." Callistus nodded and asked wittily, "And what about Antipas? Will you have him for dessert?"

"I'd rather have him crucified," my brother sighed. "But for the safety of the Romans, so I'll get him banished – along with his wife."

"Antipas is a widower, Caesar." Helicon corrected him. "His wife perished during travel."

"That served her right." Callistus smiled. "They said Herodias was a ruthless witch, and I believe it."

Sometimes I had to eavesdrop by the door of Caligula's office, while he was consulting his advisors. Yes, I even paid the guardsmen and the secretary for their silence – in pure gold.

---

[465] The governor of Syria during Caligula's reign.

"I think they're done," Tigellinus whispered. "You should hurry up, Your Highness. You know, when the council is over, Caesar has a habit to go down to culina to discuss the menu with the cookmaids."

"Bene," I gave him a money bag under the rose. " It's not that I don't trust my brother, but for the common good, I'd better keep up with his crazy ideas."

"Of course," the guardsman nodded. "Thank you, Princess."

In the portico between the official and private wings of the palace, there were other news from that region waiting for me.

"I found out everything you asked for, Your Highness." Victor recognized me with my veil on.

The Vigile and, from recently, the undercover hazzan,[466] collected information on Susannah's children with the help of his father, who was still influential in Galilee.

"Their names are Har'El and Daniel." The man informed me with a policeman's precision. "The older son is thirty-one years old and the younger is twenty-nine."

Those names, blurrily familiar, echoed in my soul like a distant memory.

"Not married yet, no children." Victor went on, a little surprised with that fact. "They reside in the house of their grandmother, Susannah's mother-in-law."

"Where is their father?" I asked with the sudden sense of restlessness. "Did he remarry?"

"Not at all," the Vigile replied sympathetically. "He never wanted another one."

Susanna's former husband died before she even left for Rome.

"He had been ill for a long time," the young man explained. "Mostly mentally – grieving for Susannah."

I wished his soul to rest in peace, and asked him whether Daniel and Har'El ever wished to see their mother.

"Many times," he replied. "But the head of the family, more precisely – their grandmother thwarted them under threat of disinheriting."

"How come a woman is a head of a family?" I was surprised. "Is she a widow with no siblings?"

---

[466] A Jewish name for a cantor.

"Yes, she is." Victor shrugged. "The old witch is called Naomi."

I smiled bitterly.

"Of course."

Son of Photice, already familiar with our secret scrolls, smiled back.

"This one is even worse."

I leaned against the motley balustrade and looked down to calm my nerves. According to the Law of Moses, Naomi's actions were legitimate, as, even abducted, Susannah was considered an adulteress. I rose up onto my toes till I could feel the burning pain, crying out inside to find a way to bring the dear family together.

"Do not worry, Princess." The young man tried to console me. "You will fulfill the promise."

Yet it was the Law, so fanatically preached by spiteful Naomi, that could turn the Wheel of Fortune in Susannah's favor.

Calvisius was screwed enough to bribe two Pharisees and then to get them drunk to learn the very truth about those family affairs. Frankly speaking, truth like that could have disgusted even late Tiberius.

"Naomi is a greedy harlot, slanderer and murderer," my friend explained. "For the sake of wealth, she cheated on her husband, and then got him killed."

"She'll get what she deserves," I said contemptuously. "Anyway, Susannah has no use for that."

The Vigile shook his head.

"No, Susannah is innocent! Naomi was the one to plan Susannah's abduction and to make sure all of Galilee believed her lies."

The old hag envied her daughter-in-law her happiness, so she decided to ruin her life. Still, there was something else Susannah didn't tell me for some reason.

"Antipas blackmailed the poor woman," the Vigile summed up. "He threatened her with murdering her sons unless she lied with him."

"But she behaved like she once loved him!" I got startled. "Why, Susannah?"

"Maybe, she is still afraid." The man shrugged. "Jester would know those women!"

"After all, it's her business." I waved aside, as I guessed. "When he got bored with her, Antipas could have given her away for stoning, but he sent her to Rome."

Pleased with the report, I opened my arms like a child.

"I owe you some great reward, Victor."

The young Vigile smiled a bit embarrassedly.

"It is our duty to serve you, Your Highness." He returned a friendly hug. "I'm glad me and my father could be helpful."

"Then," I whispered. "I have a task for Justus, too."

My friend stood to attention.

"Tell him to bring Susannah's sons to Rome by Saturnalia – along with the old hag," I ordered earnestly. "Antipas will be judged by Caesar, and Naomi will be judged by Lilith."

XXVI

None of the renegades denied their guilt. Antipas' try to justify himself with his smallness beside Artabanus was cut short immediately.

"I'm not putting you to death, because you are not worth the war," Gaius said, as he exposed the plot before the deputies. "For now, I'll have you banished to Lugdunum with your property confiscated. However, when I gather strength and beat your "Pater", you'll get yours."

"Our god and Caesar," Salome, the infamous temptress, lifted her white hands to heaven. "Please, spare me your rage! I have nothing to do with this scoundrel." She showed to Antipas – her uncle, stepfather and lover.

"She's lying!" the tetrarch shouted, flailing with his hands. "Her mother and she manipulated me to kill innocent people!"

Caligula, usually indulging for the weaker sex, showed stiffness this time.

"Take them away," he ordered to Lupus and Stella, and turned to our loyal friend Agrippa. "Galilee and Parea are yours now."

The might-have-been conspirators were leaving the palace with desperate shouts.

"It's all because of Julia Drusilla!" Antiochus cried. "She twisted around her finger them both – Tiberius and mad Caligula!"

"By our Lord!" Antipas replied in Hebrew. "Only the dark power could create a sword for a man and calamus[467] for a woman!"

This 'dark power,' as the followers of 'light' called it, decided his fate differently. On the way to Gaul, as they reached the Alps, almost impassable for eastern vehicles, the carriage with Antipas and Salome suddenly overturned, condemning the whole convoy to chilling death in the river.

Meanwhile, their long-time acquaintance Naomi met her scourge as well.

"Let me go, you beasts!" the old woman yelled, lifting up the sleeves of her suspiciously rich attire. "We are the most reputable family in Galilee!"

---

[467] The hollow shaft of a feather, also known as the quill.

When Susannah's children saw their mother, they stopped resisting. At my gesture, Calvisius and Victor untied their hands. Behind my back, I could almost feel my nursemaid's silent suffering, as she could hardly dare to take a step.

"This is Naomi bat Ephraim." Justus pushed the old woman towards me. "I thought I'd seen the Jewesses of all kinds, but this one is a vixen!"

"Damn you, you Samaritan bastard!" she hissed in her language.

I rose up from the imperial seat in the center of the atrium.

"Silence!"

Naomi, not frightened at all, still ignored me. As she notice Susannah, the old woman shuddered furiously.

"So, it's you? You harlot!"

Outraged by her effrontery, Victor rushed to the old woman.

"You were told to be quiet!" he shouted. "You are standing before Diva Augusta."

"You wish!" she replied, looking at me suspiciously. "Princess Drusilla is dead, and this one must be," she pointed at me with her bony finger, "One of Caesar's harlots!"

I burst out laughing. After that series of insults, I experienced from different traitors, the tirade of that Eve's great-granddaughter seemed so trivial and... even funny.

"Why do you hate Julia Drusilla so much, Lady?" I wondered in Hebrew. "Have you ever known her?"

"The Jews do not communicate with heathens," the old woman replied haughtily. "Yet everyone knows that she broke the old tradition, making a woman equal to a man!"

Calvisius and both his sons joined me in laughter.

"You Romans, are corrupted vermin," Naomi went on shamelessly. "Still, you can't withstand the Lord's anger, and your Empire will fall... "

"So, you're a prophetess," I said unexpectedly. "Would you like to help me judge a criminal?"

"So you're the real Julia Drusilla," she concluded grimly. "Anyway, I don't regret my words, nor am I willing to withdraw them. I am a greater woman that you and the one who gave you life."

Oh, you and Agrippina would have made good friends, I thought, returning her the gaze.

"You know, young lady," she went on self-confidently, "even wise Deborah[468] never brought to our people as much goodness as I gave my son and grandsons."

"I see," I sighed and wondered stilly. "So, what punishment should be appropriate to a wife, who deceived her lawful husband, and then killed him?"

The old woman grinned, as she believed in her dishonesty, that it was Susannah I was referring to.

"You say it right, Your Highness." She squinted contentedly. "It's her wickedness that killed my son." Then, she went on bloodthirstily, "The witch deserves stoning to death!"

"You've judged it to yourself, Naomi," I said sharply. "I have evidence and witnesses of your misdeeds."

The old Jewess turned pale and tried to deny everything. Curly Daniel, sensitive as a child, covered his eyes with his hands, while Har'El, manly and determined, asked Naomi to explain herself.

"All of Galilee know me as a decent woman, dedicated to her children!" the old Jewess yelled, tapping herself on the flat chest. "I just wanted a better life for my son and his sons! I wished them to dress like lords and to drink from topaz goblets..!"

"Calvisius," I interrupted her, as I turned to the prefect of Vigiles. "Take her out of here. The trial is over."

Naomi agonizingly recalled her husband's dumbness and her daughter-in-law's laziness, but nobody listened.

"Why are you staring at me, fellows?" I addressed Susannah's children. "Come and hug your mother!"

The young men stepped to my nursemaid half-heartedly. She knelt before them with her arms open and wept.

"You whore!" I heard Naomi cursing me, as guardsmen dragged her through the corridor. "I'm praying for the day they take your bastard child from you!"

---

[468] A prophetess of the God of the Israelites, the fourth Judge of pre-monarchic Israel and the only female judge mentioned in the Bible.

I'd definitely had enough of negative that day. Anicetus was there to shut the door, so I could happily observe a wonderful reunion.

Young men are always welcome here, I thought pragmatically. *Corbulo will train them to be warriors.* A thirty-year-old man in his prime, Roman or peregrine, with or without war experience, would come useful for the future battle of good and evil.

"Before I leave you," I stroked Daniel on his rosy cheek. "I tell you this – no woman ever treated me as kind and motherly as Susannah."

Moved and mirthful in a childish manner, Daniel helped her mother to her feet, and hugged her tightly. Har'El didn't hesitate to hug them both.

"Rejoice," I smiled, heading for the door. "No one will ever separate you from each other."

XXVII

"Volumus bellum!"[469]

They called out on the Palatine streets, while Caesar and I had our breakfast on the terrace.

Winter of AD 38 began with the uprisings in the eastern provinces, and protests of the Roman commoners. Vitellius, the procurator of Judea, wrote about the Pharisees, who, in their highest dudgeon, were destroying Roman marks and buildings all over Jerusalem.

"Tell them to erect my statue in the square by the Temple," Gaius replied – partly wittily, and partly irately. "Let's see if they dare to sue *me* before priests."

Another report, by Hosidius – a loyal commander of the army camp in Mauritania, was far from encouraging either.

"Client king Ptolemy took the side of Artabanus."

Well, I didn't have to read between the lines to see the nature of such alliance.

"Blood is thicker than water," I said. "He is not Cleopatra to break their laws for the sake of the good."

"Who knows why that is good," Caligula concluded. "The Senate has been seeking for our borders to expand, and so be it."

"Are we going to declare war on Ptolemy?" I wondered.

"No, he's not worth it," Caesar shook his head. "I'll invite him to negotiations, and kill him afterwards."

"You'll kill a kinsman of Artabanus?" I asked skeptically.

"Ptolemy formally belongs to the Antonii," Caligula explained. "So he is rather a kinsman of *ours*. I wish I never executed relatives, but traitors should be slayed."

"You're a dangerous man, Gaius," I smiled, realizing he was right. "Comparing to the other rulers, you are god of gods indeed."

---

[469](lat.) We want war!

"Thank you, Rhea Silvia." He returned a smile, and wondered wittily, "What was she to Jove?"

"A daughter-in-law," I replied, and went back to the subject. "Speaking of the wife of Mars. I must inform you, that the army, too, longs for the war."

Caligula rolled his eyes, raising his glass.

"Fuck the army!"

"Brother, it's their job." I shrugged. "Like, it's your job to raise the splendid buildings and bridges of pontoon."

The young man got earnest.

"Watch your tongue, sister."

Ever since the generals of Rome began with the significant campaigns, the stability of the constantly expanding state depended on preparedness for the new conquests. A king, a magistrate or an emperor, who would not aspire to new annexations could become ludicrous in the eyes of the neighbour rulers and even barbarians.

"I plan something big for the next year," Gaius enounced unexpectedly.

"Eugepae!" I clapped my hands. "Where are we going?"

The young emperor abruptly rose up from his couch, and came up to me.

"When the time comes, you'll know."

I pushed him aside with my shoulder a little bit angrily, but, thinking a while, I calmed down.

"Whenever Tigellinus keeps the watch, I'll, too, keep the watch by your door," I though cunningly. "Unless Callistus sing your plans away a day before the council."

Guy walked through the terrace, and stopped by the mirror, fixing his toga.

"I have to go, my dear." He spoke, occupied with his look. "Duty calls."

As I have finished my placenta, I asked wittily.

"Since when is it called duty?"

He hadn't looked at me with such vivaciousness and tenderness since we were in Misenum.

"I met an actress," he blushed. "Her name is Quintilia."

I remembered a tall, a bit sharp-featured woman, seemingly refined and meek, very convincing at playing the roles of Andromache and Alcestis.

"Now you are dating commoners," I said with irony. "What about z\the mother of your child?"

Caligula said sullenly.

"I still love Messalina… and she loves me, too."

"But?" I stood up, fixing my veil.

"Well, she is spoiled," he frowned. "Fortunately, less than you, but still, she doesn't know what a man needs."

"What *you* need, you mean?" I asked bitingly.

Gaius sighed, clasped his cloak, fixed his hair, pretending he didn't hear me. The grievance I felt in my soul turned into a nausea of my body, suppressing any humor.

"You're not looking for a wife," I stated sharply, "but a mother."

"What?" An emperor rebelled in him. ."What did you say?"

Leaving him with no answer, I left the room.

However, this quarrel hadn't lasted for too long. It didn't take me long for my suspicion towards the actress to be justified, but before that… there was something else to happen.

"Who knows why that is good," I hurried down the stairs. "I'm going to need someone to play Roxana's part."

The ground floor of the palace was hiding unexpected visitors.

"Heus, muta!" I recognized Agrippina's voice in the prothyron. "You old, ugly, fraught cow!"

I turned around. In the middle of the corridor, near the mosaic pillar, there stood my older sister.

Be quiet, Drusilla, I thought, slowly catching my breath. *Your voice can give you away.*

Fortunately, this time the flammeum was dark enough to have my face features blurred. I greeted her with a bow.

"Let's go to the viridarium," she beckoned me over with her finger. "To have a talk."

Like any other awkward moment, there was not even a shadow of a Praetorian around.

"Poor thing," Agrippina said cynically. "My brother maltreats you, does he not?"

I shook my head.

"Don't be afraid, you fool," the princess whispered. "I won't hurt you."

As I cursed, referring to the farcically absent guardsmen in my mind, I followed her to the nimfeum.

"Good puppy." Agrippina threw back her head in an unbridled manner. "Help us! Together, we can save Rome from the tyrant."

Barely audible voices from the internal garden gave away Livilla and… my 'widower.'

"Three daggers of ours will go down in history," Lepidus said unwarily.

My other sister and the stout consul were waiting for us on the bench.

"She will betray us," Livilla said timidly.

"I don't think so," Lepidus stood up, showing me a flashing blade of his dagger. "Take us to the madman!"

I shivered, and obediently walked toward the atrium. The motives of the Mithraist Lepidus were obvious. Since I had fake-married him, he had been in relationship with both my sisters. Still, I did not expect high treason from my parents' daughters.

What is their goal? What benefits are they expecting? I asked Sophia in me. *Are they those outsider assassins, chosen by senators?*

"When we're done with Caesar," Agrippina told her lover, "she is yours."

"I don't like pregnant women," Lepidus said disgustedly. "I'll kill her right away."

"I am not watching that." Livilla, so far pliable, suddenly jerked.

"Nobody is forcing you." Our sister hissed, and pushed me ahead. "Come on, move it! If someone comes along, I'll stab you in the stomach!"

I clenched my fists with my teeth gritted, trying to find out the way out of this hopeless situation. On an agonizing prayer, which had never let me down, I asked the Lord to keep my brother in his room as long as possible.

"Anyone there?" Tigellinus called out from the vestibule. I felt like I was taken out of the depths from hell.

Lepidus and Livilla fell hysteric, accusing each other, and my older sister raised her dagger, aiming it right to my face.

"Tell him to stay out!" she whispered angrily.

To win some time, and quickly removed my veil. Both sisters screamed in horror.

"What... was that?" Lepidus dropped the dagger, shocked and shaken with the sight. "By Sol Invictus!"

"Cohort, alert!" I heard saving shout of Stella. Just a moment away the prothyron was filled with the guardsmen.

"Arrest them!" I ordered the soldiers. "They planned to kill Caesar!"

"Why didn't they kill you?" Agrippina uttered through her teeth. "You damn Praetorian slut!"

Priscus, Aquila, and Tigellinus grabbed the failed conspirators and dragged them to the dungeon. Stella, confused and embarrassed, tried to explain to me the reason of their absence.

"This morning, Prefect Chaerea got a written order, sealed with the royal signet. He was urgently called to the Viminal camp, which he followed without thinking."

"And what about you, tribune?" I asked suspiciously. "Where have you been?"

With a regretful sigh, the officer replied.

"The guard was asked to leave the palace by your sisters. Supposedly, by the same behest."

"This behest was not given by Caesar." I shook my head, yet too stressed to be angry. In the passages of the palace the four traitor was hiding – a thief and a liar.

Finally, Caligula himself appeared at the top of the stairs.

"What the hell is going on?" he wondered anxiously. "What's that noise?"

I looked at him, still in high dudgeon, but relieved to see him safe and sound.

"You owe me an apology, Lord Caesar," I replied. "I saved your ass for the third time."

XXVIII

AD 39

As Gaius wished, the trial for the high treason took place at the Forum of Julius before the frightened senators and passersby. The mobs, upset by the attempt of attacking Caesar, followed the criminals to the courtroom with curses, whistles and egging.

"I sentence you to public beheading," Caligula told Lepidus, already half-dead with fear. "Thank your daughter, whose tears saved you from crucifixion."

The children's pleas saved our sisters from the worst as well. Agrippina and Livilla were banished to different islands of the Pontiac archipelago. The huge property of the princesses was sold, and the collected funds were invested in the road construction.

"Don't even think of telling anyone about your sister," Gaius warned them in secret. "I not only have islands, but swords as well."

Heavyhearted and disappointed with his kin, he behaved impetuously. Many guardsmen were demoted, and most of the servants dismissed without severance pay. However, Tigellinus, as the only person who put the false order into doubt, was promoted to the rank of tribune, despite the hierarchical and age canons.

When they executed Lepidus, Caligula addressed Vespasian.

"I have a task for you, praetor."

Confused with the new title and thousands of eyes gazing at him from all sides, the son of the Flavii no longer knew what to reply.

"When it gets dark, throw this garbage" Gaius pointed to the convict's body. "To the farthest and dirtiest ditch. Let's say, to the grotto of Cybele, the old whore."

The senator frowned, lifting his short but thick eyebrows, and reluctantly saluted.

"After you finish," My brother went on. "Borrow a broom from a street cleaner, and clean the scaffold."

This allusion to Vespasian as the main culprit made him want to die of shame – at least that very moment.

Well, there was only one thing left – to find the scoundrel, who had stolen Caesar's signet from the palace, opening the door for the intruders. Callistus, Helicon and Protogenes were only people, who kept the keys to the imperial office. During the investigation, the name of the secretary was mentioned more than once.

"That's impossible!" I denied my sister's claims. "Agrippina is lying! The senators want us to kill our loyal servants, and to plant their spies to the palace instead."

Callistus, with his eyes sad and innocent, denied the accusations, swearing there was someone, who had stole the keys from his chambers while he was sleeping; and then secretly returned them to his wardrobe.

"Protogenes has been loyal to familia for thirty and five years," Caligula was pondering. "I don't believe he would have rebelled in old age."

Helicon just kept silence, suppressing tears. No one stood in his defense, nor anyone wondered what he was doing that morning. A quiet, hard-working and prudent Egyptian, too modest to be someone's favorite in any sense, was aware of his fate in advance.

Unlike our poor servant, we were not aware of our destiny. Caligula and I accused our bodyguards and slaves of gullibility, while we ourselves were blind to see our own credulity – the fatal trustfulness, which was about to destroy his power and my wisdom.

"From now on, you only obey orders I give to you personally!" Caesar announced in the palace. "When I'm out, your god is my sister," he said to the guardsmen.

Yes, my brother gladly played his part of a deity, referring to me as to Rhea Silvia, who had given up this miserable world for the seat of the gods. After my 'death,' they erected my statues all around the city like the Korai of the Acropolis. The senators, whose influence was formally decreasing, had to pay the costs of all Caligula's endeavors, boasting to the commoners for the given honors.

"I just want to draw attention," he explained, as he was riding over a giant-length floating bridge, "to take as many people as it's possible out of Mithras' web."

"Be careful," I reminded him carefully. "Do not forget, who the real God is."

"The Romans are not ready for Him yet," I heard, while the dark veil, Caesonia's attribute, fluttered in the wind like the ominous flag.

The days passed, spring[470] was approaching, bringing the spirit of new beginnings. Favonius[471] was weakening. The meadows were slowly awakening, opening their fan of the first flowers. The murmuring of the stream was followed by the cheerful singing of spring birds. According to Alcaeus, that beauty was about to welcome my Acte.

"I'm afraid," I confessed to David at the common prayer. "Healthier and stronger women die in childbirth…"

The priest's gaze, so warm and perspicacious despite his young age, and his voice, calm like the summer sky, could soothe the highest fire of my soul… Untrammeled soul, but much too human to be pure.

"God is the giver and the ruler of our lives," he said in a low voice. "He wants us to live and to bring new lives to this world."

"I killed, rabbi," I whispered contritely. "I did bad things in the name of the good."

David pressed his index finger to his lips and gestured me to half-kneel.

"Do you repent for violating the God's Law, Chokmâh?" He changed his tone to be stricter.

"Yes, I do." I nodded. In my heart, I was forgiving my dead enemies, begging their souls to go easy on me in return.

As he finished the conceding prayer, David slightly touched my shoulder. "He who forgave the thief, the harlot, and the publican, never will reject your true contrition."

I grabbed his elbow and got to my feet.

"Still," the priest smiled to me in a friendly way, "killing in war is no murder, my lady."

"Are we in combat?" I wondered.

"Are we not?" David held his arms out. "The battle we fight is more crucial and dire than the others. It's neither wealth nor flesh we defend, but the immortal souls."

My soul sensed a sudden touch of legerity and heavenly encouragement.

"May God help us." I smiled back. "This is just the beginning."

---

[470] In Ancient Rome February was considered the first month of spring.
[471] The West wind personified.

XXIX

A strong storm woke me up in the middle of the night. The downpour noisily broke into the palace through the terraces and impluvium. The wind, latterly fresh and mild, now had been blowing heavily. It felt like the skies were about to be torn by the thunder and lightning. In my warm room I felt a sudden cold, and covered myself over my head with a blanket. In the dark, I searched for Cassius, but he was out.

The watches are changing, I thought, and turned to the side. That very moment, I was struck by pain inside my back – deeper and stronger than my usual malaise.

"Susannah!" I called out discomposedly, barely able to sit up. My strange chill suddenly turned into an instant feverish heat, until the new wave of pain encompassed my stomach. I tossed aside my blanket, and got out of the bed slowly.

My sleepy nursemaid hurried from the auxiliary room with an oil lamp.

"Has it started?" she asked anxiously.

I touched my belly. My lively girl, who was pushing and kicking inside me almost all time around, finally calmed down.

"How are you?" Susannah carefully embraced me.

Childbirth wasn't a bogey for me. Susannah, Messalina and Alfidia were always willing to retell the memories of their labors. My midwife experience at my kinswoman's bed, who delivered as quick as a cat, had had an encouraging impact on me.

"If I am what I believe I am, my soul is free from the original sin, so I probably won't suffer," I joked in a weak voice.

"You wish," the Jewess smiled. "You might be Lilith in your soul, but in your body you're the daughter of Eve, like any of us."

"Is a body that important?" I rolled my eyes, and bent over in pain.

"Tigellinus!" the nursemaid cried, while helping me out of the room. The young tribune sent two common guardsmen for the medic, and then readily lifted me up to his arms.

"What are you doing?" the Jewess asked worriedly. "The princess does not like such things!"

"It's alright," I moaned, patting my friend on his shoulder. "I trust you, fellow."

"Don't you dare drop her," Susannah threatened him. "Otherwise you'll regret you were born."

"Calm down!" I half-turned my head to hush her. "He knows what he's doing."

The pain suddenly subsided, as during my monthly.

"I guess I'm as heavy as lead." I looked sadly at Tigellinus.

The young man, boldly holding his body, walked on towards the stairs.

"Amata mea!" The voice of my betrothed broke the silence, as the light of his torch swallowed the dark.

"Cassius!" I reached out to his silhouette.

"I'm coming, too, Your Highness!" Alcaeus called out from the arcade.

"Please, Sirs, be quiet!" Susannah frowned. The sounds of footsteps and the constant slamming of the doors must have raised to dozens of slaves to their feet.

"Now they'll find out," I whispered, trying to cover my face with a sleeve. A new wave of pain gripped me from the waist down like a hoop.

"What is it?" the nursemaid exclaimed, as she showed to the large stain of red on my hem.

Bent in half with pain and horror, I touched my inner thigh, and stained my fingers with blood.

"It's no good." The medic shook his head and addressed the Praetorians. "Take her to my chambers, quickly!"

Cassius, Aquila, Priscus and Lupus crossed their arms to make a live litter. Tigellinus carefully handed me to fellow guardsmen, and raised a torch to light the way.

"No good," Alcaeus sighed as he examined me. "Athenian," he turned to Tigellinus, "keep them all out."

Without a word, Tigellinus led the other guardsmen to the hallway.

"Now, Susannah." The Cretan looked at the woman. "Bring the Rabbi and the Rabbanit."

"In here?!" the nursemaid wondered. "No man is allowed to see a childbirth!"

"Do it!" Alcaeus shouted. "Princess is in danger."

Helplessly, I looked at Cassius. My lover stroked my hand.

"You'll be alright, my love," he whispered, then turned to the medic. "I beseech you, save her!"

The Cretan came up to his desk and took a thin book with Greek letters.

"There is a certain way to save the both – the mother, and the baby. It is very risky."

"Tell me what to do!" Chaerea spoke out readily.

"Ask Caesar for permission to perform the surgery."

"What?" The prefect became bewildered. "Now?… The emperor is with his favorite."

"To hell with the permission!" I cried out, dumb with fear. "Caligula is not my husband."

Alcaeus unrolled the scroll hurriedly.

"This surgery was known to the Minoans." He showed the scheme to Cassius. "Icarus, the son of Daedalus, was born that way… so was Princess Phaedra, the daughter of Minos."

"And the mothers?" I asked, mad with uncertainty. "Did they survive?"

"Daedalus' wife died," he sighed heavily. "Yet Pasiphaë lived quite a long time afterwards."

I shivered with cold sweats and reached for a blanket to cover myself, but Alcaeus stopped me.

"It's time to act." He looked at me heartily, as he unclasped a small skin bottle from his belt. This time, it took me efforts to drink what he gave me, for the potion tasted sour, fermenting and nauseous. I coughed. There was no pain, just one more trickle of blood between my legs.

"Poppy milk mixed with wine," the Greek explained. "It will put you to sleep."

"What will you do to me?" I moaned.

Cassius was close to tears.

"Isn't there other way to save her?" he looked at the medic.

Alcaeus shook his head and headed to his workroom. As I followed him with my blurred sight, I noticed his small table from the Suburra. It was, as always, full of herbal remedies. Next to it, there was a stove with some medical tools and a pot of hot water.

"You're going to help me," he pointed at Cassius. "Saving lives in a men's thing."

My head was getting more and more inebriate. My eyelids were already swollen with a potion. Before I lost myself, I saw timorous David and his wife entering.

"What is it, Princess?" The priest raised his hands in panic.

"Go to the small room now," Alcaeus told him earnestly. "And pray to your Adonis."

"Oh my living God!" the Rabbanit cried out as she noticed an obsidian scalpel in his hands.

The fear in me grew somnolent and motionless… like me.

"I'll be alright," I said, sinking into the mist. "My time hasn't come yet."

XXX

That toxic dream took me back to my memory… a distant memory – a life before my life, the dawning of my soul. I was flying like a leaf, blown by the wind through the pinacotheca of events, landscapes and characters, as I could feel all of Sophia's joy, sadness, and pain again.

The igneous light of creation, the man I did not love, his wife, my years of being rejected and lonely, my fervent desire to love in every line of the first poem in history, and, finally, God's promise to create for me the man of my kind – a knight, a hero, a protector… semper fidelis – regardless of time and circumstances.

"*Ubi tu Cassius…*" My soul was smiling. In that interlude, I realized that death frightened me only if it would separate me from my lover. Without him, Eden felt like hell to me, and unhallowed Rome looked like the desert where I was foretold to find my peace.

"*… ego sum Sophia.*"

Then, there was something squeezing my hand to awake me. Coming to my senses was followed by pain in my stomach – yet blunt and remote, and his answer.

"*Ubi tu Sophia, ego sum Cassius.*"

From the vagueness, I came back to my lover… and the Cretan, David and… Orla?!

"Princess!" the Gaul exclaimed happily. "Thank gods you live!"

"Easy, hedgehog," the Greek interrupted her, and leaned over me. "Please, rest, Your Highness. You'll be fine. You are already fine."

"Where is my baby?" I looked at him worriedly.

"In her room, with the nursemaid and wet nurse," Cassius reassured me. "It's a girl. A very beautiful girl."

"And healthy, too," Alcaeus added. "She has your eyes, Princess."

Orla covered me with one more cashmere blanket.

"She looks like Prefect, too… a little," the young woman smiled.

David was there as well, wiping his tearful eyes with his long sleeve. "With God's help," he spoke happily, "next Saturday, we will announce her name at the synagogue."

The pain intensified abruptly, and I became sharp and nauseous.

"What have you done to me?" I asked, barely able to move my numb hand.

"We did what we had to do," Alcaeus sighed. "We'll talk of that later. Now you have to rest."

I looked at each of them in course and walked along the chamber with my eyes. On the desk I saw a wide vessel, a pile of red cloth pieces, two dozens of small amphorae, and… Orla's toolbox.

"Uncover me," I said to Cassius, startled.

The physician stopped him with a forbidding gesture.

"Princess, please." He gently touched my elbow. "We barely saved you."

"I want to see," I went on sharply. "I'm a big girl now."

Cassius took off the blankets – first the thick one, and then the thin one. David shyly mumbled about some duties he remembered at the synagogue and left the room hurriedly.

"Just relax," Alcaeus warned me. "The wound is serious; it needs time to heal."

Orla asked me to slowly lift my pelvis, so she could unroll the bandage. There was… a seam on my underbelly, suturing a distinct scar, covered with a thick layer of some green ointment.

"Your friend David called it – *'yotsei dofen,'*" the medic coughed, wiping sweat from his forehead. "That's too complex for my Greek ears, so I would rather call it – *'partus caesareus.'*"

I looked at Orla, stupefied.

"Yes," Alcaeus nodded. "Thanks to those small, dexterous fingers, you are here with us."

"Trugarez… vras," I said, bursting out crying.

The young Gaul, moved by my words, took a seat at my feet.

"Netra," she replied with her eyes wet like mine. "Me az kar."

"Why did we conquer you?" I thought aloud, pressing her tiny palm to my lips.

"I'm glad you did." She laughed sonorously. "I'm happy here in Rome. I'm doing what I love next to the one I love."

Meanwhile, the Greek mixed a new tincture for me – something colorless with a soothing taste. He helped me lift my head to drink it.

"Now I command you to rest," he said earnestly. "Let your friends think of everything else."

Stepping onto the threshold of the Dreamland, I thought of my brother.

"Does he know?" I asked Chaerea.

"Yes, of course," he replied gently. "Caesar wept with joy to see our daughter."

"He named her after you," Alcaeus added. "Announcing the birth of Augusta."

XXXI

"I name you Rebecca,"[472] David spoke thrice, and stepped off the podium to show the infant to the group of believers. "Be a bond, eternal and unbreakable – between your parents."

The parishioners rejoiced, and Victor carefully took the baby to his arms. His brother Justus, fighting jitters, tied a thin red string around her wrist.

"How good and pleasant it is when God's people live together in unity!" they sang in chorus from mechitza.

More and more Jews, who recognized Jesus as God, were finding shelter in Rome – far away from Pharisaic persecution. The refugees were given land on the outskirts of the Esquiline, separated from the Gardens of Maecenas[473] with the Servian Wall. To my delight, most of the peregrines decided to join the army, while their wives took care about new houses, controlling their construction. Safe again, those people kept their migration a secret, as well as the name of their patroness.

As for me, due to tradition and Alcaeus' recommendation, I stayed in my chambers for forty days. Cassius was allowed to visit me, but not as often as I wished.

"David told me there was a certain number of them who thanked you warmly, but refused the invitation," he said once. "They don't deny they are in danger there, but still they stay at home."

"It is because of me," I sighed bitterly. "Unmarried mothers violate the seventh commandment."

Cassius smiled, a bit confused, as he lay beside me.

"Didn't I propose to you?"

"Oh, yes, you did," I stroked his cheek, always smooth-shaven. "But we are not of the same faith."

The prefect grew earnest. "As far as I'm considered, we are now."

---

[472] (hebr.) Knitter.

[473] Maecenas – a Roman politician and patron of artists.

His deep, profound gaze took my breath away.

"Last Saturday, I became Gideon," he went on, gently touching my belly. "Since you withstood a massacre because of me, what would I be unless I do the same for you?"

I moved toward him and leaned my head on his chest. "A brave warrior," I understood the meaning. "To the point."

"Well, Rabbi had a nightdream, where he was commanded to give me that name," Cassius recollected.

"The same about me," I smiled in surprise. "I am Chokmâh! Do you know anyone else with such a name?"

The prefect shook his head, smiling back.

"What do you think of the idea to invite my uncle Philip and his wife Polyxena to our wedding?"

"It's a wonderful idea," I replied enthusiastically. "But how do we explain to them the spectacle of me playing Caesonia and with the baby?"

"They are Greeks, my love," he laughed. "Is there a nation more imaginative than the Greeks?"

"Hardly." I shrugged, and slowly got out of my bed. "Let's go to see Acte!"

"She's not here."

"What do you mean?" I jerked. This sudden move made my scar prickle. Chaerea rushed to me.

"What are you doing?" He pressed his warm palm to my belly. "Our daughter is fine."

"It's Caligula," I guessed. "Where did he take her?"

The prefect sat back on the bed and took me to his lap as if I was a child.

"Today we have Equirria,"[474] he explained calmly. "Caesar is taking her for a chariot ride around the Field of Mars."

"History repeating," I rolled my eyes. "Germanicus once took me to the battlefield to show me hostages."

---

[474] An Ancient Roman festival of chariot and horseback racing, held in honor of Mars.

"Oh I remember," Chaerea smiled. "You were a little older, though."

"I hope she likes it," I laughed. "It's better for a girl to see our soldiers than some self-important senators."

"You are right." He kissed my forehead. "But, as Caesar's heiress, Acte ought to choose a husband from the senatorial class."

"She will marry whoever she wants," I said earnestly. "I will accept her choice even if it is an *arsonist*."

Cassius burst out laughing. "You should definitely meet my aunt," he said. "You two have much in common."

"I can't wait." I cheered up and patted him on the back. "Since we are getting married, we'd better get well."

"You bet!" he whispered temptingly. "You need a clear head and a rested body to go into battle."

"A battle?" I giggled. "With who defeating whom?"

"Men of art have always compared the love skills with the warcraft," he said. "As well as their own occupation."

"True," I nodded, suddenly remembering the words of the angel. *"You, a woman with a quill, will marry a man with a sword."*

Regarding a quill... By that time, my drama was already finished, waiting to be rehearsed.

"My dear Quintilia promised to find the best actors," my brother persuaded me. Still, his new lover was not in a hurry to help me... nor even she had a nice word on my writings.

"Perhaps she's just mad about Gaius," I made up excuses for her. "She's young and so obsessed with him that she can't think of anything that is not him."

We still had time. The first smile of my daughter and the wedding planning lulled my vigilance... Alas, I had some other enemies, much more ferocious than some jealous actress.

A few days later, David rushed into my room with awful news. "Someone has stolen the scroll my brother sent from Galilee!" he cried. "The Prayer of Jesus!"

"Do not worry, we will find it," I tried to assure him. "We have found Caesar's signet, so we'll get your scroll as well… Can we remember any words of it?"

"I even managed to translate it into Latin," the priest sighed. "Pater noster qui es in coelis… sanctificetur nomen Tuum…"[475] He tried to recall with efforts. "There's no chance I remember it even in my language!"

"We will scour the palace through!" I promised him naively. "We'll turn the city upside down, believe me!"

Yet the inquest was in vain. Vespasian must have had a spy who covered his tracks artfully. As the senators found out about the secret exodus, the believers could no longer leave their homeland. With the help of his soldiers, 'Sun-Racer' controlled the departures of all eastern ports. The way across the land was not a safe alternative, because of the unstable borders between countries and the great distance.

"We are losing, Princess," David wept. "There is a Judas hiding in the palace!"

"Is that prayer so important, after all?" I asked him anxiously, as if I didn't want to see the seriousness of the damage.

"It is… everything!" The priest grew pale with suffering. "It has the core of our faith within – like the Decalogue and our ritual immersion in the mikveh!"

What we knew for sure was that the traitor wasn't Narcissus. However, many of my friends suspected him because of his dark past. To me, the young descendant of Naomi was a child, who was sincerely sorry and so willing to take the right side. I trusted him, because he told me everything he heard when Claudius held the receptions for the Flavians.

"Me, I have no idea who the thief is," Narcissus shook his head. "The bastard must be very sly and cautious. But instead, I will retell you what Vespasian told your uncle at the feast:

"'To Lord Mithras, who defeated Adonai,' the praetor toasted. He said, 'Jesus, He was crucified! I personally sent my cruelest lictors, my real beasts, to torment him.'

"Then, Sabinus said, 'Rumor has it, He has risen – Well, who knows… perhaps that whore, Sophia –'

---

[475](lat.) Our Father, who art in heaven, hallowed be thy name.

"He was interrupted by a great roar from Vespasian, 'Watch your stupid jokes! If, by a chance, she rose from ashes,' – he gazed hatefully over Claudius and guests – 'Not even Adonai himself would save her from my revenge!'"

XXXII

AD 40

On the eve of my wedding, Gaius and Cassius signed a Ketubah – a Jewish marriage contract.

"By custom, Father of the bride escorts her to the groom," David explained. "But when the bride is an orphan, it's her brother who's considered her custodian."

"Do you give your blessing to this union, Caesar?" Victor, the witness of the ceremony, asked Caligula.

My brother looked at me with the unusual tenderness and whispered, "A thousand blessings."

Justus, the other witness, smiled. "Well, *seven* are enough." He handed to the ruler an old quill and a papyrus sheet. "Marriage is a divine purpose. A man and a woman were made to cleave unto each other as one soul, and one flesh."

"Although the forefathers mention divorce and remarriage for widows and widowers," the Rabbi added, "Jesus said – what God hath joined together, let not man put apart."

For a while, my brother had been pondering over the strange document, and wondered.

"What? Cum manu?!"

"We, too, were surprised." David smiled.

"If a woman's thing is to belong to someone," I shrugged. "Let it be the one I choose myself."

Hidden in the hills and forests, the small lake Nemorensis was here to hold the secret of my wedding. Lit by the full moon myriads of stars, this coast was to host all our friends and companions, revealing a view of two magnificent ships decorated with pure gold and ivory.

My new kinsman Philip, Cassius' uncle, escorted me to the chuppah – a traditional canopy, spread above the podium, it symbolized a new home built by the newlyweds.

"I opened to my beloved…" Susannah sang in Hebrew, surprisingly clear, "but my beloved had turned away, and was gone."

"I adjure you, O daughters of Jerusalem, if ye find my beloved," I heard Rachel joining her in her deep voice. "What will ye tell him? That I am love-sick."

Harmoniously and joyfully, the women's choir from the synagogue followed them.

"What is thy beloved more than another beloved, o thou fairest among women? What is thy beloved more than another beloved, that thou dost so adjure us?"[476]

The silk roof fluttered in the wind by the turquoise-blue lake. The spring breeze gently played with my white dress and veil.

"Behold, you are consecrated to me with this ring according to the law of Adonai-Jesus," Cassius addressed me, placing the ring on my finger.

In the crowd, I heard a certain man asking the priest, in a bit upset manner, why the old formula[477] had now been changed.

"It was the Law of Jesus, which Moses brought to us," David replied. "While our Israel is everywhere where we believe in Him."

I bowed slightly to my husband, letting him remove my veil. Our lips met in a fervent kiss.

"Long live the bride and groom!" the guests exclaimed – in Latin, Greek and Hebrew. "Come let us be glad and rejoice!"

Har'El brought us two glasses of wine, and his brother showed us to a couple of high wooden chairs.

"It's time for a wedding present." Gaius stepped forward, and the guests fell silent. "When I saw those two together for the first time – twenty-seven years ago," he nodded to the newlyweds, "I noticed the deep bond between the baby girl, my sister, and the big centurion… It is no secret, I've been jealous of Chaerea since my childhood years, yet I knew the two of them would end up as a couple."

I smiled mirthfully as my husband stroked my hand. Orla, Susannah, and Alfidia couldn't hide tears of joy, and the guardsmen watched the ceremony with respect and admiration.

---

[476] The Song of Songs.

[477] The original Jewish declaration ended with the words "… *according to the law of Moses and Israel.*"

"For a long time, I've been thinking over the right gift for the best woman on earth and a man who's my role model," Gaius went on, imperceptibly nodding to someone. "Fortunately, my loyal Ioh and the old sea wolf Licinius were here to help me."

The captain, now grizzled and a little hunched because of age, joined Caesar on the improvised small scene. Anat, too, changed by the breath of time, encouraged her shy husband to come up as well.

"I've always dreamed of love aboard," my brother smiled seductively, embarrassing most of the women. "Just imagine a big floating bedroom, sprinkled with rose petals in the moonlight…"

The smaller ship, all decorated with mosaic and stained glass, resembled a palace. The bigger vessel was adorned with the round portico where they set rich tables.

"Welcome to the family, Cassius Chaerea," Caesar finally addressed the groom. He turned to the unusual company and said, "Enjoy yourselves, my friends."

The guests, excited by both the event and the cloudless mood of the emperor, quickly lined up by the boarding bridge. Licinius' job was to escort them to the unusual triclinium.

"Thank you, brother dear." I hugged Caligula, and whispered in his ear, "Why… ships?"

"Because you hate them," he giggled, and continued earnestly, "I liked the story of the Noah's ark, and I would really like to save those people from the awful things to come."

"Adiuvet nos Deus,"[478] I replied, and winked at him. "When will you, Caesar, settle down again?"

"Not soon." He shook his head. "I like to seize the moment, and I don't want anything to change."

"That's bad," I sighed, and turn around to see his new paramour in the crowd. Yet, for some reason, Quintilia was not present.

"Callistus?" I turned to the group of servants, who were patiently waiting for their turn.

---

[478] (lat.) God help us.

Anicetus responded. "He's not here... he's resting," the tall man said sadly. "He hasn't been well since last night."

"Is he ill?" I asked worriedly. "Should I send Alcaeus to the palace?"

"There's no need." The Cypriot shook his head. "He's just caught cold."

"In May?" I asked confusedly. "Was he walking in the palace naked?"

"Let him be, my love," Cassius calmed me. "He'll be fine."

"I know," I leaned my head on his shoulder. "I just wish he was with us."

"Please, next!" the captain called merrily.

"Man, wait!" I heard a woman's voice, strong but so warm. "I want to see the bride!"

On the boardwalk, I noticed a plump, bright-eyed lady of a mature, dignified beauty.

"Theia[479] Polyxena!" My husband spread his arms to meet her.

The Greek woman smiled. "You rascal!" She came up to us, jokingly threatening him with her finger. "I was afraid you would end up as a damn bachelor... and look what you did? You got yourself a princess!"

"Pleased to meet you, theia," I spoke in her language and hugged her.

"You're a little skinny, Princess." Polyxena pinched my cheek. "Come, visit us in Attica – I'll treat you like a daughter! Now remember – men of the Chaereas are so tough because of us strong women!"

I answered with a smile. I had lost weight after my child was born, but yet no Roman would have called me skinny.

"Go to your uncle," the Greek woman said to Cassius, and hugged me at the waist. "Philip and I love your husband like our own son, so I will talk to you as if you were my daughter."

I tried to thank her, but my new kinswoman outpaced me.

"Here is advice," she whispered. "Woman of the warrior is quite a special kind. Not every hen is made to be a Penelope or a Gorgo. It's not hard to please a peasant – roast some pig and bear him kids, that's it! An archon might be pleased with your big

---

[479] (anc.gr.) Aunt.

dowry, and an artist will go mad for your pretty face and sculpted smile. Still, with a soldier you must be a goddess, a true friend and a skilled lover. Do you understand me, girl?"

"Of course," I nodded. She was more free-spirited than my grandmother. Polyxena was a pure Hellene, but her bold frankness was reminiscent of the Celtic goddess Morrigan.

"There's more!" she giggled.

Well, her next advice made my cheeks blush like roses on the Esquiline. "Thank you," I chuckled back. "It was… engrossing."

"You bet, honey!" she replied, and kissed me on my forehead.

"Pame, Xena!" Old chiliarch[480] Philip called out from the deck. "We are waiting for you!"

"Don't disappoint me." Polyxena winked at me and headed to the bridge.

"Yes, Lady!" I saluted jokingly, a moment before Cassius appeared behind me with his strong, affectionate embrace… My husband, my true love and my first memory.

How could I live without him? I thought, as I squinted on his shoulder.

My knight, dressed in solemn attire, so pleasant to my touch, now without any metal or rough leather badges, took me to the bedroom on our ship. "Ready?"

I felt him lowering me down to something soft. The door was closed, so we no longer heard those merry shouts from the other ship. I opened my eyes.

The moonlight intensively flowed through the round, glazed window, bathing the silk of our bed and mosaic reliefs in its silver. On the copper tripod table, I noticed pomegranates – a symbol of love and fidelity.

"Te amo… Semper tuus…"

"Semper tua…"

We exchanged our blissful vows, feeding each other with the fruit's tart scarlet seeds.

A fresco on the wall above us represented the sacred marriage of Mars and Rhea Silvia. The god of war was giving his still mortal bride his spear – the symbol of his

---

[480] (in Ancient Greece) – a military commander of 1000 men.

power – as a proof of his deep love, while the bridesmaid, virgin deity Perenna, took off Rhea's veil.

"I wonder – what would David say about those pagan images?" Chaerea smiled.

"Maybe it's us?" I uttered the first thing that came to my mind – words from my nightmare. "Myths are the spirits' prophecies of what shall happen."

Cassius thought a little and concluded wittily, "Well… after all, it's not that bad."

XXXIII

"Happy holiday, Mama."

Another colorless and heavy nightdream was now pushed away with my sweet, dashing reality. Cassius was rocking Acte in his arms, slightly clanking with a silver rattle. As she grew, our daughter looked less like me and more like Chaerea.

"Bonum mane, Daddy's girl," I smiled as I got out of bed. "What day is it today?"

"Matralia," the prefect replied cheerfully, imitating a child's voice. "Festivity for univirae."

"Are there still any?" I noticed with irony, and kissed them both good morning.

"Sad to say, most women forgot what femininity is," Cassius sighed. "Seems like men and women swapped their roles."

"Mithras does not waste his time." I put my gown on. "He uses each and every moment to distort and to dishallow…"

"He will get his, darling. God is just," my husband calmed me down.

I approached the mirror and felt pleased with what I saw. That morning I was feeling good as well.

"Today is the open rehearsal of my play," I recalled, and turned to Cassius. "Would you like to come with me?"

"I wish I could," he replied sadly. "Caesar is convening military council."

"What?" I dropped my hairpin. "For today?"

The child observed us curiously, as if she understood what we were talking of. Chaerea fixed the small hood of her palla.

"We're going to Britannia," he softly crooned in the rhythm of a sung fairy tale. "It is a big and distant island where it often rains; the locals worship trees and never pay tribute to Rome…"

"I need to see Caligula." I headed to the corridor not to raise my voice before my daughter. "Is anyone here?" I called out.

Anicetus readily rushed for Fedlimid. The old Gaul, slim and hale like a dragonfly, quickly appeared in the prothyron.

"Take care of Acte," I told her. "I have things to do."

Susannah appeared on the other side off the hallway as she heard my voice. "Where are you going before breakfast?" she reproached me. "It is almost noon!"

"Lekh-i la azazel!"[481] I exclaimed, and ran on to the tablinum. Cassius followed me without a word and ordered the guardsmen to open the door.

"What's the matter?" Gaius wondered, still relaxed after a hot bath.

"I missed you," I joked. "Why Britannia?"

Caesar put down a scroll and looked up at the prefect. "Why did you tell her?"

"For God's sake, what a moronic question!" I said. "Every time you try to hide something from me, you fuck something up!"

"The things got fucked up long ago." Gaius motioned to the scroll.

"What is it, Sir?" Cassius asked. "The strategy of conquest?"

"Conquest is your job, Chaerea," my brother replied. "What I have here is the true Chronical History of Rome – from Aeneas to Augustus."

"Where did you find it?" I wondered.

"Let's say I borrowed it from Uncle – with the help of Narcissus." He smiled.

"So, Claudius has never really studied the Etruscans," I concluded, and moved a chair so I could sit beside him. Cassius leaned against the painted pillar next to me. We both fell silent, awaiting the story.

"Historians of past, they lied," Gaius said thoughtfully. "Our contemporaries are spreading their lies, just like those children playing 'grapewine.'"

Shortly before his death, Tiberius mentioned a certain historian Livy, who recklessly changed annals for the needs of his masters – Augustus and Mithridates.

"Do you notice, puella, that the historians of ours are mostly senators or the imperial favorites?" My grand-uncle asked me once.

"History is written by the victors," I replied, "they say."

"No, dear," he corrected me. "These men are no victors. Victory is like a racehorse – it can never be tamed by a tyrant, but the noble knight. The annals are written for the needs of losers, who exult dancing on the corpses of true victors."

---

[481] (hebr.) Go to hell!

"Are you listening?" Caligula brought me back from memories. "King Romulus did not kill his brother!"

"How?" I gasped absent-mindedly.

Caesar pointed to the line where the founder of Rome was mentioned.

"There was no Remus at all," he retold with a smile. "Romulus was the only lawful son of Numitor, King of the Latins. He inherited the throne without blood."

"I wouldn't be surprised if he did not rape the Sabine women either," Chaerea laughed.

My brother clicked his tongue and shook his head.

"Romulus was a noble and honest man," I guessed. "Like Old Caesar and Numa Pompilius."

"That's why they ended up murdered," my husband recalled. "All three were worshipped by the common people and the army but hated by the Senate."

"Sounds familiar," Caesar said wittily. "So, when they failed to put a bad king into power, they made up some flaws about the good one."

"To make people follow a bad example," I concluded and returned to the old subject, "What has it got to do with Britannia?"

Caligula took a piece of fresh parchment out of the yellow scroll – a recent report letter – and handed it to me. The ugly handwriting and smaller mistakes belonged to my Gaul servant Falcon, who once lived in a fishing village on the coast of the Oceanus Britannicus.[482]

"When I was a child, long before I got to Rome as a slave," the letter said, *"I witnessed how those strange black flamens tried to smuggle statues of some eastern god into Londinium."*

Frankly, all I knew about the Britons at that time was about a series of unresolved battles with the army of Old Caesar. After long negotiations, the proud tribe reluctantly agreed to be a Roman ally. Yet one day, during the reign of Tiberius, the Britons stopped paying tribute without explanation.

---

[482] The modern-day English channel.

"*Armoricus, the King of the Iceni and the Trinovantes,*"[483] Falcon wrote, "*he drove the uninvited guests away, but for some reason, also slammed the door in the face of the Roman messenger.*"

I tried to imagine those ominous strangers in black. Well, the picture was not strange to me. Black was the color my enemies wore in their damned place of worship.

"The Britons rejected Mithras," I said gladly. "Who is not against us is for us."

"You got it?" Caligula smiled. "We have friends across the pond!"

"Friends, Caesar?" Cassius wondered. "You said those people left our messenger outside the gates at the dead of the night!"

"*Their* messenger, not ours," I reminded him. "We are not *them*, and if it's necessary, we're no longer Rome."

The prefect nodded in approval, and Caligula reached out his hand to us. "I swear to you, all of the enemies will be defeated, and our Rome will flourish again – even stronger than it was with Pompilius!"

Cassius squeezed Caesar's palm, and I joined them as well. The fake war was was the best solution for the real great clash that was about to come. Corbulo announced the rearmament as to prepare for the campaign against Britannia. Just as we wanted it, the news shook every corner of the city and awoke the Forum gossipers.

"It's going to be tough," the soldiers spoke. "The way to the damn strait lies through the most uncertain provinces."

Caesar acted decisively and considerately. He sent two messengers north in strict secretly – one to the misty and rebellious island, and the other to Germania.

"I offered old Armoricus an alliance without tribute," he told me secretly. "I also asked Getullicus to clear our way through the Alps."

Meanwhile, Tigellinus accompanied me to the Taurus amphitheater.

"So, I have six months to prepare a spectacle," I thought aloud as we were riding in the carriage. "Will I manage to do it?"

"There's no other choice, Your Highness," the young tribune said. "Yet, you cannot rely on those actors."

---

[483] The Ancient British tribes.

"I'm not afraid as long as you're with me," I smiled. "They wouldn't dare to mess with you."

"What if they quit?" Tigellinus got earnest. "Your scenario is not for weaklings."

Shivers suddenly embraced me, as his words were echoed by my inner voice.

XXXIV

The coachman's surly face told me something had gone wrong.

"Campus Martius!" He frowned at us. "And some bunch of fools by the circus."

"Watch your mouth," Tigellinus warned him. "These are the actors of the Imperial theater."

"Watch over Lady Ceasonia," Old Rufus, who once served my grandma, warned him back. "This welcome smells like a rebellion to me."

The Greek waved aside and jumped out of the carriage. I cautiously lifted up my veil and moved off the curtain.

"He thinks I'm lying," Rufus murmured. "As if I have no other business!"

What I saw first was a fire. In the middle of the sward, between the passage and the gate, on a bronze pedestal they were burning... fifteen copies of my script, intended for the actors.

"What are you doing?" the young tribune exclaimed angrily.

Quintilia, cold-blooded as always, stepped out of the motley array.

"We are destroying some vain things," she said without pretended meekness. "Just before they destroy Rome."

"What's the slut talking about?" Balding Rufus became irate and left the carriage. I grabbed the bag with the costumes diligently made by Orla and hurried outside as well.

"You'll pay for this!" Tigellinus removed his toga and put out the flame. "All of you!"

Quintilia burst out laughing, followed by her brothers in art.

"For the Republic – without plaguesome peregrines, female writers and tyrannical rulers – we are ready to die!"

I recognized the Mithraistic pathos and reproached my brother in my heart. "From all the women, you have chosen the worst one!"

As he sensed a fight, Tigellinus nodded to Rufus. An ill-tempered coachman stepped to him, threatening Quintilia with a horse whip.

"Now," Caesar's favorite turned to the other actors. "You three will get yours."

The young Greek pulled out his gladius, and moved toward to the coachman as to cover me.

"Let's show them!" the tall actress shouted, and all the fifteen rushed to attack us. Tigellinus was dexterous enough to beat the strongest two. Rufus, with the help of his long crop, disarmed the third one.

"Leave Calliope to me!" Quintilia snarled, and she headed towards me. I removed my veil and welcomed her with a blow from my fist. The actress moaned and knelt in pain.

"Your Highness?!" Rufus recognized me. "How?"

"Watch out!" Tigellinus warned him, but it was too late. The fourth actor used the old man's instant disregard to stab him in the back.

"Rufus!" I shouted, and used all my wrath to beat Quintilia unconscious. The young tribune, with the last ounce of his strength, repelled the attack of the others.

"Help!" The plain of Campus Martius echoed my scream as I ran to my friend.

Another actor threw his head back, laughing.

"What are you going to do, Princess?" He pointed at me. "This scene was not included in your play!"

Lightning-fast, I got the coachman's whip off the ground and flapped with it, slapping the man on his chest and face.

"What about this one?" I asked theatrically.

The wounded man collapsed on the grass. Meanwhile, Tigellinus successfully defeated two more actors.

"Noli moveri!"[484] I heard Calvisius' voice and the thud of horses' hoofs behind me. "Vigiles Urbani!"

The ones who were still alive tried to escape, but the horsemen quickly surrounded them.

"What is it, Princess?" Justus hurried to dismount from his crow horse.

---

[484] (lat.) Do not move!

"The first rehearsal," I laughed nervously, pointed at Tigellinus. "Without him, it would be the last one as well."

"Your Highness," the Greek whispered, "it was *you* who saved *me*."

"Tace," I tore my veil in half and wrapped it around his wounded shoulder. "What the hell, who cares? You did your best."

Tigellinus looked at me with admiration.

"How can I repay you?"

"Teach me how to fight," I replied earnestly. "Cassius never would."

"Princess, you're already good," he smiled. "Much better than the better part of our trainees."

I waved aside. "Get in the carriage," I commanded him. "I guess someone will take us back to the palace."

Calvisius, examining the bodies, stopped beside bloody Quintilia. "The woman is alive," he said. "She isn't gravely wounded."

"Take her with the others," I ordered. "Wait until she's back to her senses, and then kill her."

The prefect put Quintilia on a horseback without question while his son gave me a startled look.

"Killing in war is no murder," I reminded Justus, and then nodded to dead Rufus. "Better take care of this old hero's funeral."

The feast on the Palatine was in its full swing. My brother wanted the whole of Rome to celebrate the military campaign. I heard the merry sounds of sistrums, flutes and tympanums from triclinium. Priscus and Lupus, already tipsy, were singing some bawdy song in the atrium.

"Tigellinus?" The blond guardsman rubbed his eyes. "What's on with you?"

"He was defending me from evildoers," I replied, annoyed. "While you were busy with worshipping Bacchus!"

"Forgive us, Princess!" Lupus straightened up his back, suppressing drunken laughter. "But, wasn't it your wish to be escorted by Tigellinus?"

"Silence!" I pushed them both away. "Now march and bring Alcaeus here or I will fuck you up!"

My ill-temper got them sober in no time. As the young men ran to peristyle, I asked Tigellinus to join me on the bench.

"Your Highness, I've been thinking," he spoke worriedly. "Would these bastards dare to challenge us if Cassius was there?"

"I don't think so." I shrugged my shoulders. "Why?"

"Someone sneaks on us," the Greek whispered. "Probably, the one who stole the signet."

"And the letter." I sighed. "You have good intuition, Tigellinus."

"Thank you." He returned the look – a little nervous and moved, and leaned his injured shoulder against the backrest. "And I also guess, you are preparing for Britannia."

"Hush!" I placed a finger before my lips. "I will not let Caligula do stupid things across the Alps."

"You're brave." The tribune smiled. "But what about your play?"

"I have my guard," I replied calmly. "I am sure you're far better actors than those peasants."

"Who will play the King?" the young man asked. "I believe…"

I looked into his eyes, slowly took the helmet off his head, and placed it on my own.

"I will."

XXXV

Before the Romans stood on a new warpath, Caesar formed the XV legion, commanded by our old acquaintance Publius Gabinius. In the times of the rebellions in Bonna and North Illyricum, Gabinius gained his fame of a conscientious and sharp-sighted fighter. My father, as well as legatus Caecina,[485] recognized the full worth of his loyalty.

"Primigenia will be the unite of the devoted warriors," Caligula opened the sitting in the Senate. "For the road across the Middle Rhine is not so easy."

Corbulo, still unaware of Caesar's peaceful goal, responded readily. "Your will is a duty to me!"

However, Gaius had another plan for his 'public brother-in-law.'

"You stay in Rome, as the temporary governor," my brother notified him.

The warlord reluctantly nodded, and then imperceptibly showed to Vespasian.

"What shall we do about him?" he whispered.

"The Praetor, as well as his brother, are going with me," Gaius said unemotionally. "As the wise warlord of Serica said – keep your friends close, but the enemies closer."

While the officers admired the madman's' prudence, his 'dead' sister also held a council with her companions. That evening, I invited to the viridarium all trusted friends, including even Dion of Misenum. To the surprise of all the women, David was the first one to support me in my war plans.

"Not every woman is made just for cooking and swaddling," the Rabbi said admiringly. "Yet the Lord created for us Deborah, the fair judge, Esther, the scholar queen, and Judith the brave heroine."

"Oh really?" Susanna frowned. "She is a mother now. How can she leave her child?"

The fresh soldier Daniel, excitedly awaiting his first war, retorted, "Look who is talking! You are paid to be a nursemaid, aren't you?"

---

[485] A Roman politician and general, a legate during the German wars.

"Easy, young man!" Rachel protested. "Do you think a weak young woman can ride on horseback over the lands just like that?"

"I admit, I am lazy like hell," I broke in. "I hate housework as much as I hate Mithras, yet even that does not make me a weakling!" Tigellinus emboldened me with a thumbs-up gesture, so I carried on. "My mentor says I'm doing fine."

"She's doing great, even left-handed," the Praetorian addressed to all the guests. "If you could see Her Highness wielding a long sword, you'd stop this prattle!"

The women, still upset, fell silent. From my early years, Susannah was suspicious of my innate left-handedness, so she tried hard to 'cure' me. Still, neither tying the wrong hand during the meal, nor telling scary tales could help her. I grew up ambidextrous, but with more confidence in my left hand.

"Does it matter?" the priest asked me again. "They say King David was left-handed, too. He struck down Goliath with a slingshot in his small left hand!"

"King Alexander and Old Caesar were left-handed," Tigellinus smiled. "I heard such people are extremely gifted."

Acte was observing us from her gilded cradle, smiling at her mother in manner that seemed strangely reasonable, for a baby.

"When you grow up, you'll understand me, girl," I said to her, perhaps the same words Annaea Helvilla told her father when he was a child. "Your parents will come back – i tan i epi tas."[486]

Actaeon, worried and amazed at the same time, wished me good luck. Callistus, seemingly preoccupied with mandates, orders, and official letters, impassively wondered what I was going to tell Caesar.

"Gaius will find out halfway," I replied. "I'll wear a military dress with a full-face helmet."

"A Greek helmet?" Actaeon asked enthusiastically.

"Sure," I nodded. "When we reach Provincia,[487] I'll give Caligula a surprise."

Orla, a bit sad, served us with the strong young wine and raised a toast.

---

[486] "With this, or upon this" – a Greek saying, which meant that a soldier could only return home either victorious (with their shield in hand) or dead (carried upon it).

[487] Narbonne (Transalpine) Gaul, modern-day Provence.

"Ave Morrigan!" she exclaimed together with Fedlimid. "Bottoms up!"

After the first sip, Callistus finally addressed me. "Are you taking Susannah with you?" he joked.

I shook my head, and slightly pushed the tribune with my elbow. "Now I have another nursemaid."

Tigellinus choked on a sip of wine, coughing and laughing at the same time.

Cassius met my decision with a lot of understanding. "We're not like the others," he said. "For us, separation might be worse than war and death."

"Mars is for war, and Libitina is for death," I replied wittily. "Do not they always go together?"

XXXVI

The presence of my husband, corky song of other horsemen, and the perfectly made lightweight equipment kept the new, mysterious decurion firm in the saddle. When our squadron took a stop for a night rest, Chaerea asked me quietly, "How are you feeling?"

"Great," I replied, intentionally in a deeper voice. "I feel like I was born a rider."

"Just be careful," Tigellinus whispered, as he took my targe and spear. "The Cretan is still far away. The Imperial troop will only join us at the border."

"I said I'm alright," I waved aside and looked toward the camp. "Better tell me when are we going to eat? I'm hungry like Charybdis!"

My husband, now Praefectus equitum and Caesar's adjutant, gave me a gentle smile and sent the tribune to set up our tent.

"By gods, dried meat!" Tigellinus exclaimed. "Our Caesar is so generous!"

Before we left, Caligula supplied all of the escorting cavalry with bags of food as heavy as lead, loaded on strong mules.

"First, you consume your personal supplies," he warned the men. "This, you shall open only as you reach Cisalpine Gaul."

"Not posca, but true Samos wine!" another horseman cheered.

"Don't overdo it with this wine!" I frowned. "Mix it with water, or you'll fall off the horses!"

"That's right, decurion!" Cassius encouraged me and addressed the whole turma. "After we have a meal, we'll decide which of us is going out on reconnaissance and who is staying here to watch the camp."

Our side of Gaul was made of bright, river-filled woodlands. Once conquered with no special efforts during the Republic's prime, the province opened our ways to the north. Its inhabitants soon became Roman allies, most of them in exchange for the citizenship.

"There is no danger of Gauls here," Cassius explained. "But from the Germans, who attack them from over the Alps."

"Germans?" The Athenian rubbed his eyes. "Didn't we drive them away to the north?"

"Yes we did... formally," I replied sadly. "Yet *the East* has helped them turn back home."

"They, too, adopted Mithras, didn't they?" the tribune whispered.

I looked up to the sky and fell thoughtful. Suddenly a blinding bright star shot from the moonless ink-colored canvas. As it fell down over the horizon, leaving a golden train behind, I got the answer from my childhood memories.

"It's midnight." My memory started with Armida's sullen face. *"Why aren't you sleeping, Domina?"*

"Susannah always tells me stories from her land," I reproached the nursemaid. *"Don't you, Germans, have some tales?"*

"Of course, we do," the German grinned. *"You want a scary tale?"*

I nodded.

"Good." She squinted cunningly. *"Once upon a time, mighty Wuotan created the first humans – out of boredom. They were small, naked, helpless like a pack of blind puppies, straggling around just to survive. Vodan's wife Skadi, to entertain her lord, immersed the middle earth in winter. The gods laughed and toasted to their ingenuity, watching those weakly creatures die of cold and hunger. This lasted for hundreds of years, until our celebrated Loki started saving fire on the bank of the Rhine."*

"It's Prometheus!" I giggled. Her legend reminded me of the famous myth. *"You stole a hero from the Greeks!"*

Armida fell silent, casting a mad look at me.

"Why are you angry?" I asked naughtily. *"Is it for what I said about the Germans, or because you failed to scare me?"*

The young woman waved aside. *"You are fearless indeed."* She frowned. *"Just like Hel, goddess of death."*

Susannah, as she heard my laughter, hurried to my room.

"If you cannot put a child to sleep," she rebuked the German, *"then be quiet and clean the library."*

I hugged the older nanny, sending the younger one off with my tongue stuck out.

"Don't listen to these hearsays," Susannah addressed me. *"God-Creator is not evil, but the one who opposes him is a seductor and a liar."*

Almost twenty years had passed since then. Soon after that, I learned from the war diaries of Tiberius that the rebellious god Loki joined the Germanic pantheon just by the end of Augustus' reign.

"Yes, they embraced him," I replied to Tigellinus. "Yet under another name."

The better part of the army joined us on the bank of Eridanus.[488]

"You live?" Alcaeus joked, taking advantage of the tumult around the emperor.

"Miracles happen," I joked back. "Look at yourself – you're back to soldier's dress."

My friend proudly pointed to the big bronze emblem on his belt.

"You like it?"

"Why a bull?" I asked, as I took a closer look at the girdle. "Isn't the emperor's symbol a lion?"

"I am Caesar's servant indeed," he said earnestly. "But, above all, I am a Cretan, a Minoan, and that makes me proud."

"I know," I tapped him on his shoulder. "I hope you're not a minotaur as well."

The medic laughed, and then lifted and lowered his eyebrow. "I guess, it depends on the woman I'm with."

"Shame on you," I pushed him with my elbow jokingly, and turned around to see my brother. Gaius was just entering his tent alone. Down on the glade, the better part of the praetorians were gathering around the fire. There was no better opportunity for me to talk to my brother unnoticed.

"Here we are in Narbo," the physician changed the subject. "We'll make it to Bonna with ease."

I nodded absently and headed for the tent.

"Where are you going, Princess?" the Greek wondered.

"Don't come near," I warned him, walking. "Zeus the thunderer will surely throw some lightnings."

---

[488] The modern-day Po River.

The warden by the tent, decanus[489] called Tigris, blocked my way.

"Watchword!" he demanded as he noticed me.

"Meow," I smiled calmly.

"Are you playing a fool, officer?" The guardsman frowned. "What is the watchword?"

"Meow-meow!" I giggled in my real voice. "What kind of *tiger* are you if you don't speak the cats' language?"

"Princess?" Tigris recognized me. "What… are you doing here?"

"Rehearsing my role," I replied. "Are you learning yours?"

"Oh, I will!" the guardsman said excitedly. "I've never been on stage, but always…"

"Great," I interrupted him, and moved a linen door aside to enter.

Curled up like a baby on a hastily made bed, Caligula was sleeping. I was startled when I noticed equestrian blisters on those gentle hands, and much dust on his trampled legionary boots.

"Just sleep, my dear," I whispered, and sat silently beside him.

"Cassius?" The young man whispered in his sleep, as he sensed someone's presence.

"Almost," I replied, and gently moved a curl from his forehead.

"What?" he muttered, waking up. "You?"

"I'm alright," I stroked his hand. "I have come with the cavalry."

Caligula, still sleepy, flinched and sat up on his bed.

"Why didn't you tell me?"

"Would you have let me then?" I answered with another question wittily.

"Of course I wouldn't," he said huffily, wrapping himself in a blanket. "This is not a pleasure trip."

"Life is no pleasure trip either," I sighed. "But still, we live it."

Caesar nodded, and then changed his tone to softer. "So you rode on horseback the whole time?"

---

[489] In Roman army – a leader of a contubernium, the squad of eight legionaries that lived in the same tent and the two support units of the contubernium.

I reached out my hands and stirred my fingers, a bit stuff from holding a bridle.

"I'm so proud of you," he whispered, reaching for my hand to kiss it. This gesture was unusual for him, yet sincere, moving me to tears.

"I am proud of you too," I replied, and fixed a blanket on his chest. "Go back to sleep. I'm going outside."

Gaius looked at me in his unrepeatable manner – warmly, with a thimbleful of daring sensuality. His charm was the reason they called him a lecher. Yet, Caligula was never vicious, he just loved this life and seized his here and now. As he leaned his head on a small pillow and squinted, I hurried to leave.

"Sister dear," his voice stopped me.

"Do you love me more… when I'm like that?" he asked uncertainly, trying to fix his rumpled sagum.

"Now you look more manly," I smiled. "As for my love, it's unconditional, but sisterly."

Caesar's blue eyes became sad and disappointed. The further conversation would have been bitter and meaningless.

"I'll never be good enough, right?" he went on. "I worshipped you, I gave you everything… Why can't I be the one?"

"Because you are not Cassius." I shook my head and left the tent.

The next morning, by the ramparts of Narbo, I was welcomed by a matchless sight. Almost all of the centuria was busy rearranging an old military rostrum to a… theatrical stage. None of the soldiers now seemed wearful, nor overoccupied with trainings.

"Hail, Augusta!" Clemens greeted me, waving with a large, dark and thick linen screen. "Look, what I've got from the Gauls – a curtain!"

"Macte!"[490] I clapped my hands and headed towards them.

"Since we are playing this, we'll do our best not to embarrass you!" Aquila spoke from under the stage stairs.

As I was coming up, Tigellinus quickly quitted polishing the shields, and rushed to meet me.

---

[490] (lat.) Well done!

"None of us were born an actor," he said shyly. "But there is no man in Rome who wouldn't like to be a warrior to Alexander – at least for a day!"

"We'll learn our lines between the trainings!" Tigris said. "You will be proud of us, Your Highness!"

"I believe in you," I smiled. "A good man is good at everything."

"That's right!" Alcaeus joined the company. "Still, don't forget that Sabinus, Vespasian and their cohorts will be close to us in Bonna."

"Fuck them all!" I spat on the ground juicily and kicked the mud with my boot. "We still have time."

The soldiers went back working, and the Cretan bowed to me theatrically.

"Now you tell me, girl – who are you?" he wondered earnestly. "Not even Alexander had your courage, grace and wisdom."

"Do not flatter me," I shook my head. "Have I achieved anything special yet?"

"… and your modesty." Alcaeus smiled and showed to our improvised stage. "Here you are, dispersing Mithras' regiment; restoring former glory of the Roman army."

"Am I?" I replied with irony, not believing in my repute.

"I am here because of you," the medic went on honestly. "You made me learn the biggest lesson of my life."

"Like what?" I asked confusedly. He came closer to my ear, and whispered.

"Omnia fieri possunt.[491] We were not made for surrender."

---

[491] (lat.) Everything is possible.

XXXVII

"Who are those people and where do they come from?" Alexander asked the priest of the Smoke Land.

"*Their skin is dark, and their eyes black,*" the man replied. "*Their bodies are hairy, and the language they speak in is strange. They do not want our tribute, nor negotiations; all they long for is our horror, pain and death! These people resemble us only by looks, for their nature is a mouth of a fire mountain, a demonic tumult...*"

"*These are the offspring of the demon, children of his son.*" I turned to Tigris, who had learned his lines extremely fast. "*God wished to wipe them out, sending the flood to earth, yet the evil one managed to hide his bastards in the lands of setting sun, where the sea pillars hold up heavens.*"

"*They are coming, my Lord King,*" one of the foreigners spoke out. "*I see turbulent waves breaking, ground cracking, and the whirlwind devastating...* "

All the actors of this act held their breath, awaiting my reply. I looked upon the guardsmen one by one, then glanced at the Gaul bodyguard by the door, and finally looked up at a gable rooftop of the tent.

"*With God's help,*" I said, minding my voice, "*This very day we will sail to the end of the world to put this plague in chains!*"

"*So mote it be!*" the priest called out, hitting the ground with his wand. "*I'm giving you the bravest soldiers of our army. If you save us, we'll be worshiping your god as the Most High!*"

"Easy, tiger." I addressed the guardsman. "Don't forget where we are staying, and who's sharing the stronghold with us."

Decanus covered his mouth with the hand to calm his fervor. Clemens ran to the tent door, and looked outside. The castrum streets were quiet. The torch-lit clepsydra was announcing the third watch of the night. It was time to finish our rehearsal.

Staying in Bonna reminded me of my childhood. Two legions, led by Gaetullicus, were constantly repelling attacks from the south, while Primigenia stayed in the settlement to protect the civilians. Caesar was staying in the tower, waiting for the fight to end. Upset about his hiding in a fortress, he amused himself with the formation games.

Both Flavians – Vespasian and Sabinus – now were separated from their cohorts, doing some humiliating work about the castle. That night, Gaius held a council with my husband and two Gallic governors.

"Don't you find it suspicious?" he said, spreading out a war map on the desk. "The Germans steered clear of us while we were moving, but they suddenly attacked the settlement, when we arrived."

"It's not about the land," Plinius spoke thoughtfully, as he pointed to the conquered area between the Weser and the Rhine. "Our legions are far stronger, we have Gauls…"

"Someone wants to hold us down in Bonna as long as it's possible," Galba estimated, "To thwart us from our plans about Britannia!"

"Is it our Praetor, or his brother?" Chaerea asked.

"Not really," My brother nodded to the quarters. "Both of them are here. Vespasian is peeling beans, and Sabinus baking some bread, while their soldiers are led by Otho."

Caesar's maneuvers weren't always understood even by our loyal warriors. As they all had a good laugh about the cooking Flavians, Cassius carefully addressed him.

"I know you hate wars, and you don't know much about the warfare," he said. "Still, I suppose that you should be more cautious, when it comes to military ranks, formation, duties and so on. Legionnaires can rebel."

"I know what I'm doing," my brother replied. "I separated oxen and the cabbage – for the common good."

"That's great, Caesar," Galba sighed. "But who incited the damn Germans now to start the fire? Who has authority on both sides?"

There was one man indeed, who managed to unite the conquered tribes of defiant Germania… yet, at a price of his loyalty.

"Lentulus Gaetullicus." Cassius figured out. "Even the barbarians, who do understand our speech, believe his lies."

My brother rolled his eyes, trying to hide his confusion.

"Chaerea," he smiled, "Which part of my notebook should I put him in? "The Dagger" or "The Sword"?"

The whole of Rome was trembling on the very mention of that notebook, which contained the names of people whom he wanted to prosecute or execute. "The Sword" usually meant decapitation or a quicker death, while "The Dagger" could have been quite... inconvenient.

"You are the judge," My husband said.

Caligula waved aside.

"Let it be sword. I'm a merciful ruler."

"Will there not be a trial?" Galba asked.

Plinius nodded.

"What if we are wrong?"

Once innocent Helicon fell a victim to our unjust accusation, for we couldn't see the real culprit.

"Sure." My brother frowned. "Now you go out and end that German circus, and bring me Getullicus."

The startled governors did as he said. Meanwhile, Gaius looked so weary, that the prefect brought him a wide chair to sit.

"I do not have time to inquiry," he said, finally leaning his back on the rest. "I'll let my sister decide on his destiny."

"Whom, Caesar?" Chaerea got astonished.

"Your wife," Gaius explained. "Since she's already here, let her expose the sleazebag, and judge him as well."

By his command, the governors sent reinforcement all to the border of two Germanias.[492] Taken aback by the sudden arrest of Gaetullicus, the barbarians retreated to the woods. Galba, motivated with the easy victory, captured Apronius, one of the officers, for he could be an ally of the culprit. Our loyal soldiers also trapped Maroboduus – the Germanic leader, who now played Arminius, uniting all the local tribes against the emperor.

---

[492] *Germania Inferior* was a Roman province, located on the west bank of the Rhine and bordering the North Sea. *Germania Superior* encompassed parts of modern-day Switzerland, southwest Germany and eastern France, while Germania Inferior encompassed much of modern-day Belgium and Netherlands.

"Quid facete?" Gaetullicus spoke out, riding behind common soldiers like a hostage.

"Caesar missed you," a young rider joked.

When they arrived to Bonna, Gaius didn't bother to show up. To make things odder, the comrades-in-arms didn't get Gaetullicus imprisoned, but without a word left him in a Praetorian tent by the stable. As he came to himself, hoping for the worst to be behind him, he addressed his neighbor.

"Do they clean this stable at all?"

A good-looking horseman looked at him indifferently and continued reading.

"Who the hell are you?" Lentulus tried to sound intrepid. "And what book is that?"

Without another glance, the guardsman pointed at the title of the scroll – "TONITRUS[493]…"

The governor burst out laughing.

"Are you damn Sulpicia?"[494]

"*I have existed from the morning of the world*," the young man read aloud, "*And I shall exist until the last star falls from the night…*"

"You are as mad as your Caesar," Gaetullicus whispered. "Who knows why that is good."

"Like Caesar my ass!" the eques laughed. "Sometimes I'm dying to dispatch him."

The old governor grew earnest, and came up to the young soldier.

"It's no good." He shook his head. "He's mad indeed, but his advisers are proficient."

"Have you tried?" The stranger winked at him.

Gaetullicus' face changed several expressions – from just curiosity through slight distrust to finally exposing jubilation.

"What is it to you?" he asked excitedly.

"Caligula knows nothing." The young man was tempting on. "You have like-minded friends here."

---

[493] (lat.) Thunder [Perfect Mind].
[494] One of the few female poets of ancient Rome.

"Tell the Sun Runner that I'm ready," the governor replied decisively.

That very moment, the mysterious knight took off his helmet and released his long light-brown curls. Gaetullicus turned pale. I turned around, so he could see me well, and called out for the guardsmen.

"Princess, please, have mercy!" the governor shouted. "I want peace!"

Alleged remorse and tears could waver Julia Drusilla, but Sophia had enough of Mithras on her way.

"I don't believe in peace with enemy," I quickly pulled my sword out of its holster, "Only in victory over him."

Meanwhile, unbridled, merry songs were coming from the castrum square. The soldiers celebrated Caesar's victory over the hated barbarians, calling my brother "Castorum Filius"[495] and "Pater Exercituum."[496] Aquila and Tigellinus took the dead body outside, and I, after long time, again felt deep fatigue and prickling of my scar.

"I'm gone to sleep," I told to the rest of the guardsmen. "See you in rehearsal tonight."

---

[495] (lat.) Son of the camp.
[496] (lat.) Father of the armies.

XXXVIII

Gallia Belgica[497] saw us off with her rocky and steep banks, smelling like tree-day rain. Caletum,[498] northern port of the Old Caesar, with its warships and lighthouse on a cliff, looked kind of dull and gray. Dark waters of the foreign sea looked so hostile, as if their fatal depths and coldness were to warn us of the fierce and proud nature of the islanders.

"Basically, the Britons are not united," the Old Caesar wrote in his War diaries. *"All of their tribes are different. The Trinovantes worship their land – they grow grains, rear cattle; they are rich in copper, too. Briefly, those are strong, hardworking, but not very clever people. Their closest neighbors, the Catuvellauni, can be drawn as skillful merchants, who believe in power of a coin. For the sake of trade, they even can pretend they're hospitable to the foreigners. The greatest warriors of the island are the Iceni. Their men are headstrong, belligerent and sharp-witted. Their patroness they trust is the War goddess. At the cost of their lives, Iceni will not bow to other gods or rulers. We will have a lot of trouble with this tribe. I must admit, those are the opponents I like."*

The sudden arrival of a Vigile messenger interrupted my reading. Corbulo was keeping a close eye on all the preparation for my brother's triumph. The senators were forced to build a large triumphant arch within six months. The slaves were not allowed to help the "masons", so the nobles had to rise and dawn and drag themselves to the Capitol and to work extremely hard. Fear for their lives turned out to be stronger than pride, so the results were even not so bad. The mobs, so happy to humiliate the odious patricians, didn't miss a chance to egg them. Along with the warlord's report, I also received a short note from my friend. Messalina had learned she was pregnant again.

"If she gives me a son," Gaius said with delight, "when we win the Great war, I will marry her, and make our child an heir."

---

[497] A province of the Roman Empire located in the north-eastern part of Roman Gaul, in what is today primarily France, Belgium, and Luxembourg, along with parts of the Netherlands and Germany.

[498] Modern-day Calais.

So optimistic and self-confident, we planned together to expose our enemies and their misdeeds at the Palatine Games. It seemed so obvious that our people, as they see Vespasian's true colors, would support us, as well as the Army. After that, uniting forces with the Britons and the Gauls, the Romans would be ready to withstand the possible invasion of Artabanus. Breaking his hellish horde, we hoped to change the world.

That day, I got some bad news, too. My loyal friend Anicetus, a kind Cypriot giant, passed away after a sudden illness. Yet my grief was more of startlement. The keeper of my chambers had been strong and healthy all the way.

"You should have stayed down in the palace," I reproached Alcaeus. "He needed your help!"

"I'm sorry for the colossus," he replied sadly. "Yet I couldn't let you go alone – across the world less that a year after a complex surgery."

"I am alright," I shook my head, and left the carriage. "More or less."

The truth was that I felt fatigue, vertigo and abdomen pain again quickly after we left Bonna. Riding on horseback became tedious, so Tigellinus had to place me to the carriage.

That is the punishment for one more death, I thought, struggling with fever. *Yet you know, my Lord, I had no choice. Unless I killed, I'd have been murdered alongside the ones I love.*

"Do you want to know what I think, Princess?" the physician asked, a little sharply. "I suggest Anicetus needed a Vigile, not a medic, to protect him."

"He was killed?!" I grabbed my head in horror, suddenly recalling thefts in the palace. "We had time for monkey business, but we haven't found a traitor."

"He is often closer than you think," Alcaeus sighed. "Sometimes as close as friend."

"Do you suspect…?" I stopped by a blue conifer – small, nice, but spiky like a hedgehog.

"Honestly…" The Greek looked up to the cobweb of clouds. "I don't believe any of those who surround you. They love you for your generosity, not for your soul. Those Jews, as well as other Greeks, especially the cinaedus…"

"Callistus?!" I burst out laughing. "Don't speak nonsense!"

"If you say so," the Cretan shrugged. "After all, they are your freedmen."

"Our friends," I corrected him. "I never treated them like servants."

Alcaeus spread his arms in disappointment, shook his head discreetly, and then headed for the tavern.

"Don't get drunk," I warned him. "I need you to be conscious in rehearsal."

He sighed and tapped himself on the chest twice.

I looked to the wharf. The sailors with "EX.GER.INF."[499] unscripted on their armors were getting the vessels ready for the navigation. By the bridge, I saw Tigellinus. A big sea lover, he even stopped his training to enjoy the sight.

"Hephaestion!" I exclaimed. "Are you learning your lines?"

The Praetorian smiled as he heard my voice, and hurried to meet me.

"I know my part by heart," he replied cheerfully. "And, training, too, of course."

"Is there some news from Armoricus?" I asked him quietly and nodded to the ships. "We're ready, if need be."

"Nothing beyond orders," the tribune replied.

Last night, while I was sleeping, a Brittonic messenger arrived. Caligula was so impatient for this meeting that he couldn't wait till dawn, and called the foreign guest right to his tent. One of our Gallic slaves volunteered as an interpreter.

"Old Armoricus is dead," the barbarian said slowly. "His daughter Boudicca is crowning her husband Prasutagus the king."

"The head of the Catuvellauni, right?" my brother wondered. "Should that mean no more discordance on the island?"

"War is bad," the messenger said timidly. "We need comrades."

The stranger, with his long and messy hair, dressed in wide braccae[500] looked at Gaius in a begging manner.

"What do I hear?" My brother shook his head. "The most rebellious people are now looking for allies."

The Briton nodded, and went on with tremor – in both Brittonic and bad Latin.

---

[499] The army of Germania Inferior.
[500] Ancient trousers made from wool.

"All the tribes of the north are uniting," the interpreter explained. "The East is threatening them."

The common enemy, Artabanus, without even knowing it turned Britons toward Rome. Our plans turned out easier to fulfill than we thought. However, those negotiations with someone's servant were far not enough for Caesar.

"Tell the new king I'll be waiting for him here in my tent," Caligula addressed the messenger. "We will discuss our alliance and…" He stopped abruptly, and looked up at the interpreter.

"Now hurry to your homeland," the Gaul spoke to the islander. "You have good news to carry."

The messenger, named Cinbell, plucked up courage to ask Caesar.

"Does this mean that Rome and the Britons are friends?"

My brother laughed, as he sensed the young man's voice naivety, not insolence.

"It depends on your leader," he joked, and corrected himself. "I mean, king."

The next step was to keep the army onshore. For our soldiers, used to breadth and movement, staying in the narrow quarts of the littoral was getting boring. The Flavians, now forced to clean the stables, try to use each opportunity inciting sailors against Caesar.

"Caligula is a coward," Sabinus spoke quietly to the captain. "He procrastinates with the invasion and calls messengers, because he knows he's losing."

Captain Severus, usually earnest and short-spoken, looked at him with a contemptuous smile.

"Caesar is Rome," Scapula, the centurion of naval infantry, spoke out instead. "The Army is Rome, too. We share both victory and fall together with the emperor. Aren't we?"

"You are repeating someone else's words," Sabinus grinned. "Or read too much. Be honest, wouldn't you prefer to be a victor or a loser?"

"Don't tempt," the captain finally replied. "My seamen are not traitors."

"It's not too late to follow my advice, Severus." Vespasian's brother grumbled through his teeth. "Barbarians are going to destroy him —"

"Titus," the young sailor interrupted him, pinching his nose. "You'd better take a bath."

Dozens of sailors and oarsmen saw the tribune off back to the stable with laughter.

"We can wait till Saturnalia, if necessary," Severus decided. "After all, we are paid well."

Meanwhile, my brother was preparing the guardsmen to welcome the important guest. He still had no idea that the person, who was on his way to Caletum, was not the king, but another supreme figure in Britannia.

XXXIX

"The ship is coming! All ashore!" Scapula ordered. Cassius placed the guardsmen in a squad around the dock.

"What kind of forecastle is that?" Severus smiled, as he noticed a raised deck at the front of a ship. "It's not bent backwards like ours, but protruding to attract attention."

The centurion waved aside.

"Silly barbarians," he frowned. Then, looking the strange vessel over, he concluded. "It is not Catuvellauni ship. We have Iceni here!"

Severus sighed and turned to the crew.

"In case of an attack… "

Chaerea, usually restrained and cautious while on duty, suddenly burst out laughing. It was one larger boat arriving. It had no platform for line thrower, so familiar to our sailors. Behind a wooden figure of a foreign goddess on the bow there stood a tall young woman. She had extremely long hair, tied with two ribbons, motley like her dress. Her long neck was adorned with a big torquis – usually a symbol of the high king's power.

"What the hell?" the captain wondered. "Who's that girl?"

"Boudicca," my husband guessed.

The sixteen-year-old daughter of Armoricus, escorted by a dozen of young servants, looked like she came here for some fishing or visiting an old friend. Shameless coughing and laughs echoed the waterfront.

"Let's help her dock," Severus ordered the crew. "It's our guest."

"Well, she's not ugly," the seamen joked. "It's a question of time before Caligula fucks her."

"Do your job and be quiet!" Cassius exclaimed. The young sailors jerked and got earnest in accord.

Boudicca deftly walked on sand and stones, without fear or unrest. Curious about the noise, Caligula left his shore tent. The unexpected sight did not confuse him, on the contrary – it made him very glad.

The queen calmly greeted my brother in Latin, mentioning all the allied tribes of her lands, and then fell silent, waiting for reply.

"Degemer mat, *Buddug*." Caesar smiled and took a closer look at her entourage. "You are brave indeed."

"And you are modest," Boudicca replied, as she accepted his welcoming gesture to the tent. "Your kings are famous for high castles and big palaces they built in every province…"

"I do have it all," My brother yawned. "I'm bored of it."

Two Gauls served Caesar and his guest some seafood appetizers and wine. The host took a seat on a couch and toasted.

"May I ask, my Lady," he winked at the girl. "Why didn't your husband, Prasutagus, honor me with his presence?"

Boudicca, like a child, replied to him with her mouth full.

"In our homeland, the king and queen consort are equal. They support each other in both peace and war. The queen is often a king's deputy."

Caligula observed his lovely guest with curiosity, filling his mouth like her.

"I must admit, this custom is a little odd to me," he smiled. "Yet my sister would have liked it."

Boudicca's eyes, dark blue and wild as sea, took on an expression of sadness.

"I am sorry, Caesar," she whispered. "I know you loved each other very much."

"Let's change the subject," Gaius smiled, and handed her a bowl of dried fruit. "I'm still admiring that courage of yours, dear Buddug. You sailed alone across the seas without a single soldier…"

The young queen straightened her back and said, "*Andraste* is protecting me."

"Who?" Gaius wondered.

That moment, when Armoricus' daughter thought about how she would describe the patroness of the Iceni, someone moved velarium aside. Who was that bold to enter uninvited? A decurion… videlicet a decurioness.

"Oh!" Boudicca turned pale with amazement.

"Calm down, girl. I'm not a ghost," I said in Briton. "I've just played my death, because –"

"Andraste!" Boudicca jumped up to her feet, performing a ritual dance. "O, invincible one!"

"What's going on here?" Caesar was astonished, and said to her, "I did really enjoy watching you, Buddug, but I think you're mixed the things up. That's my sister."

The young queen gave him a bit of an offensive look and stepped to me.

"It is a sign!" She raised her hands. "I saw you in my dream the night my father died."

I reassured my brother with a calming gesture and reached out to Boudicca.

"My name is Julia Drusilla, married Chaerea." I smiled. "Optionally, Morrigan, Andraste et cetera."

"It's crazy!" Gaius grabbed his head. "Have you come here to mess up my negotiations?"

With the twinkling of an eye, the queen pulled out from her girdle a small dagger – thin, but sharp like a Gallic needle, and extended it in the direction of his chest.

"How you dare you, mortal man, insult the goddess!" she exclaimed indignantly.

Caligula jerked back in panic.

"Toss this, Buddug, now!" I ordered her. "I'm not a goddess of the murderers."

The girl obeyed and spoke embarrassedly.

"Protect us, venerated one! The dark-skinned people want to capture us and take our newborns!"

"First, calm down." I hugged her and glanced at my brother. "You, too. What a sissy are you to be scared of a child!"

"A child has almost killed me!" Gaius went upset. "How can you hug her?"

"Now shut up, and let me work it out," I whispered.

Reckless and open-minded like all the adolescents, Boudicca shared with us the story of her people, mentioning the Old Caesar's visit to Britannia.

"My great-grandfather told my father how noble and wise man he was," she said warmly. "Old Caesar respected out warriors, and didn't want our king to obey Rome, but to be allies."

The Romans helped the islanders rebuild fortifications, and the strong-willed Iceni didn't protest against paying tribute to new friends. The alliance had lasted for decades, even some years after the Old Caesar's death – until Augustus started his secret campaign on the behalf of Mithridates. The new ruler spoke of Pax Romana – the cessation of hostilities with the barbarians, but this policy was just to serve his plans of spreading the new cult among the provinces and allied lands.

"We didn't want to worship a bloodthirsty deity," the queen explained. "So my grandfather said, and broke the alliance with Rome."

"And what about Tiberius?" My brother asked. "What do your people say about him?"

"He didn't care about us," Boudicca shook her head, "He only fought the Germans."

Gaius didn't hide astonishment.

"How is it possible that they just let you be?"

The young woman smiled mysteriously, nodding towards me.

"Our Patroness was watching over us."

On behalf of the united Briton tribes, Boudicca renewed the allegiance, so Caligula appointed her a client ruler.

"From now on, Caesar, my entire army is at your disposal," the young woman said contentedly. "Let us welcome Artabanus with the Briton spears."

"And Roman swords," Gaius went on.

"And Gallic arrows, Sir." One of the servants spoke excitedly.

"Do not forget about the Greeks," I hugged them both – my brother, and our guest. "There will be more!"

Boudicca clapped her hands with joy, reminding me of three-year-old Octavia. After we escorted her alongside with her maids-in-waiting to the summerhouse, Gaius and I went back to the port.

"What will we do about them?" I nodded to the soldiers. "The fellows will be very disappointed."

"Don't worry, little sister," Gaius replied calmly. "Bring me Chaerea."

"Have you just commanded me?" I laughed and put my helmet on.

"You're a decurion, and I'm your emperor," he spoke out after me, while I was riding off.

Cassius mounted his black horse, and galloped to the ruler's tent, while I, as "ordered" by my brother, hid in the port tavern.

The makeshift garrison on the foreland began humming.

"There will be war." Sabinus rubbed his bony hands. "I cannot stand to pluck those weeds."

"You're talking like a peasant," Alcaeus replied. "I'm not surprised why women do not like you."

Vespasian's brother prepared for another tirade, but my husband's return forestalled him.

"Forma – ad aciem!"[501] Cassius shouted, raising his sword.

Taken aback by a combat orders, the officers looked to the ships, and all around. It seemed that Caesar suddenly changed strategy, appointing a new legate… or warlord.

"Parati!!!"

Forming a column hastily, both cavalry and infantry started their clumsy march toward the sea.

"Pugna! Celeriter!"[502] Cassius pointed to the sea. "Impetus!"[503]

The hundreds of soldiers rushed forward, brandishing their weapons. Only Alcaeus still remained in place, exchanging merry glances with Chaerea.

"Meus caparum Romanus – ad Victoria!"[504] The Cretan called after the fighters.

Caligula was laughing, watching them through the small window.

"You want to kick ass," he spoke lazily, so proud of his idea. "Go attack Neptune."

On the other side of the sea coast, in front of the rotunda tavern, cooks and fishermen lined up like the spectators at the theater to observe the battle with the waves.

---

[501] (lat.) Form battle lines!

[502] (lat.) Battle! Quickly!

[503] (lat.) Attack!

[504] (lat.) My Roman troops - To Victory!

"What trophies will they bring to Rome?" An old man with no teeth giggled to me. "Some mermaid tails?"

"How dare you!" I laughed back. "We're bringing a hundred of chests with the seashells as a gift to Roman Senate."

XL

Traveling exhaustion was growing into insomnia. The sleepless nights of early winter fed my ailments, bringing back the hardest thoughts. As we passed Genua and its surroundings, I finally agreed to drink Alcaeus' new tincture, which I wanted him to keep as long as possible in case one of the soldiers got some heavy injuries. The bitter liquid and moonlit pointed roofs of some Ligurian settlement insensibly submerged me into a deep dream.

On the dark side of the moon, I saw the outlines of a strange city – grimy and noisy, full of *Trojan horses* and apathetic figures. The silhouettes were moving fast, but with no visible enthusiasm or even goal around the large steel squares, as if some evil spirits chased them. Despite the distance between me and them, I was able to feel their despair.

Am I in hell? I thought, trying to suppress my fear with curiosity.

"No. You are not." Someone invisible replied. His voice was so unearthly pleasant and familiar.

"What's wrong with them?" I pointed to the leaden crowd. "Who is making them flee?"

"Nobody is." There was the answer. "They have chosen it."

"Wait," I looked up. "How can anyone love it?"

"They can't love anymore." The calm voice gained a note of grief. "They do not want to."

It sent shivers down my spine.

"Where am I?" I exclaimed. "Who are you?"

"It doesn't matter where, but when," the Voice replied. "This is the end of time."

I fell thoughtful and silent. Suddenly, one of the apparitions noticed me, and pointed a finger at me. The better part of passers-by stopped and stared at me, whispering. Another moment someone brought the vision closer, so I could see their faces. Some of them were making fun of me, the others hated me, the rest… was raising their weapons.

"Why?" I jerked, trying to hide behind the Invisible One. "They do not even know me!"

"You are not their kind," the Voice responded. "If they knew who you are, the things would be a whole lot worse."

"Semangelof?!" My soul recognized one of the angels.

The baleful sight disappeared on the spur of the moment, but my guardian did not appear embodied.

Does this mean that Vespasian is going to win? I asked in my heart. *Are all our efforts in vain?*

The old acquaintance read my mind and answered, "In the God's name, nothing is in vain."

I laughed. "You never knew how to console."

"You were impatient," he explained. "You never wanted to go with the flow."

The sounds, images and smells of the ominous future dulled my senses.

"You have seen the end, but not *the endless*," Semangelof said. "There might be a lot of people, but not all. Those days won't come tomorrow."

"Will it change…?" I whispered with the last ounce of my strength.

The answer came within another apparition. The huge book of a divine look came down to fill the whole space in front of me. In awe, I touched its handle. The scroll opened on its own, like in a legend.

"The Mother of Rome gave birth to a righteous woman," I read it aloud. *"The one of great deeds and deep faith. Her offspring will bring back the peace to the house of her father. The good lineage will be carried on in centuries."*

Having uttered the last word, I felt the heat under my fingers, and jerked back. The book disappeared, as it left two burns – on my thumb and forefinger.

"Photice told me," I recalled, addressing to the angel, "she will meet my daughter and my daughter's daughter to baptize them…"

"You will not be there," Semangelof replied.

The sensation of burning left my fingers, swiftly entering my heart. The wormwood of tomorrow echoed in my head with one and only question – more painful than hell.

"Me and Cassius…" I gasped.

Semangelof did not let me choke in my tears.

"The man, who was created for your sake, will follow you," he said. *"For in the Father's house are many mansions."*

As I calmed down a bit, I asked about the fate of our uprising, but I got no answer, but a warning.

"He, who shares the table with a sinner, will taste the wine of betrayal."

The morning gleam breaks my vision, and the angelic voice mixes with the human sounds.

"An enemy to God can't be your friend."

I finally woke up. The horses in the carriage were still resting, and Alcaeus was sitting by me to watch over.

"Bonum mane, Princess." He rubbed his swollen eyes. "How are you feeling?"

I reached out and moved the small curtain aside. Through the bare branches of the deciduous forest, I saw the town walls.

"While you were sleeping like a log," Alcaeus smiled, "here we are in Tarquinia."

As I didn't feel a trace of my recent helplessness, I jumped out of the carriage.

"Little Owl, where are you going?" the Greek asked me worriedly, following me outside.

I stepped on the ground of Latium[505] still thinking of the last words of the angel.

"You are right." I turned to the physician. "It's my friend who betrayed me."

Alcaeus squinted in confusion and came closer. He must have known how I felt, so he hugged me in a fatherly manner, leaning my head on his shoulder.

"We'll thrash it all out," he sighed. "There is no mystery. Helicon was executed, Protogenes is too old for plots, so…"

"Callistus."

My eyes filled with tears. Despite both human logic and heavenly warning, I still did not want to believe he was guilty. While the Cretan was enumerating all the sins

---

[505] The region of central western Italy, which was the cradle to Roman Empire.

of Callistus' past, my blind and deaf heart of a friend recalled those nice and witty moments.

"I can't accuse him just like that," I stated sadly. "He has been with me when all the others…"

"Callistus is no fool," the Greek retorted. "Your rise helped him feather his nest. Now, as he is free and rich, the senators can take him seriously."

My insight let my confidence grasp at the very last straw.

"Narcissus was a spy too," I concluded. "I'll put him to the test as well."

"Minoans say – stay far away from those who don't love anyone," Alcaeus said. "But, above all, avoid a fool who loves the worthless."

I turned my back on him, so I no longer so the quite reproach in the Greek eyes. It was so easy to suppress the voice of conscience, and even easier to deceive myself.

"Do not destroy us all with your forgiveness," he advised me in the end.

I was no longer listening, as I noticed Cassius next to the forest grotto, so I hurried towards him. He didn't hear my footsteps, but he felt my presence with his heart.

"Decurion, how are you doing?" he asked joyfully. Towards the end of our journey, those role-playing games became unbearable. I longed for home, for Acte, for my friends, my books and… dresses, too. I missed my life, careless, being someone's Little Owl.

I'll tell Callistus I know everything, I thought. *If he repents, I'll give him one more chance.*

Three years ago, in the middle of the dark and stuffy Mithraeum, Vespasian, possessed by demons called me fool and a naif… He must have laughed a lot, as he found Alexander's spear left by the entrance of the cave.

"I don't regret my choices," Sophia retorted every time when Mithras tried to tempt or frighten her. *"I'm following my heart."*

XLI

The triumph of my brother opened the Saturnalia of AD 40. Despite the cold and rainy weather, thousands of people were welcoming Caesar back home by the red marble arch. As to surpass both Augustus and our father, Gaius prolonged fasti and nefesti, merging the yearly festivities in the honor of Saturn with the Palatine Games. The Vigiles were ordered to return a certain part of the collected taxes to the citizens, as well as to share manumissions to a hundred slaves.

"Long live God of the gods!" they praised him on the streets. "Our valiant victor!"

Caligula's parade chariot was escorted by his soldiers and… actors from Gaul, disguised as the conquered Britons. Each of the horsemen held a helmet full of 'spoils of war' in his left hand.

"Will this dementia ever end?" Patricians deprecated. "This shameful man derides the pride and honor of our fathers!"

"When the night is gone, there comes the Sun," Vespasian reassured them. "Wait until the Equinox."

In the palace the musicians were playing all the foreign instruments, the dancers were performing the best figures, and the most beautiful Roman girls lined up in the nymphaeum to throw light silk shawls to Caesar's feet.

"My Princess!" Messalina greeted me with a warm hug. "I'm so happy you're here!"

"Where is Acte?" I asked mirthfully.

"Still sleeping," she smiled, secretly observing Gaius. "I treasure her like a jewel."

This moment I heard tiny stomping and Fedlimid's grumbling from upstairs.

"Auntie! Auntie!"

Octavia had not forgotten me. I took her in my arms and stroked her fair curls.

"Baby Acte is growing so fast!" the girl said happily. "I love her very much!"

"A little bird told me, you are going to become an elder sister," I said to her ear.

"A bird?" My niece smiled. "From the tale of a honeybread man?"

"Yes," I nodded, as I saw Callistus at the end of the hall by the stairs. The Greek, busy with planning Caligula's feast, didn't notice me.

"I have to go, my dear." I kissed Octavia. "We'll play tomorrow."

Octavia embraced me gently, and reached out her small hand to the nursemaid.

"Do you want them to prepare the bath?" Messalina asked me carefully.

"Later," I replied, keeping an eye at the secretary. "I need to talk to someone first."

Too anxious to wait for servants to withdraw, I grabbed Callistus by the toga.

"Let's go to tablinum."

The Greek, a little startled, greeted me with a groveling smile. As he realized I wasn't joking, he accelerated steps. When they closed the door behind us, Callistus tried to make jokes. I was silent, following that icy look and his chaotic speech. That was no longer my old friend. His witty efforts got no answer, so he grew more and more restless.

"Jati,[506] filo mu?" I finally broke the silence.

Callistus' fear turned to apathy, as my quite disbelief became nauseous.

"You're losing, Princess." He shook his head. "Rome will never follow the minority."

"Since when are you Roman?" I smiled bitterly.

"A Roman citizen, from recently." He shrugged. "An independent man."

"You wish!" I laughed. "Neither Vespasian nor Artabanus himself are free."

"I am not talking of the afterlife." He waved aside. "Nor do I really believe in it. I live my life right now and try to get advantages of it as long as possible."

"What did they promise you?" I caught his look. "When did you turn into a traitor?"

He didn't hide cold irony.

"Life is a gamble, Princess," he said knowingly. "An honest player never wins. His strategy is boring."

In my heart I was comparing all my enemies – dead and alive. They might be different, but yet they had in common two bad features – cowardice and pride. Even now, exposed and frightened, Callistus behaved like he would live a hundred years.

"What did you tell them?" I exclaimed.

---

[506] (anc.gr.) Why?

"Not much." The secretary crossed his arms over his chest. "I keep you for the end."

The death of Julia Drusilla turned to his advantage. On the first day of the mourning, Vespasian covertly sent gifts to Callistus' chambers. Always cautious and artful, the Greek was still keeping my secret, yet for his own purpose, actively participating in the plots against my brother.

"Your protector left you," was the message. "Caesar will fall soon. *Non est dies sine lumine.*[507] It is not too late to change the side."

Callistus knew of the Mithrasts more than any other freedmen in the palace. Still, the reason of his assentation wasn't fear of the dark forces, nor was it avarice.

"I thought," the secretary said. "What would become of Rome, and my beloved Hellas, if the world was ruled by bland Jewish religion?"

"You disgust me," I stood up to leave. "I won't get my hands dirty condemning you."

Callistus fell silent. He didn't utter a word when they were taking him to the dungeon.

"You'll stay imprisoned till the end of war," I told him in the end. "After we win, I'll let Vespasian kill you… or whatever."

Just in case, I decided to shorten the Palatine Games.

"Let it be January 24th." I chose the day for my performance. At that time, many years ago, Numa Pompilius tricked Jove.

The preparations for the festival went well. The actors learned their lines during our unusual campaign, and now proudly quoted them on duty. Orla, with the help of other seamstresses, made new costumes, even lighter and more beautiful. Six months we spent abroad were enough for the Egyptian slaves to build the stage for the complex play.

"Will we prolong the intermission, Princess?" Narcissus suggested. "People love the treat as much as they love theater."

"Thanks for an idea," I agreed with him. "We won't skimp on this event."

---

[507] (lat.) There's no day without light.

The son of Artabanus and Pyrallis played Roxana – the only female character in my drama play.

"A man pretends to be a woman, and a woman figures like a man!" Susannah scolded me. "What are you doing, Little Owl?"

"The coup is coming, mother," Daniel, one of the actors, spoke. "It's time to break dissembling rules and write the new ones."

The first act was telling of the notorious events of Alexander's life. As an adolescent he tamed an indomitable stallion, then conquered a great number of the eastern lands in early twenties, and won out over cruel Darius. The second act was going to unveil the secret part of his adventures. I prepared for the spectators an amazing story of the King, who visited Jerusalem, converted to the true faith, and fulfilled his sacred mission on the end of the world.

"Pure luck, cinaedus did not tell anyone about you," Aquila thought aloud. "Friends like that are worse than enemies."

"Be careful whom you trust," Lupus advised. "Most people think the truth is what is paying off the most."

"Of course," I joked. "That's why I'll double your salary."

The extraordinary troupe supported me with joyful smiles.

XLII

AD 41

That morning, when the sounds of drums and trumpets announced the final day of the festivities, I was standing on the terrace by my husband's side. We were rocking our daughter's cradle… for the last time.

"We will make it," Cassius assured me, feeling my distress. "We'll show these bastards who we are."

I stroked his hand and fixed the baby's dress. The visions of the future couldn't leave my mind. The voice of Semangelof and his prophecy followed me everywhere.

"If we fall," I said, nodding to Acte. "This girl will avenge us."

The prefect gently pulled me closer towards him.

"Semper simul, aeternus et umquam."[508]

Our daughter babbled happily, not realizing she was going to become an orphan soon. When Chaerea left to give the orders to the guard about the emperor's day out, I hurriedly sent Lupus for Messalina.

"Listen to me carefully," I told her, "A great war is coming, and I won't survive it."

Caesar's favorite got pale and uttered a weak moan, but Lupus gestured to her to be quiet.

"Sister," I embraced her. "Please, take care of Acte… Hide her away as soon as possible."

The woman's eyes got red with silent tears.

"You are the wife of Claudius," the young centurion explained. "Victory or defeat, you will be safe and sound."

Messalina nodded, and took a baby from the cradle, trembling.

"Find her a good home," I turned my back, not to observe them leave. "Take all my gold, make sure no one finds out who she is – not even her."

---

[508] (lat.) Always together – forever and ever.

When my Messalina's steps dissolved into singing from the Forum, I took a small white dress out of the cradle and reached out to Lupus.

"Don't wait for them to break into the palace," I squeezed his fist with my both hands. "Go to nymphaeum, find my cat… A slab beneath the cathouse is the entrance to cloaca."

The guardsman saluted without any questions.

Two and a half hours later I was going up on stage, dressed like the king with the greasepaint, stuffier than any mask. I still believed the lines I spoke could help me invoke victory.

"There is nothing impossible to him who will try," I addressed Tigellinus. "Heaven cannot brook two suns, nor earth two masters."

"My king and my friend," Loyal Hephaestion said. "The cavalry of Darius is more numerous, and his infantry more skilled. I beg you; let me go on battlefield instead of you!"

"Be not afraid of an army of lions led by a sheep," Alexander retorted. "But an army of sheep led by a lion."

The diverse and cheerful audience watched our performance with respect and warm approval. They could recognize all actors, but the leading one. Only two of them, Caligula and Cassius were smiling to their princess from the goldwork loge.

"You are right, my lord." Tigellinus got more encouraged. "Please, forgive me."

I looked up and squinted at the upper rows. Vespasian, Asiaticus and Sabinus were here as well, among the pleased spectators.

"No one on earth can beat me," I said word by word. "But myself."

Even short-sighted, I noticed confusion in their wicked eyes. I felt them radiating bitterness just like those people in the future. The Sun-Runner recognized me.

"I will break you," I addressed him in my heart. *"One day."*

The first act finished with applause and bright evergreen flowers, thrown down to the stage.

"Who is that fellow?" I heard from the benches. "He is playing the part like a god!"

I winked at Gaius warily and left the scene to take a little rest and to change my clothes in cryptoporticus.

"Your Highness," Someone touched my shoulder timidly. I turned around and smiled.

"Narcissus!"

My friend was still wearing his read dress.

"I must admit, you acted great," I praised him.

The Parthian's plump lips began to twitch. He seemed to have goosebumps all over his body.

"When I left the stage," he uttered fearfully, "before you did… I heard the Vigiles talk."

I shook my head and rubbed my eyes.

"Callistus… he escaped the dungeon!" Narcissus exclaimed, almost in tears.

That meant the only one thing – a conspiracy among the guardsmen and policemen.

"Bring Caesar here!" I shoved the Parthian. "Now!"

The panic in my body turned to fever. I opened the door to the passageway, trying to find but a single soul there.

"Orla?" I called out into the darkness. "Actaeon!"

The corridor was empty. The wall torches were dying down slowly. The heartache started choking me, as I could sense what had been happening.

"Amici mei!" I curled up in a corner and cried. *"Mea culpa!"*

The sound of footsteps eased my torments for the moment.

"Sister dear!" Caligula helped me stand up, and hugged me tight.

"Don't be afraid!" Cassius shouted. "We have the first cohort!"

"No, you don't," I heard the Parthian's voice. "Forgive me, Princess."

The stone door behind us suddenly slammed shut, and the wrought-iron latch rattled heavily on the thick chain.

"What does that mean?" My husband fell on the barrier, but vainly.

Caligula quickly blocked the door from the inside, and pointed to the other door across the portico.

"Now barricade the exit," he commanded to the prefect. "We will not do runners."

It was noon, but the space around us was slowly consumed by darkness. In the weak light of the last torch, three figures, holding hands, were waiting for their doom.

"Sooner or later they will break in here," I looked at Chaerea.

"Any moment now," he sighed. "People are surely wondering why the play stopped, and where their Caesar is."

Gaius fell thoughtful, and then whispered calmly and decisively, "I'm not giving up. I want to die for Rome."

"Death will be nasty," I reminded him. "Mithraists have no sympathy."

The torch was burning more and more unsteadily. Caligula turned to the prefect. "Kill me. That's an order."

Cassius pulled out his sword reluctantly. I suddenly recalled the way Tiberius had gone, and then I heard Antonia's last words inside my head.

"When Father realized they were surrounded by the enemies, he pulled out his dagger and took Cleopatra's life, not to let her suffer in the hands of the bloodthirsty Parthians..."

The heavy banging from outside and tainted swearing broke my vision. The enemies were coming.

"Vivo!"[509] Gaius screamed. "Hoc age!"[510]

The prefect followed the command. My brother looked at me as he was leaving.

The noise was getting louder. I took Cassius' hand, and pressed it to my chest.

"Mi Bellator,"[511] I said softly. "Elevasti me ad Aetnam."[512]

"I will follow you." My soul could hear his soul. "I will be killed with the same sword."

The pain was short... the turmoil subsided, and the lights went out.

---

[509] (lat.) I [still] live!

[510] (lat.) Do this!

[511] (lat.) My warrior.

[512] (lat.) Ascend me to Etna.

EPILOGUE

While the startled audience was leaving the big circus, senators with the help of the renegade guardsmen broke into the underground hall. Asprenas lifted up a lamp to light the passageway. Cassius was kneeling in the cold slabs next to the two corpses, holding his breathless wife's hand.

"Euge, Chaerea!" Vespasian clapped his hands. "You've done the dirty work."

Four of the Praetorians forcibly separated my husband from me. Sabinus came up to the lifeless emperor, drew the dagger, and thrust him in the neck.

"Accipe ratum!"[513]

The wild horde left thirty-three wounds on Gaius' body.

"Take the murderer to prison," Vespasian ordered. "Let the new ruler judge him."

"What about her?" Sabinus asked, nodding at me.

"Do what you want." The praetor waved aside. *"Drusilla is long dead."*

That day's events were passing with a hellish pace. The outlaw praetorians attacked their fellow cohort Lupus, searching for the child.

"Where is the bastard?" Clemens struck him. "You were seen with her dress in your hands!"

Lupus was loyal till the end.

"The girl is dead."

The unveiled passage through to cloaca and cat's blood on a small tunic were not convincing enough to the Flavians.

"You will end up like Chaerea," the Sun-Runner said to Lupus when they dragged him to the dungeon.

In the meantime, at the Forum, Vitellius announced the tragic news with would-be sadness. "Lord Caesar is dead! He was killed in a conspiracy of the Praetorian Guard. His wife and daughter are dead too."

---

[513] (lat.) Take that!

The upset Romans flooded to the rostrum like a stormy river, almost ready to strangle the senator. Their mournful and furious shout echoed through the whole city.

"Death to the assassins! Damnatio memoriae!"

As he sensed the trouble, Claudius fled to the palace and crawled under Messalina's bed as fast as he could.

"What are you doing?" Messalina wondered. "What is going on?"

"C-c-caligula…" the censor muttered.

The cries from outside made the things clearer than Claudius would do. Startled to the edge of reason, the young woman sat down on the edge of bed and hugged her sleeping daughter.

In two hours, the Vigiles impudently broke into cubiculum.

"Where is your husband?" the stranger, who looked like their commander, shouted.

Messalina looked up to him, depressed by pain.

"You don't look like Calvisius," she uttered. "Who are you?"

"Praefectus urbi Aurelius," the Vigile introduced himself and went on with his search.

It took his companions turning the room upside down to find Claudius.

"Come out, Caesar!" Aurelius grinned. "People are waiting for you to judge Cassius Chaerea."

"What… C-c-caesar?" My uncle turned pale. "What do you mean?"

The younger Vigile helped him to his feet.

"Your blood has saved you," the new prefect of the policemen explained. "They want you for the emperor."

It was too late when, overwhelmed with grief, Tigellinus told Corbulo about our death. The warlord wept, striking the stone wall with his fists.

"We must avenge them!" Tigellinus tried to encourage him. "Shall we let the beasts rule the Empire?"

"Rome will never be the same again," Corbulo prophesied. "Ever."

The only chance for the disaster to be mitigated was to declare Claudius emperor, so the Army had no other choice. This decision, somewhat strange but logical, was welcomed by the Romans. Formally, my uncle was the only offspring of the ruling dynasty, excluding my two banished sisters.

Messalina sighed with weak relief. The fate of Caligula's children, as well as her own, was, for now, safe and certain. The young empress wrapped her husband, torpid with lying curled up on the floor, in a toga, and left the room quietly.

Where are Calvisius and his sons? she thought, passing by the new guardsmen.

The empty chambers of the palace gave her the bitter answer. All my loyal freedmen, Vigiles and Praetorians were executed less than an hour before I was dead. The hand of fate painted the shining white marble of the atrium red, and replaced Messalina's yellow dress with a black mourning stola.

"The enemy of the Senate deserves the worst funeral," Claudius announced, too clear and daring for his nature. "All the three should be buried like murderers."

Wise from the experience of living on the Palatine, Messalina pretended to support her husband. In her heart, however, she decided to call for the only person who had power to protect the memory of her beloved. Herod Agrippa, the prince of Judea, sailed to Rome with the first ship, willing to take care of our remains and to protect the Jews from the Esquiline.

"Requiescat in pace, mi amici," Agrippa bade us farewell. "What's immortal may never be killed."

The ashes of Gaius, the third Roman Emperor, were buried in the gardens of Libitina. All our friends found their peace beside their Caesar. Tigellinus, the only one survivor of the palace massacre, was banished to Tyrrhenia.

"The truth will always come out," Messalina whispered as she kissed the urn.

The ashes of the princess and her warrior were scattered at Lake Nemorensis, the cradle of two gilded ships – the symbol of their endless journey.

Here is where the story ends… the story of Drusilla, but not Sophia.

> *For I am the one who is disgraced and the great one.*
> *Give heed to my poverty and my wealth.*
> *Do not be arrogant to me when I am cast out upon the earth,*
> *and you will find me in those that are to come.*

Do not look upon me on the dung heap
nor go and leave me cast out,
and you will find me in the kingdoms.

Do not look upon me when I am cast out among those
Who are disgraced and in the least places,
nor laugh at me.

And do not cast me out among those who are slain in violence.
For I, I am compassionate and I am cruel.
Be on your guard!

Do not judge me,
You who are vanquished, judge the ones who vanquished you
before they give judgment against you,
because the judge and partiality exist in you.
If you are condemned by God, who will acquit you?
Or, if you are acquitted by Him, who will be able to detain you?

Hear me, you hearers
and learn of my words, you who know me.
I am the hearing that is attainable to everything;
I am the speech that cannot be grasped.

Look then at his words
and all the writings which have been completed!
For many are the pleasant forms which exist in numerous sins,
and incontinences,
and disgraceful passions,
and fleeting pleasures
which men embrace.

Grow sober,
Don't try to be wise out of selfishness!
For God is Love,
And Man is perfect as a duality,

Because the two are one.
Remember this until you go up to your resting place.
And you will live,
and never die again.

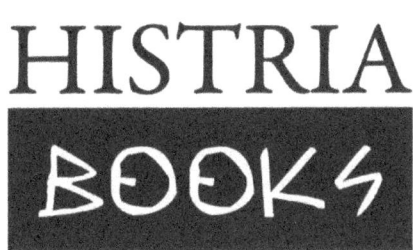 

Other fine works of fiction available from Addison & Highsmith Publishers:

 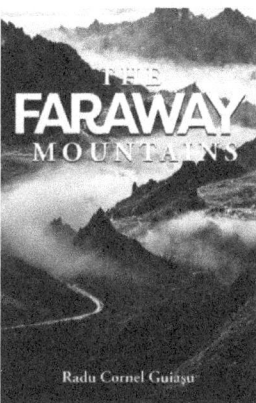 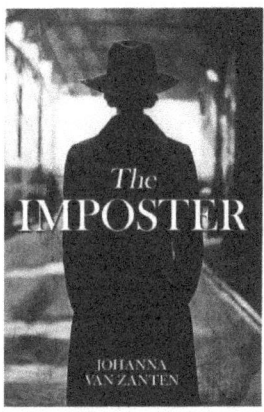

For these and many other great books visit
HistriaBooks.com

Addison & Highsmith

Other fine works of fiction available
from Addison & Highsmith Publishers:

For these and many other great books
visit
HistriaBooks.com